S0-ASI-223

"Taylor writes a tasty little novel!"
—*Publishers Weekly*

CHARMED LIFE
By Bernard Taylor

Bestselling author of *Mother's Boys*

Mourning the loss of his beloved wife and sons, Guy Holman returns to the tiny English village where his wife grew up. But the little peace he finds there is shattered when he becomes the innocent victim of an attempted murder. Soon Guy realizes that what at first seemed a random act of violence is really part of a diabolical plot. An unwilling pawn in a battle between unknown supernatural forces, Holman races to change a fate that could bring life or death to thousands.

"Taylor is capable of making your hair stand on end! Fascinating!"

—*Newsday*

Other *Leisure Books* by Bernard Taylor:

MADELEINE
THE REAPING
SWEETHEART, SWEETHEART
THE GODSEND

BERNARD TAYLOR

LEISURE BOOKS ⬛ NEW YORK CITY

In dear memory of Roy

A LEISURE BOOK®

January 1994

Published by

Dorchester Publishing Co., Inc.
276 Fifth Avenue
New York, NY 10001

In the course of writing this book I have had occasion to be grateful for assistance in several instances. To those who have given me such valuable help I offer my thanks; in particular they go to Dr. Sylvia Gardner of the Public Health Laboratory, Colinadale, and to Detective Constable Clive Blake and Detective Superintendent Douglas Campbell, both of the Metropolitan police.

The best of men cannot suspend their fate...
—Daniel DeFoe

Why I hold fate
Clapsed in my fist, and could command the course
of time's eternal motion...
—John Ford

Part One

Gonna take a sentimental journey;
Gonna set my heart at ease . . .
'Sentimental Journey' –
Brown, Homer, Green

1

'Why this place? What's the significance of it?'

The young man, freckled and sandy-haired, spoke as if the thought had just occurred to him. The woman sitting on his right, agent Mary Hughes, blonde, over-made-up, and inclining to fat in her middle years, said shortly, not moving her gaze from their focus before her:

'The subject was baptized here. He was born and raised in this town.'

The young man drew a breath to speak again, but she forestalled him, flapping a red-nailed hand in a gesture for silence. 'Just watch – and you'll learn what there is to know.' The young man was a new member of the conclave and she was short of patience for his present ignorance.

The group of seven sat in the narrow confines of the crypt of a little church on the outskirts of Norwalk, Connecticut. Agent Hughes, like the others, sat tense, waiting with anxious anticipation. She had not the least idea of what they might see. She knew only that the meeting had been urgently called, and that the matter was of considerable importance. She sighed and shifted uncomfortably on her chair. They had been waiting for more than an hour now, and still from behind them in the hushed, candlelit interior came the sounds of the whirring, clicking beads as the old man worked at his frame. On the seat of a chair beside the man lay a pair of worn football boots and every so often he would turn from the frame and put his thin hands close to them as if warming himself

11

over a fire – or as if drawing from them some special power. Taken years ago from among the forgotten belongings in a nearby attic, the boots had once been the property of the subject of the gathering, Guy Holman, last worn when he had been a high-school student in the town.

Almost a year earlier some of the conclave had sat in this same church, while the same old man had worked at his frame in the shadows. The reason then for their presence had been as it was today. The man Holman. At that time they had sat and watched the occurrence of his death. He had been hit by a truck that had roared around a corner, striking him head on and dragging him for fifty yards before leaving him lying, bloody and mangled, in the middle of the road. There was no question but that he had been killed outright; his head had been smashed like a dropped melon.

The watchers had been horrified by the vision – but nevertheless they had also been much relieved.

Their feelings of relief had not lasted long, however. When, weeks later, the incident had occurred in reality, Holman had survived.

Hughes stirred and drew herself straighter in her chair. At last something was happening. The scene before them was changing. The cramped interior of the crypt was dissolving in smoke, while in its place appeared a view that was wide, sunlit, and open to the skies, its outer edges stretching away on either side, far beyond where, minutes before, had stood the crypt's walls. To Hughes the conjured scene looked as solid and three-dimensional as the hard wooden chair on which she sat; she knew, however, that it was as insubstantial as the wreaths of smoke that blurred its edges.

In the centre of the scene was the rear exterior of a small hotel, white-walled and sun-drenched. Judging by

12

the flora in the garden beneath the terrace and the architecture of the hotel and the buildings beyond, it appeared to be situated in some North African country.

'Tunisia? Libya?' said Paxton, a lean, middle-aged black man sitting on Hughes's right. 'Could be, I guess. Or Morocco possibly . . .'

Hughes nodded, eyes not moving from the vision before her. One of the extraordinary things about the scene was the low level of sound emanating from it. Strange too was its relative lack of colour; she was reminded of movies in which filters were used to reduce colour content to a general sepia tint, or of plays in which a designer has limited himself almost to a single colour, relying for effect on varying tones.

'There he is,' came Paxton's voice again. 'There's Holman.'

As one, the watchers now focused on the figure of a man who emerged from the hotel onto the sunlit terrace. Of Western appearance, tall, slim, fair-haired, he wore grey jeans and a white shirt; he had a denim jacket slung over his arm and carried a travel bag. From their briefings the seven knew that he was American and thirty-eight years old.

As the seven continued to watch, the man moved to a table, dropped his jacket and bag onto a chair and sat down. A few moments later a young, dark-skinned waiter appeared and placed a cup and saucer before him. The two men exchanged a few words – words unheard by the watchers – then the waiter moved away and vanished into the hotel's interior.

Left alone, the American took up the cup, sipped from it and replaced it in the saucer. As he did so a little dog got up from the shade, padded towards him and sat at his side. Smiling, Holman turned and spoke to the animal, bending low to it, murmuring softly and fondling its ears. Tail wagging, the dog stretched up and licked his face. With a laugh, Holman jerked his head back and wiped at his cheek.

As the dog moved away again Holman glanced at his watch. A moment later another man, a little younger, a little shorter, entered. He joined Holman at the table and they sat facing one another, their mouths moving in unheard conversation.

'Who's the guy with him?' asked one of the watchers, a short, balding man with rimless spectacles.

'That we don't know, Doctor,' Paxton replied. 'It may not be important. Perhaps we'll learn.'

As he spoke the scene began to disintegrate and fade, its wavering lines obscured by rising, swirling wreaths of vapour.

'Was that *it*?' the sandy-haired young man asked. 'Is that all there is?'

'We'll soon know,' said Paxton. Turning, he looked over his shoulder at the old man who worked hunched over the frame, hands moving rapidly over the rows of discs and beads strung upon the wires before him. Paxton observed his actions for a few seconds then, satisfied, turned to face the front again.

A new scene was emerging. Now before the watchers appeared a sunlit street. On the far side stood the façade of what appeared to be the hotel in the previous scene. On either side of it were shops, cafés and bars. Cars and taxis sped by, while in the foreground at a bus stop a number of people stood waiting. As before, the level of sound was low, the colours muted.

After a few seconds the attention of the watchers was drawn to the figures of Holman and his companion as they appeared at the top of the steps at the hotel's

14

entrance. Holman, now wearing his jacket, carried a suitcase and had his travel bag slung over his shoulder. The other man carried a holdall and bore a backpack. After a moment or two the pair descended the steps and came across the street to the bus stop. Setting down their heavier baggage on the pavement they lit cigarettes and settled to wait. After a while a crowded bus appeared and pulled up. With the opening of its doors its passengers began to alight from the front entrance while the people waiting began to pile on board at the rear. Following the others, Holman and his companion took up their baggage and moved forward.

The incident happened as the shorter man was climbing onto the bus. Holman, behind him, had put down his suitcase and was stooping to pick up something from the pavement when the greyish-brown shape of the dog appeared, dashing around the rear end of the bus. Violently, ferociously, teeth bared and snarling, it rushed at Holman's stooping figure, jaws snapping at his reaching arm. Startled, Holman leapt back, swinging his bag in an attempt to ward the animal off. Then, as abruptly as it had begun, the attack was over and the dog was running away again, dashing back around the end of the bus.

With the dog gone from sight the eyes of the seven focused on Holman. Clearly shaken by the incident he touched at the torn fabric of his jacket then pulled up his sleeve to look at his arm. In the bus's doorway his companion stood, mouth opening in unheard speech. Then, moving quickly, Holman picked up his case, adjusted the bag over his shoulder and climbed onto the bus. Seconds later the doors were closing and the bus was moving away.

Watching as the scene faded the sandy-haired young man said, 'What happened? Did he get bitten?'

15

Hughes said, 'It looked that way. He got bitten on the arm, didn't he?' She turned to Paxton. 'Did you see whether the dog drew blood? I couldn't see.'

Paxton shook his head. 'I couldn't either.'

'Is it possible to see it again?'

Paxton briefly considered the question. 'I think we'd better continue. There might be a lot to get through.' Turning to the old man, he said, 'We'll move on, if you don't mind.'

The clicking and whirring of the beads began again, and after several minutes the screen of smoke before them faded to reveal a sunlit square which one of the watchers immediately placed in Marrakech. The scene held for only half a minute, but it was time enough for the watchers to seek out and locate the two men looking relaxed and content as they sat over beers at a café table.

'Well,' observed Hughes, 'he doesn't seem to be any the worse for it – the dog's attack.'

Like a slow-moving montage in a film, a series of visions came and went before the seven watchers. Scenes before them were identified in Casablanca and Rabat, after which came others set in southern Europe. It was not possible for the watchers to identify every location, but among those they identified were scenes in Spain and Portugal. And there always were the two men: walking along the streets, looking in shop windows, consulting maps in sunlit squares, eating and drinking in restaurants and cafés. Observing Holman and his companion wandering into a public park, Mrs Hughes adjusted her buttocks on her seat and muttered, 'Dear God, I hope they're enjoying this tour more than I am. How much longer is it going on? This chair's breaking my butt.' One of the other watching women, small, thin, wearing an elegant grey suit, shot her a glance and drew in a disapproving little

16

breath. Hughes ignored it. 'I'm hungry, too,' she added. 'We've been here for hours. Can't we send out for pizzas or something?'

After a while the scene changed again, this time to what appeared to be a small hotel room. With his concerned friend standing nearby, Holman lay on a bed, his clothed body covered with a blanket. As the seven watched, Holman threw off the blanket, sat up and began agitatedly to shake his head from side to side. After a while he sank down again.

'He's fallen sick,' observed the doctor, Coombes.

In the scenario played out before the watchers it became night, the room lit by a single bedside lamp. Holman still lay on the bed. In a burgeoning fever he tossed and turned, his eyes and mouth spasmodically opening and closing. The door opened and his companion entered holding a tumbler of water. As he moved towards the bed Holman turned and saw him. At once Holman sat bolt upright, and with an expression registering abject terror he cried out in unheard protest while he pressed himself back against the bed-head.

Dr Coombes, eyes riveted to the scene, gave a nod. 'Ah, yes,' he breathed.

He watched as Holman's body suddenly twisted and turned in a violent muscular spasm that arched his back and sent his arms shooting out before him. 'Classic,' Coombes murmured. 'It's classic.'

Paxton turned to him and said in a low voice: 'You've made your diagnosis?'

'Oh, yes, indeed.'

'Rabies. Yes?'

'Unless I'm very much mistaken.'

After a while the scene changed once more, now to the interior of a cool, shaded room with white walls whose

17

only adornment was a crucifix. Through a gap between half-closed shutters a narrow shaft of brilliant sunlight slanted into the room, striking in a patch of brightness the stone-tiled floor. On a bed Holman lay quiet and still beneath the sheets. 'So he's in a hospital,' murmured Coombes. 'And sedated. Standard therapy.'

Before the conclave's gaze the shaft of sunlight moved across the floor till it began to fade, and with the lighting of a lamp was obliterated altogether. From time to time a nurse – a nun in a white-winged headdress – entered the room to tend to the patient. On one occasion she was accompanied by Holman's companion. After standing for some moments looking down sadly at the still form of his friend the young man turned and left the room.

Time passed; Holman stirred, opening his eyes, consciousness returning. The door opened again and once more the nurse was there, this time standing aside to be preceded by an elderly man.

As they reached the bedside Holman gave them a tired smile. The doctor bent and spoke to him, and Holman answered, and in his face the watchers saw an expression of pleading, followed by what appeared to be the weariness of resignation. While the nurse stood a little to one side the doctor drew up a chair and sat down beside the bed. After a time Holman began to show signs of agitation and the doctor turned and spoke to the nurse. At once she moved to a small table nearby and began to prepare a hypodermic syringe.

'They'll sedate him again,' Coombes said. 'It's necessary in such a situation.'

The seven watched as the nurse, the syringe ready, approached the bed. As she did so Holman was suddenly stricken by a violent spasm. His body twisting and writhing beneath the sheets he clutched at his throat,

18

mouth gaping, snatching at the air. Then, shoulders and feet pressing into the mattress, he flung his arms out while his back arched, the greater part of his body lifting clear of the bed, almost as if he possessed the power of levitation. He remained there for two, three seconds, his eyes wide and staring, then suddenly collapsed.

Bending over the now-still form of the man, the doctor lifted one of his eyelids. He felt for a pulse, then bent lower and put an ear to Holman's chest. Straightening, he shook his head, murmured something and pulled up the sheet and covered the dead face. The nurse crossed herself and set down the unused hypodermic. Taking up a clipboard she began to write.

Agent Mary Hughes expelled the air from her lungs in a long sigh of released tension. Shifting her eyes from the scene, she turned to look at Paxton. His lips were pressed together in satisfaction.

'I don't need to ask how you feel about it,' she said.

Keeping his eyes on the scene ahead he gave two or three swift, brief nods. 'Relieved,' he said. 'Very relieved – so far.' He turned to the old man in the shadows. 'Hold it there, can you?'

A few seconds went by, then all movement in the scene before them ceased, leaving the figures fixed like wax-works in a museum tableau.

Paxton rose from his seat and stepped forward. 'Don't worry,' he reassured the others, briefly turning back to them as he reached the edge of the scene. 'I shan't do any harm. But if it's possible I want to get some indication of where this is taking place, and also when it's due to happen.'

The others watched as, like a spectator leaving the auditorium to join the cast of a play on stage, Paxton stepped through the band of curling smoke into the scene.

19

Stepping to the side of the transfixed figure of the nurse – and careful not to touch anything – he bent his head to peer at the clipboard in her hands. After studying the paper for a moment he moved to the bed and gazed down at the sheet-covered body of the American. Then, turning, he started back again.

As he reached his chair the scene was already fading. 'Well . . .?' asked the thin woman in grey as he sat down.

'The date is there,' he said. 'May 11th. And this year.'

'Did you find out where it was happening?' asked Hughes.

He nodded. 'According to the paper on the nurse's clipboard it's the Hospital Santa Maria in a place called Tufacino. Probably somewhere in Italy or Spain. We'll check on that.'

The young sandy-haired man spoke up at this. 'Are we to assume that his death was connected with – ' he broke off and corrected himself: ' – *is to be* connected with the earlier scene? That the dog was rabid and Holman contracted rabies?'

Briefly Hughes raised her eyes. 'No,' she said, covering her exasperation with a little laugh, 'the poor bastard died from contracting a hangnail.'

'Patience, Mrs Hughes,' said Paxton. 'We can't all have equal experience, and there isn't one of us who still hasn't everything to learn.'

Seeing that no new scene had formed to replace the hospital room, Paxton turned to the old man. 'Is there nothing else?'

Hands still moving over the strings, the old man shook his head. 'I can't get anything else at present.'

'Then it looks as if that's it,' Paxton said. 'Anyway, we'll stop now and continue in the morning.' Directing his attention to Coombes, he went on: 'Just to be sure,

20

Doctor, you're quite convinced that Holman died as a result of the dog bite?'

Coombes nodded. 'He must have done.' His glance took in the other members of the assembly. 'The symptoms and the pattern of the illness were classic. The malaise, the sensitivity, the acute anxiety followed by the spasms, the manifestation of hydrophobia – which is actually caused by spasms of the pharynx – and the evidence of periods of rationality between spasms. It was all there. Almost a textbook case in the symptoms and the pattern. Oh, there's no doubt as to the cause of his death. In this case it would appear to be due, specifically, to respiratory failure. It's usually that or cardiac failure. Either one in this case would be due to his having contracted rabies.'

'Don't you find it astonishing that such a thing can still happen?' said the thin woman in grey. 'I mean, in this day and age, with all our progress in medical science. There's treatment for rabies, isn't there?'

'Yes, if it comes soon enough,' Coombes said. 'But in this case, with Holman, it obviously didn't. Though it's hardly surprising when you think about it. We watched him and his friend wandering around Morocco and southern Europe, going wherever the whim took them and with nobody knowing where they were. Even if it were suspected that Holman might have been infected I doubt there'd be any way of contacting him in such a situation.' He shrugged. 'You can see how he could come to die.'

'Yes,' Paxton said, 'though of course, we mustn't forget that it hasn't happened yet. He's destined to die like that yes, but not just yet. Not until May 11th. At 3.20 in the afternoon to be precise.'

* * *

21

They met at the church again the following day and sat patiently while the old man managed to conjure a few more images. There was nothing, however, that seemed to be of any importance.

That evening they gathered around a couple of adjacent tables in a small bar just off the town's main street.

'Oh, by the way,' Paxton said, 'I checked on the name of that place. Tufacino is a village in southern Spain.' He took a swallow from his beer glass. 'And,' he added, 'going by the few fragments we managed to get today I think we can be sure that Holman's death is not going to affect anything or anyone of any great moment. Oh, there are bound to be *some* effects, of course, but no great, far-reaching ramifications.'

'Ripples,' observed Coombes, 'as opposed to tidal waves.'

Paxton nodded. 'You could say that. And it's something we can be grateful for. Okay, it's awful to see someone suffer like that – but at the same time it's a tremendous relief to get these loose ends tied up and out of the way.' He gave a sigh of satisfaction. 'I can't tell you – I'm very glad to see the end of this business in sight – to know that it'll soon be finished with, once and for all. God knows, this man's been an itch between our shoulder blades for too damned long.'

The sandy-haired young man said, 'Obviously I don't know as much as the rest of you about all this – but I understand that he's escaped in the past.'

'Twice,' Paxton said. 'Once at his birth and then again just last year – last July.'

Briefly he outlined for the young man the incident of Holman's accident with the truck; his escape from death.

'But miraculously he survived,' he said. 'Somehow it didn't happen exactly the way it was supposed to, the way

22

it was *meant* to happen. He was severely injured but not killed. God knows how. He just wasn't in exactly the right place at the time. He suffered a fractured skull, broken collar bone, broken ribs, broken leg and a ruptured spleen. And he survived.'

'But he was *meant* to *die*,' said the young man.

'Oh, yes, he was meant to die all right. But he didn't. He seems to be a law unto himself; to have some ability to move around outside the natural laws. He's like some – some wild card in a game. Don't ask me how he does it – he just *does*. And of course we've been very anxious about him. There's just no knowing which way he's going to move next. It's got to stop sometime, though. Our only hope has been that it would stop before he does any real harm.' He gave a sigh of relief. 'But now, *again*, we can see an end in sight. And, please God, this time it'll work out the way it's meant to.'

'What if it doesn't?' The young man voiced the question that neither Paxton nor anyone else wanted to face.

'In that case,' said Paxton, pushing long black fingers through his kinky hair, 'we're back to square one. But somehow – I don't know – this time I have the feeling it's going to be all right. I feel somehow that this time he won't escape. Anyway,' he added, 'it won't be long before we know.' He glanced from one to the other. 'Are there any more questions?'

'Yes,' Hughes said. 'When was he bitten – infected by the dog?'

'He hasn't been,' Paxton replied. 'Not yet.'

'Then – '

'It's due to happen tomorrow. Tomorrow morning.'

'I see.' Hughes nodded. 'Tomorrow's the 13th – so if he's to die on May 11th that gives the poor son of a bitch just four weeks left to live.'

23

2

At the moment that Mrs Hughes, in the New England bar, was observing the little time left for Guy Holman to live, he, all unaware of the great interest in him, was sitting in a small café in Agadir.

The café – which owned the dual merits of being handy and inexpensive – was about a third full. Sitting alone, Guy faced out onto Avenue Hassan II, the main street of the town. Beyond the window and the figures who drank coffee and beer at the pavement tables the evening traffic went back and forth. Above the bar a TV set with blurred picture and garish colour blasted away in Arabic a programme of sports news. Unfazed by the quality of the image, a row of Moroccan men stood leaning on the bar, gazing avidly up at the screen, empty coffee cups in a row before them.

After eating a mediocre meal of vegetable soup and bread, followed by a cheese omelette, Guy now smoked and sipped a glass of mineral water. He wondered vaguely where Jack was. Probably drinking at one of the large package tour hotels. Guy had declined Jack's urging to accompany him; tonight he preferred to be alone.

Over by the door the waiter, taking advantage of a lull in the evening's business, stood picking his nose, forefinger up to the first knuckle. Guy pushed his plate an inch further away. And, he thought, there would almost certainly be cockroaches in the kitchen.

He put out his cigarette, got up and moved to the cash register at the end of the bar. As he waited for his change

24

he glanced up at the television screen just in time to see a golfer address the ball and swing. *Thwuck*. Memory flared and Guy winced and quickly looked away. He took his change, dropped a tip onto the plate and moved past the waiter – now working on the left nostril – out into the mild April air. He would get back to the hotel and get on with his packing.

As he walked along the main street he was struck again by his lack of any sense of peace. It was inexplicable, for there were no pressures now. The very worst that could happen to him had happened. Sylvie was lost to him for ever – as were Davie and Luke – and he should be learning to live with the fact. But he could not. Those brief, clutched-at feelings of peace were proving more elusive by the day, by the hour, and in their place he was left only with melancholy feelings of business unfinished, of loose ends left untied.

But be patient, he urged himself. It had been less than a year. It was still early days. Peace would come in time, and as for the rest it would all pass. Everything passed eventually.

With the thought he stepped out more firmly. One had no choice but to make the best of one's life. And, he reminded himself, he had been given a second chance to do just that. After all, he had survived the accident with the truck. His life had been saved when he could so easily have died. But he had not. Against all the odds he had survived and made a miraculous recovery.

Turning to the right he made his way along a side street, heading for the hotel. Tomorrow he and Jack would be off to Marrakech, the next stage of their tour. He liked Agadir with its fine beach and friendly people but there was little to see. Marrakech held a different promise: other faces, other sights. *Yes*, said a voice in his

25

head, *and other diversions*. No matter, he thought; just so long as it worked. Given enough time, enough distance and enough new sights he could, surely he could, leave Sylvie and the past behind.

Standing in his small, simply furnished hotel room, Guy took the little leather-framed photograph of Sylvie and David from the bedside table and placed it carefully in the suitcase where it lay on the bed. He looked at his watch – new, inexpensive and bought that day in Agadir's main street. Not yet nine o'clock. The time was passing so slowly this evening. He became aware yet again of his growing sense of restlessness. He would feel better come the morning when he and Jack left for Marrakech.

His packing was just about finished now. There remained only those items that he would need before leaving in the morning. Closing the case he placed it beside the bed. Now what to do? For a moment or two he considered going out again, to take a walk and get some air, but eventually he decided to get a leisurely drink and then have an early night.

Downstairs in the small bar he moved to a corner table. The only other customers in the place were four Germans who sat in animated conversation at a table nearby and an English couple sitting on stools at the matchbox-sized bar. He ordered a beer and when it came sat taking desultory swallows and smoking. His feeling of restlessness and disorientation was growing more acute and now, in addition, he felt a slight ache taking hold in his head, not at the front where the scar was, but towards the back of his skull.

He remained sitting there for some minutes longer, hoping the ache would fade. But it did not. In the end he got up and, leaving his unfinished drink on the table, left the bar and went upstairs.

Back in his room he took a couple of pills and sat on the bed and tried to think about the morning departure. After staying in Marrakech for a few days he and Jack would set off for Casablanca – he had been looking forward to that – then to Rabat, then on to Tangier. From Tangier they would probably leave Morocco and go to Portugal, and so resume their leisurely, wandering tour of southern Europe. No definite plans; that wasn't the way they were doing it; they had decided simply to go where the mood and the inclination took them.

He lay back on the bed. Instead of his headache receding it was growing worse. After a minute or two he got up and went into the bathroom. Flicking on the light he stood before the mirror above the hand-basin. The discomfort in his head was increasing by the second. Briefly he shut his eyes against the pain then, opening them again, lifted a hand to touch fingertips to the fine mesh of scars that marked his upper forehead and ran into his hairline. The source of the pain, though, was elsewhere.

As he gazed at his reflection he felt a strange pressure beginning to build up inside his head. It seemed to be something quite apart from the headache. It touched him first only as the faintest murmur, but in less than a minute it had grown so that his head was pounding, while deep inside his brain it felt as if some expanding core was about to explode.

The pain grew, and it was all he could do not to cry out. He clutched at the rim of the basin while he screwed up his eyes against the burgeoning onslaught. There was a taste in his mouth – bitter, yet at the same time laden with an intense sweetness – and for a split second a part

27

of his mind acknowledged that he had known it before. He spun, heading for the doorway; he must get to the bed. But there was no time. A moment later the bitter-sweet taste was flooding his mouth and the expanding core in his brain was exploding.

When he opened his eyes he found himself looking at the ceiling. He was lying half in the bathroom and half in the hall. He realized, dully, that he had passed out. He moved his hand to his head. There was only a very slight ache there now – and that was the result of the fall. There was no vestige of the earlier devastating pain he had felt.

He sat up. Looking at his watch he saw that it was coming up to eleven o'clock. He had been lying there for over an hour.

He got to his feet. The strange taste in his mouth was almost gone. Standing at the basin in the bathroom he looked at his reflection. There was a slight graze low on his right cheekbone; a little bloody, but the blood was dry. It would soon heal. Looking back into the hall he saw there an overturned wicker wastebasket and realized that in the fall his head must have struck it – luckily though, for it had probably saved him from greater injury on the hard tiles.

He turned on the cold tap and splashed water over his face, dried himself with a towel then went back into the bedroom. At the window he stood for some moments gazing out across the shadowed rectangle of the hotel's small garden. Within him he felt nothing but turmoil.

Turning, he glanced over at his packed travel bag and suitcase, staring at them as if seeing them for the first time. Then, moving across the room, he dipped a hand into one of the bag's pockets and drew out his address

28

book. Sitting on the edge of the bed he consulted the book and reached for the telephone.

As he waited for the call to come through he thought again of the inexplicable blackout. And suddenly he remembered that the same thing had happened before. It had been like that on the day of his accident the previous summer. He had been at his desk making arrangements for the flight to England when that same excruciating pain in his head had come on and suddenly the room had swum before his eyes. He had later recovered to find himself half lying, half sitting in the chair and with the discovery that over an hour had gone by. There had been no accounting for it. All he had been left with was that strange, bittersweet taste in his mouth. It was then that he had gone out into the street and narrowly escaped death in the accident with the truck . . .

The call came through after a few minutes. When it was completed he lay back against the pillow. As he did so he became aware that his feelings of inner turmoil were going, fading away, leaving in their place a swiftly dawning peace.

The following morning Guy emerged onto the little terrace that looked out over the hotel's rear garden. Dropping his jacket and travel bag onto a chair he sat down at a table. The April sun shone down. The air was warm, building up to another hot day. The heat was pleasant, though – a dry heat, not like the humid, energy-sapping heat of a New York summer.

A young waiter appeared after a little while bringing the coffee Guy had ordered on his way out. Guy thanked him, tipped him.

'You're leaving this morning, sir?' said the waiter.

'Yes, quite soon.'

29

'And your friend, Mr Shaw?'

'Yes, we're both leaving.'

When the waiter had gone Guy sipped at the dark coffee, stretched his legs and sighed. A movement caught his eye, and turning he saw the familiar shape of a small greyish-brown mongrel dog coming towards him. Stopping in front of him, the dog looked up at him, tail wagging. A friendly little animal, it belonged, Guy guessed, to the hotel proprietor.

'So how are you, today, you little mutt?'

Bending low, Guy patted the dog and fondled its ears. The dog stretched up and licked at his face. 'No, thanks,' Guy laughed, moving his head back, 'I've already washed.' The dog sat looking at him for a few moments then turned and padded away, back into the shade. Guy looked at his watch. Jack should be up and ready if he intended to catch the bus.

'I should have known you'd be up bright and early.'

Turning, Guy saw Jack coming towards him across the terrace. Uncertainly, Guy smiled at him, watching as he tossed his jacket down beside Guy's own and lowered himself into the opposite chair. Jack wore blue jeans and an open-necked shirt. His hair, even lighter than Guy's, was sun-bleached, like the hair on his tanned arms. He was thirty-four years old, and a little hungover.

'I was just about to come looking for you,' Guy said.

'Yeh, I slept late,' Jack said, then added, gesturing to Guy's cheek, 'What happened? Did you try to shave in the dark?'

'Oh – this . . .' Guy put fingertips to the graze. 'I had a run-in with the wastebasket in my room.' He paused. 'Have you packed?'

'Just about. I've settled my bill, too. Have you?'

'Last night. Have you had breakfast?'

30

'I don't want anything.'

'Where did you go last night?'

'That's a good question.'

Guy laughed. 'You have a good time?'

'Pretty good. I think.' Catching sight of the watch on Guy's wrist he said, 'Ah, I see you found your watch.'

'No such luck, I'm afraid.' Guy displayed the new watch. 'I bought this here in town yesterday. It's cheap, but it'll do. I can't travel without one.'

'You still have no idea where it might be?'

'No. I could have lost it anywhere – in the hotel or out in the town. I don't know.'

'Too bad. I doubt you'll see it again. Though it might turn up.'

'Sure, and I might find a million dollars.' The lost watch had been a present from Sylvie, and could never now be replaced. 'Shit!' Guy said in a sudden burst of anger. 'It's my own fault. I knew the strap needed fixing.'

Feeling something brush against his knee, Guy looked down and saw that the dog had come back and now sat gazing up at him with misty, doleful eyes. He reached out to pat the animal but it started away, turned in an erratic little circle then settled once more in the shade. Guy drank the last of his coffee. Nearby on the terrace wall a small lizard made a sudden darting little movement and was still again. Guy, silent, realized that he was putting off telling Jack of his decision.

Across the table Jack stretched in his chair. 'I'm not looking forward to that goddamn bus ride, are you?' he said. 'Moroccan buses – Jesus! I mean – okay for a short journey, but for anything more, forget it.' He shook his head. 'Still, we'll manage. We don't have any choice.'

Guy said: 'Listen – I'm not going on the bus.'

Jack blinked at him. 'Come again?'

31

'I've – decided not to go on with the trip.'

'Huh?' Jack was gazing at him with a disbelieving smile. 'Are you serious? What are you talking about?'

'I'm ducking out,' Guy said. 'I'm sorry, Jack. I'm not going on with it.'

' – When did you decide this?'

'Last night.' Guy did not elaborate. *I passed out and after I came round I changed my mind.* Jack would never understand; he couldn't understand it himself. 'I'm sorry,' he said.

'But – I don't get it. What happened?'

'Nothing. It's just not – working out for me.'

A little silence. Jack said with a shrug, 'Well, it's your decision. What do you plan to do instead? Go back to New York?'

'No. I've decided to go to England.'

'England?' Jack's tone was slightly incredulous. 'You said you didn't want to go back there – not yet, anyway. Not this trip.'

' – I know.'

'But now you've changed your mind. Why?'

Guy did not answer.

'What d'you plan to do when you get there?' Jack said.

'I don't know yet, exactly.'

'You know how long you'll stay?'

'No.'

'You don't seem to know a hell of a lot, do you?' Jack frowned. 'Your decision is so sudden. I mean – you were so keen. All those places we talked about. Marrakech . . . Casablanca. Don't you want to see Casablanca?' He smiled now. 'Play it again, Sam? No? Well, forget Casablanca. How about Portugal, Spain, Italy . . .? You wanted to see those places.'

Guy made no response.

32

'Ah, what the hell,' Jack said, 'if you've made up your mind you've made up your mind.'

'I'm sorry, Jack – ducking out like this. But you'll have a better time on your own, anyway. The way I feel right now I'd only be a drag.'

Jack said, 'Is it something I did?'

'Christ, no!' Guy protested. 'It's just that – I think I need to be on my own a little.' Words, just words, he knew. He couldn't just admit that he simply felt compelled to abandon the trip and go to England instead.

He had intended to go to England the previous July – though not for what anyone would call a vacation. But then he had had the accident, and that had finished everything for a while. Then this year, following his general recovery, his doctor had advised him to think of taking a vacation: 'It's what you need – to get away for a while. Find a change of scene. Learn to relax again.' And Guy had seen it as the answer and had toyed with thoughts of journeys to foreign lands – though not to England, of course; never again to England. The money his father had left him the year before ensured that he had the finances – if he was careful – and as he would not resume teaching until the new semester in September he also had the time; time and opportunity to get away from the confinement of familiar surroundings, to find a change of scene that would take his mind off things and allow him to relax and fully recover his health and strength.

It was while he had been sifting through the various options that Jack, an old friend, had appeared on the scene. Newly freed from an unhappy marriage, Jack was planning to take a trip to southern Europe. When he suggested that they went together Guy had quickly taken to the idea, grateful to be presented with an almost ready-made package. After months of frustration – through the early months following his accident he had been quite incapacitated – it was a relief to have something positive and new to look forward to.

And the trip had gone well. They had spent a week in Portugal and ten days in Spain, after which Jack had suggested that they go further south, to Morocco, for a while. Guy, eager to see everything, had at once agreed, and they had come to Agadir and booked into the hotel *Le Fieste de Sud*. Now, a week after their arrival, Guy was backing out and going his own way.

'So,' Jack said, 'when d'you plan to go there – to England?'

'There's a plane leaving for Heathrow this morning. At eleven-twenty. I reserved a seat last night.'

Jack's eyebrows lifted. 'You don't waste time, do you? Where will you stay when you get there?'

'I called a hotel in London – where I stayed once before – and managed to get a reservation.'

A little silence. Jack said, 'Maybe the trip's proving a little too much for you – physically. After all, you've been through a pretty rough time. Maybe we've been trying to do too much.'

'No, I feel fine. Listen – it's not the trip. I've enjoyed it. And I've enjoyed your company. It's just . . .' He shook his head, at a loss.

Jack gazed at him for a moment then nodded and gave a resigned smile. 'Well, if that's it, that's it. You're sure I can't change your mind?'

'I'm sorry.'

'Well,' Jack said, 'I'm sorry about it too, but you have to do what you want.'

Guy said awkwardly, 'Will you continue with the trip as we planned it?'

'I don't know. After Marrakech I might just go straight back to Spain.'

In the little silence that fell Guy noticed that the dog was still resting in the shade of the wall. It lay with its head on its paws, eyes closed, occasionally twitching in its sleep.

'It won't be long before my bus is here,' Jack said. He was glancing at his watch. 'I'll have to get going.'

From his pocket Guy took a small notepad, wrote in it, tore out the page and handed it to Jack. 'My hotel in London. Just in case you decide to come visit.' He knew that Jack would not. Somehow, with their parting he felt that a chapter was ending; they might never meet again.

They got to their feet. As they put on their jackets Jack said, 'You'll be leaving for the airport soon, I guess.'

'Yes, I've ordered a cab.'

'So – I guess this is it. If I don't see you in London I'll see you back in Rockland County.'

'Yes. I don't think I'll be away that long. But anyway, we'll keep in touch.'

'Sure.'

Guy picked up his travel bag and together they left the terrace and went into the lobby. Guy's suitcase stood beside Jack's baggage near the desk. As they approached it the young Moroccan receptionist smiled and told Guy in his accented English that the taxi would be there in a few minutes. Guy thanked him. The Moroccan gestured to the new watch on Guy's wrist.

'It is a great pity about your other watch, sir. But if it is found we will let you know.'

Guy thanked him, then turned to Jack who was pulling on his backpack. 'I'll walk across the street with you,' he said. 'I've got time.'

His travel bag over his shoulder, Guy left his suitcase

where it was and followed Jack through the main doors. As they stood side by side looking onto the street Jack said quietly:

'Listen – I know you've been through a bad time, what with one thing and another, but . . .' He came to a halt.

'But what?'

'You've got to start getting on with your life, Guy. I mean – starting now. Easy for me to say, I know, but – the past is over.'

'I'm okay. I feel great.'

'Yeh – well . . .' Jack shrugged. 'Anyway, I'd better get going. I don't want to miss my bus.'

They moved down the steps and across the street to the bus stop and joined the Moroccans who waited in a straggling group about the shelter. Jack put down his holdall. 'You don't need to wait,' he said.

'It's okay. I've got a minute or two before my cab gets here.'

They lit cigarettes, and Guy stood turning his cigarette lighter over in his palm in rhythm with the words that Jack had spoken. *The past is over*.

Eventually a dusty bus arrived and pulled up at the kerb. The people surged forward. Giving Guy's shoulder a pat, Jack moved towards the bus and climbed up behind the others. In the doorway he turned back to Guy. As they faced one another Guy's cigarette lighter fell from his hand. Quickly he stooped to pick it up. In the same moment the little dog came dashing around the end of the bus, flew at him and snapped ferociously at his arm.

Guy's cry was not from pain but from the shock of the attack. Springing back he swung at the animal with his travel bag. 'Get away, you bastard!' Dodging the blows the dog backed off and crouched, snarling. Then, suddenly whirling, it was off again, dashing back along the

36

pavement and across the road. Guy stood there gasping slightly from shock, hardly aware of the bus pulling out and moving away.

Eyed by curious passersby who had seen the incident he pulled up the torn sleeve of his jacket and looked at his arm. There was no mark there. The dog's teeth had not touched him. He pulled his sleeve down, pocketed his lighter, hoisted his bag over his shoulder and started back across the street. As he went up the steps to the hotel he was aware of a taxicab pulling up at the kerb behind him.

In the lobby Guy picked up his suitcase and wished the young Moroccan clerk goodbye. As he turned to the door the taxi driver was there waiting. Taking Guy's case from him, the driver led the way to the cab. Moments later they were setting off for the airport.

3

On the flight Guy found himself relaxing further. He was also aware of a slight edge of excitement at the knowledge that he would soon be in England again. The last time he had visited the country had been six years ago, when he had tried to persuade Sylvie to return with him to the States. He closed his eyes for a moment, dwelling on the memory, then, with an effort, thrust it aside. As Jack had said, the past was over.

He took a copy of the *Independent* from the stewardess with the realization that for the duration of his trip he had been unaware of what was happening in the world. But of course nothing had really changed; here and there all over the globe the usual violent unrest was going on. And as one people edged towards peace so another seemed to be heading for bloodshed. The present news was not only of the continuing conflict in Lebanon and the occupied West Bank and Gaza but also of the growing strife in Larinas, the small republic sandwiched between Colombia and Venezuela. The country seemed to be suffering increasingly under the dictatorship of its premier, Perreiros, who had come to power in a military coup. Guy did not finish the article; such problems, occurring so far away, had no part in his life. Turning the pages he settled to study the theatre listings, mentally marking a few of the London shows he thought he might like to see.

After lunch he read a book for a while, following which he closed his eyes and tried to doze. Eventually the plane touched down at Heathrow, and after collecting his baggage and moving through Passport Control and Customs he left the airport and caught the tube to Bayswater in London's West End.

St John's Hotel, where he had stayed on his last visit, was a small family concern situated in Inverness Terrace, just over a hundred yards from Bayswater Underground Station. After checking in he was shown to a room on the third floor. It looked comfortable enough, and he considered himself lucky to have got it at such short notice. In any case, all he really needed for the moment was a base of some kind while he collected himself and decided what he was going to do.

When the porter had gone Guy took off his jacket and shoes and lay on the bed, unwinding. Then, stirring himself after a while, he got up, unpacked his bags and hung up his clothes. The torn denim jacket was beyond repair, and he threw it into the trash can. After taking a soothing shower he put on his bathrobe, lay on the bed again, pulled the covers over him and closed his eyes and slept.

It was after six when he awoke. He rinsed his face with cold water, got dressed, went downstairs and set off along Bayswater Road to Marble Arch where he went into a pub and drank a glass of lager. Afterwards he found a small restaurant where he ate a quiet, solitary dinner.

He got back to the hotel just after eleven and was soon in bed. Regardless of his rest in the late afternoon, he quite quickly fell asleep.

In the living room of a flat in Lewisham, south London, a telephone rang. In the bedroom Crane's wife stirred at her husband's side. He laid a brief, reassuring touch on her shoulder and sat up. 'It'll be for me,' he murmured. 'Go on back to sleep.'

From the bedroom he padded through the apartment in his slippers and dressing gown and lifted the receiver. 'Hello?' He spoke with a cultured British accent.

'Crane?' the caller said.

'Yes.' The Englishman recognized the owner of the voice and pictured the lean black American. 'Paxton,' he observed.

'Yes. Did I wake you?'

'Of course you woke me. Don't you realize what time it is here in London?'

'I know what time it is here in Connecticut.'

'Yes, well it's still the middle of the night here. You got me out of bed.'

'I'm sorry,' Paxton said. 'Anyway, isn't it time you got a telephone installed in your bedroom?'

'And encourage this sort of thing?' Crane sighed and ran a palm over his rough chin. He was a tall man, thin and angular. 'Anyway, what's up?' he said. 'This *is* important, I gather.'

'Yes.' Paxton paused then said: 'It appears that there's been some kind of – anomaly.'

' – Go on . . .'

'The subject, male, is one of ours. His name is Holman. Guy Holman. You'll be hearing from your own superiors first thing in the morning, but I've been instructed to inform you – to warn you in the meantime. You'll need to set up a meeting as soon as possible.'

'What's it got to do with us?'

'Because it looks as if he's going to be your responsibility for a while.'

Crane groaned. He felt suddenly weary – a weariness that had nothing to do with having been aroused from his

40

sleep. The fleeting thought went through his mind that at sixty-two it was time to rest from the constant necessity for vigilance; the constant, never-ending series of conflicts.

'Yes,' Paxton was saying, 'the subject, Holman, was attacked in Morocco yesterday morning – by a rabid dog.'

'And it wasn't supposed to happen?'

'Oh, yes, it was – and it did. And afterwards he was supposed to get on a bus with his friend and go off on a tour of Morocco and southern Europe.'

'Yes – go on.'

'And then in a month or so he was due to die of rabies in some little place in Spain.'

'So? What happened?'

'The problem is, he got attacked by the dog but he didn't get on the bus. His friend did, but not him.'

'How can he do it?' said Crane. 'If he's due to die in Spain then that's it. There's no getting away from that.'

'Try telling that to Holman,' Paxton said. 'Look, I'm almost as much in the dark as you are. All I know is that it's happened – and that for some unknown reason he cancelled his plans to travel through Morocco and southern Europe and took a plane for London instead.' He paused. 'I should also tell you that he's done it before.'

'He *has*?'

'A year ago. He was meant to die in a traffic accident – but he survived.'

Crane was silent for a moment while he took this in. 'Where is he now?' he said.

'In London. At a small hotel in Bayswater.'

Crane nodded. 'We shall have to get busy right away.'

'Sorry to dump this on you,' Paxton said, 'but you'll need to get your team together. By the way, it's being arranged for a couple of our people to be sent over to

41

give you assistance. It'll probably be agent Hughes and myself. In the meantime you'll be given whatever information is available.'

'Thanks,' Crane said. He added, 'This is all I needed.'

'Again, I'm sorry,' Paxton said. 'And I'm sorry to get you out of bed. Still – you can go back to sleep now.'

'Sleep?' Crane said. 'You think I can get back to sleep after this?' He was silent for a moment, then he said:

'The other side – will they know about this?'

'I'm afraid your guess is as good as mine. But if they don't know already it'll be only a matter of time before they do. You can be sure of that. They'll be on to it like a shot – to see how they can exploit it for their own ends.'

'Without doubt,' Crane said. 'Still, let's not start to worry too much just yet. After all, this may not lead to anything.'

'No, it may not,' Paxton replied. 'But on the other hand we can't afford to take any chances.'

Even before Crane had replaced the receiver a telephone was ringing in the bedroom of a house a few miles away in London's Mayfair. In the bed a small, corpulent man with silver hair roused himself and sat up. There were two telephones on the bedside table, a red and a black. He took up the red receiver.

'Yes?'

'Mr Rawlinson?' The caller, Pitman, spoke with a slight Cockney accent.

'Of course. Who the fuck d'you think it is.'

'Sorry, sir. Anyway – word has just come to us. I've been told to call you. Apparently something's happened.'

'What do you mean, something's happened?' Rawlinson's tone was brusque, impatient. 'Explain what you mean.'

42

'There's this American come to our notice . . .'

' – Yes?'

'Well, it looks as though – ' Pitman hesitated, 'as though he's – avoided his fate.'

' – I'm listening.'

'It seems he was attacked by a rabid dog – which was all on the cards – and afterwards, so we've learned, he was meant to leave for a tour of Morocco and southern Europe . . .'

Rawlinson was becoming aware of his full bladder. 'And?' he prompted.

'Well, for some reason he had a change of heart. He's come to England instead.'

'*Ah.*' Rawlinson nodded, thoughtfully putting a plump hand up to his smooth, pink chin. 'Who is this man?'

'His name is Holman. From the USA. New York state.'

'Holman. I know that name.' Rawlinson sat up straighter in the bed. 'It's happened before, hasn't it? With the same man, I mean.'

'Yes, sir. Last summer, to our knowledge.'

'And what's the picture this time?'

'Well, as I say, apparently he was on holiday with a friend of his whom he used to work with. Apparently they started off in Portugal, then decided to move down to Morocco before going back to southern Europe. They were going to – '

'For Christ's sake get to the point,' said Rawlinson. 'I haven't got all night and I need to piss.'

'Sorry, sir.' Pitman took a breath. 'It appears that when he goes off on this tour, moving from one place to another, he doesn't take any medical advice or get treatment – '

'This is what's *supposed* to happen, you mean.'

43

'Right. And as a result of not getting treatment he comes down with rabies.'

'Which of course proves fatal.'

'Yes.'

'But now you say he's gone off course – and he's come to England instead.'

'He's here in London at this moment.'

'Does he know the dog was rabid?'

'Apparently not.'

'So he's sought no treatment or advice?'

'Not so far.'

'Then perhaps he won't, if he hasn't done so already. In which case he *still* might die of rabies. He's sure to unless he gets the proper treatment.' In growing discomfort Rawlinson swung his bare feet to the floor and half stood, blind white toes groping for his slippers. 'Anyway, what's being done about it? Have you got him under surveillance?'

'Oh, yes, sir.'

'And what are you doing about looking into the ramifications of it – his change of plan? Have you got that in hand?'

'We're setting it up now. I don't know how long it'll take, but it shouldn't be too long.'

'If there's anything there we must get on to it.'

'Of course, sir.'

'And *soon*. Before anyone else does. By the way, what faith is he? Christian? Jew? Do we know?'

'On paper a Christian, I believe, sir.'

'Not that it makes any difference in the long run. Is he a believer?'

'We don't know.'

'I see. Anything else?'

44

'Not right now, sir.'

'Right. Keep me informed.'

Guy awoke just after eight.

After breakfasting in his room he showered and shaved and was soon out walking along Bayswater Road. It was a fine, clear morning. Over to his right people were walking their dogs on the green expanse of Hyde Park. On an impulse he crossed the busy street and made his way into the park. There after walking for a while he found a vacant bench and sat with the April sun on his face.

Three boys came walking by, chattering animatedly. Guy focused on two of them, a tall boy of about twelve or thirteen, and the smallest of the three who looked to be about seven. Luke's age – if he had lived. Luke, their second chance. Into his mind came a picture of the little churchyard at Forham Green – and Sylvie standing there, so cold, so remote, so anxious to get away. Between them, Luke's little grave. Where baby Luke was concerned it was his only memory.

Not so with David. Memories of Davie were so numerous they were never out of his consciousness for long; he had the power of thrusting himself – but oh so gently – into the most banal situation or prosaic, unrelated thought. So suddenly he would be there, full of life; a small boy with Sylvie's dark chestnut hair, wide smile and infectious laugh. And then, suddenly, *thwuck* – there would echo in Guy's brain the impact of the club, and he would hear again the strange choking sound Davie had made; an odd little noise; not nearly dramatic enough for what it had meant.

Closing his eyes, Guy tried to thrust the pictures away. It did no good to think about the past. *The past is over*.

45

Nothing could be changed. Think about something else. Getting to his feet he made his way with quickening step along the asphalt path and out on to the pavement.

In and around Oxford Street he did a little shopping, buying a new casual jacket to replace the one torn by the dog, some groceries and a fresh supply of disposable razors. Back at the hotel he made a lunch of cold cuts, potato salad and crisp-crusted French bread, finishing off with a slice of cheesecake and a small bottle of Perrier water.

He lay down on the bed when he had eaten. The question went through his mind: What am I doing here? But he dismissed the thought as quickly as it came.

He found he had a slight headache, the pain nagging dully somewhere behind the scar that marked his forehead. After a while he got up and swallowed a couple of pills. Then, drawing the curtains over the light, he lay down again, closing his eyes and waiting for the ache to fade.

It was after three when he got up off the bed. His headache was gone now. He washed, put on his jacket and went out into the warm afternoon. At the foot of Queensway he went into a café and drank a cup of coffee. Couples sat at three of the other tables, and as he glanced at them he became aware of his solitariness. A vacation was best shared. But was that what he was on – a vacation? Hardly. In any case, he was used to solitude.

Later he went to Marble Arch, to a cinema showing a new Woody Allen movie. He watched it without involvement and afterwards returned to the restaurant where he had eaten the previous evening. After finishing his meal he wandered into a crowded pub nearby and there sat at a side table nursing a glass of lager.

And all at once, he became sharply alert. Idly raising his head, his glance roaming over the throng, his eyes had fallen upon the face of a girl.

Sylvie . . .

She stood on the far side of the room, near the bar, a red headscarf over her dark chestnut hair. Then, as suddenly as she had come into his sight she was gone again, hidden by the moving crowd that passed between. He got to his feet. And there she was again.

But it wasn't possible; his mind and eyes were playing tricks. He craned his neck trying to keep her in view beyond the heads and shoulders that moved between. Now she was moving towards the door.

He started forward, pushing his way through the crowd, and moments later was outside, looking up and down the street. She was nowhere in sight.

As he stood there he dimly realized that he was almost breathless and that his heart was thudding in his chest. It was Sylvie he had seen. It was she. At the same time, though, he knew that it could not be. He knew that Sylvie was dead.

4

He kept thinking of the girl as he walked back to the hotel, and later as he lay in bed. The sight of her in the pub had swept away all reality; for moments he had been convinced that it was she, Sylvie. Just those fleeting glimpses of her, taking in her height, her build, the line of her cheek, the dark hair hanging below the scarlet of the kerchief – it could only have been Sylvie. And yet he knew that it could not be.

Changing into pyjamas and bathrobe he switched on the television and lay on the bed. There was an old Clint Eastwood movie playing, some epic with cars chasing cars. He had no interest in trying to follow its plot and very quickly his mind wandered to the image of the girl in the pub. And from her, of course, to Sylvie.

Giving himself up to the memories and images that crowded his mind he thought of Sylvie – picturing her as she had stood cold and ungiving beside Luke's grave. That Sylvie, though, was not the Sylvie he had first known, the *real* Sylvie, the Sylvie he had loved and who, at the start, had loved him in return . . .

Taking up the remote control from the bedside table he pressed Clint Eastwood into oblivion. Then, crawling under the covers, he turned off the light and closed his eyes.

When sleep would not come he eventually gave up the effort and let his thoughts have rein. Untouched by the distant hum of the traffic, his mind roved in the dark to their meeting – that summertime, fourteen years ago,

48

when he had been on his first trip to ... been twenty-four and not long graduated from ... the September of that year he was to begin as a teacher of English and English literature at a New York high school. It was that, his forthcoming job, that had prompted the trip to Britain, and in the company of a friend he had flown in, all callow eagerness and looking forward to five weeks of sightseeing and other pleasures.

He had met Sylvie during the first week. Left to himself while his friend Ian was off on his own pursuits he had got a train to the old Wiltshire town of Salisbury, with the intention of taking a bus to Stonehenge, which was no great distance away. After checking on the times of buses he had wandered around the town for a while and then returned to the centre. Still having twenty minutes in hand he had wandered into a nearby bookshop. He had been there only a few minutes when she had come in. He had noticed her at once, in a glance taking in her slim figure, her shining hair and the smooth oval of her face. Later, taking a paperback to the checkout, he had found her standing before him. After she had paid and gone and he had made his own purchase he saw that she had left a wrapped package behind on the counter.

'I'll take it to her,' he had said.

Without waiting for any protest from the cashier he had picked up the package and hurried out onto the pavement. Looking about him he saw the girl moving away along the street. He set off in pursuit, and had almost reached her when she turned in at a doorway and disappeared from view. Arriving at the doorway a few moments later he saw that it was the entrance to apartments above a stationery store. But which apartment? – there were two bells. Turning, looking quickly over to the bus stop, he saw that the Stonehenge bus was in. Without

49

...s. After he had waited ... opening and the girl was ...gan to speak she caught sight of ...nds.

...s!' she said. She took them from him, ...m warmly. Half-turning, he saw the bus start o... ...ving out into the road. He took a half step across the pavement and stopped. 'There goes my bus – ' He watched as the bus moved into the stream of traffic. He stood looking after it for a few seconds then turned back to the girl in the doorway. At his rueful grin she shook her head sympathetically.

'Oh, I'm so sorry. That was my fault – my carelessness.'

'It doesn't matter.' He shrugged.

'It *does* matter. If it weren't for me you'd be on it now. Is there another one soon?'

'Not for a while. It won't leave me enough time, though – I have to get a train back to London. It doesn't matter, though. I imagine Stonehenge will be there for a while yet.'

While the other pedestrians moved by on the pavement behind him he told her, in answer to her questions, that he was on vacation from America. She in turn said she was in Salisbury visiting a friend. Her eyes, hazel, were wide, with fine, arching brows. Her mouth, devoid of lipstick, was full-lipped. After a little while, as he prepared to say his goodbyes, she said:

'Are you really set on seeing Stonehenge?'

'Well – sure, I'd like to see it. But I can make it another day.'

She was silent for a moment, then: 'I'll drive you there,' she said. 'I was about to start home anyway.'

'Oh, no,' he protested, 'I couldn't think of taking you out of your way . . .'

'It's not far out of my way. It wo
you can catch a bus back, can't you?'

'Oh, I'm sure I can.'

She stepped back into the doorway. 'Look, you wait here a minute. I'll just get my things and say cheerio. I won't be a second.'

Twenty minutes later, travelling north in her Austin Mini through the Wiltshire countryside below a darkening sky, Guy saw the ancient stones rising up from the level of the plain.

When they reached the site they parked the car and followed the other little groups of tourists wandering slowly around the perimeter gazing at the mysterious monoliths. As they completed their circuit they felt the first drops of rain. Within a minute or two it was raining heavily.

They sought refuge in the cafeteria where they sat drinking coffee and looking out at the rain that fell on the sweeping landscape. The girl's name was Sylvie Bennett, he learned. She lived with her widowed mother in Forham Green, a village not far from Trowbridge. She had one sister, Marianne, older by two years. She herself was twenty-four – just four months younger than himself. A graduate in biology, she worked at a horticultural nursery from which at present she was on vacation.

When the rain stopped they left the cafeteria and Guy walked with her to her car. 'Where will you go now?' he asked, ' – home?'

'Yes.' She paused briefly. 'I could drop you off in Trowbridge if you like. If you're going back to London you could easily get a train from there . . .'

He had bought a round-trip ticket from London to Salisbury but he said at once, 'Thanks, that would suit me fine.'

51

...ed the main highways ... – 'The scenic route,' she ... wheat were ripening and the ... with the white and mauve blossoms ... the occasional cottage gardens they ... bright with the brilliant orange of nasturtiums ... velvet yellow and purple pansies. Bringing the car ... a halt at the top of a hill she showed him the panoramic view spread out below. Climbing onto a five-barred gate they sat talking of this and that, while every now and again she would point out various birds and summer flowers; she seemed to know the names of them all. By the time they moved back to the car Guy was feeling reluctant to return so soon to London.

As they drove on he drew up his courage and, without looking at her, said that perhaps he would not return to London that day after all; perhaps, he said, he would spend a day or two in Trowbridge. And if he did, he asked a moment later, was it possible that she might be free that evening? If so, perhaps they could have dinner together . . .?

She did not reply at once and looking at her profile he saw her draw in her lower lip as she considered his proposal. She gave an awkward little laugh. 'My mother will say, How can you? You don't even know the man.' Turning her head she flicked the touch of a smile at him before looking back to the road again. 'But thank you,' she added. 'I'd like that.'

Arriving in Trowbridge, they found a hotel where he booked a room for the night. Afterwards he saw Sylvie back to her car and waved her off, happy and not a little excited in the knowledge that they would meet again that evening. Left to himself he bought a razor and toothbrush and then telephoned a message to Ian at their London hotel not to expect him back until the following day.

He and Sylvie dined together that evening, and met again the following day. It was then he met for the first time – and briefly – her mother. Although Mrs Bennett's manners were impeccable, however, she showed him no warmth, and he was relieved when the meeting was over.

For the remainder of his stay in England Guy saw little of London but a great deal of Trowbridge and Forham Green and the surrounding areas. He met Sylvie's mother on several further occasions, too, and also Sylvie's sister Marianne and Marianne's husband Geoff. The latter meeting was a happy one, but those with Mrs Bennett left him under no illusions about her resentment of him. He refused to let her thinly-veiled antipathy disturb him, however, or to get in the way of what he wanted. When the day came for him to return to America he knew that for him it had to be Sylvie or no one.

That autumn he flew from New York to be with her for two short weeks, and after returning home again proposed to her over the telephone. And – clearly in spite of her mother's wishes – she accepted.

He realized later that he should have heeded the warning of Mrs Bennett's disapproval and possessiveness. Yet he would not have acted differently. And in any case, he had won, for that November he and Sylvie were married in the small village church of St Peter's, near her home. Mrs Bennett, having lost the first round, then attempted to dissuade Sylvie from leaving England, trying to convince her that she and Guy could be equally happy in Forham Green, living at The Willows, Sylvie's home, and that he, Guy, could easily find a worthwhile teaching job in Trowbridge or some other nearby town. Guy of course had resisted. Observing the situation he knew well

53

that if he and Sylvie were to have any chance of happiness it would have to be well away from her mother's influence. Apart from that, he had his work in New York and his studies for his Master's degree.

So, as he had planned, he took Sylvie back with him to America, to New York, to his small fourth-floor apartment on West 81st Street, an act for which Mrs Bennett – and it was no real surprise to him – never forgave him.

Throughout their years together in New York Mrs Bennett paid less than lip-service to their marriage, and used any means – including her supposed loneliness and her oft-extolled love for Sylvie as her favourite daughter – to entice Sylvie back again. At the same time Guy tried not to let her hostility get to him, or get between him and Sylvie; he was already having enough problems keeping the marriage afloat.

Over the weeks, the months, while he taught during the day and studied for his degree during the evenings, he had watched Sylvie making efforts to come to terms with her situation – and at last had reluctantly come to the realization that she was not cut out for her new life. Not that she didn't try; she did; having got herself a job in the office of a Manhattan department store she made every effort to adjust and shape for herself a new kind of existence. But her efforts were largely unavailing, and after a while Guy became aware of the inroads that her inability to cope was making on her peace of mind. So he waited, hoping. She would get used to it in time, and everything would be all right. And later, once he had got his degree, they could move away – perhaps out to the country. If they could just hold out until then . . .

He was wrong; she never got used to it. But he had been wrong about so many things. His greatest mistake, he came to realize, had been in taking her away in the

54

first place from all she had known and still expecting her to thrive. That it could ever constitute any real problem for them had been something he had never contemplated. Ostrich-like he had refused to face it. As it was, everything was different for her. She had spent all her life till then in a large house in the English countryside, her working life spent amid plants and flowers. From that environment she had been transplanted into a fourth-floor, one-bedroom walk-up with six locks on the door and a window box for a garden. In place of the panoramic patchwork of fields and sweeping plains that had been the background to her habitual walks, she now found herself living in the grey, concrete environment of Manhattan. It was, Guy later reflected, like uprooting some fragile flower and expecting it to flourish in an alien, inhospitable soil.

And yet there were still times when he believed that everything would still be all right. David was born late in the July of '77, almost two years after their marriage. He was a beautiful child, bright, winning, and all that they could ever have dreamed of. And with his coming Sylvie at last found a contentment – a peace which banished the shadows from her eyes and gave Guy hope for the future. At the same time, by dint of saving and scraping, they were nearing the time when they could begin to look for a property in some rural area beyond the city.

But then, one fine and terrible August day in 1980, David died.

The following summer, almost a year later, a year during which Sylvie had grown increasingly withdrawn, she left him and returned to England.

He followed three days later in pursuit. Arriving at The Willows he met hostility from Mrs Bennett, and only reluctantly did she even allow him in. As he entered she

55

told him that Sylvie was home to stay and, for good measure, that Sylvie would not want to see him.

He did see her, though. When told that he was there she came downstairs to him. And while she wept in his arms her mother reluctantly left the room – loath to leave them alone together, clearly afraid of allowing Guy an opportunity to use any powers of persuasion he owned.

Mrs Bennett did not give up, though. When she made it clear that he was not welcome to stay overnight he had no choice but to check in at a bed-and-breakfast place in the village. He was not overly concerned, though; by the time he left Sylvie later that evening he felt sure that he had managed to win her round. They had spoken of her returning to New York with him and had even made some tentative plans for the future. On his return the next morning, however, he found that she had changed her mind. Now she would not return immediately with him, but would follow in a few weeks. And in spite of his efforts to persuade her to the contrary he had to be content. Next day when he returned to New York he went alone.

Back in Manhattan he waited. And as the time of her expected arrival approached she telephoned to say that she wanted to stay a while longer. But that while stretched into weeks and at the end of September, unannounced, he flew back to England again – this time with the news that he had sold the lease of the apartment and found a small house in Valley Cottage, Rockland County – as close to the rural scene as he could find.

On his arrival he found her in some strange way changed. She had a new, unaccustomed air of contentment. He sensed a new excitement within her, and saw a joy shining in her eyes that she could not hide.

Together they went out into the mild September air. She said little as they walked, but all the while he could

56

detect that difference about her. In the sunlight they wandered beside the brook where the willows hung, and then down to the orchard. He watched as she moved a little ahead of him and reached up to the apples clustered on the bough. And as she did so he saw the way the fabric of her skirt tightened across her belly.

'You're going to have a baby,' he said, his breath catching in his throat, the words coming only a second behind the realization.

She turned to him, the plucked apple red in her hand. 'Yes!' she breathed, laughing. There was the shine of tears of happiness in her eyes. 'Yes, I am.'

He moved to her, wrapping her in his arms. 'Why didn't you tell me?'

'I only just found out myself. I couldn't say anything before – not until I was sure.' She laughed again. 'Oh, Guy, isn't it wonderful!'

As Sylvie was happy, Guy was happy; so happy and excited at the prospect of another child. This child, he thought, this new life, would bring them together if nothing else could; it would make them complete again.

When Sylvie later insisted that she have the baby in England he reluctantly agreed. He was confident in the belief that after the birth Sylvie and the baby would rejoin him in the States, in their new home.

It did not happen, though, for he later learned that the baby had died within just days of his birth. And so with Luke's death Guy's second chance had gone, his last real remaining hopes for Sylvie and himself.

He had seen her on further occasions, travelling to England for the purpose; and he had written and tele-phoned her many times. She responded to his letters at

57

first, but gradually her letters dried up, and then when he tried telephoning she was never available.

As time went by it became increasingly clear to him that it was over; as far as Sylvie was concerned their marriage was finished. Any love she had had for him had died. Perhaps, he thought, she blamed him for everything that had happened, all the sorrow she had known. Whatever it was, it was clear that she no longer wanted him to be a part of her life.

In the end, getting nowhere, and gaining nothing for his pains but anguish, he had given up all attempts at a reconciliation and tried, without much success, to build a new life for himself. Then, almost a year ago, just this past July, there had come the telephone call from Sylvie's sister Marianne.

'Aren't you coming?' she had said, her tone cold with anger, at him. 'Sylvie is worse – much worse.'

The words had taken his breath away. 'Worse? She's *sick*?'

'Didn't you know? I thought you knew.' She caught her breath. 'Sylvie's got cancer, she's – not expected to live. She's been asking for you. She wants you to come to her. Please – get here as soon as you can.'

'Yes,' he had said, ' – yes, of course.' He could hardly get the words out. 'I'll leave at once.'

Sylvie . . . She was dying. She wanted him. In a lather of sweat and panic he had made immediate preparations to fly out. But then that very day, just an hour after receiving Marianne's call and making his flight reservation, he had been hit by the truck. When he had recovered consciousness he had been given the news that Sylvie was dead.

58

5

An elderly, grey-haired woman working in her front garden in the little village of Forham Green paused to watch a middle-aged couple coming down the lane. They looked out of place against the background of the old stone cottages. The woman, plump and too brightly blonde, wore a cobalt-blue coat with matching hat and self-consciously toning accessories. The man at her side was as black as coal and wore a dark-blue blazer and Black Watch tartan slacks. He carried a Burberry over his arm, while around his neck hung a camera.

Beside the wall that bordered the garden the blonde woman came to a stop and fumblingly extricated a small stone from her shoe. 'I hope the church isn't much further,' she said. Her accent was American. 'These shoes weren't made for walking.' As she put her shoe back on she caught the eye of the grey-haired woman who stood watching. They smiled at one another.

'Beautiful afternoon, isn't it?' said the grey-haired woman.

The blonde woman nodded. 'Just beautiful.' After a pause she added, 'I guess we're going the right way for St Peter's church, are we? I think maybe we parked too far away.'

'Oh, it's just along there.' The grey-haired woman gestured ahead. 'You can see it from the bend in the lane here.'

Moving forward a few paces the American woman peered past a shield of evergreens and caught sight of the walls of the small church. She clapped her hands in a foolish-looking little gesture of ecstasy. 'Well, will you look at that. That has to be just about the cutest thing I've ever seen.'

As she stood there enthusing an elderly man in a cap and dungarees appeared around the side of the house. He came to a stop, regarding the strangers. 'You're going to the church too, are you?' he said. 'We've seen several going by in that direction. There's no wedding nor nothing on today, is there?'

His wife spoke up at this. 'No, I'm sure there's not.' To the Americans she added, 'The church is hardly used these days. Mostly just for weddings, funerals and christenings. There's only a service there once a month now. On other Sundays we have to go to St Mark's in Lower Hesting.' She paused. 'We've been wondering what all the sudden interest is for. All the strangers.'

The blonde woman smiled. 'Oh, but it's the grave.'

'The grave?' The older woman frowned. 'Which grave is that?' Then: 'Oh – you mean the poet?'

'That's right.' The black man nodded. 'It's his grave we've come to see.'

'We sometimes get the odd one or two coming by to see it,' the Englishwoman said. 'But it's rare – and I've never seen so many as there've been today.'

'Well,' the blonde woman shrugged, 'we're members of a society, you see.'

'Oh – all interested in him – Albinson.'

'Yes,' the blonde woman said. 'You probably think it's pretty silly. I know he's regarded by many as a very *minor* poet but – well, we're great admirers of his work.' For a moment she looked as if she was about to get launched on the subject, but the black man touched her arm and said with an indulgent smile:

60

'Come on, you'd better not get started or we'll be here all day. And I'm sure these nice people have better things to do than listen to us.'

'Yes, I guess you're right.' The woman gave a fluttery little laugh. 'And we mustn't keep the others waiting.'

Saying their goodbyes, the American pair continued on up the lane while the couple in the garden watched them. 'Pack of fools, if you ask me,' the old man muttered, ' – getting all worked up over somethin' like that.'

As Paxton and Hughes entered the churchyard they saw two men standing beside a horizontal gravestone. Stepping carefully between the graves, the two Americans moved towards them.

Stopping before the flat, rectangular stone with its lichen-blotched, time-eroded inscription, Hughes and Paxton exchanged greetings with the two men whose accents revealed them to be English. The taller of the two, Simon Levin, had pockmarked cheeks, dark hair and a curving nose. He looked to be somewhere in his early forties, though his leather pants and bomber jacket, with their plethora of zippers, chains, studs and rings, would have looked more at home on a man twenty years younger. Hughes and Paxton, however, were not misled by his flamboyant style of dress and rather effeminate manner.

Next to Levin stood Harold Trevorson, a shorter, stocky man of fifty. With mousy, greying hair his near-classical features were only marred by a slight fleshiness about the jaw. He carried a grey trilby and wore a shabby raincoat over a dark, shapeless suit which was fraying at the cuffs.

The four chatted for a while and then Paxton consulted his watch and murmured that it was time to go in. Levin

61

nodded, adding that others had already entered. With his words he turned and led the way towards the church. It was just coming up to two o'clock.

Just outside the door they passed a middle-aged man who was down on one knee cleaning the weeds from between the flags of the path. They did not acknowledge him, nor he them. They went on by; they knew he would remain there, at his post.

Entering the cool interior, the four saw a tall, thin, dark-haired, elderly man in brown cords bent over a brass tablet, making a rubbing from it on paper with a thick, waxy crayon. He, Crane, lifted his head, smiled and nodded as the four passed by. His eyes were a piercing blue, the more noticeable for the heavy black brows.

The American pair sat in one of the pews near the front while the two Englishmen moved across and sat on their left. There were two English women already seated at the other end. One was Mrs Jane Haddon. Tall, heavily built, red-haired, round-faced, in her mid-forties, she wore a loose-fitting coat and a small black hat with a little bunch of silk poppies attached to its narrow brim.

The other woman, Miss Heather Crawley, was, at twenty-eight, the youngest member of the gathering. She wore a blue coat over jeans and sweater, and a pale-blue kerchief tied over her dark hair. Her large, round-lensed spectacles only slightly detracted from her prettiness.

Seeing that everyone was seated Crane left his brass-rubbing, walked up the aisle and turned to face the small assembly. He looked at them each in turn, then nodded and gave a grave little smile.

'Thank you for coming,' he said.

Mrs Haddon, chewing on a toffee, said, her own smile ironic, 'I wasn't aware that we had any choice.'

'We don't,' Crane said. 'But I thank you anyway.' He

62

looked at Paxton and Hughes. 'And my thanks also to our two American friends who've so promptly come to help out.' He smiled at them. 'I hope your trip wasn't too exhausting.'

Paxton shrugged and spread his hands as if to say exhaustion was something to be borne under the circumstances, while Hughes said, 'Ask me again in a few hours. I think I'm still numb.'

After Crane had introduced the British members to the Americans he said, 'We won't be disturbed here, but our time is limited so we must get on.' He paused while the others gazed at him expectantly, then continued:

'Although our chapter forms only a small part of an organization the boundaries of which are known to only a few, nevertheless the work we have to do is of the greatest importance. I've been instructed to summon you here not, of course, to celebrate some minor, fifth-rate poet who died deservedly unsung at the turn of the century, but to discuss a matter which could have the gravest consequences. Precisely how grave we don't know yet.' His glance moved over the faces of the small assembly. 'As you're aware – a certain anomaly has occurred. In short, a particular individual looks set to avoid his destiny. Exactly how, we don't know. Maybe we'll find out. It could have a definite bearing on the outcome.'

'Is there much known about him, the subject?' asked the stocky, mousy-haired Trevorson. 'From the briefing we've had we know a little about the situation, but hardly anything about the subject himself.'

'I'm coming to that,' Crane said. He consulted notes in a file. 'As you know, his name is Guy Holman. He's American – which is why we have our American colleagues joining us at the meeting.' Here he gestured to Paxton and Hughes. 'Holman is thirty-eight years old. He

63

was born in Norwalk, Connecticut, from which place he and his father later moved to New York. Holman's home – his father died not long ago – is now in Valley Cottage, a small place just outside New York City in Rockland County. He's a lecturer in English at New York University. In 1975 he met and married an English girl, by name Sylvie Bennett. Their first son, David, was born in America in July 1977.' He turned a page of his notes. 'Three years later Holman was responsible for his son's death. A second son was born in 1982. At present the subject, Guy Holman, is in London.'

'If I might ask,' said Levin, ' – why did we have to come all the way out here? Was this house the only one he ever had any contact with?'

'In England, yes,' Crane replied. 'I'm sorry about the journey, and the inconvenience, but it couldn't be helped. The subject is not much for religion, in any formal sense. This venue was chosen as he was married here. However, once we're able to focus on him clearly enough we hope it'll be possible to meet a little more centrally.'

'You say he's not much for religion,' said Mrs Haddon. 'D'you mean he's not a believer?'

Crane shook his head. 'I think not. But in any case, that's irrelevant.'

Mrs Haddon shook her head, making the silk poppies flutter. 'I just can't understand how such a thing could happen. How can a man escape his fate?'

'No, it's not easy to understand,' said Crane, ' – for any of us. But it has happened and we have to deal with it as best we can. And we have to try to deal with it before anyone else gets onto it.'

Levin nodded grimly. 'If they find that it holds anything for them they won't stop at half-measures to exploit the situation.' He paused. 'Are they aware of it, d'you think?'

64

'We don't know yet,' said Crane. 'But we must act on the assumption that they are – or soon will be – and work accordingly. Our task is to try to find out what the repercussions might be – in all their alternatives – and, if there is reason to, to effect a correction of the anomaly as best we can. *If* we can, that is.'

Miss Crawley said, her eyes wide behind the lenses of her spectacles, 'You're quite sure of all this. I mean, there can't be any doubt, can there?'

'None whatsoever. The situation has been demonstrated by all possible means. And there's something else – it's happened *before* with him.'

'The *same subject*?' said Levin.

'The same.'

There was a faint murmur of surprise from two or three of the assembly at this. Crane went on:

'It occurred first at the time of his birth, and again in July of last year when he was involved in a road accident.'

'*Twice* before,' said Trevorson. 'My God. How does he manage it?'

'We don't know,' said Crane. 'Perhaps it's the result of the circumstances of his birth. I'm afraid we just don't know, and it's possible we'll never know. All we know is that he has some particular power that enables him to do what he has done.'

'What was that about his birth?' Miss Crawley said. 'Can you tell us what happened then?'

Crane turned some of the papers in the file before him. 'His mother died when he was born,' he said. 'She was eight months pregnant with him when she was injured in an accident in the kitchen of her home. Apparently she fell and struck her head and shortly afterwards went into a coma. She was rushed to the hospital, but while the doctor was determining whether or not to induce the

65

baby's birth she died. The doctor didn't waste any time. He performed a caesarian section immediately.'

'Untimely ripped,' murmured Mrs Hughes who knew her Shakespeare.

Crane nodded. 'Untimely ripped, indeed. And it would appear, from what we know, that he himself is not aware of the particular circumstances of his birth.'

'His father kept it from him,' observed Levin.

'D'you think he's aware of this power he has?' This from Trevorson.

'We don't know. It's very likely that he doesn't.'

'Well,' said Miss Crawley, 'if he doesn't know he has this power, then he's not able to manipulate it – use it at will.'

'It would seem not. It's almost certainly something that just happens – without his knowing about it.'

'How did it happen this time?' asked Levin.

'Some of you already know this,' said Crane. 'He came into contact with a rabid dog in Morocco. At that time Holman had been planning to travel through Morocco and parts of Europe – but he changed his plans and came to London instead.'

'And he wasn't meant to,' said Haddon.

'No, he was not.'

'And if he'd kept to his plans – ?' said Levin.

'Then,' said Crane, 'he would have remained beyond help until it was too late. Without treatment for the disease he would surely die. But now – well, we just don't know what will happen.'

'Of course, it still might happen,' said Hughes.

'Oh, yes, it might. But as I said, we don't know.'

Haddon said: 'I gather he doesn't know that the dog was rabid.'

'No, he doesn't.'

'Then how will he know? There's no way he can find out, surely. And if he doesn't find out he'll still die at the time he's meant to.'

Crane sighed. 'We don't have all the answers yet.'

'Surely he's bound to find out,' Levin said. 'I know very well that if I were bitten by a dog in Morocco or some such country I'd start to panic immediately.'

'He wasn't bitten,' Crane said.

'But I thought you said – '

'I said he came in contact with a rabid dog. He was indeed attacked by the dog. But he was not bitten.'

'Then how – ?'

Crane looked over at Paxton. 'Mr Paxton, would you be kind enough to give all of us the information you gave me yesterday?'

Paxton nodded, the eyes of the other members fixed upon him.

'We too,' he said, 'assumed that Holman was bitten by the dog. But yesterday, before we left – Agent Hughes and I – we found that it wasn't so. In the attack upon him the dog only tore his sleeve.'

'Then how could he contract rabies?' asked Crawley.

'He contracted it through a small wound on his face,' Paxton said. He spread his large hands, pink palms up. 'We don't know how he came by it, but it wasn't much – probably a little cut or a graze. Anyway, it was through that small wound that the virus entered.' He paused. 'Transmitted when the animal licked his face.'

Silence greeted Paxton's words, then Haddon said:

'So of course he sees no reason to worry. The dog didn't bite him, so as far as he's concerned that's the end of it.'

'Right.' Paxton nodded.

67

As Paxton sat down again Levin said, directing his question at Crane:

'So it's possible that it might still happen as ordained – that he'll die as he's fated to . . .'

'Yes,' said Paxton. 'But the fact remains that so far he's persistently evaded his fate – which for anyone else, of course, is inescapable.' He shook his head. 'We don't know the answers. We only know it's happened to this man before and now it's happened again. I hope we'll find more answers in time.'

'Time,' said Hughes wryly. 'We may not have too much of that. This guy seems to be able to move every which way.'

'True,' said Crane with a sigh. 'But we must do what we can. As you know, on those earlier occasions the situation was examined in the States, and as far ahead as anyone could see there was nothing to worry about. Oh, granted there were going to be changes all over the place – and other individuals were going to be affected by it. Nevertheless, there was nothing of any great seriousness; there was no – *peril* in the situation – nothing that warranted any intervention. But, as I say, that was as far as could be seen at the time. Now it might be different. That's something we'll have to find out.' He closed the file. 'I know you must have many questions. But bear with me for a while longer. We'll find out as much as we can – and nothing will be kept from you. You'll be contacted again in a few days, and we shall meet again shortly. In the meantime, we must be vigilant. Others might well be ahead of us in knowledge, in which case there's no telling how they might move.'

He nodded to the gathering, turned to face the altar, bowed his head and then walked to the door and exited. After some moments the others rose and, singly or in pairs, followed him out into the air of the bright April afternoon.

Later that afternoon Guy was riding on a bus along Oxford Street when he saw the girl again. She was walking on the pavement near the junction of Regent Street.

As soon as the bus stopped he got off and walked back in the direction from which he had come. There was no longer any sign of her. Turning again, he wandered slowly on towards Marble Arch.

Rain began to fall before he got back to the hotel and once inside he decided to stay in for the rest of the evening. After reading for a while he lay back on the bed while the radio softly played and a BBC disc jockey spun up records from the forties and fifties.

Ah! the apple trees, blossoms in the breeze, where the hammock swung . . .

For a while he let the music wash over him, but in the end Dinah Shore's soft velvet voice, all wistful yearning, was too much for his mood, and he switched it off and lay in silence with his thoughts.

He had a simple meal brought to his room around seven. Afterwards he watched television, first part of an old British movie – in which the speech was like a different language – and then an investigative documentary on the repressive situation in Larinas. In it, men and women from the nation's capital, Castelandú, spoke of the sufferings they had endured at the hands of the country's security forces; some exhibiting the scars they carried as a result of their interrogations.

Guy watched it through to the end, then switched off and got into bed.

Towards midnight, when he lay still awake, one of his headaches came on and he took a couple of pills. As he

69

waited for the dull pain to subside he let his thoughts wander. And inevitably Sylvie returns again. She is nursing David. He sees once more the softness and peace in her face as the baby sucks at her breast. Other pictures swim on to the screen of his memory – Sylvie during his first summer in England, in a small glade, before her on a cloth the remains of an impromptu picnic. As if looking at an old movie he watches her brush a lock of hair from her face while the dandelion she holds reflects gold in her smooth cheek. In another flashing memory he stands at the foot of a green slope while she runs down towards him. And breathless and laughing he sweeps her up in his arms and presses his face to hers.

He would choose always, if he could, to recall only the happy times, but those other memories always insinuate themselves into his recollections sooner or later. And so again he sees her at Davie's funeral in New York with the devastation in her face as she follows the little coffin. Yet another memory brings her to him as he had seen her after the death of Luke – seven years ago now – when she had stood at the graveside avoiding his glance and clearly so anxious to get away. And then once more he is sitting beside her in her car outside the railway station at Trowbridge. 'I love you still,' he says. 'I always shall.'

As he lay there in the silence of the room he answered the unspoken question that had been at the back of his mind since he had decided to come back to England. He would go to Forham Green, to Sylvie. He had told himself all along that he would not, but he would. He knew now that it was the reason for his return.

The vision, the last one, hovered shimmering before the small assembly. It was of a large house, with a brook running by and willows bending over the water. As the

70

image faded the lights in the room came back on. The gathering, after many hours in deep concentration, shifted on their seats, cleared their throats and murmured to each other. Rawlinson got up from his seat, his short, corpulent figure standing hardly taller than when he had been sitting. Raising a pale, soft hand to his immaculate silver hair he looked around him.

'Well,' he said, 'I think we've seen enough to know in which direction we have to go.'

There were nods, murmurs of assent.

'And one thing that must now be clear to all of us,' Rawlinson added, 'is that love will be the key.'

'Love?' said one of those present, a tall Scot with a beard and a gold earring. His tone echoed Rawlinson's expression of distaste.

'Yes, love,' Rawlinson replied. 'Crane, Paxton and their holy crowd claim that love is their greatest weapon. It might well be – and it's what we shall use against them.'

The others in the room nodded approval.

'With love,' Rawlinson added, 'and with agents in place, the man will be ours.'

71

6

After breakfast Guy made inquiries as to the times of trains then caught a tube to Paddington Station where he bought a return ticket for Trowbridge, via Bath. As he sat waiting for the train to start he realized that his decision to go to Forham Green had brought him a kind of peace. Perhaps now, by going there one last time, he would finally be able to come to terms with the past.

When the train began to move he became aware of the beating of his heart and in an effort to relax he tried to breathe more deeply, letting the air out in slow, steady exhalations. It would not be long now.

Arriving in Trowbridge he bought some daffodils and then, after waiting for several minutes, caught a bus for Forham Green. A little later, as the vehicle wound through the green, rolling Wiltshire hills, he found himself coming upon familiar scenes and landmarks. Seeing them he found that his palms were damp.

At last the bus had reached Forham Green and was drawing to a halt outside the Hen and Hare public house. Moments later Guy was stepping down onto the pavement. He stood unmoving for some moments as the bus started away again, then, turning, set off through the narrow streets of the village. Taking a path that skirted the green, he made his way along a lane between stone cottages. The signs of yesterday's rain had gone now, and the day was sunny and warm. The neat gardens that lay on either side were bright with the blossom of cherry and magnolia, while the green buds on the birches and the sycamores were bursting into moist new leaf.

When the little church of St Peter's came in view his steps briefly slowed. Then, moving on again, he arrived at the church gate and came to a halt.

It had been seven years since he had stood upon this spot. At that time, too, he had carried daffodils. Then, however, Sylvie had been with him.

After arriving in London on that occasion he had at once telephoned Sylvie and arranged to meet her. The following day he had gone to Trowbridge and taken a taxi to The Willows. Sylvie had opened the door to him; she had been watching for him, she said. He had learned with relief that her mother was out and together he and Sylvie had sat drinking coffee in a silence that lay like a fog between them. Later, after Sylvie had picked some flowers, she had driven them to the church.

He could recall it all so clearly. The day had been grey, and although the heavy rain of the morning had ceased, scudding clouds still hung low and heavy and threatening more rain to come. As it was now, the churchyard had been deserted. Following in her steps he had walked over the grass between the graves until she had stopped beside that particular one. Beneath the leaden skies the smallness of the grave had taken his breath away; that, and its newly-cut, simple little stone:

IN MEMORY OF

LUKE

BORN MARCH 20TH 1982

DIED MARCH 25TH 1982

And the tears had sprung to his eyes and run down his cheeks.

73

He had remained standing there with his head bowed while his tears dried in the wind and Sylvie took the dying forsythia from a small earthenware pot set in the soil and replaced them with the grape hyacinths she had brought. When she had arranged them she straightened beside him and said, almost in a whisper:

'Are you all right?'

'Yes.' He nodded, raising a hand and brushing at his cheek. When he lifted his head to look at her a moment later she moved her own glance away. He watched as she gave an awkward little shrug.

'Well – ' she said, 'shall we go . . .?'

They had only been there a minute. She seemed ill at ease, anxious to be gone. But was it any wonder, he asked himself.

' – Just a moment more.' he said. 'A little longer.'

'Of course. I'm sorry.'

She turned to him. There was a strange expression on her face. He saw misery there, and the shine of tears in her eyes, and something else as well, something he could not read. The April wind was chill and he pulled the collar of his raincoat closer to his throat. They remained side by side in silence in the wet, short-cropped grass. 'I never even had the chance to see him,' Guy said. He realized he was still holding the daffodils.

'Why?' he said after a while. 'Oh, why didn't you let me know? Why didn't you let me know right away that – that he was born? Oh, Sylvie – ' the words came out in a groan, 'I would at least have had the chance to get here – to see him in time. Before it was too late. I've got nothing now. Not even a memory.' Bitterness growing beside his grief, he went on: 'I get a letter from you – and that's it. Not even a phone call. Just a letter telling me that he had been born – and that he had died five days later.'

74

Looking at her as she stood there like an anxious bird poised for flight he saw unease in every line of her body. 'Can you imagine what it was like,' he said, ' – to learn about it all in a single letter? His birth *and* his death? And even then not to learn about it till days after he had died.'

She said nothing.

'Why?' he said. 'Why didn't you let me know?'

'You don't understand,' she said, not looking at him.

'No,' he said bitterly, 'I don't.'

'D'you think it was easy even to write you the letter I did?'

'But you have a telephone. Couldn't you or your mother or your sister have called me on the phone?'

'Oh, please, Guy – please. It's over and I don't want to talk about it.' She took a step away.

'We can't leave it like this. We have to talk about it.'

'Haven't we talked enough?'

'Sylvie – please . . .'

A pause. 'Well – not here anyway.'

'No – well – okay.'

'Anyway, I'm cold,' she said. She turned and started towards the gate. Stooping, he put the daffodils – their stems sweat-damp from his palms – into the pot along with the grape hyacinths. Then he straightened and followed in her footsteps.

When he reached the car he found her already sitting inside. He opened the door and got into the seat beside her. Behind the steering wheel she sat looking silently ahead.

'Why didn't you tell me?' he said after a few seconds.

When no answer came he said quickly, the words coming out in a rush:

'Sylvie – do you hate me so much?'

She shook her head, turning her gaze to her right, even

further away from him. 'No, I – no, of course not.' A little silence, then she added wearily, 'Of course I don't. Anyway, what difference does it make now. What does it matter.' They were not questions.

'Don't say that,' he said. 'Of course it makes a difference. And it matters a great deal. You must know that. Doesn't it matter to you how I feel?'

She said nothing. The line of her cheek was cold, impassive. He said:

'Sylvie – they were my sons too.'

There was silence in the car, touched only by the sounds of their breathing, while from outside came the sounds of rooks cawing in the high elms beside the church wall.

'Please, Sylvie, don't shut me out for ever,' he said. He could feel the pricking of tears in his eyes again – not only for Luke now, not only for Davie, but for the grief they had all known, and the loss, the waste. 'It's been so long,' he said. 'I had hoped that our – our being apart these months might have changed things.'

She didn't answer.

'It's still Davie, isn't it?' he said. He shook his head. 'It's been nearly two years now since – since . . .' His voice trailed off.

She said quickly, flatly, 'D'you think I'm not aware of how long it is?'

'Oh, yes,' he replied, 'I'm sure you're only too aware of it.'

'I think about him every day.'

After a moment he said:

'It wasn't my fault, Sylvie. I wasn't to know.'

She said dully, 'I know that. But it doesn't make any difference. I'm sorry, but – it doesn't change things. I only wish it could.' She shrugged. 'Who knows – perhaps in time . . .'

He gazed at her. 'Was it – revenge?'

'Revenge?'

'For what I did. Is that why you didn't let me know about Luke? Was it because of David?'

She turned to him at this and he saw the despair in her face. 'Oh, Guy,' she muttered, 'you don't understand. You just don't understand. You never will.'

Then all at once she was leaning forward over the steering wheel, tears pouring down her cheeks, her sobs racking her body. He reached out and tentatively laid an arm across her shaking shoulders. After a few minutes, when her tears had stopped, she shrugged his arm away and straightened in her seat. 'Well – I must get back,' she said. She started the car and pulled away from the kerb.

In silence they drove alongside the green. When they reached the junction she turned left, heading for Trowbridge and the station.

'I thought we were going back to the house,' he said lamely. When she didn't answer he added, ' – To talk.'

'Haven't we done enough talking?' She kept her eyes on the road ahead. 'Is there anything left to say?'

Near the station entrance she pulled up and sat looking down at her hands on the wheel – waiting for him to say his goodbyes and leave. He felt as much apart from her as he ever had. But how could they leave it like that? They had to be left with *something*; there had to be something between them other than their unhappiness and her continuing blame of him. 'Listen,' he said, his voice hoarse, 'later on, when you're feeling better, I'll write to you. And I'll come back and see you.' He paused. 'We loved each other, Sylvie. Don't forget that.'

She turned to him, hazel eyes huge in her tear-streaked face. Her mouth moved as if she would speak, but in the end she just turned away and looked ahead of her again.

77

'I love you still,' he said. 'I always shall.'

In silence she kept her eyes on the street ahead.

'That must count for something . . .' he persisted.

Still she didn't respond.

'Or maybe it doesn't.' He gave a sigh. 'Anyway,' he said, 'I'll come and see you.'

She shook her head. The movement was slight but decisive. 'No, Guy, please,' she said. 'There wouldn't be any point.'

The last words had carried a note of finality that he was too tired and too distressed to try to breach. After gazing at her for a moment he got out of the car. Inside the station he waited for over an hour for his train.

He had seen Sylvie on two further occasions over the next couple of years. Each time he wrote saying he wanted to see her, and each time she reluctantly complied. And so he had flown to England, and although he would have preferred to meet her in Forham Green he had bowed to her wish to meet in London, she catching the train up from Trowbridge for the purpose. They met at the Savoy Hotel – which she referred to as 'Tom Tiddler's ground', a neutral place where, as she put it, neither would be compromised or at a disadvantage – and on both occasions he tried to persuade her to return with him to the States.

Both times, though, he had soon realized that his journey was futile. Sitting facing him over coffee, Sylvie – clearly ill at ease and eager to be gone again – had refused all his entreaties. It mattered not at all how he described the attractions of the house in the woodland of Valley Cottage. No, she told him, she was settled now; and more than that, she was happy – or happier than she had been for a long time. And he had had to admit that there might be truth in her words. In spite of her obvious unease, he

78

could see behind her anxious glances a look that told of something else. Something that gave to her a little spark of life, a spark that he had not seen there for so long. He wondered at its source. It was on their second meeting that a thought had suddenly struck him, and with it he wondered why it had not occurred to him before.

'There's someone else, isn't there,' he said a moment after the realization came to him.

'What?'

'You've met someone else.'

' – I?'

'Yes. There's someone else in your life.'

'Oh – Guy, no.' In spite of her protest she appeared slightly flustered.

'I can see it. I can tell. There's some other man.'

'No, no.' She shook her head. 'No, there's not. Believe me.'

'No?' He had been sure that he was right. 'Truly?'

'Truly. I swear it.'

Hearing her words the hope had come surging back and he tried once more to persuade her to give their marriage another chance. If she wanted him to he would give up his work in America and move to England, he said. It didn't matter to him; all that mattered was that they were together. No, she said, avoiding his eyes, it was too late. Afterwards when he saw her into the taxi that would take her to the station he knew that he had lost again. And this time he knew it was irrevocable.

Over the years that followed he had tried to form other relationships. He had had a few affairs, and in some cases had found himself thinking there was a chance that he could banish Sylvie's power, lay her ghost for good and all. But it never happened. She always managed to get in the way. And in spite of his knowing that he had lost, that

79

all her love for him had died, one part of his mind continued to nag at him, insisting that there was still a chance; that one day everything would all be right again, and they would be back together, where they belonged.

And so it had gone on until that July day last summer when he had learned that Sylvie was dead.

He stood at the churchyard gate with the daffodils in his hand while the memories came flooding back. And he could stand there for ever; there was no shortage of memories. Pushing open the gate and closing it behind him, he walked through into the churchyard. He stood for a moment getting his bearings, then started off along the path, leaving it after several yards to cross the grass that skirted the south side of the church, moving towards the site of Luke's little grave. And there at last, close to the shade of an old yew tree, it lay before him.

The first thing he noticed as he stepped towards the grave was its look of neglect. There were no flowers; even the earthenware pot had gone. The soil of the grave was choked with weeds, while the stone, through subsidence, had shifted, so that it stood slightly tilted. Moss and lichen had taken a hold on part of the stone's surface, while a creeping ivy had twined about it, hiding part of its inscription from view.

Crouching in the grass at the grave's side he pulled the ivy away from the stone, then began to uproot the weeds, laying them beside him. After a while the grave bore something of its appearance on his previous visit.

Picking up the little pile of weeds, he carried them to a small rubbish tip in the corner of the churchyard. In amongst the dead flowers and weeds and old grass cuttings he found a tin can. Carrying it to a tap near the church wall he filled it with water. He checked that it was sound

80

then moved back to the grave and placed it on the newly weeded earth, pressing it in. Carefully he divided the daffodils, placing half of their number in the tin, arranging them as well as he could. They looked pathetic but it was the best he could do.

Holding the remaining daffodils he straightened and scanned the surrounding graves, searching out the newer ones. As his eyes roamed across the serried rows of stones a question suddenly came to him: Why had Sylvie not been buried with Luke? He looked down at Luke's grave. Sylvie should have been buried there, with her son. Clearly, though, judging by the size of the grave, baby Luke lay there alone.

He moved away, searching for Sylvie's grave.

Thirty-five minutes later he stood once more beside the little grave of baby Luke. He had looked at every gravestone and every grave in the churchyard, even reading many of the inscriptions on those stones which, quite evidently by their appearance, were too old to be Sylvie's. And Sylvie's grave was not there. If it was, then it was among those graves without stones. But this he found hard to accept. The idea that she had been laid to rest in some unmarked grave just didn't fit in with the social status and lifestyle of her family. Her mother, if no one else, would have erected a stone to Sylvie's memory; in Sylvie's death, as during her life, nothing would have been too good for Sylvie where her mother was concerned.

The thought occurred to him that there might be someone about who could give him the information he sought, or access to some register of burials. Turning, he moved towards the church.

Reaching the double doors he turned the handle of the left-hand one, pushed it open and moved through the

81

porch into the cool interior. Closing the inner door behind him he remained still for a moment in the silence then moved down the aisle and stopped before the altar.

The last time he had stood there had been over thirteen years ago, at his marriage to Sylvie. The church's interior had been crowded with her family and friends and people from the village. There had been a little choir, he remembered, made up of half a dozen local lads, cold in their cassocks and surplices, their treble voices ringing out sweetly in the November chill of the inadequately-heated building. *The Lord's my Shepherd; I'll not want* . . . Now he stood alone, and the only sound was that of his breathing, hollow in the emptiness. He noticed too that the atmosphere had a faint musty smell about it; on that earlier occasion he had only been aware of the scent of the roses in Sylvie's hands, the chrysanthemums that had adorned the altar – that, and how Sylvie had stood beside him, looking fragile and breathtakingly beautiful in her white Empire wedding gown. In an almost overwhelming rush of tenderness and love for her he had felt himself to be the most fortunate man on earth. It had been a time of such promise. Everything had been before them.

And now . . . Now their lives together were over. There was nothing left to show for what had been between them, of the little happiness they had known.

Turning, he retraced his steps to the door. Passing through into the porch he glanced at the notice board and saw there a typewritten announcement to the effect that until further notice Sunday services would be held at St Peter's only on the first Sunday in every month, and that on other Sundays worshippers should go to St Mark's in Lower Hesting, the next village. So much for the necessity and power of the Church, he thought; there was no longer

82

enough business in Forham Green to support its own incumbent.

He moved out into the air again and closed the door behind him. He looked at his watch. It was after three. He had not eaten since breakfast that morning. He would get something to eat when he got back to Trowbridge.

The question of the whereabouts of Sylvie's grave remained on his mind as he walked back along the lane. The person who could give him the answer, of course, was Sylvie's mother. With the thought he came to a stop, deliberating. He had no wish to see her; she was the last person he wanted to see, but he needed to know . . .

Striding out, he moved past the green, heading for the western side of the village. At last he came to a halt before a large house standing in spacious grounds, set apart from its nearest neighbour by some forty or fifty yards. To the side of the garden a brook rippled by with willows hanging over the water. At the head of the short drive the double gates – one bearing the house's name, The Willows – were closed. He opened one of them and moved towards the forecourt with the monkey puzzle tree in its centre. Intentionally avoiding looking at any of the windows – in case he should glimpse Mrs Bennett looking out at him – he went to the front door and rang the bell.

After a few moments the door was opened and a dark-haired woman was standing there. In her forties, she wore a smock and held a duster in her hand. She looked at him inquiringly.

'Yes . . .? Can I help you?' Her voice had the flat vowels of the West Country. Obviously Mrs Bennett's cleaning woman.

'Hello . . .' He smiled at her. 'I'd like to see Mrs Bennett, please . . .'

83

She shook her head. 'I'm sorry, but she's not at home right now.'

'Do you expect her back soon?'

'No, I'm afraid not. She's gone away for a few days. She won't be back till Wednesday. I can take a message for her if you like.'

'Uh – no – that's okay, thanks.' He backed off the step.

'I'll tell her you called, shall I? Mr – ?' She waited for his name. Guy smiled and gave a little shake of his head. 'It's not important. But thank you.'

He heard the door closing behind him as he moved back across the forecourt towards the gate.

In his sleep that night he dreamed that he was wandering through a vast churchyard, looking for Sylvie's grave. When he awoke in the early hours of the morning the images from his dream were imprinted on his brain.

7

Sylvie had once sent to him a picture postcard bearing a reproduction of Millais's *The Death of Ophelia*. The painting had held a fascination for him ever since. Now, before him in the Pre-Raphaelite room of the Tate Gallery, hung the painter's original creation.

He had set off for the Tate fairly early that morning, having made a decision over breakfast to do something positive with his time. If he did not, he had told himself, he would end up just wandering aimlessly about the city.

He stood gazing at the deranged Ophelia. Bedecked with flowers, she lay supine, eternally drifting down the stream, red hair floating, a pillow of waterweed beneath her air-billowed skirts. Her hands were lifted just above the water, fingers curled, palms up in an unconscious gesture of submission to her fate. There was no fear in her eyes.

And suddenly he saw in the glass that covered the painting the reflection of a still figure standing in the background beyond the throng of constantly moving people. He spun, and there was the girl before him, turning away on the far side of the room. Almost involuntarily he stepped towards her, as he did so colliding heavily with one of the viewers. Guy apologized and the man, wearing a black leather jacket, stooped, rubbed his shin and gave Guy a look that was without charity. A second later when Guy turned to look at the girl again he found she had gone.

Quickly he moved out of the room in search of her. She

was nowhere in sight. After a brief hesitation he set off to the foyer. There was no sign of her there either, and after debating whether to look for her in some of the other rooms, he went outside. At the top of the wide steps he stood looking up and down the street. After a few minutes he gave up and went back inside.

In the gallery's cafeteria he bought a cup of coffee and carried it to a vacant table where he sat drinking and thinking of the girl. The sight of her had been unsettling. It might have been Sylvie herself standing there . . .

Thinking of Sylvie, he saw himself once again in Forham Green, moving from gravestone to gravestone in the search for the one that bore her name. His failure to find it, he realized, had left him with a sense of business unfinished . . .

It was universally acknowledged that the bereaved had a need to mourn; more – that they had a need to find some focus for their mourning. He recalled reading a moving account in a newspaper a few years earlier of a number of elderly British women who had travelled thousands of miles to Burma to see the place where their husbands had died during World War II, broken in body and spirit by the Japanese in the construction of the Burma–Siam Railway. The women's pilgrimage had been a search for peace of mind; they had been possessed by an inescapable feeling that they could never rest until they had seen the spot where their loved ones – forever young and vital – had died as the result of unspeakable brutality, in deprivation and misery, in an alien land, so far from home.

Sylvie's passing had known no such attendant horrors. Death had come to her while she was in the company of her loving mother and sister, but the end result was the

86

same. And Guy knew now why the British widows had gone. For the same reason he had to find Sylvie.

But where was she buried? And, why was she not buried with Luke?

He ate lunch in the West End, did some browsing among the stores in Oxford Street and got back to the hotel just after five-thirty. As he approached the desk the porter held out his key along with a slip of paper.

'There've been two phone calls for you while you were out, sir,' the porter said, gesturing to the note. 'Both long distance – from Morocco. The caller said he's the manager of the hotel where you stayed in Agadir. He wants you to call him back as soon as possible. Says it's urgent.'

Guy thanked him and went up to his room where he threw aside his raincoat and jacket and sat on the edge of the bed. He looked at the slip of paper bearing the telephone number of the Moroccan hotel. Why was the hotel manager trying to contact him? Then the answer came to him. His watch. Of course. His watch had been found.

Lifting the telephone receiver he gave the Agadir number. While he waited for the call to come through he undressed and got into his bathrobe, ready to shower. A few minutes later the call came through. Guy thanked the porter and the next moment heard a foreign-accented voice on the other end of the line.

'Hello – is that Mr Holman?' The line was bad, the man's voice distorted by crackle and static.

'Yes, this is he.'

'Hello? Mr Holman?'

'Yes. Who is this?'

'Ah, Mr Holman. Good. This is Mr Al Kasri. Mr

87

Hassan Al Kasri – of the hotel *Le Fieste de Sud*. You left your London address with the porter . . .'

'Yes – right,' Guy said, then added happily, 'Did you find my watch?'

'Your watch?' The other's tone reflected puzzlement, then he said: 'Oh, yes, your *watch*. Yes, I remember. No, it is not *that* – not your watch I telephoned about. I telephoned you because . . .' The rest of his words were lost in a static crackle.

'What?' Guy said. 'What did you say?'

The line became clearer. 'I am telephoning about the dog.'

'The *dog*?' Guy was puzzled. 'What do you mean?'

'The dog in the hotel. The little dog. You remember? We have just learned that it attacked you when you left.'

' – Ah, yes . . .'

'Yes, someone on the street saw it happen. And fortunately we had your address in London, so I telephoned you at once.'

Guy, puzzled, wondered what the fuss was about. 'It's okay,' he said. 'The dog didn't hurt me. He just ripped my sleeve, that's all.'

'It didn't hurt you?'

'Not at all. Why, what's the matter?'

'Well, after the dog attacked you it came back into the hotel and tried to bite one of the waiters. The dog was sick, you understand.'

'Sick?'

'Yes. It ran out of the hotel, but came back the next day, and it was – ' the man paused, searching for words, 'it was – was beating its head against the wall. We trapped the dog, then someone came to shoot it and it was taken away for tests to be made. We don't know the result of

88

the tests yet, but it is almost certain that the dog was – *rage*. I don't know the English word for it.'

'Oh – you mean *rabid*,' said Guy.

'Ah, yes – rabid.'

Guy was aware of the faster beating of his heart; he had come so *close*. 'Anyway,' he said, 'I thank you very much for telling me, but like I said, the dog didn't hurt me.'

'You are quite sure of that.'

'Oh, yes, absolutely.'

'Because even a *little* bite could be very dangerous. I am told that it is in the animal's spit – er – saliva, you understand?'

'Yes, I understand. But don't worry. He didn't hurt me – thank God.'

'Well, that's good. That's very good.' Mr Al Kasri sounded much relieved. 'And the other gentleman – your friend. He was all right too?'

'Oh, yes, he was already on the bus.'

'Ah, I see. And you are okay?'

'Yes, I'm fine.'

'Good. I had to be sure, you understand?'

'Oh, indeed. I'm very grateful to you.'

'Not at all.' A brief pause. 'Well, I wish you goodbye, Mr Holman.'

'Goodbye, Mr Al Kasri – and thank you again.'

When Guy had hung up the receiver he at once hitched up the sleeve of his bathrobe and examined his arm. There was not the faintest mark there. He sighed with relief at his narrow escape. He had forgotten all about the dog's wild, surprise attack. Rabies. That accounted for the animal's inexplicable behaviour, its suddenly becoming so vicious when only minutes before it had been so friendly.

89

In the bathroom he took off his robe and took a long, soothing shower. Afterwards he put his robe back on, wiped the steam from the face of the mirror and began to comb his hair.

And all at once his action came to a halt. He stared, his eyes focused on the small, healing graze on his lower cheek. Suddenly he was back on the hotel terrace in Morocco; he could see again the dog as he had bent to stroke it; could feel again the dog's rough, wet tongue as it had licked at the wound. But it had been such a small wound; and now it was almost gone . . . He wiped the mirror again, leaning forward, peering more closely. He became aware that his mouth was dry while his hand holding the comb was clammy with perspiration; he could feel, too, the cold sweat in his armpits and the rapid beating of his heart.

Moving to the bed he sat down as if dazed. Then, swiftly, he was picking up the telephone receiver and telling the porter that he had to see a doctor, urgently. The porter said he would try to contact the doctor who looked after the hotel residents. Guy thanked him, replaced the receiver and began to get dressed.

Within five minutes the porter was back on the telephone. The doctor, he said, was out, but was expected back very soon. A message had been left for him to contact the hotel on his return.

In the dimly lit room Rawlinson's short, corpulent body pivoted slowly as he turned on the dais taking in the rapt faces of the small assembly.

'*He knows.*'

His voice held a note of deep satisfaction. After a pause he continued, his words measured:

'He knows now that the dog was rabid. So, with luck,

90

he'll get treatment and he will survive. And with a little more luck and a great deal of care and vigilance we'll have him where we want him.' He pursed his pink lips. 'In the meantime we must keep him safe.'

8

Forty-five minutes went by before the doctor, who gave his name as Powell, telephoned and asked Guy the nature of his problem. Trying to remain calm, Guy told him briefly of the situation. After questioning him for a few minutes in order to get a clearer picture, the doctor told him to stay in his room and wait; he would get back to him again as soon as he could.

While waiting for the doctor to call back Guy nervously paced the room, watching the minutes going by and trying to recollect the past five days for any signs of symptoms that might be cause for alarm. Then, almost an hour later the telephone rang and the porter announced that the doctor had arrived and was on his way up.

Dr James Powell was in his early forties, heavy-set, dark and bespectacled, and, Guy silently observed, with a manner which in other circumstances was probably found to be calm and reassuring.

Guy sat on the bed while Powell looked at the small, almost-healed wound on his cheek and took his pulse and temperature. Afterwards Powell nodded: 'Fine,' and moved to a chair and sat down. 'I'm sorry to have left you worrying for so long after our initial chat,' he said, 'but I had to do a little checking. Rabies was eradicated here several years ago so it's not a disease that many British doctors have experience of.'

Impatience and fear growing, Guy thought, This is great; I get someone who hasn't the first idea about anything.

92

The doctor continued: 'Anyway, the first thing I want to tell you is that you're not to worry, you understand?'

'Not to worry?' Guy said. 'The dog was rabid and it licked the wound on my face.'

'Oh, don't think I'm underestimating the seriousness of it,' Powell said. 'We won't take any chances. You'll get the very best treatment, believe me. And you're going to be okay.'

Guy said nothing. He desperately wanted to accept the man's reassurance, but against it were all the legendary horror stories associated with the disease.

Powell, seeing his concern, got up and put a hand on his shoulder. 'You're going to be okay. Believe me.'

Turning, he took a notebook from his case, consulted it and moved to the telephone. After dialling a number he asked for a messenger to come at once to the hotel. As he replaced the receiver he turned to Guy and said:

'As soon as the courier gets here I'll send him to Colindale in north London for the vaccine. Colindale,' he explained, ' – that's where the Public Health Laboratory is. The vaccine is kept there. The courier will be here in a minute. We'll soon get you fixed up.'

As he moved back to the chair he asked, 'Are you in London on your own, or have you got family along?'

'I don't have any family.'

'You're not married?'

'Not now.'

'No parents? – brothers and sisters?'

'No one.'

After a little time had passed the porter rang to say that the courier was there. Powell went from the room and returned a few minutes later.

'He's gone off now on his motor bike,' he said, 'he'll pick up the vaccine and bring it to me. I'll go on home

93

now and phone the Duty Officer at Colindale to let him know he's on his way. Then when I get the vaccine I'll meet you at my surgery. It's very close by.'

'*Surgery?*' Guy said.

Powell smiled. 'Don't be alarmed – that's a doctor's consulting room here in England.' He handed Guy a card then looked at his watch. 'Half-past seven now. Come round to my office at nine. I should have the vaccine by then and I can give you the injection right away.'

He picked up his case and moved to the door, Guy following. In the doorway Powell turned and shook Guy's hand. With a grave but reassuring smile, he said, 'And don't worry. Everything's going to be all right.'

Shortly before nine o'clock Guy, after a brief walk from the hotel, arrived at the doctor's office in Queensborough Terrace. On his arrival Powell ushered him in.

'I've got the vaccine,' Powell said. He waved a hand. 'Go over to the couch and take off your coat and jacket and drop your trousers and underpants. This evening you'll get three injections – which are the first part of your course of treatment. After that it gets easier.'

He took from a package a couple of small containers, studied the labels, then began to fill a hypodermic syringe from one of them. When it was ready he came towards Guy. 'Right – turn round. You get the first jab in your backside.'

'I thought you gave the injections in the stomach,' Guy said as he turned.

'Oh, no,' Powell replied, 'those infamous injections in, the abdomen are a thing of the past. *And* most of the pain associated with them. You'll feel no pain from this. Now – just relax your leg.' Guy felt the wipe of a cold swab on his right buttock then winced as he felt the prick of the

94

needle and fluid surging into his flesh. 'Well,' Powell said, 'almost no pain.' He withdrew the needle, dabbed again with the swab. 'One down, two to go. Pull up your trousers and sit on the couch.'

The doctor changed the needle in the syringe and came back to Guy's side. 'Lift your chin a little. This one has to be given directly into the wound. It will hurt a little more, I'm afraid, but the pain shouldn't last long.'

Head up, eyes closed, Guy felt the cold of the antiseptic swab on his cheek and seconds later the sharp sting of the needle as it entered the site of the small wound. Powell withdrew the needle. 'Sorry about that,' he said as Guy opened his eyes. 'Was it very painful?'

Guy forced a smile. The site of the injection was burning. 'Well, let's say I wouldn't care to have it every hour on the hour.'

Powell smiled sympathetically. 'Anyway, the last one won't be so bad.'

Guy received the third injection – which was relatively painless – in his upper left arm. Afterwards, with his jacket back on, he sat beside the desk while Powell wrote in a file. After a few moments' concentration on his notes Powell looked up and said:

'I've learned quite a bit since I got your message earlier this evening. Had what you might call a crash course in rabies and its treatment. And I'm very glad to say that medicine's come a long way in the last few years where rabies is concerned. I believe the administration of the old type of vaccine was very painful. And that's what so many people still think of – those painful injections. The treatment, it seems, was feared almost as much as the disease.'

'You said there would be a course of injections,' Guy said.

95

'Yes.' Powell took up a printed leaflet, consulted it. 'There are six injections altogether of the vaccine. You had the first one just now, in your arm. The other five are given over a period, spaced apart. Four in the first fortnight, and then two boosters.'

'What were the other two shots I had? – the one in my butt, and the one here?' Guy indicated his face.

'Those were immuno globulin.'

'Immuno what?'

'Immuno globulin. It's a blood product taken from people who have already received the rabies vaccine. You had half the dose in the buttock, the other half in the site of the wound. You won't be having any more, though. From now on it'll just be the vaccine itself – given in your upper arm like the one you just had.' Powell looked back to the leaflet. 'Your next injection will be in three days. They run at three, seven, fourteen, thirty and ninety days from the time of the first injection. Then that's it. Finished.'

'And it's more effective than the old one, is it? This new vaccine?'

Powell gave an emphatic nod. 'Oh, yes. There've been very few failures since it was first used several years ago. And now that the immuno globulin is given as well as the vaccine it's even safer. Though, of course, the treatment has to be started in time. It was developed in France.'

'And it's cured nearly every case of rabies that's been treated.'

'We believe so.'

'Don't you know?'

Powell hesitated, searching for words. 'You have to understand that very few persons *strongly suspected* of having contracted rabies and who have been given the

96

course of treatment have ever gone on to develop symptoms of the disease and die.'

Guy looked at him blankly. Powell explained:

'You see, at present the only means of being certain that a person has actually contracted rabies is when the symptoms appear. But by then it's too late. It's *always* too late. Every person who has ever shown the symptoms of the disease has gone on to die from it. So – the answer is to get treatment as soon as possible – *before any symptoms appear*. As I say, if one waits until the symptoms appear it's invariably too late. The patient invariably dies.'

'So how will I know whether I've been infected or not?'

'With luck you'll never know. The only certain way would be *not to take the treatment* and wait to see whether you develop the symptoms.'

'I see. But if I developed symptoms it would be too late for the vaccine to do me any good, right?'

'Right.'

'I'd be a dead man, right?'

'Quite. Once the symptoms told us that you'd been infected it would be too late; no vaccine would help you. No, we have to work on the *assumption* that you've been infected, and treat you accordingly. The only people who have ever known that they were infected have then gone on to die of it.'

'My God.' Guy shook his head. 'And what if this treatment hasn't been given to me soon enough? You said it has to be started in time. What if it hasn't been? I'm going to be a nervous wreck, waiting every minute for symptoms to appear.'

Powell put a hand on his arm. 'Don't be pessimistic. You're not showing any symptoms at all, and when the

97

vaccine is given *before* symptoms appear it's *extremely* rare for a patient to go on and develop those symptoms.'

'I see. But there *is* a *chance*.'

'Well – the *very slightest* chance.'

'I see. Would I be able to spot the symptoms?'

'Oh, indeed. You'd be feeling very much under the weather.'

'When will I know – whether I'm out of the woods?'

'Within a few days. If you're not showing any symptoms within a few days then either you never contracted the disease in the first place, or the vaccine has been successful. But as I told you, it's very rare indeed for a person to develop symptoms *after treatment has begun*.'

'Is this vaccine available in the States?'

'Oh, yes. Apparently they used to use a different one, but now they use the same one. I was coming to that. When I told them at the Public Health Lab that you were from the States they suggested that you stay here at least for the first four injections of the vaccine – all to be given within the next two weeks – and then, if you want, return home for the last two – the two boosters.' He paused. 'Where is home?'

'Just outside New York City.'

Powell nodded. 'Of course if you want to return to New York at once you could go *tomorrow*. I understand there's a very slight difference in the method of treatment there, but it's not of any real significance. It wouldn't affect you at all. So there'd be no problem in your continuing your treatment in New York. If you wanted to, you could take the rest of the vaccine with you.'

Guy said nothing; he didn't know what to say.

'You don't have to make up your mind now,' Powell said. 'Think about it. But decide soon. Personally, I wouldn't advise your returning home immediately. I think you should stay at least for the early part of the treatment. Would that present a problem?'

'Oh, no – no . . .'

'Fine. Well, let me know what you decide. D'you think you'll want to return home before your next jab? That's in three days from now. Thursday.'

'No, I wouldn't think so.'

Powell consulted a calendar, made notes in a diary and on a sheet of paper. He handed the paper to Guy. 'These are the dates for your treatment – whether you stay here or go back to New York. As I say, your next injection has to be this coming Thursday. So come along here in the evening – say seven-thirty. Can you manage that?'

'Of course.'

'Good. And in the meantime, try to relax.' He looked at Guy somewhat appraisingly. 'You look as if you could do with a course in relaxation too.'

'I'll work on it.'

'Fine.' Powell smiled. 'Well, that's it for now.'

'Oh,' Guy said as he stood up, 'I must settle my bill.'

'Don't worry about that right now,' Powell said. 'It'll keep till next time. You'll be back.'

At the front door Guy shook the doctor's offered hand. 'I don't know how to thank you.'

'Not at all. It's what we're here for.'

As the door closed behind him Guy went down the front steps, out of the gate and onto the pavement. It was a fine evening. Walking along the street he became aware of the slight soreness in his cheek and buttock and a dull ache in his upper arm. Reminders of his probable salvation.

The short, powerfully-built man, Trevorson, had followed Guy from the doctor's home and now stood before the St

99

John hotel, eyes focused on a third-floor window. A light had just gone on behind the curtains. Trevorson stood there for a while longer then, satisfied, lowered his glance and moved on.

'We've just received word,' said Crane, speaking on the telephone to Paxton, 'that a quantity of anti-rabies vaccine has been issued at the medical centre in north London, and that the subject, Holman, has received treatment.'

'Well,' said Paxton with a sigh, 'we were afraid that might happen when we saw that he'd changed his plans. Anything was on the cards then.'

'Yes. Anyway, a meeting is to be set up.'

'For when?'

'Sometime over the next few days. We must try to find out what the consequences are likely to be.'

'Do you know the venue?'

'The same place, I should think. But I'll confirm that very soon.'

'Fine.'

'In the meantime a watch is being maintained. Trevorson is one of the team. I don't envy him. Such a boring bloody job. Got to be done, though.'

100

9

In the cafeteria of the Tate Gallery Guy sat bent over a cup of coffee. Open beside his cup lay a little, old, red-leather-covered book: Elizabeth Barrett Browning's *Sonnets from the Portuguese*. It had been Sylvie's, bought second-hand while she was a teenager; she had given it to him on the day of his return to England during that November of their marriage. Its pages lay open now at the sonnet, *If Thou Must Love Me*. His eyes lingered over the so-familiar words, then, turning the pages back to the fly leaf, he read again the inscription, written in her round hand – *For my most dear Guy, with my love, always* – followed by the sonnet's last line which she had written beneath:

> . . . love me for love's sake, that evermore
> Thou mayst love on, through love's eternity.

Through love's eternity . . . He closed the cover of the little volume, blotting out the words, while he wondered why he had chosen to bring the book with him. For comfort? If so, its comfort was of the bitterest kind.

He looked at his watch. Almost three o'clock. He would leave the gallery soon and make his way back to the hotel. He had already spent over an hour-and-a-half looking at the exhibits. It was enough for today.

From all around him came the sounds of clinking china and the chattering of voices. The cafeteria, like the exhibition rooms above, was crowded. Why he was there again, so soon after his last visit, he wasn't sure. At least, though, it was preferable to wandering about the streets or sitting in his hotel room waiting for symptoms of rabies to appear. He had done his share of the latter following the start of his treatment two days ago. Since then there had been a vigilant monitor at the back of his mind constantly checking every facet of his well being. In spite of his worries and his searching for symptoms, though, he felt well, very well. He had no feelings of lassitude, no nausea, no lack of appetite. There had not even been a sign of one of his headaches.

He hadn't decided yet, but he was almost sure that he would return to New York over the next few days. He must make up his mind and tell the doctor when he saw him tomorrow for the second injection of the vaccine. Then, as Powell had told him he might, he would take the rest of the vaccine with him and continue his treatment at home. He would feel more at ease if he returned. With the anxiety he felt as a result of his brush with the dog, wasn't it natural that he should want to go back? Didn't most animals make for their lairs when they were injured or sick? Besides, what reason did he have for hanging on?

There was, of course, still the matter of Sylvie's grave, but there was no doubt that it was there somewhere. Mrs Bennett would be returning to her home today and all he had to do was ask her. But what was the point? Would it change anything? It wouldn't bring Sylvie back. Nothing could do that. And wasn't it madness to spend so much emotional energy fretting and worrying over something that was over and done with? In the end his continual questioning would become nothing more than an exercise in self-indulgence, a bogus means of reviving yet again the ghosts that came to haunt him. Sylvie – like David

102

and Luke – was a part of his past. It was time to accept the fact and get on with his life.

And yet, for all his silent injunctions there still remained in him that desire, that ache, that *need* to find and see the spot where Sylvie lay. And he thought again of the English women and their trip to Burma.

He thrust the thoughts aside. He would go back, go back home. And for the last time. His business here was finished now for good and all. He would never return.

His coffee was finished; he set down his cup. A moment later, glancing over to the door, he saw the girl.

He had just a glimpse of her as she hovered in the doorway for a second before turning and moving away, but he recognized her at once.

He hesitated briefly, then, slipping the little volume of sonnets into his pocket, he picked up his raincoat from the seat beside him, got up from the table and moved out of the cafeteria in her wake.

He found her in the Pre-Raphaelite room, standing before Millais's *The Death of Ophelia*.

As she stood before the painting, seemingly oblivious of the other viewers who moved about her, Guy stood to one side and covertly studied her.

Her hair was styled in what he assumed was a kind of long 'twenties cut; a little shorter at the back; at the front a heavy wing of dark hair swinging in a graceful curve against her cheek. She wore a simple grey skirt, to her mid-calves, and a dark-blue sweater that showed the swell of her breasts. Slung over her shoulder was a bag with a red tartan design, while over her arm she carried a raincoat. The resemblance between her and Sylvie was astonishing, though there were of course differences. She was perhaps a shade taller than Sylvie. Perhaps her nose

103

was slightly shorter, her eyes a little less deep-set. Not-withstanding the differences, however, the resemblance was almost uncanny.

The girl hadn't moved. Feet a little apart, she stood looking intently at the study of the drowning Ophelia. Guy, realizing that he was staring, quickly turned away. With a pretence of looking at the other paintings he turned to the canvas closest at hand and found himself gazing at a sentimental study of a consumptive girl coming face to face with her newly-returned lover. He moved to the next picture, all the while keeping the girl within his peripheral vision. After another minute he saw her turn and, as if the Millais had been her sole purpose for being in the room, start towards the doorway. He waited for a moment then followed her out of the room.

Out in the hall he saw her walking ahead of him and soon realized that she was going to the cafeteria again. He followed her – it was more crowded now – and joined the line at the counter, separated from her by a couple with a child. He watched as she was served with a cup of coffee and carried it to a vacant table. He bought a pastry and a cup of coffee. Turning, holding his tray, he could see only two or three vacant tables in the whole place. Ignoring them, he moved towards the girl's table, hovered beside it for a moment then said:

'Pardon me – d'you mind if I sit here?'

She glanced up from the newspaper she was opening and gave a little shrug. 'Not at all.'

'Thank you.' He set down his tray, slid into the seat and laid his raincoat beside him. 'Pretty crowded in here,' he said. She raised her eyes from her newspaper and gave a slight nod and an even slighter smile. It was not encouraging.

He sipped at the coffee, at the same time covertly

104

eyeing her over the rim of the cup. He was seeing her full-face and at close proximity for the first time. She was strikingly beautiful. Her lowered eyes were rimmed with the darkest lashes. Her mouth with its full lower lip was wide. Her skin was flawless. She looked to be about twenty-seven or twenty-eight. Setting down his cup, he cleared his throat and said,

'I guess you like Millais, do you?'

She looked up, a slight frown on her brow. 'I'm sorry?' There was no humour in the trace of the smile that lifted the corners of her mouth.

'I noticed you in the room where they have the English Romantics – or the Pre-Raphaelites as you call them.' He smiled. 'Standing in front of the Millais painting of Ophelia.'

She gazed at him for a moment then said coolly, again with a hint of the rather patronizing smile: 'So I was.'

Not giving up, he said, 'Yes, I noticed you – and the other day, too – on Monday. You seemed quite engrossed in the painting . . .'

She nodded. 'How observant.'

He felt embarrassed, and felt his embarrassment growing. 'It's just that – you seemed so intent on it.'

She nodded again. 'So?'

Not knowing when to stop, he gave a shrug and added lamely, 'Well – I couldn't help noticing you. And having seen you there twice . . .'

She gave a slow nod, no smile of any kind on her mouth now. 'What are you doing – following me?'

At the cool tone of her voice he felt his cheeks flushing. He said quickly, 'Of course not. It's just that I thought how odd it was that I should see you twice in the same spot. Odd in a place the size of London, I mean . . .' He

105

didn't mention also having seen her in a pub and on the street.

She gave a disdainful little shrug, as if to say What does that matter? and then looked to her newspaper again.

Guy's lips were set tight. He was angry with himself for getting into the situation, and also with the girl for adding to his discomfort. There was no way to save it now, though; with every word he only made it worse. Hot with embarrassment, he drank from his cup and chewed on a piece of the pastry. He became aware of the girl folding her newspaper, lifting her bag and thrusting the paper inside. She was not even bothering to finish her coffee. Next moment she was rising to her feet and then, suddenly, in a brief flurry of movement, her cup was going over, its contents splashing out and running across the table and into Guy's lap. He leapt to his feet. Opposite him the girl's face was a study in horror and dismay.

'Oh, my God! I'm so sorry!' Dropping her bag back onto the table she raised both hands, fingers spread, to her face. Guy took out his handkerchief and began to dab at his jeans. 'It's all right,' he said.

'Here . . .' The girl opened her bag and got out some tissues. 'Use these . . .'

'It's okay, thanks. I think I'd better go and sponge myself down.' He moved away from the table, aware of the attention of the people around him.

In the men's room he wetted his handkerchief and did what he could to get rid of the coffee stain. Afterwards he used paper towels to dry himself as best he could. The rest was a job for the cleaners.

Approaching the table a few moments later he saw to his surprise that the girl was still there. He had somehow expected her to take advantage of his absence and make her escape. As he reached the table and bent to pick up

106

his coat she gave him an apologetic smile. He returned it half-heartedly; with her earlier coldness she had dispelled a good deal of her fascination for him.

'Are your clothes okay?' she asked.

'Yes, thanks.'

'I really am so sorry.'

'Don't worry about it.' He draped his coat over his arm. 'Forget it.'

' – And your coffee's cold now.'

'That's okay.'

'I'm really so sorry about it – my clumsiness.'

'It doesn't matter. Forget it.'

Still standing, he shifted his cup and saucer to one side and used one of the tissues the girl had given him to dab at the remaining traces of spilt coffee on the table top. He forced a smile. 'I guess I'll leave the rest for the cleaning lady.'

As he put the sodden tissue into his saucer the girl said, 'At least let me buy you another cup of coffee.'

'It's all right, thanks.'

Her fine eyebrows lifted in a little expression of supplication. 'I promise you'll be safe this time.'

He hesitated, smiled more warmly, then tossed his coat onto the seat and sat down beside it. 'Why not. Thank you.'

The girl – she gave her name as Ann Milburn – 'But I'm called Annie' – went back to the counter and brought coffee for them. They talked as they lingered over the cups. She came from Bradford in Yorkshire, she told him, and worked as a supply teacher – 'What you'd call a substitute teacher, I think' – teaching general subjects to primary school grades. At present, she said, she was enjoying a few extra days following the Easter holidays

107

but was soon to start work at a school in London's East End.

She went on to say that her own particular subject was Fine Arts – 'Though I don't paint anymore' – and that she had done her graduate thesis on the Pre-Raphaelites. 'I've always been fascinated by them,' she said, 'their work *and* their lives. That's why I come here quite often to the Pre-Raphaelite room. I love the Tate anyway, and whatever else I look at, sooner or later I find myself looking at those particular paintings.'

In answer to questions he told her that he lived in Rockland County, New York, that he had come to England for a vacation and would soon be leaving to return home.

When at last he replaced his empty cup in the saucer she asked if he would like some more. He smiled and shook his head. 'No, thanks. I really think I've had enough for now.'

'How terrible,' she said with a little grimace, 'to do that to you – and after behaving towards you like that. You must have thought me so rude.'

With a shrug he said, 'Well, you don't know me.' He grinned. 'You're not to know that I'm a perfectly harmless guy trying to make his way in a difficult world.'

'Are you?' she said.

'Trying to make my way?'

'A perfectly harmless guy.'

They laughed, then, looking at her watch she said she supposed she had better think about catching a bus home to Hammersmith. They got up from the table, left the gallery and walked along the pavement to a bus stop. As Guy waited with her their conversation continued, but then too soon she was saying, 'Ah, here's my bus,' and their brief meeting was coming to an end. He said quickly:

'I'd like to see you again. Are you doing anything later on?'

'I'm afraid I'm tied up this evening.'

He nodded. Tomorrow would probably be his last full day in London. 'Tomorrow?' he said.

' – I'm sorry.'

' – Ah, well . . .'

A little silence. The bus was very close now. 'I'm free on Saturday,' she said.

Saturday. If he went through with his half-formed plans he could be on the way back to New York by then. But what difference would another day make? 'Saturday would be good,' he said. 'Perhaps we could have dinner together.'

She smiled. 'I'd like that.'

'I'll call you.'

She recited her telephone number. 'Hang on,' he said, dipping into his pocket for pen and paper. The bus was pulling up. He found a pen but no paper. 'Tell me again,' he said. She repeated the number and he wrote it on the palm of his left hand. 'Got it. I'll call you.'

'Good.' She was stepping onto the bus. 'Don't wash your hands before you do.'

'I won't.' He stood smiling after her as the bus pulled away.

That night, as he lay in bed in the dark, he thought about his meeting with the girl. He looked forward to Saturday. The little thrill of anticipation he felt brought in its wake a slight sense of guilt, as if he were somehow being untrue to Sylvie's memory. He thrust the feeling aside.

Consulting his watch Trevorson saw that it was coming up to quarter-past eleven. He sighed, yawned, wishing the

109

time gone by. Holman had stayed in for most of the evening, and there had been no light at his window for the last fifteen minutes. He must have gone to bed – bed, where he, Trevorson, would like to be, and would be before too long.

Trevorson was sitting in the passenger seat of a Ford van, keeping an eye on the face of the hotel across the street. At midnight one of the others would be coming to relieve him and he could make his report and get some rest. Holman wasn't likely to be going anywhere now.

Trevorson needed to pee, and his need was growing stronger with every moment. He knew that he was not going to be able to hold out till his replacement came. He should have brought a bottle with him, he told himself; added to which he shouldn't have drunk the can of lager. But one needed some help in passing the time.

Turning his head, he looked up and down the street. The signs of life were diminishing. The pubs had closed, and the restaurants were beginning to wind up their business. Apart from the traffic that kept up its regular flow back and forth, and the occasional pedestrian who moved past, there was only the old bag-woman and the drunk. The woman had just finished making up a bed on a bench that stood close to a telephone kiosk. Now she lay down, a shapeless bundle wrapped in layers of old rags and newspapers. The drunk – who hadn't made it more than a few yards since leaving a nearby pub – had spent the past twenty minutes sitting on the kerb, hanging his head.

A few yards down the street on the right Trevorson saw the shadow of a slight recess beside a shop. Probably the entrance to a yard. He could slip in there. No one would see him.

Still he remained sitting there, unwilling to commit

110

himself to the move. But he would have to. His bladder was on the point of bursting.

Another few moments of indecision and he was slipping the catch, opening the door and stepping down onto the road. Closing the door behind him he glanced quickly up and down the street then stepped across the pavement. In a few seconds he had reached the shadowed spot beside the shop.

As he stood urinating against one of the tall wooden gates he closed his eyes with relief. When he opened them again a moment later he glanced to his right and with a wary eye saw the tramp get unsteadily to his feet and begin to stagger along the pavement towards him.

The drunk showed no interest in him, however, but lurched over to the seat where the old bag-woman lay and clumsily fell across her legs. Trevorson, still urinating, watched half-amused as she rose up with a wail of protest and struck out, first with her bare hands and then with a rolled-up newspaper. The drunk suffered the violence for a few moments, then, his patience giving out, he snatched the paper from the woman's hand and began to rain down blows upon her unprotected head. Muttering, she briefly raised her arms to fend him off then lurched from the bench and staggered away, her rags, rugs and papers falling around her. Glancing over at Trevorson she caught his eye. Her expression of distress changed; she grinned at him and altered her direction, moving unsteadily towards him. Quickly he zipped up his fly.

They met as he stepped towards the van, her arms reaching out to embrace him while she murmured something he couldn't catch. With a low laugh he tried to ward her off, but she was surprisingly fast and her arms came up again, wrapping about him. She held him close, her head on a level with his own, her smell – old wine and

111

urine – an assault to his nostrils. He tried to thrust her away, one hand reaching out to the door of the van, but she was too strong. Next moment her hand was on his head, pulling it down towards the dark, disgusting pit of her mouth.

He had no time to be fully aware of what happened next. It was all over and done with in seconds. As he struggled to free himself from her embrace he became aware that the tramp was there beside them. And in that second realization came. But it was too late. Suddenly he felt his arms held from behind, while in the same moment the woman's hand was reaching up to his face. The prick of the fine, fine blade was so sharp, so fast, that he barely felt the pain. So quickly it pierced his left eye and slid up through his eye socket into his brain. His eyes widened slightly, as if in surprise at the strange, cold, numbing feeling, and then fixed, unmoving. Just as swiftly the fine, razor-sharp blade was withdrawn. As the life fled from him he was half-dragged, half-carried into the shadows. Only then was he allowed to fall.

Part Two

The wind doth blow today, my love,
And a few small drops of rain;
I never had but one true love,
And in cold grave she was lain.

'Waly Waly' – Anonymous

10

Soon after breakfast the next morning Guy left the hotel to walk in Hyde Park. The day was warm and he sat down on a vacant bench taking in the sun. He thought with pleasure of Annie, and their date on Saturday, but more importantly, and with continuing relief, of the fact that he still felt *well*. Every day that passed without the appearance of any symptomatic feelings of illness the safer he became. He felt more relaxed, more positive, than he had for days.

After a time he got up, left the park and went into a pub where he ordered a glass of lager and carried it to a small table beneath one of the patterned windows. As he drank he took out the little volume of sonnets that Sylvie had given him. All he needed now, he said to himself, was to know where Sylvie lay buried. Once he had seen her grave and had said his last goodbye he could go back to New York in peace . . .

Into his mind came the thought that Mrs Bennett would have returned by now to Forham Green. He could telephone her . . .

He sorted out some loose change, went over to the telephone in a small alcove on the far side of the room and dialled Mrs Bennett's number. After a few rings the receiver was lifted and the pips were sounding in his ear. He pressed a coin into the slot and the next moment Mrs Bennett's voice was on the line:

'Hello?'

'Mrs Bennett . . .?'

' – Yes?' She had recognized his voice and her tone was at once wary.

'This is Guy.'

A brief pause. 'Yes?'

No 'How are you? Have you quite recovered from your accident?' – just the one cold interrogative word. Some promising start, he thought. And now that he had her on the phone he didn't know how to begin.

'I don't want to bother you,' he said, 'but do you have a minute? There's something I'd like to ask you.'

Another brief pause. 'Yes?'

'I wanted to see Sylvie's grave,' he said, 'but I couldn't find it. I thought she'd be buried with Luke, but she's not.'

He waited but she said nothing.

'Why aren't they buried together?' he said.

More silence. 'Hello?' he said. 'Mrs Bennett . . .?'

Another moment of silence and then he heard a click as she replaced the receiver.

When he dialled the number again the ringing went on and on, unanswered.

He returned to his seat, sat down. He had not exactly expected her to dance with joy at the sound of his voice, but he hadn't expected her to hang up on him either. He sat there for some minutes thinking about it. He looked at his watch. Then, making a decision, he downed the rest of his beer, put his cigarettes and lighter into his pocket, and left the pub.

He had gone a hundred yards along the street when he realized he hadn't picked up his book. Returning to the pub he went to the table at which he had sat. A man and a woman were sitting there now, but there was no sign of the volume of sonnets. To his questions the couple replied that they had seen nothing of any book. An inquiry at the bar brought no better result. Puzzled, he left the pub again and set off for Paddington Station.

Standing at the open gates of The Willows a few hours later he saw that there was a car in the open garage, a dark-blue saloon. He walked across the forecourt to the front door of the house and rang the bell.

At once from inside came the yapping of a dog, and he recalled that Mrs Bennett had kept a couple of wire-haired terriers – nervous creatures that seemed to be in a perpetual state of anxiety. Going by the sound of the frantic barking coming from behind the door she still had a penchant for the particular breed. He waited. The barking ceased and then, suddenly, on the periphery of his vision to his left, he became aware of movement. Turning his head he saw the curtain at the window swing back into place.

He waited another minute and rang the bell again. Still no answer. He wondered what to do. He was quite sure that Mrs Bennett was at home. Leaving the porch he went round by the side of the house to the rear. On the small terrace at the back he looked about him for signs of life – there was none. He rapped on the back door. From inside the dog's sharp barking began again.

He knocked again, and on the other side of the door the dog threatened to bark himself into a fit. After a moment's hesitation Guy grasped the door-knob and turned it. The door opened into the familiar scene of the rear passage, with a kitchen opening off. As he pushed the door wider there was a flurry of movement and suddenly the dog was rushing towards him. Guy stepped aside in alarm, and the animal dashed past him and ran down the garden path.

Guy watched as it disappeared from view beyond a

117

bank of yew shrubbery, then turned and started down the path in the dog's wake.

He found Mrs Bennett beside a herbaceous border at the side of a lawn. Clearly aware of his presence she was making a show of tending a rose-tree. Guy came to a stop and stood there. She straightened, turned and looked him up and down. Notwithstanding her pretended occupation Guy saw that in her elegant two-tone blue woollen dress she was dressed for anything but gardening. Having tried to avoid meeting him, the slight flush in her cheeks gave evidence of her embarrassment at being caught out. Her discomfiture didn't last long, though. After a moment of silence she said, fixing him with a cool gaze:

'Well, now, to what do we owe this great honour?'

'I wanted to see you,' Guy said evenly.

She nodded. 'I thought you might pay us a visit. When my daily woman said there'd been a visitor, and described him, I knew at once it was you. And then your phone call.'

Her eyes, much darker than Sylvie's, and owning nothing of Sylvie's warmth, gave evidence of her part-Italian parenthood. They gazed at him now with a glance as hard and as ungiving as the thin, implacable line of her mouth. She was in her mid-sixties, a tall woman whose age seemed to have done nothing to bend the straightness of her spine, or show any hint of compromise in the square set of her shoulders. She stood before him, aloof and unapproachable.

'How did you know I was here?' she said. 'And how did the dog get out?'

'I let him out. And followed him.'

She raised an eyebrow in overdone surprise. 'You let yourself into the house, did you?'

'No, I didn't let myself in. I merely opened the back

118

door. I knew somebody was in – I saw somebody at the window while I was ringing the bell.'

She dropped her glance at this and took a few steps away across the grass, coming to a halt beneath the branches of a flowering cherry. Standing before him she was all hard, uncompromising lines against the contours of the tree with its delicate pink blossom.

'Well,' she said, 'why did you come here?'

'Because I wanted to talk to you. I tried calling you on the phone, but if you remember you hung up on me.'

Looking at her expression as he spoke he found himself touched again by the reality of her dislike of him.

'I've got nothing I want to say to you,' she said.

'You made that fairly obvious.'

'Exactly what are you expecting here?'

He gave a humourless smile. 'Certainly not any kind of a warm welcome.'

'Listen,' she said, unfazed, 'I haven't got time to play games. What do you want? I'm expecting company.'

That, Guy thought, explained the elegance of her dress. He watched as she raised a hand to touch unnecessarily at her immaculate dark hair – only beginning now to grey – and the thought flashed through his mind that she was nervous, a little afraid. Afraid? Of him? He could not imagine Mrs Bennett being afraid of anyone.

'Don't worry,' he said, 'I won't keep you more than a few minutes. I'm quite aware that my presence doesn't exactly bring you any pleasure.'

She gave a silent nod of agreement, at the same time turning her head to glance at the terrier where it sniffed among the plants at the lawn's edge.

'Though I don't really understand why,' Guy added. 'I never could.' He paused. 'But even so, now that it's all over, I thought that – '

119

'Yes,' she cut in, 'it *is* all over. Thanks to you.'

'To me?'

'Yes, to you.'

He became aware of a nervous fluttering in his chest. Surely she did not blame him for Sylvie's death.

'If Sylvie hadn't met you,' she said, 'she might be alive today.'

'Please . . .' Guy half-turned from her gaze. 'Don't say that.'

'You can't bear to live with the truth, can you?' There was the sudden gleam of tears springing to her eyes. 'You made my daughter unhappy – so unhappy – and I'll never forgive you for it.'

Hearing her words Guy knew that he could not win. Whatever he said would make no difference.

'Anyway,' she said, 'why have you come?'

Before he could answer he heard the pattering of feet, and turning, he saw two children, a girl and a bespectacled boy, running down the path from the house. The girl looked to be about eight or nine, the boy a year or two younger. They came to a halt at the sight of him – the girl a few yards in front – and stood looking from him to the woman. Both children had her dark eyes and dark hair. Raising her hand to the girl Mrs Bennett said, 'Cressida, dear – you and John go on back indoors at once. And tell your mother I'll be there in a moment.'

The children did not move, but continued to look at Guy with curiosity in their eyes.

'Did you hear me?' Mrs Bennett said. 'Go on back into the house, both of you. Gramma's talking right now. I'll be in in a minute. Go on now.'

They turned, first the boy, then the girl, and moved back along the path towards the house. Mrs Bennett watched them go, one hand fluttering to her hair again.

'Marianne's children are a handful at times, I can tell you . . .'

There was a slight change in her manner. It did not last, though. 'Anyway,' she said after a moment, 'say what you have to say.' Her eyes did not meet his.

Abruptly he said, 'Why didn't you tell me that Sylvie was so sick?'

When she did not answer he went on:

'Can you imagine what a shock it was to me – to hear out of the blue from Marianne that Sylvie was so – so near to death? And then after my accident I find a telegram from you waiting for me – telling me that she's dead.' He shook his head. 'A telegram.'

Mrs Bennett said, shaking her head, 'I'm – I'm sorry about that. Believe me. But when one is – overwrought one doesn't always do the right thing. I'm sorry.'

She was sorry. And that was supposed to explain it all. He felt suddenly sickened with the whole thing. What was the point in pursuing it? 'Just tell me one thing,' he said.

'Yes . . .?' The wariness was back in her voice. 'What is it?'

'Just tell me where she's buried. I went to the church but although I searched I couldn't find her grave. I found Luke's grave all right – I could remember where that was – but I couldn't find Sylvie's.'

'No,' she said after a moment, not looking at him, 'you wouldn't.'

'I wouldn't? What does that mean? I expected her to be buried with Luke – but she's not anywhere there.'

She sighed. 'Sylvie wasn't buried in the churchyard at St Peter's. She was buried at St Mark's.'

'St Mark's?'

'In Lower Hesting, the next village.' She gestured off.

He nodded, remembering the note on the church notice

121

board about services being held at St Mark's. Moving a couple of steps across the grass he stopped and turned back to face her. She stood watching him, incongruous against the cherry blossom.

'Why isn't Sylvie buried with Luke?' he said.

As she looked at him now he read alarm in her eyes, while her hand once again touched nervously at her hair.

'You'd never understand,' she said.

'Tell me.' His voice rose slightly. 'To hell with whether or not you think I'd understand. Just tell me.'

'Listen to him,' she said. 'Such passion. I don't like this conversation, the way you come here making your demands, asking your questions – and without a thought as to the effect it might have on other people.'

'Tell me,' he said evenly. 'I have a right to know. Sylvie was my wife.'

'True.' She nodded. 'The worse for her.'

'She was my wife,' he repeated, 'and Luke was my son.'

She spoke now as she turned away again, her voice so low that he barely heard the words:

'Was he?'

He stared at her.

'What? What did you say?'

Without answering she suddenly stepped forward, pushing past him. He stood there, as if stricken, then spun, moving after her, catching her by the wrist, bringing her to a halt. She glared at him, then lowered her eyes to his restraining hand. 'Do you mind?'

He let go of her wrist. 'What did you mean just now?'

'Listen,' she said, hissing the word at him. 'I never liked you. Never. I knew what it would be like if Sylvie married you. And I was right. Unfortunately she never had the judgement that I possessed. She never could make the right choices.' She paused. 'I'll tell you one or two things

122

and then that's it. No more. I don't want to see you again, ever.'

' – Go on.'

'First of all – yes, I had Sylvie buried in a different place from – from Luke. And my reasons for that are my own. Don't ask me what they are, because I'm not about to tell you. And secondly – and I know this may hurt you – but you've asked me. But perhaps it's time you knew the truth. I told you I don't like you; I never have. I could see at once that you were totally selfish. I never thought, though, that you were naïve.'

'Naïve . . .?'

Avoiding his eyes she turned from him again. He could only see the line of her cheek as she continued:

'One reason Sylvie was so unhappy – and why she left you to come home . . .' Her voice trailed off.

' – Yes? Go on.'

She paused. 'She had met someone else.'

He stared at her. 'I don't believe you.'

'It's true.'

'I don't believe you,' he said again.

'You don't believe me.' Her tone was withering as she turned to him. 'Oh, the arrogance. It couldn't happen to you, could it? Not to the great Mr Guy Holman.' She paused. 'Listen – during the last few months of her time in New York with you Sylvie was – was seeing someone else. Oh, I didn't approve of it when she told me, don't think that. But what could I do? Anyway, by the time she told me, it was all over – she had come home. That's one of the reasons she came back – because of the – the relationship ending.'

Guy had not moved throughout her revelation. When she had finished he remained there, as if stunned. It was impossible to take in. It couldn't be true. It couldn't.

123

'I know how you feel about me,' he said, 'but – ' he had difficulty finding the words, ' – you wouldn't make up something like this, would you? To get back at me?'

She bent her head, silent.

'Is it true?' he said.

She gave a deep sigh. 'I'm sorry. I never meant to tell you.'

He still could not take it in. He must have been blind. Sylvie's growing unhappiness over those last months; those times when he had felt that her misery was so acute that she could not continue to bear it – he had thought it was all due to the death of David, and homesickness, and her inability to settle in the city. It had been more. She had been unhappily in love with another man.

'Who was he?' Guy asked.

' – I don't know.'

'Didn't she say who it was?'

'No.'

'Never?' He looked at her in disbelief while his mind raced, searching faces, names. 'Didn't she ever mention him by name?'

'No, never. She never said, and I didn't ask her. I didn't want to know. I was just glad that it was over, and that she'd come home.' She stood looking unseeingly into the distance. After a moment she said dully:

'And it *is* over now. My Sylvie's gone.' She sighed. 'Like the other two persons in this world whom I cared most about.'

They stood in their own silence while the birds sang and the bees buzzed among the cherry blossoms. Guy shrank from grasping the full implication of Mrs Bennett's words. Though she had already said enough.

'And – and Luke?' His voice was hoarse. 'Do you mean – I was not his father . . .'

124

She bent her head, studying her clasped hands.

He closed his eyes in anguish. When he opened them a moment later she was looking at him with an expression of sympathy on her face. Her eyes were moist. He had never thought to see such a thing.

'I'm sorry,' she said sadly. 'Believe me. And I'm sorry you had to learn it like this. But you insisted. Anyway – ' she shrugged, 'you know it now.'

As she finished speaking there came a voice, a man's voice, calling softly from the direction of the house.

'Anna . . .?'

She turned her head at the sound; lifted her hands and wiped at her eyes. 'I must go in,' she said. 'My guest is here.'

Moving past Guy she set off along the path, the terrier trotting at her heels. After a moment Guy followed. Turning a bend in the path he saw a man standing on the terrace, watching their approach. He looked to be about Mrs Bennett's age, in his mid-sixties. Wearing a sports jacket and cord trousers, he was of middle height and trimly built. He had thick, greying hair and a faint look of the Mediterranean about him.

'I was just about to come looking for you,' the man said to Mrs Bennett, smiling, showing even white teeth. He spoke with an Italian accent.

Halting before him, Mrs Bennett patted her hair and touched hands to her cheeks. 'I had an unexpected visitor,' she said. Turning towards Guy she said, 'This is Mr Holman.' She gestured to the Italian. 'Mr Rossi.'

As Guy and the other man shook hands Mrs Bennett said, 'Mr Holman is just leaving.' She hesitated then moved past them towards the house. In the open doorway she turned and looked back at Guy. 'Goodbye . . .'

'Goodbye . . .' Guy nodded to her, nodded affably to

125

the man and then left them, moving around the side of the house.

When Guy Holman had moved out of sight Mr Rossi turned to Mrs Bennett. 'Who was that?' he said.

She was still standing in the doorway. 'He used to be my son-in-law,' she said.

'Ah, yes.' Rossi moved to her. 'Your daughter Sylvie. I remember you told me she'd been married to an American.'

'Yes. I'm afraid I let his coming here upset me.' She sighed. 'It brings everything back.'

'Don't let it upset you,' he said gently.

'No, I mustn't.' She sighed again. 'Anyway, he's gone now.' She forced a smile. 'Let's go on in. I'll get us some tea.'

11

Mrs Bennett's revelation weighed on Guy's spirits like a lead weight as he walked, as if in a dream, around the side of the house. As he got to the front he was brought to a halt by the sight of a woman moving across the forecourt to a white car parked there. He watched as she opened the door, leaned in and placed a box on the front passenger seat. As she straightened she caught sight of him. Her eyes widened in surprise.

'Hello, Guy.'

'Hello, Marianne.'

He went towards her.

'Well, this is a surprise,' she said.

Her tone was not altogether warm, and Guy thought she looked as unsettled by his appearance as had Mrs Bennett.

She stood beside the car, looking at him. She was two years older than Sylvie and very like her in physical appearance. She wore a woollen sweater and blue jeans, her dark hair tied at the nape of her neck with a red ribbon.

'The children told me that Mother had a visitor,' she said, 'but I didn't imagine for a minute it was you. Are you over here on holiday?'

'Kind of.'

She nodded. 'What are you doing in Forham Green?'

He paused. 'I came to find out where Sylvie's buried. I couldn't find her grave at St Peter's.'

'No – she was buried at Lower Hesting – at St Mark's.'

127

'Yes, I know now. Your mother told me.'

Silence; awkward; then: 'Are you better now? Are you quite recovered from your accident?'

'Yes, thank you.'

'Good. I'm very glad. It must have been terrible.' She closed the car door. 'Well . . .' She did not seem eager to prolong the conversation but she did not move away.

Guy hesitated, then said abruptly:

'I just learned – about Sylvie.'

Marianne frowned. 'Learned what?' She sounded wary. 'What d'you mean?'

'Your mother told me.' He took a breath. 'That Luke was not my son.'

'What?'

'She said Sylvie had a – a lover in New York.'

She was gazing at him with eyes wide with surprise.

'Didn't you know either?' he said.

' – No. No, I didn't.'

He watched as she slowly shook her head, taking it in. The revelation was new to her too, he could see.

'I thought you would have been told,' he said with a sigh. 'I thought you might know who – who it was.'

'No.' There was anguish now in her face.

'Neither your mother nor Sylvie – they never mentioned anything?'

'No, nothing.'

'Nothing at all? No hint of any kind?'

'No, really. But my mother's never confided in me a great deal.' She groaned. 'Oh, Guy . . .'

'I must have been blind,' he said. 'I had no idea. I asked your mother who he was – the man – but she said she didn't know. She said Sylvie never told her.' A little silence, then he added, 'I don't know what to do.'

'Do?' She shook her head in a gesture of hopelessness.

128

'There's nothing you *can* do, is there? I mean . . .' Her words trailed off in a sigh.

'No, I suppose not. I guess it's just come as such a – a shock. I can't seem to take it in.'

'I'm not surprised.' She reached out, as if she would touch him, but her hand stayed, fell back to her side. 'I don't know what to say.'

'I'd like to find out who it is,' he said.

'Will it make any difference – to anything?'

'I guess not. Oh, God, I don't know.'

She gazed at him in silence for a moment, then she said in a rush: 'Guy, why don't you leave it? Just – just leave it alone. It'll be much better if you do. There's been so much unhappiness. For everyone. And not least for you.'

'Oh, but – ' he began to protest, but she broke in:

'We can't put the clock back. It's too late.'

'I know that,' he said. 'I know that nothing will bring Sylvie back, but even so – '

'Then why don't you just accept it. Stop tormenting yourself.'

'Yes.'

'Go on back home. There's nothing more for you here, you must realize that.'

'I know. But it's not that easy.'

A movement at one of the lower windows drew his eye and he turned and saw the two children looking curiously out at him. Marianne followed his glance, then agitatedly flapped a hand at them. They withdrew.

'You're right,' he said, 'there's nothing more for me here.' He half-turned, a prologue to his departure. Marianne said:

'Where are you going now? To catch your bus?'

'No, I'm going to Lower Hesting.'

'Ah – yes. How will you get there?'

'Walk, I guess.'

'It's a longish way.'

'I'll manage.'

'I'd offer to drive you, only . . .'

'That's okay.'

'When are you going back to the States?'

'In a few days.'

She hesitated, then, making a decision, said: 'Come on, get in. I'll drive you to Lower Hesting.'

'What? No, really, I can manage.'

'I'm sure you can. But, I told you, it's a tidy walk. I'll let you off at St Mark's, then afterwards you can get your bus back into Trowbridge.'

'Well – if you're sure.'

'I'm sure. It'll only take a few minutes.'

Moments later Guy was sitting beside her as she drove the car through the gateway onto the road. His last image as he looked back was of the girl and the boy, watching from the window.

As the car left the village and wound through the winding roads of the open countryside, he said:

'Tell me something, will you?'

'What's that?'

'Why does your mother hate me so much?'

Marianne flicked a swift glance at him. 'Isn't it obvious? You took Sylvie away from her.'

'But – but surely she didn't expect Sylvie to stay around for ever, did she?'

'I don't know. Maybe she *hoped* she would.'

'She must have known that at sometime or other Sylvie would get married and go away.'

'Oh, yes, of course she must have thought about it. But I'm sure she never dreamed that when it happened Sylvie would go to the other side of the world.'

130

'No, I guess not.'

'You mustn't take it personally, Guy. She would have felt the same about anybody who did it. It just happened to be you.'

They drove on in silence. After a little while Marianne said:

'You must try to understand. Sylvie was all my mother had left.'

Guy looked at her, studying her profile. Her lips were set.

'I don't understand,' he said. 'She had you.'

'Oh, no, I'd already gone by that time.' She gave a little shake of her head; there was a faint look of melancholy in the gesture. 'But even if I hadn't married Geoff and gone to live in Bath, starting a family of my own – even if I'd stayed at home it would still have been Sylvie. Where my mother was concerned it was always Sylvie.'

'Oh,' he said, 'that's such a – a sad thing to say.'

'It's all right,' she said. 'I got used to it. And I'm not telling tales out of school. I'm not being disloyal. At least I hope I'm not. But it's all to do with it – with you and Sylvie and – oh – everything.' She paused. 'No, I think, truthfully speaking, that I realized from quite an early age that there were three people of *prime* importance in my mother's life – and I wasn't one of them.'

Guy said nothing. Marianne added:

'The important people in my mother's life were my father, Sylvie, and my brother.'

Sylvie had often spoken of her brother who had died as a child.

'Your brother, Jonathan,' Guy said, 'he was older than you, wasn't he?'

'A little more than four years. Where my mother was concerned you'd have thought the sun rose and set in his

131

eyes. And I think, when he died – he was eight when he got meningitis – she couldn't understand why it should be him and not me.'

'Oh, don't say that. You can't mean that.'

'I do. I've always thought so. I know that when I was little I was very much second best. It was always Jonathan. And then of course after me she had Sylvie. When Jonathan died she seemed to give to Sylvie all the love that she could no longer give to him.'

'What about your father? How did he fit into all this . . . ?'

'My father . . . He was a wonderful man.' There was warmth in her voice now. 'At least I had *him*. And – he seemed to understand the situation. But he was never one to make waves. And he loved my mother, there's no doubt of that. And I suppose because of the way Jonathan's death affected her – she was absolutely devastated – well, he gave in to her, indulged her – and probably sometimes against his better judgement.' She shrugged. 'I don't know. And I don't suppose it matters much now. It's all water under the bridge.'

'Did you miss him when he died – your father?'

'Oh, yes, enormously.' She sighed. 'I still miss him in a way – sometimes. Though it's been so many years now. I was only ten.'

Beyond the line of Marianne's profile the trees and the meadows wound by in the sunlit afternoon. Everywhere was green; fresh green splashed with the new, bright colours of spring.

'Perhaps if my father had lived,' Marianne said, 'my mother wouldn't have been so possessive of Sylvie. Perhaps eventually she'd have accepted her going away.'

'Did your mother never think of remarrying?'

'Oh, God, I wish she *had*.' This was spoken with some

132

spirit. 'I've always thought she's the kind of woman who needs a man in her life. And perhaps if the right man had been there at the right time it might have happened. But that's the way it goes – living out here in the country there aren't the opportunities for meeting people. And she was never one to get out and about that much.'

'Who's the man I met? Rossi – is that his name?'

'Yes. Alberto Rossi. He's a widower who's come to live in the village. He seems all right. He's Italian – which of course is something of a plus for him – she being half Italian herself. And he's got a wire-haired terrier like hers. That's helped. She hasn't known him long, but they're talking of breeding puppies. That'll be a nice little interest for her. A little diversion. For which I'm grateful. Though we get on all right now. Much better, anyway. We've grown a good bit closer since Geoff and I split up.'

'Oh – I'm sorry,' Guy said, 'I didn't know . . .'

She nodded, shrugged. 'He found other pastures greener. It happens – and life has to go on, right? But which is not to say I don't miss him – and would be glad if he came back. Though there's no chance of that, I'm afraid.' She sighed, gave a flicker of a smile. 'You see, I do understand something of what it's been like for you.'

They were entering the village of Lower Hesting now, and a minute later Marianne was drawing the car to a halt near the gates of St Mark's church. She turned to him.

'Well – here you are.'

'Thank you.'

He made no move to get out. 'You know,' he said, 'on our few meetings we never ever really got to talk, did we?'

'No.' She shrugged. 'But that's the way it happens, isn't it.'

133

'I guess so.' He paused. 'Anyway – I'm glad we were able to talk today.'

'I'm glad too.'

'I think I understand things a little better. *Some* things.'

She smiled, and it was Sylvie's smile. 'Something's better than nothing.'

'Yes.' He smiled back at her.

She looked at him in silence for a moment, then she said: 'I think we could have been good friends. If things had been a little different.'

'I'm sure of it.'

'Oh, Guy,' she said, 'I know you loved Sylvie, and I know what you must have gone through. I don't think I truly realized it before.'

'You were so cold to me,' he said. 'That time when you telephoned and told me that Sylvie was – was so sick – that she was dying.'

'Yes, perhaps I was. I couldn't understand why you hadn't come sooner.'

'I told you – I didn't even know she was sick.'

'She didn't let you know?

'No. She didn't answer a single one of my letters towards the end.'

Marianne gazed at him in silence for a moment, lips compressed, then looking at her watch, she said: 'Listen – I must get going. We have to get back to Bath.' Turning, she gestured towards the church. 'You'll find Sylvie's grave on the other side. You can't miss it. It's close to a little sycamore tree. She's lying next to my father and Jonathan.'

'Right.' He held out his hand; she took it in hers. 'Goodbye, Marianne.'

'Goodbye.' Still holding his hand she said: 'When you've seen it – Sylvie's grave – go on home to America.'

134

'I intend to.'

'And don't – ' her words were gentle, 'don't come back. There'd only be more pain.'

'No, I shan't come back. There'd be no point, would there?' He turned his face away, gazing unseeing at the ivy-covered churchyard wall. 'I loved her, Marianne. So much. She was my life to me. And I don't seem to have had any – any purpose since she went.' He shook his head. 'No, I shan't come back.'

It didn't take long to find Sylvie's grave.

As Marianne had said, it lay beside the grave of their father and brother, who shared a stone with words lovingly inscribed to their memories.

The plot of Sylvie's grave, unlike Luke's at St Peter's, was well cared for – apart from the fact that the daffodils in the vase were dead; but that was to be expected, he thought, since Mrs Bennett had been away. The stone looked so new. The inscription on it read:

IN MOST LOVING MEMORY OF

SYLVIE JULIA

BORN 5 JUNE 1951

DIED 12 JULY 1988

DEARLY BELOVED DAUGHTER OF

JAMES AND ANNA BENNETT

Guy stood looking at the inscription. She was referred to simply as *Sylvie Julia* – with the implication that her last name was Bennett. There was no hint of the fact that she had had a husband. Mrs Bennett's decision and design, of course.

He thought again of Mrs Bennett's revelation. *Oh,*

135

Sylvie . . . how could I have been so wrong about so much?

He had never dreamed that there was such a story behind Sylvie's unhappiness. Another man. He thought of their walk into the garden and down to the orchard. And with the memory he wondered at the warmth she had shown him – while all the time she had been hiding her secret.

A chill breeze had sprung up, touching at the leaves of the nearby sycamore and briefly stirring the heads of the dead daffodils. *Sylvie* . . . He bent his head and wept.

After some time, the tears dry on his cheeks, he turned and moved away towards the path.

He reached Dr Powell's office ten minutes late that evening. Powell was not concerned. As he examined Guy he asked him how he was feeling. 'Fine, just fine,' Guy answered.

'No ill effects of any kind?'

'None. I feel fine.'

'You're sure?'

'Oh, yes.'

After Guy had received the injection he settled the bill. Powell asked him whether he had yet decided when he wished to return to New York.

Guy hesitated. 'No, not yet,' he said.

'You're due to get your third shot next Monday. Will you be here for that?'

Guy gave a nod. 'Yes, I will.'

'And afterwards?'

' – I'll let you know.'

'I've been informed that Trevorson is dead,' Paxton said. He was speaking over the telephone to Crane.

'Yes.' Crane's tone was grave. 'His body was found this morning in a back yard in Bayswater.'

'How did he die?'

'He was murdered. He was stabbed through the eye. His wallet was missing, though, so the official view is that he was mugged.'

'Is that what *you* think?'

'What *I* think is that we've got to be very careful. Before Trevorson was killed we had no idea whether the Holman anomaly was likely to have any grave consequences. There was always a chance that it would prove to be a quite innocuous incident; that there'd be no serious ramifications. Trevorson's murder, though, has put paid to that idea. We know that he wasn't mugged by any opportunist yob.'

Paxton said: 'Obviously they know something that *we* don't. They've discovered something.'

'Evidently,' said Crane. 'And whatever it is it must be pretty momentous.' He sighed; he sounded weary. 'It makes me sick – to find we're always one step behind. It's always the same. Anyway, we'll be meeting tomorrow. Maybe we'll find out more then.'

'Where is it to be?' Paxton asked. 'The church where we met before?'

'Yes. I'll call you back with details of the time.'

Lying in his hotel bed that night Guy thought back on his trip to Forham Green. He had to face it now: Sylvie and Luke had never been his. Neither one had belonged to him. He had come back for nothing. All this time he had been holding on to something that was made of illusion and shadow. Even the few golden memories he had treasured had turned out to be tinsel.

137

12

In the little church of St Peter's Crane faced the small assembly: Paxton, Hughes, Levin, Haddon and Crawley.

'This conclave,' he said, 'was formed solely to deal with the case of one man, the American, Holman; to ensure that his continuing survival is not going to pose any kind of threat. So far we don't know what the consequences of his survival might be. We've all been hoping that it would be nothing extraordinary – in which case we could all pack up and go home. But the indications now are that the situation might be very serious. As you know, since we last met one of our members has been murdered. And it was no random, motiveless killing, or for some purpose such as robbery. Agent Trevorson's murder is indication that the future of Holman is interwoven with some larger event. It shows also that those who killed him are aware of the nature of that event, and that its outcome is of vital importance to them. Accepting that, then there's also the fact that they're ahead of us in their knowledge. So obviously we've got no time to lose.' He looked at his watch then glanced over at the door. 'Miss Donahue should be here by now.'

A moment after he finished speaking there was a sound from the door and the conclave turned to see a small, thin woman in her early sixties step into the church's gloom. Over her shoulder was slung a canvas bag while in her hand she carried a very large, long, flower-patterned holdall.

'Ah . . .' said Crane, moving to help her. 'We wondered where you'd got to.'

'I'm terribly sorry,' Miss Donahue said as she closed the door behind her. 'I couldn't get my car started.'

Crane picked up her holdall and started back down the aisle. With the others rising and following, he led the way down to the crypt. There in the dimly-lit interior Miss Donahue took off her coat and got to work, taking from the large holdall pieces of a contraption which she, Crane and Levin began to assemble. While this was going on the others drew up chairs, placing them in a row near the centre of the north-facing wall. Then they sat down and waited.

After some time the construction of the frame was complete. In a last check, Miss Donahue ran her hands over the wires strung with the large beads of varied shapes, each one bearing some arcane design. 'I think we can start now.'

At her words Crane moved to a small table on which stood a candelabra holding seven candles. He struck a match and put the flame to the wicks, then, moving to the wall he switched off the main, overhead lighting.

'Ready now,' he said, taking a seat beside the others.

With the space now lit only by the burning candles, Miss Donahue bent to her canvas shoulder bag that lay on a chair at her side and took out a small red-leather-covered volume: *Sonnets from the Portuguese*. Straightening she lifted the book and pressed it to her forehead. Her eyes were shut tight. Opening her mouth she began to speak strange and unfamiliar words. This went on for several minutes, then she put down the book and bent to the frame before her.

While the watchers directed their glances ahead they heard from behind them the sounds of whirring and

139

clicking as beneath Miss Donahue's moving fingers the large, strangely-patterned beads began to slide along the strings.

Up and down the beads moved, sometimes so swiftly that their shapes were blurred. As they struck one against the other little sprays of sparks erupted, while at the same time the points on their surfaces picked up the glow of the candles and threw it onto the walls of the crypt in tumbling, coloured patterns of light.

Miss Donahue's voice came again, softly but taking on a strange echo, as if the enclosed space of the crypt was slowly expanding. And along with it, the sense of growing space, the watchers smelled the faint odour of something indefinable – like the smell of flowers, and shaded pools, of ozone and wide, open terrains on which the sun never set.

Although Miss Donahue kept her voice at little more than a whisper it began to increase in volume – as if she were speaking into a microphone. And all the while beneath the sounds of the words there came the whirrings and the clickings of the beads as they flew back and forth on the strings. Then into the symphony of sounds there came the beating of a drum, which, keeping up a steady rhythm, increased in volume along with the woman's voice. The sound grew, growing in volume and intensity, echoing back and forth off the walls and ringing in the ears of the men and women who sat there.

And then, all at once, the sounds ceased; the whole cacophony of noise ended abruptly, being sliced off so sharply that a reverberating echo rang in the air. Then the echo faded until the silence was absolute but for the sound of Miss Donahue's breathing as she stood with her eyes closed tight, the great beads now unmoving on the strings beneath her still fingers.

Before them, the watchers saw rising up a wall of smoke-like mist that obscured the far and side walls of the interior, the vapour twisting and writhing in curling ribbons that seemed to grow out of the stone flags and reach up towards a roof that was no longer in sight.

Minutes went by. And still there was nothing before them but the curling ribbons of grey smoke. Miss Donahue opened her eyes, took a breath and started again. Throwing back her head she began to chant the strange, unintelligible words. Then her voice ceased and she bent over the frame, her fingers manipulating the flying beads, sending them clicking against each other and whirring on the wires. The drumbeat began again.

The result, after almost half-an-hour, was the same. Nothing. She tried once more. Again there came the sound of her voice, growing in volume, supplemented by the noises of the beads and by the heartbeat-like drum, the sounds growing until they reached an almost deafening pitch. As before, the sound suddenly ceased, leaving in its wake a silence which was almost palpable. Then, all at once, the smoke-like haze began to clear.

Shifting and wavering, shapes began to form out of the grey; at first slowly, but then more swiftly. The area before the watchers opened out, giving way to space and open air, and they found themselves looking at a dusty, sun-drenched street. To Paxton and Hughes the scene was familiar; they had viewed the same scene in the crypt of the church in Connecticut. To the others the scene was new. They watched as a bus pulled up, saw Holman stoop to pick up something from the ground, saw the small dog come rushing around the end of the bus and fly at him.

'The whole thing's exactly the same,' observed Paxton.

As Holman recovered himself after the attack, Crane turned to Miss Donahue.

'Bring it forward a little, can you?'

Head bent in concentration, she sent the beads flying on the strings. The forms of the scene shimmered and wavered as if viewed through moving water, the lines fragmented, dissolved, and the scene disappeared. Seconds later new forms began to take shape.

The watchers now saw before them a small churchyard with a church in the background – which they recognized as the one in which they now sat. Holman, looking a few years younger, stood beside a small grave. There was a young woman there too. She and Holman stood apart while raindrops dripped from the trees and a breeze touched at the leaves of the evergreens.

'Forward – come forward,' Crane said to Miss Donahue.

The scene dissolved, the lines re-forming to show a garden with a small boy playing. Mrs Hughes murmured speculatively, 'Holman as a child? It could be,' while Levin shook his head in impatience and said, turning to Miss Donahue, 'He said *come forward* in time – not go *back*.'

Crane quickly raised a hand in a demand for silence. 'She's doing the best she can. Remember, the man's a law unto himself. It's difficult to get a fix upon him.'

The scene faded and in its place appeared a little woodland glade. In the centre sat Holman and a young woman. Holman leaned over and kissed the girl on the mouth.

'Who's she?' Paxton said. 'Is that his wife?'

'His wife is dead,' said Crane. 'That was his wife before, I think – just now in the churchyard.'

'Who's this, then? She *looks* like his wife.'

'Maybe so – but his wife is dead.'

142

They continued to gaze at the scene for a minute or two longer, then Crane turned again to Miss Donahue.

'Continue, please. Forward.'

Under Miss Donahue's fingers the beads flew: whir, click, whir, click, whir, click . . . The scene before them shook and faded. A churchyard took shape before them; but not the one that had appeared earlier. Holman was seen standing above a grave.

Crane shook his head. 'I've no idea what it means – or if it has any significance.'

The image slowly dissolved. The scene that now appeared seemed to be a corner section of a city square. Beyond a fountain, around which a number of teenagers gathered, were shops, cafés, apartment houses and restaurants, intersected here and there by street entrances. It was evening, and in the glow of lamps and brightly-lit windows people milled about.

'Must be somewhere in Italy,' said Haddon.

'I think it's in Milan,' said Levin. 'I'm sure I recognize it.'

They watched as the people moved back and forth. 'Ask her to move on,' Haddon said. 'There's nothing in this.'

'Wait,' Crane said. 'Give it a chance.'

The minutes ticked by. The scene remained as it was; people moved easily about the piazza, an old flower-seller sold her wares, boys rode on bicycles, couples strolled hand in hand, two lovers stopped, embraced, kissed; a little boy fell, was picked up by a woman and comforted.

Crane watched the scene for a while then said to Miss Donahue, 'Go forward in time a little, can you?'

The scene shimmered and dissolved, only to reappear a few moments later unchanged. The lovers stopped again, embraced and kissed. The child fell once more, the same

143

teenagers rode their bicycles. 'Bring it forward,' Crane instructed.

The scene shimmered and dissolved into the ribbons of smoky haze, and re-formed once more, exactly as it had been. And once again the watchers saw the same scene; the same couples walked hand in hand, the lovers kissed, the child fell. 'Tell her to move on,' Levin said, but Crane hushed him to silence. 'Wait. There must be something.'

Then, suddenly, into the general light-hearted murmur of the comings and goings, there was the sound of a report, followed just two or three seconds later by a second one. The sounds were muted, as were all the sounds emanating from the scene, but the watchers were in no doubt that they were gunshots. This was borne out by the people, many of whom, amid cries and screams, threw themselves to the ground or ran from the scene.

Crane leant forward in his seat watching the pandemonium. Then, as the scene began to dissolve into the smoke he said urgently, 'Go back to it! Get it back.'

After a few seconds the scene reappeared and the watchers saw the same things happen, the same sequence of events culminating in the firing of the shots and the panic in the square. Again the scene dissolved and faded away.

'Again!' Crane rapped out. 'And keep it going.'

Once more the scene was conjured up; people walked in the square, the shots rang out, the people reacted in panic. But this time the scene continued, and the watchers observed the panic-stricken people recover themselves, get to their feet and swiftly converge about an area near the corner of the street that ran into the square. The curious crowd was gathering outside a restaurant, *La Primavera*, which stood near the corner of a street entrance, their attention focused on something on the ground.

'Obviously somebody's been shot there,' Crane said; then to Miss Donahue: 'Can you go back?'

The scene halted, dissolved, and began again. Now the watchers' eyes were directed towards the restaurant at the rear. The shots rang out and beyond the moving throng they caught a glimpse of a man falling to the ground. As the people recovered themselves and began to gather about the fallen figure, Crawley voiced the question that was in the mind of each of them:

'Is it Holman? Is he the victim?'

Crane shook his head. 'It's impossible to see anything through that crowd.' He turned to Miss Donahue. 'Show it again, can you? And this time try to hold it. Let's see if we can get a look at him.'

Miss Donahue nodded and moved her hands down to the wires. The familiar clicking and whirring sounds came again and the scene re-formed out of the smoke. This time the watchers concentrated on the figures in the background, and this time they saw the man as he fell.

At Crane's insistence the scene was called up again and now the man was observed as he emerged from the restaurant. Of fairly short stature, he was tanned and dark-haired, wearing a dark-blue suit and carrying a light raincoat over his arm. Beside him walked an elegant, well-dressed blonde woman.

'That's certainly not Holman,' said Hughes.

'Hold it there!' Crane rapped out to Miss Donahue; then to the small assembly in general: 'Keep your eyes on the man – the one to be shot . . .'

Moments after he had spoken the scene froze, everyone on the huge stage becoming fixed in mid-move, so that it suddenly resembled an enormous wax-works tableau.

145

The eyes of the watchers stayed on the man in the dark-blue suit, held in the act of turning from the restaurant door. He could just be seen beyond the figures of the other people who stood frozen in motion.

Crane said, turning to Miss Donahue, 'There's no reason we shouldn't go in there, is there?' He gestured to the scene. 'So long as we don't disturb anything, I mean.'

She nodded. 'It won't do any harm.'

'*We* can move into the scene?' Miss Crawley said.

'Strictly as an observer,' said Miss Donahue. 'And if you're extremely careful and don't take too long. I can't hold it indefinitely.'

Led by Crane, the group rose, stepped forward and gingerly entered the scene. Moving quickly but with caution they wove a path among the people until they reached the little group towards the rear. There they stopped, peering at the man in the blue suit. Crane said with a shake of his head:

'I'm still no wiser. Who is he, for God's sake?'

'I don't recognize him,' Paxton said. 'I don't think I've ever seen him before.'

'Is there any reason we *should* know who he is?' asked Hughes.

Crane replied with a shrug: 'Your guess is as good as mine. But he's obviously somebody of importance in Holman's scenario.'

'Who's the blonde woman?' said Haddon. 'His wife? His girl friend?'

'Who knows,' said Crane. He glanced anxiously around him. 'I think we'd better start back.'

They turned and walked back to the side of the arena, taking their seats again. Crane turned to Miss Donahue. 'Can you continue it from here for a few moments? And get ready to stop it again after the shot has been fired.'

146

As he turned back to face the front the scene came to life once more. The lovers stopped to hold one another and kiss, the boy ran for a few yards and fell, the cyclists rode by. Gazing at the restaurant, the watchers saw the door open and the man appear, the woman behind him. The two shots rang out and the man fell. At once the air was filled with the muted sounds of screaming and shouting.

'*Hold it there*,' Crane said. The scene came to a halt, the figures freezing, the dulled sound of the tumult abruptly dying.

'Let's see it close to.' Crane turned to the others on either side of him. 'Wait here. I'll go in . . .'

He rose and stepped forward into the tableau, moving carefully past the figures, many of whom were frozen in attitudes of horror and fear. Reaching the small nucleus towards the rear he stopped and bent over the fallen man. He lay on his back just before the open restaurant door, right leg bent, right arm thrown out to his side. His head lay with his right cheek on the pavement. The blonde woman had been caught on her knees beside him, one hand raised, fingers outspread, caught in a gesture of shock and horror. Her other hand reached out to the man, fingers spread.

Crane saw that both bullets had struck the man; one in his right shoulder, the second in the centre of his forehead. The latter had made its exit at the back of his skull, leaving a gaping hole through which his blood and brains had exploded.

Crane straightened, turned and made his way back to the group. 'The man is quite dead,' he said. As he sat down the scene came to life once more, the pandemonium starting up along with the muted cries of horror as the people tried to shield themselves from harm or dashed

147

away out of the square. A minute later the scene was disappearing from view.

A new scene was revealed. Before the watchers appeared the lush interior of a palatial house with a lofty marble staircase sweeping down to a wide hall. An elderly man was descending the stairs. Paxton said at once:

'It's Perreiros – the President of Larinas. Surely it is.'

As he finished speaking the man suddenly tripped, staggered and fell headlong, his body coming to a halt several steps down. People appeared and gathered around him, bending over his still body.

Even as the watchers were taking in the scene it was fading, changing. In seconds it had become a wide square, but different from the one where the shots had been fired. In the background stood an imposing white building. Armed guards stood at attention at tall gates at the entrance to a wide, palm-fringed forecourt. In the square a vast crowd waited.

'Larinas again,' said Hughes. 'The Presidential Palace in Castelandú. It was on TV the other night.'

After some moments the watchers saw a funeral cortege moving through the crowd. To the accompaniment of pipes and drums, and flanked by armed guards, a draped coffin was borne slowly by.

'Must be Perreiros's funeral,' Crane observed.

The procession moved on through the silent crowd. The scene faded.

'So Perreiros is to die unexpectedly – accidentally,' said Crawley. 'But what's the significance of it? What's it got to do with Holman?'

The square vanished and reappeared – though clearly now at a different time. It was again crowded with people, but now there was a light-heartedness about them; they laughed and talked animatedly, appearing relaxed and

148

happy. Many of the children carried the Larinas flag while others carried small flags bearing the stars and stripes of the USA. There were numerous policemen in evidence, keeping the crowds from the gates and preventing them from spilling onto the road. All the while the guards remained at attention, unthreatening.

After a few minutes a fleet of open cars was seen driving slowly towards the palace gates. The cheering crowd surged forward, waving hands and flags, many carrying placards bearing the name *Juan Aranco*. In one of the first cars a wiry, middle-aged, grey-haired man sat beside an attractive dark-haired woman, smiling about him at the crowd of well-wishers who took up the cry – muted but distinct to the watchers: '*Viva* Aranco!'

'Aranco,' said Paxton. 'Never heard of the man. But it looks as if he's the new President – Perreiros's successor.'

'And,' Mrs Hughes remarked, 'obviously a popular one.'

As the cars drove in through the gates onto the fore-court of the palace Paxton fixed his glance on the man and woman sitting opposite Aranco and his wife. 'My God,' he said, 'it's the President of the United States. It's Bush. Well, Aranco's got the seal of approval there.'

Crane nodded. 'So that, it appears, is to be the outcome of Perreiros's death. Aranco becomes President. And with the full support and approval of the West.'

On the forecourt the first limousine had stopped and attendants were moving forward to open the doors. From the car stepped the neat figure of Aranco, followed by his wife. Immediately afterwards the American President and First Lady stepped out onto the waiting red carpet. There they were officially welcomed to the palace by Aranco and his wife.

The cars that followed drew to a halt and various

149

officials and security officers got out. Aranco, his wife and the American President and First Lady went into the palace. Minutes later they appeared on a high balcony, the sight of them raising a great roar of approval.

The scene faded. Crane was silent for a few moments then said, 'Well, it seems clear enough, doesn't it? I never heard of Aranco before – but clearly he's going to be what Larinas needs. And after what the country's gone through it won't be before time, either.'

Levin nodded. 'Right – but what the hell does it all have to do with Holman?'

Crane nodded. 'That I'd like to know.' He turned to Miss Donahue. 'Can you tell us anything else?'

Miss Donahue started slightly as if coming out of a dream. 'Oh, yes,' she said, 'there's more to come – though it might take a little while.'

Crane tilted his head in sympathy. 'You're tired,' he said. 'I'm not surprised. I should think you must be exhausted.'

She wiped the back of a thin wrist across her forehead. 'I am,' she confessed.

Crawley looked at her watch. 'It's after ten.'

'I'm sorry,' said Crane. 'I wasn't aware of the time.' He looked around at the others. 'I think we'll call it a day for the time being – unless anyone objects.'

No one made any objection. It had been a long day and everyone was tired and hungry.

Crane got to his feet. 'We'll continue tomorrow.' He turned to Miss Donahue. 'What about your equipment? Will you dismantle it or leave it here?'

'I'd like to leave it if it'll be safe overnight.'

'Oh, it'll be safe; there'll be guards posted.' He was already moving away. 'Let's get to the hotel and get some rest. It might be another long day tomorrow.'

* * *

150

They drove in their cars to Trowbridge where reservations had been made for them at The Swan Hotel. On checking in they learned that the restaurant was about to close so without bothering to go to their rooms to change they washed their hands and went straight into the dining room. At their request two tables were placed together to accommodate them and with relief they sat down and ordered much-needed drinks from the bar. That done they gave their orders for dinner from the rather limited menu. The only others in the room were a middle-aged couple who soon paid their bill and vacated their table, leaving the seven alone. In the foyer the couple stopped at the desk where the woman, giving a friendly smile, asked the elderly porter if a Miss Donahue was staying at the hotel. The porter replied that she was, adding that she had just checked in and was at that moment in the restaurant. 'You must have walked straight past her,' he said.

'Oh, really?' the woman said. 'I'm afraid I didn't notice.'

'If you go back in,' said the porter, 'you'll find her at one of the tables.'

The woman hesitated for a moment, exchanged a look of concern with the man at her side then shook her head. 'No, I don't want to bother her when she's just about to eat. I'll see her in the morning. What room is she in?'

The porter consulted the hotel register. 'Room fourteen.'

The woman thanked him, then together she and the man made their way across the floor and up the stairs.

When the members of the conclave had eaten, Miss Donahue, yawning, made her excuses and said she must go and sleep. Room key in one hand and overnight bag in the other, she got up from her chair, said her goodnights and left.

'She's earned her rest,' Paxton said as he watched her move out of sight beyond the restaurant door. 'What an amazing woman. Who'd ever think it possible – that slight figure, and so much power.'

The others murmured in agreement. 'D'you think we shall need to continue tomorrow?' Levin asked.

Crane nodded. 'You heard what Miss Donahue said: there's more to come. Why – don't you think we shall?'

'I don't know.' Levin frowned. 'We don't seem to be learning anything. I can't see that any of it has any relevance to what we're doing.'

Crane looked concerned. 'You might well be right, of course. But that's something we've got to find out.'

'It doesn't seem to be getting us anywhere,' said Levin, 'for all our hours of sitting there, watching those images.'

'I agree,' said Haddon. 'The whole thing seems to have gone off at a tangent.' She picked up a mint from a small dish and put it into her mouth. 'Granted there were things to do with Holman at the start today – which were possibly relevant – but this later business – the shooting, Perreiros's death and Aranco getting the premiership – it seems to belong to a different scenario altogether.'

Levin said, 'That's what I think. What's it got to do with Holman? Is it possible that Miss Donahue's getting her wires crossed?' He smiled, raised a protesting hand. 'No pun intended.'

Crawley nodded as she set down her coffee cup. 'Let's face it – it wouldn't be the first time it's happened, and I doubt it'll be the last.'

'Right,' said Levin. 'I'm not criticizing Miss Donahue. I'm sure she's first-rate. But everyone can make mistakes. And,' he added, 'although that whole thing with the

152

images is supposed to be *selective*, we don't know that it is. Some of those scenes we witnessed might not have any significance at all where Holman is concerned.'

Haddon, helping herself to another mint, said, 'Maybe we've had all the relevant information there is about Holman. For myself I can't see what those other images have to do with him. Perhaps we should just take what information we have on him and see where it leads. After all, it's up to us to work out what it means.'

'But we didn't really find out anything about him,' Hughes said. 'And that's what we came here for. I think there's got to be a connection. I'm sure that somehow Holman ties in with all that other business – Perreiros and Aranco and everything. I'm sure there's more to this if we care to look.'

Levin shook his head. 'I think we've been witnessing things that have no relevance. And we haven't got time to waste, have we?'

'Perhaps there's nothing more to learn,' said Haddon. 'Perhaps, quite simply, there *are no consequences of importance*. No consequences that can be seen as yet, anyway. And remember we can only see just so far ahead. We can't see ahead indefinitely, can we.'

'Quite,' Levin said. 'However clearly we can see, there is a limit. It might well be that *if* there *is* some kind of disastrous consequence as a result of Holman slipping through the system, that consequence is too far away for us to discover as yet. But as agent Haddon says, we don't know that there are serious consequences. We might just be looking for things that don't exist.'

'That's true,' said Crane. 'And we might well have to wait some considerable time – perhaps years – before we can see ahead to any particularly *vital* time.'

153

Hughes said: 'But we can't be *sure* it has nothing to do with Holman. And can we afford to take a chance?'

Crawley said quickly, 'What *can* it have to do with him? Look at it – the shooting of some man outside a restaurant in Italy, and then all that about Larinas, a rather remote foreign country that has no particular power in the world. In respect of Larinas we learned of the accidental death of Perreiros, the President, and the popularity of his successor. But what can Holman have to do with that? I mean, from all the information we have – and no one's questioned it – Holman's never had anything whatever to do with Larinas. He has no political connections either. He's a teacher of English, a youngish widower who keeps himself to himself and lives quietly alone in upstate New York.'

'With regard to that assassination,' said Haddon, 'we might have been shown it simply because Holman was there at the time. Isn't that possible?'

'Right,' said Levin. 'And later on, when Aranco was welcoming President Bush, Holman might just have been in the crowd. There on holiday, perhaps.'

'I guess it's possible,' Paxton said. 'With all those thousands of people there's no way you could pick out just one guy.'

'We also have to bear in mind,' Levin said, 'that he's a law unto himself. We're all aware of how difficult it's been to get any kind of focus on him – let alone anything that appears to have any significance.' He shook his head. 'I agree with Haddon and Crawley. I don't think Holman's got anything to do with Larinas – except perhaps coincidentally.'

Mrs Hughes said: 'If you're right, and Holman has no vital part to play in coming events, then why was agent Trevorson eliminated?'

154

Crane nodded. 'That's a question that must be addressed.'

Levin said quickly, 'Ah, but we've been *assuming* that he was killed by the opposition. We don't know that he was. There's no evidence of it.' He sighed. 'I think we're in great danger of seeing problems where none exists – of seeing conflict where there's none. And once we get bees like that in our bonnets we can go on for ever finding factors to fit a scenario – without any of it being valid.'

'So you're doubtful about the wisdom of going on tomorrow,' Crane said. 'Even though Miss Donahue says there's more to come.'

'More of what?' said Levin. 'If it's more of this then I'm just not convinced of its relevance. What's to be gained? Particularly if, as you say, this is a matter of some urgency.'

'Mr Paxton?' Crane said.

'Well . . .' Paxton shrugged. 'I don't want to waste time, and I wouldn't want to put Miss Donahue through more work than is necessary. Though, of course, that shouldn't be a consideration.'

There was a little silence, then Crane said, 'Well, my own inclination is to continue – which, I believe, is shared by agent Hughes.' A nod from Hughes at this and Crane went on: 'But perhaps I'm merely being over-cautious. Perhaps we're looking too hard when in fact there's nothing to be found. Anyway,' he moved his glance from one to the other, 'I'll give it some further thought tonight and decide in the morning. And of course, if anything transpires at a later date we can always reconvene.'

He got to his feet and took up his room key. 'And now I think I too must get some rest. It's been a long day.'

Soon after Crane had made his departure Hughes, Haddon and Levin said their goodnights and went off to their rooms. Paxton, left alone with Miss Crawley, felt almost too tired to get up. He looked at his watch. After midnight. He poured himself another glass of water.

'So,' Crawley said, 'is it back to the States for you if you're not needed here any more?'

He nodded. 'I guess so. Or maybe I'll stay on for a while. Visit some old friends and try to relax a little. How about you?'

'Oh, if it's all clear by the end of the week I'll go on home.' She took off her spectacles, polished them. Without them she looked very pretty and barely twenty.

'Where is that – home?'

'Norfolk. A little village just outside of Norwich. I won't be sorry to get back.'

Paxton smiled. 'You sound as if you mean that.'

'I do. I don't think I'm cut out for this.'

'What d'you mean?'

She shrugged, gave a rueful little smile. 'I don't think I'm up to it.'

'Oh – you really feel that?'

'Yes.' She sighed. 'Anyway – it won't be long now. This is my last job with the organization.'

'You're getting out.'

She nodded. 'Yes. Getting out.'

'To do better things?'

A little laugh. 'I don't know about *better*. But more enjoyable, I hope. For one thing, I'm getting married.'

'Well, that's very nice.' Paxton smiled warmly at her. 'When will that be?'

'In the summer – if this business is all finished.'

The waiter entered to ask if they needed anything further. He too was eager to get to bed. 'Would you like anything?' Paxton asked Crawley. 'Coffee or anything, or another drink?'

156

She shook her head. 'No, thank you. One coffee's my limit. I'll never sleep if I have any more.'

When the waiter had gone away again Crawley said:

'You're not convinced, are you?'

'About what?'

'Leaving this Holman business where it is for now . . .'

'Not totally.'

'It's very difficult, isn't it? Working in the dark so much.'

'It certainly is.'

'Anyway, perhaps things will look a little clearer in the morning – once we've all had some sleep.' She picked up the room key from beside her empty coffee cup, looked at it more closely, then said with a groan: 'Oh, shit, someone's taken my key and left me theirs.'

'Really?'

'I was given room twelve.' She held out the key in her hand. 'I've got the key for fourteen.'

'Who has your key, then?'

'Either Miss Donahue or Mr Levin, I suppose. They were sitting either side of me.' She shrugged. 'Anyway, it won't make any difference. I imagine one room's pretty much like another, and I've got everything I need.' She took up her overnight bag. 'All I want is to get to sleep. And the way I feel right now I could sleep on a clothesline.'

Unlocking the door of room fourteen Crawley let herself in, switched on the light then went to the bathroom and turned on the taps. While the water was running she unpacked her bag, set out her toilet things and laid out her nightdress. When the bath was full she added a little oil to the water then got undressed and climbed in. She lay back, relaxing, soaking away the dust of the crypt.

157

With the radio on she didn't hear the faint click of the lock, while the intruder's feet on the carpet made no sound at all.

Entering the bedroom, and keeping out of sight of the open bathroom door, the woman looked around her. On the back of a chair hung a grey silk scarf. Taking it up she silently let herself out of the room.

Her bath finished, Crawley pulled the plug, wrapped a towel around herself and got out. Bending over the tub she washed her hair, using the shower attachment to rinse away the suds.

As she rubbed her hair with a towel she noticed that the bath water was not running away. Damn. Bending over the tub she reached down into the water and felt at the plughole. There was nothing stopping it. She shrugged; it was a job for the hotel plumber, but not tonight. Moving into the bedroom she took up her hairdryer and connected the plug of its extension lead to a socket near the bathroom door. Back in the bathroom she stood before the mirror drying her thick, dark hair.

She had been using the dryer for less than a minute when she felt the first touch. It was like a heavy hand upon her chest, roughly pushing her, so that she gave a little cry of surprise and staggered back. A second later it came again, much harder this time, striking at her with force, like the blow of a fist, so that she staggered violently under the impact. She cried out and raised her hands – still clutching the whirring hairdryer – in an attempt to protect herself.

'*What's happening? Something's happ* – ' She didn't finish the word. A third blow came, the unseen fist striking her with such force that it knocked the breath from her body and sent her reeling. Before she could recover her breath or her balance she was struck again, a thudding

158

blow to her sternum that slammed her staggering backwards. A split second later she felt the edge of the bathtub against the backs of her knees. Arms flailing, she fell back into the tub.

13

Agents Paxton, Hughes, Haddon and Levin sat subdued in the church crypt, facing Crane who stood with his face lowered, his mouth set.

It was Hughes who had discovered Crawley's death. When Crawley had not appeared for breakfast Hughes had gone to her room and, getting no answer to her knock, had called for the maid to unlock the door. They had found the young woman dead in the bath, her hairdryer still clutched in her hand. The police and a doctor had at once been summoned. The death however had not been viewed with any suspicion and following routine questioning everyone had been allowed to leave. The remains of the conclave had at once made their way to St Peter's church.

Now, raising his head to the little assembly, Crane said, tears shining in his eyes:

'We discussed last night the question of whether we should leave this business here, as some of you were of the opinion that we were only being presented with irrelevancies. Since then, as you know, another much-respected member of our company has been murdered.' He paused. 'The second to die in a matter of days. I trust you no longer think we're wasting our time.' Silence followed his words. He went on:

'We know now, of course – if there was any doubt – that Trevorson was also murdered. And what agent Crawley's death has told us is that we must continue. When she was electrocuted she was in the room assigned to Miss Donahue, so it would appear that the assassin believed that Miss Donahue was the occupant of the room. It's only by chance she wasn't. Which must lead us to the conclusion that others, having made certain discoveries, believed that we, with the assistance of Miss Donahue, were about to make those same discoveries for ourselves. And, clearly, they wanted to prevent this. It's our job now to find out what they wished to keep hidden.' He gestured to the door to the crypt. 'Miss Donahue's already down there, so let's begin.'

As the four members rose, Levin said, his voice tight, controlled:

'What will happen about Miss Crawley's death?'

Crane shook his head. 'Nothing. It will be the subject of an inquest, of course. And they'll find for accidental death. Only *we* shall know that it was not – we and those who were responsible. After that it's out of our hands; it's finished. It's not our way to seek revenge.' He sighed. 'Anyway – let's go downstairs now and do what we can.'

In the crypt they found Miss Donahue making last-minute preparations at her frame. As they approached they saw that her expression was grave. The death of Miss Crawley and her own narrow escape had shocked her greatly. Crane asked her whether she felt ready to resume.

She nodded. 'Of course.'

As Crane moved to take his seat, Haddon said to him:

'Mr Crane – there's something I meant to tell you.'

'What's that?'

She sat down, fished in her bag and drew out a copy of that morning's *Guardian*. 'The man who was shot in the square. I think I know who he is.'

'You do?' Crane gave her all his attention now.

'I meant to tell you earlier but not surprisingly it got

161

driven out of my head.' She passed the folded-back newspaper to him, at the same time tapping a forefinger against a photograph. 'There.'

Crane peered at the photograph in the dim light. There were several faces in it. In the centre was Perreiros. Grey-haired and benign-looking, he had been frozen by the photographer's camera with one hand raised, his mouth open in speech to some out-of-shot journalist.

'There's Aranco,' Crane said, pointing to the profile of a man on the right of Perreiros. His gaze shifted, focused on a face set back a little in the shadows. He recognized at once the square jaw, the heavy moustache and the thick, dark hair. Eyes moving to the accompanying text, he read:

President Guido Perreiros is shown leaving a press conference in Castelandú, Larinas yesterday. In a departure from usual custom over past years members of the Western press were invited, a move clearly in accord with Perreiros's proclaimed shift to a more openly democratic system of government. To the President's left in the photograph is Chioro Belliros, recently named as Perreiros's deputy. A little-known figure to those in the West, Belliros, it is now known, was head of the military force which originally brought Perreiros to power.

Crane studied the photograph then passed the news-paper to the others, who had been listening with interest. 'That's him all right,' he said. 'Belliros.'

Upwards of an hour passed, and at last the watchers saw the first image materialize before them: the now-familiar square with the fountain in the centre. Seconds after it had taken shape Levin said: 'Yes! Of course. It's the piazza dei Fiori in Milan. I remember it now.'

About the square milled the people: the youths on their

162

bicycles, the lovers strolling hand-in-hand, the old folk. The watchers found themselves anticipating the action; they would see a child fall, see two young lovers kiss. After that would come the shots, and the man, Belliros, would fall dead.

The banal performance continued in its predicted pattern. Then, as the watchers tensed in anticipation of the gunfire there came a slight gasp from Hughes and her voice rang out in a sharp whisper:

'*Look!*'

Turning their heads the other watchers followed the line of her finger.

'Good God!' Paxton breathed. 'It's Holman.'

The American, Guy Holman, was now in the scene.

He was moving across the square from the rear, from left to right, walking alone. Coming to the fountain he disappeared from view as he passed on the far side of it, but then he came in sight again, emerging from behind the straggling group of youths and girls who clustered about the fountain steps. The watchers had a clear view of him and even though he was some distance away they could detect an anxious expression on his face. He came on, looking about him as he walked. He appeared to be searching for something.

'I'm sure he wasn't there before,' Crane whispered. 'He wasn't there yesterday when we watched the scene.'

'No, he wasn't,' Hughes murmured. 'We couldn't have missed him. We were looking out for him.'

Before the watchers' collective gaze Holman moved further to the right, seconds later vanishing from sight beyond the confines of the image. The two lovers strolled, self-absorbed; the child walked at his mother's side. And then, suddenly, Holman was there again, bursting into the scene and running across the piazza. As he drew near

163

the fountain he collided with a youth, collected himself and ran on again. In the same moments the lovers stopped to kiss, the child ran from his mother and fell. At the far side near the restaurant Holman came to a stop where, turning abruptly, he narrowly missed being struck by a passing cyclist. Behind him the restaurant door opened, and Belliros, followed by his wife, emerged. A moment later the first shot rang out. Then, just visible through the moving figures between, the watchers saw the two men, Holman and Belliros, in a sudden, confused flurry of movement, like some weird, impromptu dance routine. Then together they fell.

Pandemonium broke out. Screaming, crying out, panic-stricken people began to run in all directions while others threw themselves to the ground and lay cowering, hands covering their heads. Then, as before, the panicked crowd began to recover, getting warily to their feet, while some of those who had fled began to reappear. In seconds they were converging about the spot before the restaurant door.

The watchers leant forward in their chairs. And this time they saw the short, blue-suited figure of Belliros rise to his feet.

'I don't believe it!' Paxton breathed, 'the man's alive!'

'What's going on?' said Crane, his words joined by murmurs of bewilderment from the others at his side. He turned to Miss Donahue. 'Can you stop it and go back? We need to halt it at an earlier point – before the crowd starts to converge on that spot.'

Miss Donahue's hands flew over the wires. The scene dissolved and reappeared. The watchers gazed as the people milled casually about and the familiar incidents were enacted. And there was Holman again, emerging from the left, looking about him as he moved across the

164

square. They watched as he briefly disappeared from view behind the fountain with the gathering of youths and girls and reappeared on the other side. He moved on, out of sight beyond the borders of the image. The lovers came strolling together; the child hand in hand with his mother. Then suddenly Holman was back in the scene again, dashing back across the piazza.

'Get ready,' said Crane to Miss Donahue. 'Stop it after the second shot.'

Near the fountain steps Holman collided with the youth, recovered himself, ran on. Reaching the restaurant he stopped, turned and abruptly stepped back to avoid the cyclist. Behind him Belliros emerged from the restaurant doorway.

The first shot rang out. The second.

'*Now!*' Crane said. 'Stop it *now!*'

In a moment all movement was halted.

'We must move quickly,' Crane said, rising, beckoning to the others.

With Crane leading the way, they made a cautious, winding path among the still figures in the square. Reaching the entrance to the restaurant they peered down. Belliros and Holman lay on the ground, supine, Holman's body lying partly across that of Belliros. Belliros's right hand was frozen in the act of clutching at Holman's shoulder, fingertips digging into the fabric of his jacket. Holman lay with arms outstretched. A little to the right the blonde woman had been caught in the act of throwing herself to the ground. She was just halfway there, arms reaching out before her, one foot off the paving stone, defying the laws of gravity.

The attention of the five, however, was on the two men who lay on their backs.

165

'He's been hit,' observed Haddon, looking down at Belliros, 'but it's not much more than a scratch.'

There was a bullet wound in the soft flesh of Belliros's upper left arm. The bullet had cut through the fabric of his suit and lay embedded in the wood of the lower part of the door surround. Apart from Belliros's superficial wound he appeared to be unhurt. His face, though bearing an expression of shock and desperation, was unmarked.

Not so Holman.

'Oh, my God – the poor bastard,' said Hughes.

Crane nodded. 'Lucky for Belliros, though. There he is, the target of an assassin, and along comes Holman and steps in the way.'

The second bullet had struck Holman just above the right cheekbone. Emerging at the back of his skull it had left a wide, gaping hole through which a mess of blood and brains still oozed. His dead eyes, fixed, vacant and dulled, gazed off into his own infinity.

On the way back across the square Crane and Levin briefly paused to examine a couple of newspapers that lay discarded on the ground. At the same time Paxton bent to look at the wristwatches of two of the transfixed pedestrians.

Reaching the front again Crane turned to Levin.

'Friday, May twelfth?'

Levin nodded. 'Friday, May twelfth.'

The two turned to Paxton.

'Seven minutes past ten,' he said.

After a break to stretch their legs and take a little refreshment the five resumed their seats while Miss Donahue took her place at her frame. There was, she told them, still more to come.

166

There was much more. And while the vision of the death of Holman had been tragic and shocking, it was nothing to that which came after. Over the hours that followed the watchers found themselves witnessing scenes of increasing horror.

The first of the scenes was set outside the Presidential Palace in Castelandú. The ambience of ease and content-ment that had been there earlier, however, was no longer in evidence. There were crowds in the square as before, but now they were shouting angrily. In the earlier scene the guards had appeared to be almost incidental; now they had taken on a sinister aspect, standing tense and threatening. As the swarms of people pressed forward the guards suddenly raised their rifles and fired into the mass. In seconds the terrified citizens were routed from the square, leaving dead, dying and injured in their wake.

From then on the scene-changes took place rapidly. The watchers saw the city streets of Castelandú dark and almost deserted with the sinking of the sun. No carefree groups of adults or teenagers chatted on the street cor-ners, no couples wandered hand-in-hand, window-shop-ping at the store windows; few cars moved in the wide streets, no young men rode by on motor cycles. The few individual citizens in sight appeared furtive and afraid. Only the figures of the uniformed military seemed at ease.

The repression and the fear grew more intense. Through a montage of swiftly changing scenes the con-clave watched as men and women were snatched from their homes by the military and taken away in jeeps to be incarcerated in strongly guarded buildings. They saw scenes of torture played out in dark cellars – victims strung up by their limbs or subjected to other agonizing and terrifying horrors. Of those who were fortunate enough to be eventually released many appeared to be

167

irreparably crippled, in both mind and body. They, however, at least escaped with their lives. There were many who simply disappeared, to which fact grieving parents, wives and siblings could be seen attesting, and which was further borne out by the images of graves beyond the city's limits. In two separate scenes in the Larinas countryside the watchers saw buses halted by armed soldiers and the peasants on board – on the way to their labours in the fields – forced out and lined up while identification papers were checked. In each case some of the passengers were taken away and summarily shot.

As one horrific vision after another went by, and over what was clearly a period of several years, the watchers witnessed the gradual, but total, subjugation of a nation's citizens. Ordinary men and women were too terrified to protest, while newspapers no longer dared speak out against the outrages, outrages which, eventually, were not even solely directed against what the government termed 'the people's enemies'. In the end the powers of the regime were used against anyone deemed undesirable, for whatever reason. And so along with the rebels and the protesters, the teachers and the writers went the homosexuals, the disabled, the beggars and the gypsies. Supporting Belliros, and supported by him, the military was all-powerful, and the people walked in fear.

In a hotel room on the outskirts of Swindon the five members of the conclave sat facing each other around a table. They had left the church more than two hours before. There, when the last conjured scene had vanished and no other had formed in its place, Miss Donahue – hands now moving ineffectively over the wires – had informed the gathering that she was unable to raise anything else.

Eventually convinced that nothing more was likely to

be forthcoming, Crane had thanked her for her work and let her go.

Now, sitting at the table in the hotel room he took a swallow from his scotch and soda and said:

'Would anyone care to say anything . . .?'

Haddon sighed. 'Well – I don't think there can be much doubt about what happens, can there?'

'I don't think so,' said Crane. 'The way I see it, the first scenario shows that soon after the sudden and unexpected death of Perreiros, Belliros, his second-in-command, is assassinated. Which is due to happen in Milan on May the twelfth. As a result Juan Aranco comes from behind in the government to succeed to the premiership. Eventually under his leadership the country gains a measure of peace and prosperity it hasn't known for years.' He looked from one to the other. 'Do you go along with that scenario?'

'Yes,' Levin said, 'but if Belliros is *not* killed then he'll take over on Perreiros's death and plunge the country into even greater bloodshed and economic and social disaster than it knows at present.'

'But that's not what's *meant* to happen, is it?' said Hughes, putting down her gin and tonic. 'Belliros is *meant to die*, to be assassinated. By rights Aranco is meant to succeed to the premiership.'

Paxton said, 'Yes, and he would do, except that Holman looks like screwing everything up, by being where he's not meant to be.'

Hughes said, 'What can Belliros be doing in Milan?'

'Who knows,' Paxton said. 'He's there on vacation, or on business. It's not important, is it?'

'But surely,' said Haddon, 'if he's about to take over the running of his country he wouldn't be off taking holidays in other places. He'd stay where it's all happening, ready to step in.'

169

'Yes,' said Crane, 'but only *we* know that Perreiros is about to have his fall, his fatal accident. Belliros doesn't know that. There's no reason he shouldn't travel abroad.'

'He must feel pretty safe, too,' said Levin, absently fingering one of the metal rings on the sleeve of his jacket, 'wandering around freely like that.'

'Well,' said Hughes, 'if he's kept a low profile up till now then he's probably not known outside of Larinas. You saw what the newspaper had to say about him.'

'That's right,' Crane said, 'though of course he's misjudged the situation, hasn't he? He's *not* safe. As we saw earlier on. Obviously there's some disaffected Larinasian who's got it in for him, and manages to assassinate him.'

'Will it help us to find out who the man is, the assassin?' said Haddon.

Crane shook his head. 'I don't think so for a moment. He's basically unimportant. He'll fire the shots – which is what he's meant to do, but what happens to him after that is of no concern to us. Our concern is Holman being there when he's not supposed to be there.'

Paxton said: 'Yes, by rights Holman should be dead by May twelfth. But instead he's managed to escape the inescapable – his *fate*. And now, no longer having any ordained part in the scheme of things, he's wandering around, his presence a threat to everything else that's going on. May twelfth is less than three weeks away, and it's Belliros's fate to be assassinated in Milan on that date. And there's no doubt that it would take place. Only now – with Holman coming on the scene, it looks as if it's not going to happen after all.'

'It's incredible how Holman upsets it all,' said Crane, shaking his head in wonder at the magnitude and the simplicity of it. 'It's incredible, isn't it? Having escaped his own fate he now wanders into that square in Milan

170

and changes everything. At any other time his actions would probably have no bearing whatsoever upon anything, but in this case – simply by moving in that particular second, on that particular spot, he's able to change the course of history.'

Silence in the room.

'So,' said Paxton, 'what's to happen?'

'Yes,' Levin said, 'what can be done about it?'

No one answered his question. Haddon said:

'Anyway, who's to say that it actually *will* happen the way it appeared? The man's a law unto himself. He could still change his plans, even now. When the twelfth of May comes round he might be miles away from that place.'

'He might indeed,' Crane said. 'As you say, there's no knowing. He's repeatedly managed to defy his destiny, and there's no saying that he won't do it again. Going by what we've seen this afternoon, though, it appears that this is to be the general pattern of his movements in the near future, taking into account his maverick existence. We must also bear in mind that others have been convinced by the scenario we've seen. And convinced to the extent that they haven't hesitated to kill rather than allow us to discover it for ourselves.'

'Not to be wondered at,' said Hughes. 'The discord and misery that will come about as the result of Belliros's presidency will be exactly what they want.'

'Which brings us back to agent Levin's question,' Crane said. 'The question of what can be done about it.'

No one spoke. After a second or two Crane added:

'Belliros can't be allowed to escape his fate. He cannot. He *must* die as he has been fated to die.'

'So?' Levin said.

'So Holman must be prevented from being there. From being in the same spot at the same time.'

171

14

Guy had telephoned Annie the evening before, and now, at 6.45 on Saturday, he was making his way along Hammersmith's King Street. Turning onto Parker Lane he stopped at the door of number fourteen and rang the top bell. A minute later Annie, wearing her coat, was opening the door to him.

'Well, hello. Glad you found your way all right.'

'Am I too early?'

'Oh, no, I'm ready.' She pulled the door shut behind her, locked it. 'As you asked me to, I booked a table at a place just down the road. For half-past seven. That okay?'

'Fine.'

'It's not far from here. I thought maybe we could go and have a drink somewhere first. If you'd like that.'

They set off along the pavement. Stopping at a corner pub they went into the lounge bar and ordered gin-and-tonics. Taking the drinks over to a soft bench near the window they took off their coats. Annie wore a long-sleeved, pale-yellow dress with a white silk scarf at her throat. It was the kind of outfit Sylvie might have worn.

In their conversation they spoke again of the Pre-Raphaelites and she asked him whether he knew the story behind the painting of Ophelia, that Millais had used a model named Elizabeth Siddall who had posed for many hours lying in a bathtub, as a result of which she had caught pneumonia.

'Did she survive?' Guy asked, to which Annie replied

that the story went that she didn't. 'Though the whole story might be apocryphal,' she added.

They talked of tourism, vacations, and he said he would probably return to New York during the coming week. They spoke of their families, and he learned that she had one sister and that her parents resided in Bradford where they had spent their lives. Asked about his own family he told her that his father had died just over a year ago; his mother, he added, had died shortly after his birth.

She shook her head in sympathy at this. 'Oh, that's very sad. What was it – complications with your birth? Something like that?'

He nodded. 'Something like that. My father never wanted to talk about it.'

They got back to the subject of his vacation. He told her of his original plans to travel in Spain and other parts of southern Europe, then of how he had decided to change those plans and come to England. When she asked how he had spent his time since his arrival he replied, 'Doing very, very little, I'm afraid.'

It emerged from their conversation after a while that Annie had once been married, but had since – not too long before, obviously – got a divorce. She didn't elaborate on the few basic facts she let go and he felt that the subject was a matter of some distress for her. She, shifting the conversation from herself, asked him whether he was married.

'Not now,' he said.

'Are you divorced?'

'No – my wife died.'

'Oh – I'm very sorry . . .' She hesitated, searching his face for a moment, then asked, 'When did it happen?'

'Last year. Last summer.'

' – What was her name?'

173

'Sylvie.'

'That's a lovely name.'

'I think so.' He paused. 'She was English. I met her over here.'

'Have you got any children?'

He hesitated before answering. 'Not now.'

She gazed at him.

'I had two sons,' he said. 'They both died.'

'Oh, God – I'm so sorry. I'm really so sorry.'

'That's all right.'

'I don't always ask the wrong questions.'

'You weren't to know.'

He smiled at her. She smiled in return, then rose and picked up their glasses. 'I'll get us another drink.'

He watched her as she moved to the bar and gave the order to the bartender. She looked so like Sylvie standing there.

Sitting at a candlelit corner table in the restaurant they ate slowly, while talking a great deal, and Guy found himself becoming increasingly drawn to her. There were so many things about her that attracted him – her hazel eyes with their dark lashes, her laugh, the smile that lifted her cheeks and crinkled her eyes, the way the dark wing of her hair swung forward slightly when she bent her head, her voice with its very English accent, the sound of his name on her tongue.

Music softly played as they ate – orchestral music from Italian opera. Guy heard the sounds in snatches, in the relaxed lulls in their conversation or coming faintly behind their words. He recognized the drinking song from *La Traviata*, an aria from *La Rondine*; another from *La Bohème* – at which latter Annie sighed with delight, lifting her hand, poised, while the strains of the bittersweet

174

melody washed over them. 'Oh, I know they say Puccini is second rate,' she said. 'But it's beautiful isn't it? I usually hate music in restaurants, but when it's like this, done to create an effect, it's a little different.'

To their surprise the lamps that lit the room faded to nothing while new lamps came on that left everything in shadow but for the whites and the palest colours – the napkins, the collar and cuffs of Guy's shirt, Annie's scarf and pale-lemon dress – bathing them in a fluorescent glow. At the same time the music swelled, and the monks' chorus from *Nabucco* filled the room. Annie laughed. 'God, what a cheap effect. But it's fun, isn't it?' The dramatic change in the lighting had briefly arrested her actions so that she paused with her hand on the tablecloth in the act of replacing her wine glass. Reaching out, Guy laid his fingertips on hers. At his touch she looked down at their two hands, while he watched her eyes, searching them for disapproval or acceptance. She raised her head, looked into his eyes and smiled. Only after another moment or two did she draw her hand away.

Later, way after midnight, they stood at her front door while she turned her key in the lock. 'How will you get back to your hotel?' she asked.

He didn't want the night to end yet, but it appeared that it had. Yet over his momentary disappointment came the realization that he didn't mind; it had been wonderful.

'I'll get a train,' he said, ' – a tube.'

She made a face. 'I think they'll have stopped by now, or they will at any minute. This isn't New York, or Paris.' She paused. 'You'd better come up and we'll phone for a minicab.'

The Victorian house was tall and narrow. He followed her up two flights of stairs to the top landing where she

175

unlocked the door to her flat and led him inside. Going before him, she switched on a couple of lamps. He was standing in her living room. It was comfortably furnished, with patterned covers on the two armchairs and the sofa. Framed prints hung on the walls; on the coffee table lay books, magazines, and a couple of record albums. She took off her coat, urging him to do the same, and lit an ornate little gas fire. 'Would you like some more coffee before we phone for your cab?' she asked, and he answered yes, though more coffee was the last thing he wanted.

She went out of the room and he sat down on the small sofa. When she came in again a few minutes later she was carrying a tray holding mugs of coffee. Guy took one and set it down on the coffee table. Leaving her own coffee on the tray she went to the telephone, dialled a number and asked for a cab to go into the West End. 'It'll be here in ten minutes,' she said as she replaced the receiver. She sat facing him in one of the armchairs and picked up her mug. 'Why are you uncertain about how long you'll be in London?' she asked.

He hesitated for a moment. 'Well, you see,' he said, 'I'm receiving medical treatment.'

'Medical treatment? What for?'

A longer pause before he answered. 'For rabies.'

'*What?*' Although her voice was low she sounded horrified.

He told her about the dog in Morocco, the telephone call that had set him in a panic and led to him seeking treatment.

'It must have been terrible for you,' she said.

'It was at the time. Though I'm okay now. I'm feeling just fine and the doctor doesn't think I have anything to worry about.'

He told her then about the possibility of his continuing his treatment in New York, and she said:

'Well, I'm sure you'll feel more comfortable if you do that.'

'I think so.'

'So when d'you think you'll go back?'

'I'm due to get my third shot on Monday. I could go right away after that.'

'You think you might?'

'I haven't decided yet.'

They were talking of other things when there came a ring at the front door bell. The cab had arrived. As they stood up Guy said:

'This has been one of the very best evenings.'

'Well . . .' She nodded, gave a grave little half-smile. 'It's been good for me too. It was a lovely evening.'

'Can I see you again?'

'But – you're going away.'

'I still have two or three days.'

She hesitated, then smiled. 'Okay – phone me. In the early evening.'

'I will.'

He turned from her and went out onto the landing. As he went softly down the stairs he looked back and saw her bent over the banister, watching him. He waved and smiled and saw her smile back.

Guy called Annie the following evening just after six o'clock. 'I half guessed it might be you,' she said when she heard his voice.

'I wanted to tell you again what a good time I had last night,' he said.

'Well, I liked it too.'

'Are you busy tonight?'

177

'No – not particularly.'

'Can we meet?'

'Okay. What would you like to do?'

'Whatever you want. We could go to the theatre. Or to the movies and watch men tapping into secret computer systems. There's always at least three of those showing. Or we could just go out and eat.'

'*That* sounds good.'

'Fine.'

'And it's on me this time.'

'Well, we'll talk about that.' He smiled. 'I'll be with you in an hour or so.'

She was ready when he arrived at her flat. They went to an Indian restaurant a short distance away. Guy had never eaten Indian food before, and he enjoyed the spicy dishes. Afterwards Annie tried to insist on picking up the bill but Guy would not hear of it.

Back in her flat she lit the fire and made coffee and they sat facing one another, she in the armchair, he on the sofa. In the little silence that fell in the room he smiled at her and she smiled back, just the flicker, a little uncertain. Leaning forward, he took her left hand as it rested on the chair-arm. She did not resist. Glancing down at her cool hand held in his he saw that her little finger was imperfect; it was slightly bent at an angle at the lower joint. He had not noticed it before. She, becoming aware of his attention, quickly withdrew her hand.

'I'm sorry,' he said, looking up into her face.

She flicked a glance at him. Her smile came and went. 'It's okay.'

'Did you have an accident?' he asked.

'Well, yes – you could say that.'

As soon as she had spoken she got up from the chair and moved past him to the telephone. 'I'd better call your

178

cab for you,' she said, 'or you're going to be very late.' The relaxed sound that had earlier been in her voice had gone. Guy watched her, not understanding. 'I'm in no hurry,' he said.

'Still – even so . . .'

She picked up the receiver, held it for a moment, then put it down again. She leaned over the desk, eyes shut tight. Guy got up and moved to her; stood looking at the anguish in her face. 'Annie, what's wrong?'

She didn't answer, merely shook her head.

'Is it something I said?'

'No – of course not.'

'Then what is it?'

She shook her head again, turned and began to search the desk top. 'I had some cab numbers here,' she said. 'God knows where they are now.'

'I don't care about a cab. I can find one along the street.'

'Yes,' she nodded, 'I'm sure you can.' She half turned, the gesture signalling their imminent separation, the winding-up of the evening. 'Well – if that's all right with you. There should be cabs up by the station.'

He didn't move. 'I'll go in a minute,' he said. 'Not for a minute, though. Not yet.'

A pause. 'I think you should, Guy. It would be better.'

'Why?'

She didn't answer.

'Can I see you tomorrow?' he said.

'Well, I . . . D'you really want to?'

'I wouldn't ask if I didn't.'

She gave a worried little shake of her head. 'Is there any point in it? For either of us?'

He did not know what to say. She moved away, touching at the magazines on the coffee table, adjusting a cushion. 'God, I'm so tired,' she said. 'I must get some sleep.'

He gazed at her for a moment longer, then picked up his coat and moved to the door. Facing her from the open doorway he said:

'Thank you for the evening. I don't know what the hell happened, but I won't give you any further cause for concern. Good luck.'

Turning, he passed through onto the landing and down the stairs.

Downstairs he closed the front door behind him, put on his Burberry and started along the street. A wind had sprung up but he barely noticed it as he strode along; the evening that had started so well, with so much promise, had turned sour and he did not know why. It did not matter how he urged himself to be rational, told himself that he hardly knew her, that they had met only a few times; he felt weighed down with melancholy.

He had walked only a hundred yards along the street when he became aware of the sound of hurrying footsteps behind him. As the steps drew nearer he heard her voice:

'Guy . . .'

He stopped, turned. She hurried towards him, coming to a halt four or five yards away, a little out of breath. She had come out without a coat.

He frowned. 'Did I forget something?'

She shook her head, her mouth open, getting her breath back. 'No, I came to say that . . .' Her words tailed off. 'Don't go,' she said. 'Don't go yet.'

'I don't understand . . .'

'Of course you don't. Who could. I'm a fool.'

She moved towards him, stopping just a yard away. 'Come back and finish your coffee.'

He didn't speak.

180

'Come on,' she gently urged him. 'Please.'

He smiled back at her. 'Oh, Annie . . .'

He stepped forward, looking into her smiling face. Her hand came up, touched his arm. 'Let's hurry,' she said. 'I'm getting cold.'

15

She had turned up the flame on the gas fire and the warm glow supplemented the mellow light from the single lamp that shone. Sitting in her chair, facing Guy as he sat on the sofa, she said simply:

'I – I was afraid.'

'Afraid? What of?' He was still a little wary.

She hesitated. 'You.'

'Of me? Why? I wouldn't hurt you.'

'Oh, I know that.' She fell silent. In the stillness the fire gave out a gentle hiss. 'No – afraid more of myself, I suppose, really. Afraid of – of liking somebody too much.'

'I don't understand . . .'

She sighed. 'Afraid of even the possibility of getting involved again. I've had that and all I got was a lot of unhappiness.'

'You mean – your husband?'

'Harry – yes. You know – when we had dinner last night I had a wonderful time. And I knew right away that I liked you.' She gave a helpless little shrug. 'And tonight too. And realizing it I suppose I just became – a little afraid.'

'. . . Go on.'

'I grew afraid that – well, that I could get *too involved*. Even with your only being here for such a short while.' She raised her hands in a gesture of protest. 'Oh, I know that must sound very presumptuous, because I'm quite sure it's the last thing you'd want, anyway. After all, you're here on holiday, you've only got a couple of days left, and you're just out for a good time.'

'Is that how I come over?'

'No, of course not. It must sound really foolish to you but – it suddenly struck me when we were here earlier, that it was crazy. There I was, wanting to see you again and – and you're going away. In another day or two you'll be gone. So I thought – stop it now. Before it has a chance of going any further. But then after you'd gone I realized that I couldn't let you just walk out like that. That wasn't the way to end it. *You* hadn't done anything. It was me.' She sighed. 'You know, it's been so long since I was – with anyone. To be close, I mean. And I just suddenly became – afraid. Now, though, I'm not so sure. After all, you can't go through life like that, can you?' She looked down at her hands, touched the little finger of her left hand. 'My husband did it,' she said. 'He broke it. I can't straighten it now.'

Guy frowned. 'Did he – mistreat you frequently?'

'It happened occasionally. Mostly I was just left with bruises, a black eye or whatever. Sometimes it was more serious. He broke three of my fingers – the little one so badly that it couldn't be set properly. And there was a time I got a perforated eardrum in a restaurant when we had a little disagreement. He just leaned across the table and swung at me with his fist – in front of everyone.' She gave a bitter smile. 'But most of the things he did left no scars. Other things did. I'm not talking about broken fingers.'

In the silence that fell Guy became aware again of the faint hiss of the fire. After a few moments she went on:

'I loved him so much at the start. And there was no sign at the beginning of how things would turn out. Oh, I knew he had a quick temper – I'd seen it turned in other

183

directions – on objects, strangers. But there was never any hint of what was to happen between *us*. Anyway, I took it for as long as I could, then got out. I haven't seen him now for a while. Over two years, in fact. He didn't contest the divorce.' She sighed. 'I suppose in the end you come to believe that you can't depend on your own sense, trust your emotions. I mean – Harry was the first and only man I ever loved – and to find out after our marriage that I had never known him, that he was a different person from the man I thought I knew . . . And it wasn't as if I was a child. I was twenty-four. Old enough to have some sense of judgement. Anyway, one gains something, I suppose. Wisdom of a kind.' A little smile. 'But I was determined never to make the same mistake again. Does that make sense?'

He nodded. 'Oh, yes.'

Another little silence passed. He looked at his watch. Close on eleven-forty. 'I'd better go,' he said. 'Let you get to sleep.'

She said quickly, 'You don't have to go yet – unless you want to.'

'No, I don't want to.'

She tried a smile. 'Would you like some more coffee? Or tea?'

'Tea would be nice.'

'I'll make some.' She got up from the chair. 'Milk or lemon?'

'How do you drink it?'

'With milk.'

'I'll try milk.'

When she had gone from the room he sat thinking of the things she had told him; the horrors perpetrated by one human being on another – they never ceased to amaze. It was no wonder that she had become afraid of

184

taking a chance, of any kind of emotional involvement. How could she feel free? – she was still harnessed to the memory of her marriage. He found himself checked by the thought. In that, he ruefully told himself, they had something in common. As she had Harry, so he had Sylvie. In their own ways they were both governed by their pasts.

When Annie came back into the room she set the tray down and poured the tea. She handed Guy a cup, took her own and sat in the chair. They looked at one another in silence for a second then Guy patted the sofa seat at his side. 'Come – sit here . . .' She hesitated briefly then got up and sat beside him.

He watched her as she leant forward slightly, contemplatively stirring her tea. The soft light from the lamp and the fire reflected mellowly in her hair. He set down his tea and put an arm around her shoulder. Leaving her own cup and saucer on the table she let him draw her to him. He held her. She was tense at first, but then, gradually, he could feel her tension going, seeping away.

Later, lying naked beside her in the bed in the soft glow of the lamp, he kissed her and moved his hand gently over the smoothness of her body. She gave no sign of wanting more but it did not matter. For now it was enough just to be so close. After a while she turned from him and he cupped her naked body with his. She reached out and switched off the light, then took his hand and brought it to her mouth. Softly planting a kiss in his palm she burrowed back into his warmth. After a time he heard the pattern of her breathing change into the rhythmic pattern of sleep.

He awoke as the first light of dawn filtered past the drawn curtains and gave shape to the objects in the room.

The fact that he had slept surprised him; for so long now he was accustomed to sleeping alone. Annie was still sleeping soundly. Her body, close against him, was like warm silk. He moved his hand, gently tracing the contours of her flesh, the curve of her arm, her hip, the swell of her small breasts. She stirred under his touch, turned her head and smiled up into his face.

He kissed her, gently at first, and then more urgently. In his arms she was like a flower, awakening, opening to the light. When the time was right, and when he could wait no longer, he began, slowly, to enter her. At first he felt her body tense; felt her hands on his shoulders as if she would thrust him away. But then her hands were holding him to her, and the little sounds of protest that had formed on her lips became little gasping moans of ecstasy. 'Yes,' she murmured. 'Yes. Oh, Guy – yes, oh yes . . .'

He used her razor to shave in the morning, and afterwards, freshly showered, put on the towelling bathrobe she had given him. Long and loose-fitting on her it came to mid-thigh on his tall frame. As he came from the bathroom he was met by the smell of fresh coffee, scrambled eggs and toast.

They ate at the little kitchen table. She wore a blue wrapper, belted at the waist. Her face looked newly washed, her hair brushed. 'I'll have my shower when I've finished my coffee,' she said. She smiled, reached across and gently ran fingers through his damp hair. Guy felt her fingertips touch the scars that ran into his hairline. Seeing them, the scars, she frowned. 'What happened?' she asked.

'Oh – ' he shrugged, 'I had a little accident.'

'A *little* accident?'

186

'OK, a *big* accident.'

'How?'

'I had a run-in with a truck. We both tried to be in the same place at the same time.'

'Do you hate talking about it?'

'It doesn't matter. There's nothing much to tell. It was last summer. Last July. I was crossing the road when this truck came roaring around the corner. The offside wing caught me.'

She drew in her breath. 'God, how awful. Were you badly hurt?'

'Yes, I was – rather.'

' – You don't want to talk about it, do you?'

'I don't mind. It doesn't matter now; it's over. Though it was tough at the time.'

'Were you *very* badly injured?'

'You could say that. I had some internal injuries along with a fractured skull, broken collar bone, broken ribs and broken leg.' He slapped his thigh. 'I've got a few scars on my leg, too. I was unconscious for eight days. I think some people thought I wouldn't come through it, but I did.' He smiled. 'And here I am.'

'Here you are.' She touched his cheek in a little caress. 'It must have taken you a while to recover.'

'Oh, yes, months. I was in the hospital for ages, and then my convalescence took time too. Fortunately I was covered by insurance. This vacation – it's part of my convalescence. I'm okay now, though. I could have gone back to my teaching a little earlier, but they insisted – my doctor and my principal at NYU – that I take a little more time off. It wasn't really necessary, not this length of time, I'm sure. I feel a bit of a fraud sometimes – though I've been glad of the break.'

'You were lucky you weren't killed,' she said.

187

'Oh, I know that. If I'd been in the middle of the road a second sooner I *would* have been. But I got there a second *late* – and I was saved.'

'What do you mean, you got there late?'

He was silent for a second, thinking back to that July afternoon. 'It was a terrible day,' he said. 'I'd just heard that my wife was very sick here in England, and I was rushing around making arrangements to fly over to see her. I was starting across the street, when, for no reason that I can recall, I stopped, hesitated. Don't ask me why; I don't know. *Maybe* I had a reason; I can't remember one now. Anyway, it was that moment of hesitation that saved me. Without that happening I would have been right in the truck's path.'

'You say you don't know why you hesitated. But you must have had some reason.'

He shrugged. 'I don't know what it was.'

'Was it a – a premonition or something like that?'

'I don't think so. I don't remember anything about the actual collision – about being hit, though I remember everything pretty clearly up until that moment. I can remember thinking: What am I doing? What am I stopping for? But I still don't know why, even now. I just did it, that's all.'

As he sipped at his coffee he thought of the events that had comprised the catastrophe, the inexplicable happening that had occurred earlier when he had fallen unconscious – just as he had in Morocco before he changed his travel plans. There was no accounting for it.

'First an accident with a truck,' he said, 'then a meeting with a rabid dog – I'm like Macbeth; I bear a charmed life.' He shook his head in a little gesture of incredulity. 'When I think of that dog, and what *could* have happened . . . If I hadn't changed my plans on that last night in

188

Morocco I wouldn't have had the treatment from the doctor. I'd still be wandering around Spain or Portugal or somewhere. And if I hadn't lost my watch . . . It was that – losing my watch, changing my plans and then leaving my London hotel number at the hotel in Agadir – in case my watch turned up. It's amazing how one thing leads to another – the sequence of events. But I guess that's fate. If I hadn't left a phone number there wouldn't have been any way of getting in touch with me when they found out the dog was rabid, and, not knowing, I would have just gone on, and after a while it would have been too late.'

'Don't,' Annie said. 'It's too awful.'

He laughed. 'No, that's the marvellous thing. Everything worked out for the best. I'm here.' He leaned across the table, kissed her. 'And I'm here with you.'

That evening he saw Dr Powell for his third injection. During his examination Powell asked him how he was feeling.

'I feel great,' Guy said, smiling. 'Every morning I wake and I look for signs – whatever they are – but there's never anything. I feel really good.'

Powell was pleased. 'So,' he said as he prepared the syringe, 'have you decided yet when you're going home? You talked about going tomorrow.'

'I've changed my mind,' Guy said. 'I've decided to hang on for a while.'

'Well,' Powell said, 'if you've got nothing to rush back for there's not much point. You'll be as well off here as you will anywhere.' He gave Guy the injection, withdrew the needle and dabbed at the site. 'So what are your plans?'

Guy shrugged. 'Nothing definite. I just thought I'd stay

189

on maybe another week or two. Visit a few places here and there. I'll see how it goes.'

As Powell disposed of the needle he said, 'Your fourth jab is due in a week. Next Thursday.' He opened his diary. 'The 1st of May. The fifth one's due two weeks afterwards, so you'll have plenty of opportunity to make your plans as to when you'll go home. In the meantime I'll expect you next Thursday.'

After leaving the doctor's office Guy set off for Hammersmith to have dinner with Annie.

Arriving at her flat he rang the bell and after a short wait the door opened and she was standing there in a long grey dress patterned with large red roses. 'Oh,' he said, 'you look so good.'

'I hoped you'd like it,' she said, smiling. 'After all, this could be your last night in London.'

He drew her towards him. 'No. I'm not leaving just yet. I'm staying on for a while longer.'

'I'm glad,' she said. 'I'm very glad.'

'Who's the girl?' asked Haddon.

Crane shook his head. 'I don't know. We haven't got a line on her yet. We'll get one, though. The important thing right now is Holman's decision to stay on.'

'He looks like keeping to this new pattern,' said Levin, shaking his head. 'He's got to be stopped.'

'Stopped,' echoed Hughes sharply. 'And how do you propose to do that?'

Levin shrugged. 'We'll have to find *some* way.' He paused, added: 'If necessary he'll have to die.'

Hughes shook her head. 'Just like that. As simple as that. Don't you have any feelings for the man?'

Without looking at her Levin replied, 'Mrs Hughes,

190

you know very well we can't allow feelings to get in the way of what has to be done.'

'Mr Levin is right, of course,' said Crane. 'We can't consider one single individual when so much else is at stake.'

Hughes sighed. 'No, I know you're right,' she said. 'It's just – oh, I don't know – that poor bastard, he's had so much unhappiness in his life. You'd have thought that a little contentment was due him by now.'

'I understand your feelings,' Crane said. 'And I'm sure we all agree with you. But if he keeps on his present course he's going to die anyway. You saw that yourself; you saw him shot down. We've got to stop him before it happens.'

'I know, I know.' Hughes nodded, then angrily clenched her fists and struck impotently at the air. 'This fucking job! Sometimes I think I'd like to be doing anything else but this.'

16

Tuesday. It was just before noon. Guy prepared to take his leave of Annie. On the landing outside her flat he stood and wrapped her in his arms. The past night had been wonderful and he was reluctant to go. He had no choice, though; she was to leave that afternoon for Bradford where her father was to go into the hospital for a hernia operation the next morning.

'I shall miss you,' Guy said.

'Will you?'

'Oh, yes.'

She sighed. 'I want to see my Dad, of course, but at the same time I wish I didn't have to go.'

Her words lifted his spirits. 'Anyway, you'll be back on Saturday,' he said; it was part question, part statement.

'Yes, on Saturday. What will you do in the meantime?'

'Oh, I guess I'll think of something.'

That evening he went to the theatre to see an Alan Ayckbourn play and afterwards ate supper at a pasta restaurant. Back at the hotel he lay on his bed watching television – an Italian movie with English subtitles. It was difficult to concentrate, however; thoughts of Annie kept coming into his head. He wondered what he might do in the time till her return. Perhaps he'd go to a few galleries, the British Museum, see a few of the sights he had never gotten around to on those earlier trips. He should begin to *use* his time here. He had wasted so much of it up till now. He thought of his two journeys to the West Country.

They had brought him the satisfaction of seeing Sylvie's grave, but he had found no consolation.

And why, he wondered, had Sylvie and Luke been buried in separate graves? And why had Mrs Bennett refused to tell him the reason? The questions led him to that other inevitable question: who had been Luke's father?

He would never understand how it could have happened that Sylvie had taken a lover. Though God knew she'd had every reason to seek happiness and comfort and he could never truly reproach her for it. It was just so hard to believe that she had done such a thing. And who was the man? One of his friends? No; he would have seen that something was going on between them; they couldn't have hidden it from him. Who, then? One of her colleagues at work? Possibly. There was any number of men in her office whom he had never met, men whom he knew merely as names. If it was one of them he would never know. The more he thought about it the more convinced he became that Mrs Bennett *did* know the man's identity. Sylvie, he was sure, would not have kept it from her.

Over the following three days he spent his time visiting the cinema, galleries and museums. And then, on the third day, Friday, a day earlier than he had expected, Annie telephoned to say that she was back in London. Her call came in the early evening as he got out of the shower in preparation for another visit to a cinema. 'Where are you calling from?' he asked.

'From Hammersmith.'

'That's great. How's your Dad?'

'He's fine, just fine. Making good progress. I realized I wasn't really needed there any longer, so – I came back.'

'That was a good idea.'

'I thought so. I'll probably go up and see Dad again in a few days, but for now I'm back here. What are you doing?'

'At the moment? Standing dripping over the carpet.'

She laughed. 'And when you're dry?'

'I don't know. Seeing you, I hope.'

'I was hoping you'd say that.'

' – I'll leave in fifteen minutes.'

'Good. I'll see you soon.'

'See you soon.'

The following morning, Saturday, Guy and Annie went shopping together along Hammersmith's King Street, and in the afternoon into the West End to catch a Saturday matinee of a musical that turned out to be a disappointment. Returning to Hammersmith they ate dinner at a small Greek restaurant. As they emerged onto the street afterwards Annie looked up at the clear night sky and said, 'If it's fine tomorrow we could go for a picnic.'

When morning came Guy would have liked to stay in bed beside her – their two nights together since her return had been so sweet – but she was firm: they must get up, get ready and leave. By ten-forty-five they were in her car and, after stopping to pick up a few things they needed at a nearby supermarket, were driving west along the M4 motorway.

Leaving the motorway after a while they followed side roads that wound through the countryside. Nearing a village they saw a sign advertising a boot fair. What was a boot fair? Guy asked, and Annie replied: 'A sale of people's junk. Stalls and stalls of people's junk.'

'Like a garage sale, I guess.'

'Really?' Annie shrugged. 'I wouldn't know. You want to go to it?'

'Sure. Why not. We've got time, haven't we?'

She smiled. 'We've got all the time we want.'

The signs led them into a large field just off the main road. They parked the car and joined the other punters wandering around the scores of stalls piled with old clothes, books, records, china and bric-a-brac. Guy bought for Annie a little ceramic figure of a dolphin and she bought for him a volume of poems by Wilfred Owen.

Back in the car they set off again, and as they drove Guy leaned back in the seat aware of his contentment. He looked at Annie beside him as she concentrated on the road. Beyond her profile the trees and hedges passed by in a sunlit blur.

'You okay?' he asked, and she flicked him a glance and smiled. 'Yes, I'm okay. Are you okay?'

'Yes, indeed.'

She turned on the radio, pressed in a cassette and the interior of the little car was filled with the sound of Orff's *Carmina Burana*.

After a time they turned on to a narrower way that led between fields and stretches of wooded areas. Eventually, on the edge of a wooded hillside, Annie drew the car onto the shoulder, braked, and switched off the music.

'How about this?'

'Fine.'

She glanced at her watch. 'After three. We'll look for a nice spot around here, shall we?'

They got out of the car. As they did so a blue Ford van with the sound of heavy rock blasting from its interior roared past. Annie frowned at the intrusion. 'You can't get away from it, can you?' she said, watching as the van disappeared around the bend ahead.

On the side of the road on which they stood the woodland stretched away. On the other side, beyond a

195

narrow fringe of trees, lay rolling meadows. The green of the grass, like the leaves, was rich and fresh, while the hawthorn blossoms in the hedgerows that bordered the near fields were like snow. Guy drew in the air, sweet in his lungs with the scent of the spring-growing things, while from all around came the chirping murmur of birds.

Taking the rug and the packed holdall from the back seat they left the car and walked along the roadside, the woods on their left. After a short distance they found a bridle path that led through the trees. They followed it for half an hour, then left it to walk through the woods. Eventually they emerged into a sunlit clearing. 'How's this?' Annie said. 'We'll be worn out if we go much further.'

'It's perfect.'

At the edge of the clearing stood a magnificent horse chestnut tree in full flower, its blossoms like deep pink candles. Coming to a stop Guy watched Annie as she moved ahead. It could be Sylvie walking there, he thought. He moved to her side, put down the holdall, took her in his arms and kissed her.

Sitting on the rug watching while Annie set out the picnic things on a cloth, Guy felt a sense of peace that he had not known in a long time. It was all due to her, he knew.

Raising her head, finding his eyes upon her, she smiled at him. 'I hope you're hungry.'

'Yes, I am.'

She had brought a large slice of game pie, some slices of ham, a green salad with a French dressing, a French loaf and butter, cole-slaw, potato chips, pickles, and an assortment of cheeses. There was also a cherry pie and cream, fresh fruit, beer, a bottle of red wine – 'At least we won't need to chill it,' she said – and a flask of coffee.

196

As they ate – from plates with exotic birds painted on them – Annie said:

'You get another of your vaccine injections soon, don't you?'

'Tomorrow.'

'Do you dread it?'

'No, not at all. It's a small price to pay.'

'And you're still feeling okay, are you?'

He nodded. 'I feel great. Better than I have for a long, long time.'

When they had eaten Annie poured coffee. She handed him a cup and said, her question taking him somewhat by surprise:

'Have you got a photograph of Sylvie?'

He hesitated, afraid that Annie, seeing Sylvie's likeness to herself, might somehow misinterpret his motives for his interest in her.

'No,' he lied, 'not here.'

'You don't carry a picture of her with you?'

'No,' he said, and thought of the colour photograph of Sylvie that even at that moment lay in his wallet next to his chest.

'I'm sorry,' she said, 'I shouldn't have asked. I was just curious, that's all. I wonder sometimes what she was like.' She smiled. 'Was she pretty?'

'Oh, yes.'

'I knew she would be.' She paused. 'Tell me about her . . . won't you?'

He was silent for a moment, then he began, haltingly, to tell something of their story. He told of his meeting with Sylvie and of how he had taken her to New York after their marriage. He told of her unhappiness there, and the birth of David, and of how, following David's death – from an illness, he said – Sylvie had come back to

197

England for the birth of Luke. And he told of how Luke had died within days of his birth and how Sylvie herself had died, less than a year ago. He told the story simply, and using only half-truths. He said nothing of the fact that he and Sylvie had remained apart all those years after her return to England, or of Mrs Bennett's revelation that Luke was not his son.

'So,' Annie said when he had finished, 'you never saw your baby, Luke.'

'No.'

'Oh, that's so sad.'

He set down his cup and from the inside pocket of his jacket took out his wallet. Holding it away from Annie, he opened it – and there was Sylvie, framed in a little plastic window, smiling out at him. From behind the photograph he pulled out another. It showed a child laughing beneath a green, summer tree, holding a ball in one hand and pointing off with the other.

'Davie,' he said, passing the photograph to Annie. 'I took it in Central Park. On his third birthday. Just before we went up to the Cape for our vacation.'

'The Cape? Cape Cod, is that?'

'Yes.'

She looked at the picture. 'He's beautiful.'

'Yes, he was.'

'How long afterwards was it that he – ?' She broke off and added quickly, 'I'm sorry; I can't imagine you want to talk about it.'

'I *haven't* talked about it,' he said. 'Sylvie and I – we never talked about it.'

Annie handed the snapshot back. He gazed at it. 'It was the last picture I took of him,' he said. 'Less than a week later he was dead.' He put the photograph back in the wallet, returned the wallet to his pocket. With a shake

198

of his head, he said, 'It's been nine years since he died. And sometimes it still seems like yesterday.'

'What was his illness?' she said.

He paused. 'Illness,' he repeated. 'That's what I said, wasn't it? No. He wasn't sick. I lied. He – he had an accident.'

Annie said nothing. He added, keeping his eyes lowered, picking at the blades of grass:

'There was an accident. He was killed.'

Raising his eyes he saw that she was looking at him with an expression of pain on her face.

'I killed him,' he said.

Reaching out, Annie laid her hand on his.

'I loved him so much,' he said. 'He was everything I wanted, everything I'd ever hoped to have in a son. And I had him, and he was mine, and I killed him.'

He moved his hand within hers, briefly pressed it for a moment then released it.

'It was a summer day,' he said. 'A beautiful day on the Cape. We'd gone up to Cape Cod for two weeks' vacation, and it was our first week there. I was off school for the summer vacation, of course. New York is impossible in the summer. It's so humid you can hardly move. That day on the Cape, though, it was fantastic.' He came to a halt, seeing the scene before him. After a moment he went on:

'It was a Thursday afternoon. We were at the beach. Sylvie, Davie and I. We ate a picnic lunch and then just relaxed. There was hardly anybody else around. There were two or three other families a little further down the beach, but we were pretty much on our own. Sylvie was relaxing in the shade, Davie was playing in the sand. It was one of those really peaceful days – and it was one of

199

the happier times Sylvie and I had known since our marriage.'

He pulled himself up a little, leaning on his right forearm. With his left hand he began to pull at the blades of grass; they squeaked beneath his fingers.

'In New York we only had the apartment,' he said, 'but we were hoping for better things. And we were having a good time on the Cape that day, and the weather was good. Things were looking up. Well, we had Davie. And he made up for so much for us. I know that as far as Sylvie was concerned he made her whole life worth the living. Without him I don't think she'd have stuck it there at all. New York, I mean.'

He fell silent, shifting his gaze to look off into the distance. His hand had stopped plucking at the grass. 'I'd brought some golf clubs along,' he said. 'They were in the trunk of the car. I went and got one. Sylvie was asleep on the rug. Davie was digging in the sand. I whispered to him to stay where he was, not to come near me, then moved off a little way and stood there practising my swing, knocking the odd shell and things out into the surf.'

He closed his eyes. In a whisper Annie said:

'Don't talk about it.'

'I have to now,' he said. After a moment he went on: 'I remember swinging the club for a while and then picking up another bunch of shells and setting them out in a row. It just took a minute or so. He, Davie, was so quiet on the sand I didn't hear him. His little feet . . . He made no sound at all as he ran to me. Anyway, as I said, I set the shells out, and then, straightening up, I swung the club. And then I heard him. A kind of little – choking sound as the head of the club hit him. It was just a tiny little sound. The club – it caught him in the throat. And that was it.

200

Just like that. One single movement and it was all over. He died within minutes – in my arms, as Sylvie and I were running with him to the car.'

There was silence but for the birdsong. Guy shook his head. 'I fucked everything up. Everything.'

'Oh, Guy . . .' Annie moved to him, wrapping her arms around him. He let himself be held, giving in to the warmth of her comfort, her closeness.

Later, beneath the arms of the chestnut, they made love. Afterwards they lay there side by side while the shadows lengthened. And at last it was time to pack up, time to go.

As they moved back along the tree-shaded path towards the roadway Guy was aware that he felt a little easier, a little lighter. He had never before spoken voluntarily of Davie's death.

Emerging from the bridle path onto the quiet roadside, they turned to the right and made their way, hand in hand, towards the car. They were within fifty yards of it when Guy heard the sound of an automobile swiftly coming up behind them. He flicked a glance over his shoulder and saw the blue Ford van approaching. Riding the crown of the road the vehicle was moving at such a pace that Guy drew Annie nearer to the shrubbery at the side. Then, even as he was silently remarking on the van's dangerous speed it seemed to change course and come swerving across the road. Guy caught a brief glimpse of two men sitting in the cab as with a screeching of tyres the van came roaring towards them. Annie screamed. Guy cried, '*Look out!*' and letting fall the holdall, thrust an arm around Annie's shoulder and, dragging her with him, hurled himself into the shrubbery.

201

As they fell they heard the van roar past, so close that they could feel the current of air caused by its motion. For a second the two of them sprawled there, then with difficulty Guy pulled himself out of the bushes and brambles. The van was no longer in sight. Gasping from the shock and the sudden exertion Guy held out a scratched, grazed hand to Annie and helped her back onto the grass. 'Crazy bastards,' he said, 'they damn near killed us.' Annie's hands were touched with little spots of blood and there were fragments of leaves and twigs in her hair. She stood there for a second in shocked silence, then burst into tears. He wrapped his arms around her. Close to his foot the holdall lay crushed, the broken china bursting through the fabric. The rug lay ploughed into the earth. Guy held her while she wept. 'It's all right,' he said, holding her close. 'It's all right.'

After salvaging what they could from the holdall they moved to the car and, with Guy driving, set off. A few minutes later they entered a small village – Dunstead by name – and as they came to a pub Guy slowed the car and turned it onto the forecourt. 'What are you doing?' Annie said.

'I think we could do with a drink,' he said as he braked. 'And we can clean up as well.'

With obvious reluctance she nodded. 'Okay, but let's not stay long, all right?'

'Only for a minute or two.' He thought she still looked tense, shocked. He pressed her hand. 'Let's go have a beer. You'll feel better when you've relaxed for a while.'

The pub – The Four Sisters – had few customers and was gratifyingly quiet. While Annie made her way to the women's room Guy went to the bar and ordered beers. Then, leaving the barman filling the glasses he went to the men's room to clean himself up and to wash clean the

202

scratches caused by the brambles. They were not serious, but investigating a soreness in his right palm he found a thorn embedded deep in the flesh. He tried to pull it out but could not.

Returning to the bar he took out money to pay for the drinks. As he did so the barman said, 'You look a bit better now. You looked like you'd been in the wars.'

Guy nodded. 'Some idiot in a van almost hit us. We had to dive into the hedge to get out of his way or he'd have run us down.' He probed the thorn in his palm. The barman said, putting change on the bar, 'You need a nurse,' and looked over to a neat, grey-haired little woman who sat at a table nearby. 'Nora?' he called. 'Looks like there's a job for you.'

The elderly woman – who turned out to be a retired nurse – needed no second summons. She examined Guy's hand and then with brisk efficiency quickly acquired a needle, tweezers, antiseptic and cotton wool from the publican's wife. By the time Annie returned the woman was tending Guy's hand and they were chatting together like old friends.

'Annie – meet Nora,' he said. They smiled hellos to one another. Annie, he saw, had cleaned the scratches on her hands and combed her hair. He smiled at her. 'You look better now.' Her returning smile was faint. She stood beside the table watching as the woman, squinting through her spectacles, finished cleaning Guy's hand and began to probe the thorn with the needle. 'Sit down,' Guy urged Annie. 'This won't take long.' He gestured to her glass of beer which he had placed on the adjacent table. 'Drink your beer and relax for a minute.'

Annie sat down and picked up her glass while Guy told the woman of their encounter with the van. Without raising her glance she clicked her tongue in sympathy and disapproval. 'The way some people drive . . .'

'You're telling me.'

'Are you over here on holiday?' she asked. She lifted her head now, looking into his eyes.

'Just for a few more days.'

'Staying in London, I suppose. All the tourists do.'

'Yes.'

She bent her head again to his palm, worked for some moments in silence, and then, gripping the thorn with the tweezers, pulled it out. 'There!' She gave Guy's palm a final wipe with a piece of the cotton wool. 'You'll live.'

He thanked her, adding as he got to his feet, 'Now you must let me buy you a drink.'

She thanked him in turn, saying that she would have a gin and tonic. As Guy turned towards the bar Annie frowned at him, clearly anxious for them to be on their way again. In response he silently pleaded with her for a further minute's patience.

'Do you live here in Dunstead?' Guy asked the woman when he brought her drink.

She gestured with her hand. 'Yes, I live in the lane next to the pub.' She thanked him for the drink, drank from her glass and added, 'I used to live in London when I was young. I couldn't live there now, though. Which part of London are you staying in?'

'Bayswater.'

'Oh, I know Bayswater quite well. There are some rather grand hotels around there.'

He smiled. 'Oh, I don't think anyone could ever describe my hotel as grand.'

'Which one is that?'

'The St John. D'you know it?'

'No, I don't. It's comfortable, though, is it?'

204

'Yes. If you don't expect too much.'

'Well,' she laughed, 'that's all right, then.'

While Annie barely hid her impatience, Guy listened while the woman spoke of the two passions in her life – her painting and her cats. 'I paint flowers mostly,' she said. 'I'd like to paint people, but I'm afraid I'm not good enough. Children,' she added, sipping at her gin, 'that's what I'd really like to paint. Trouble is, they never keep still – and they always have their mouths open and I could never paint teeth.' She chuckled. 'Mind you, I try to paint my cats – after a fashion.'

'How many do you have?' Guy asked.

'Eight.'

'Eight!' He turned to Annie. 'Can you believe that?'

'Yes, I can believe it.' Annie pushed her beer – barely touched – away from her. 'Guy, can we go? Please?'

'She was so kind,' Guy said when they were in the car. 'I couldn't just get up and walk away.'

'I'm sorry,' Annie said. 'I didn't mean to be rude, but I just want to get home.'

Guy studied her as she sat at the wheel, tense, her lips compressed. 'It really upset you, didn't it?' he said. 'That business with the van. But it's over now. And we're okay. Don't let it get to you.'

She turned the key in the ignition, gave a nod. 'No, it's stupid, I know. I'll be all right soon.'

As they drew into Hammersmith Annie said, without looking at him:

'Guy – if you don't mind terribly I'll drop you near the station so you can get your train . . .'

' – Of course. Whatever you want.'

'Well, it's Monday tomorrow and I've got a lot of work

205

to do before then. Besides – I think I'd like to be on my own for a while.'

'I understand. No problem.'

In a side street near Ravenscourt Park Station she brought the car to a halt. Turning, she pressed his hand. 'I've got some things to do tomorrow evening, but phone me, will you? Then if you're free we can arrange something for Tuesday.'

'I will.'

'You promise?'

'I promise.'

'You're not pissed off with me, are you?'

'What?' He smiled. 'No, of course not.'

Cupping his face in her hands she kissed him on the mouth. 'Good. I'll talk to you tomorrow.'

Part Three

What of soul was left, I wonder,
When the kissing had to stop?

Robert Browning

17

In the morning he went into Hyde Park where he sat on a bench and tried to read. As he sat there a child's ball came rolling across the turf to fetch up at his foot. He picked it up and held it out to a small boy who came running in pursuit, the child's mother standing watching from some distance away. With a shy smile and words of thanks, the boy snatched the ball and dashed off again. Watching as he ran across the grass Guy thought at once of Davie, and Luke. And then, of course, of Sylvie.

Her deception was the bitterest of pills. And he still could not imagine how he had been so wrong. How could he not have seen what had been going on almost under his nose? But he had not; he had not dreamed that such a thing was happening. Yet in the year following Davie's death Sylvie had met someone else – and had embarked on an affair which she had managed to keep secret. And later, after her return to England and the discovery that she was pregnant she had let him believe that the child in her womb was his.

Learning of Sylvie's deception from Mrs Bennett had made it even harder to accept. He could see Mrs Bennett's face as she had told him; hear her voice. Had she taken some perverse pleasure in stripping him of those last vestiges of comfort to which he had clung? Had she enjoyed bringing him so low, watching him suddenly floundering?

Yet still, even with his intellectual acceptance of Mrs Bennett's words he found it all but impossible to believe in his heart that Sylvie could have done such a thing. He would never have believed such an act to be within her nature. But it had happened, and he had been blind. Blind to everything; blind to her secret love affair, and blind, so blind, to the needs that had driven her to it. He was not a little touched by the sour irony of it all; when at last he had been forced to acknowledge Sylvie's needs it had been too late; someone else had come upon the scene, bringing to her the comfort that he had not.

And who was it? That was the question that prodded at him now. And whoever the man was, did he know that Sylvie had borne his child, and that that child now lay in his grave in an English country churchyard?

Seeing again in his mind the little grave he was struck by the thought: why had it been left untended? And, again, there was the question of why Sylvie had not been buried with him. Instead she lay miles apart in another churchyard. Mrs Bennett said she had her reasons for it, reasons which she would not divulge – but what were they, and why would she not reveal them? He had a right to know. Sylvie had been his wife.

Leaving the park he walked around for a while till he came to a restaurant where he stopped to eat an indifferent lunch of pizza and salad. He got back to the hotel just before two o'clock. After picking up his key from the desk he started to move away, then stopped. The porter looked at him questioningly. 'Sir?'

'Can you tell me,' Guy said, 'if there's some place in London where they keep records of births and deaths?'

'Oh, yes,' the man answered at once, 'you want St Catherine's House. They keep all those records there.'

'Can anybody go in?'

'Yes, I'm sure they can. You know where it is?'

'No, I don't.'

210

'It's at the bottom of Kingsway – near Holborn tube station.'

St Catherine's House was a modest-looking building set at the busy intersection of Aldwych and Kingsway. Inside he made inquiries at the information desk and was directed to where the various records were housed.

He made his way to the right, to the Births section, where cabinets of metal shelves bore row upon row of large volumes. The place seemed hardly adequate to hold the number of people who were there seeking information, bending over the volumes on the sloping-topped reading tables and writing in notebooks or on scraps of paper. For a few moments he stood watching the activity, not a little astonished at the casual treatment meted out to the volumes by some of the researchers, seeing how they tossed them around with no apparent consideration as to their value. None of the officials seemed to mind, however, and anyway it was none of his business.

Pushing his way between the researchers, he found the volumes for the year 1982. Casting his eye along them he located the register for the period January to March. He drew out the one covering the letter H, carried it to a spot on a desk that had just become vacant and opened it up. Turning the pages he came to the section covering the letters HO. He ran his finger down the names: Hollowell, Hollyman, Hollywell, Hollywood, Holm.

And there was Holman.

There were fourteen Holman births registered. He ran his eye swiftly down the list of first names.

Luke was not one of them.

It couldn't be. He must have missed it. He read down the column again. No, there was no Luke Holman. Once more he read down the list of names. No. He checked the

211

date on the spine of the volume: January to March 1982. No mistake there.

While the other researchers milled about him he stood gazing down unseeingly at the cover of the closed volume, and wondering at the mystery. For some reason Luke's birth had not been registered.

'Ex*cuse* me . . .'

He came to with a slight start, and became aware of a thin-faced woman eyeing him impatiently as she stood beside him holding a volume in her hands.

'If you've finished there,' she said, 'I'd like to put this down.'

'Of course. I'm sorry . . .'

He picked up the volume, moved away and replaced it on the shelf. He felt at a loss. After a few moments he turned and headed for the section holding the registers of deaths.

A minute later he had before him the relevant volume covering deaths for the period of January to March 1982. Three, four times he ran his finger down the list of Holmans. Nineteen Holman deaths were registered for the period. Under *L* there was a Leslie Alfred, and beneath that a Leslie Frank. But there was no Luke.

Making inquiries of a young man at the information desk he was told that births and deaths had, by law, to be registered; therefore, the birth and death that Guy sought should be noted in the registers.

There was a bench over to one side and Guy sat down to think over the matter. Where to go from here? He had not the faintest idea. Was it possible that Luke's birth and death had been registered under his father's name? If so at present he had no hope of finding it.

'You look as if you've got a problem.'

212

He turned and saw sitting beside him the woman who had spoken to him earlier.

'Yes,' he said. 'I'm trying to find the entries for a birth and death that occurred in 1982 – but they don't seem to be registered.'

'They must be. They have to be, by law.' The woman, tall, angular, middle-aged, put down her exercise book and pencil, then took off her spectacles and began to polish them. 'You must be looking in the wrong place,' she added. 'I've done a lot of this – searching these records – and I always find what I want eventually. Are you sure you've got the right name?'

'Why, yes, I – ' He stopped. He had only looked under Holman. 'I've thought of something else,' he said, getting up from the bench. 'Thank you very much.'

'Not at all.'

Moving back to the birth registers he looked under the letter B for the first three months of 1982. He turned to the name Bennett. Perhaps for some reason Sylvie had registered Luke's birth under her maiden name. He found the first names beginning with L: Laurie, Lavinia, Lawrence, Lester, Lester, Lucy, Lucy, Ludovic. No Luke.

Without hope he moved to the deaths registers and looked under Bennett. No Luke.

A few minutes later, disappointed and bewildered, he was walking along the Strand. He had had the vague hope that by acquiring a copy of Luke's birth certificate he might find some clue as to the identity of the father. Instead there was not even a record of the baby's brief existence. He had gone there to find answers and had left with more questions than he had started with.

He was glad to get back to the hotel, and once in his room he threw off his jacket, kicked off his shoes and lay back on the bed. As he lay there he kept thinking back

213

over his search through the registers. Could he have made some mistake as to the year or the month? No, he was sure he had not. What, then, was the explanation? It was as if Luke had never existed.

There was, he thought, one person who might know the truth. After a moment's hesitation he lifted the telephone receiver and dialled Mrs Bennett's number in Forham Green.

The housekeeper answered; he recognized her voice at once. Mrs Bennett, she said, was away on holiday and was not expected back till Thursday. When he asked where she was staying the housekeeper told him that she was not at liberty to say. He had to be content with that. He thanked her and put down the receiver. Maybe, he thought, he should try to contact Marianne. But no, he felt sure she wouldn't be able to tell him anything. He would wait for Mrs Bennett's return.

That evening when Guy went for his fourth anti-rabies shot Dr Powell showed continuing satisfaction with his state of health. As he prepared the syringe he asked Guy whether he had come to any decision regarding his return to America.

'Not yet,' Guy said. 'I'll probably go back in a week or so.'

Powell smiled. 'Perhaps you're getting attached to the place. Perhaps you'll end up staying for good.'

'Oh, no, I shall go back,' Guy said. He had to see Sylvie's mother, however, before he could leave, for he knew he would never come back.

'You've got two weeks before your fifth jab is due,' Powell said. 'So let me know.'

'I will.'

* * *

214

'I understand,' said Mrs Hughes, drawing on her cigarette, 'that it didn't work.'

'No,' Paxton said, 'but it was a close thing.'

'Was he alone?'

'No, he was with the girl.'

'So they might both have been killed.'

'True.' Paxton was silent for a moment, then he said, 'Listen, Mary, you know damn well there's no room for niceties in this business.'

'You're telling me.'

'The man is dangerous. He's like some goddamn time bomb set to go off at a particular time.'

'And he has to be defused, I know. So I guess they'll just keep trying till they get it right, yes?'

'*They?*'

'All right, then – *we.*'

'You don't think anybody enjoys this, do you?'

'No, of course not. I just wish it wasn't necessary.'

'So do I.'

'I came into this job to protect life, not to destroy it.' She ground out her cigarette in the ashtray.

'We all did,' Paxton said. 'But sometimes we have to make choices.'

She said nothing.

'We're doing a job of work,' he added. 'It's the only way to look at it. Some people work computers, some paint pictures, some wait on tables. We do what we have to do.'

That evening Guy dialled Annie's number but the ringing went unanswered. Later, after a visit to a nearby restaurant he tried again. Still no answer. Then, ten minutes after he had put down the receiver, she called. She was phoning from Bradford, she said.

215

'What are you doing back in Bradford? Is it your dad?'

'I'm afraid so. My mother called me late last night to say that he'd had something of a set-back, so I thought I'd better come up and see him. I'm sorry I didn't let you know before.'

'That's okay. How is he now?'

'Well – his blood pressure suddenly dropped quite dramatically yesterday – which is not so good in somebody his age. But I think he's going to be all right. He's a tough old man.' She sighed. 'Of course, there's nothing I can do here but he's so pleased to see me. And it helps my mother to have me around at such a time.'

'I'm sure it does. D'you know when you'll be back?'

'No, but I don't think it'll be long. I'll phone you.'

'You won't forget?'

He could hear the smile in her voice: 'No, I won't forget.'

For lunch the following day Guy bought sandwiches at a delicatessen and took them in the park. He ate mechanically, finishing them almost without being aware of it. He continued to sit there while the people came and went on the path before him. Before leaving the hotel he had debated whether to call the Forham Green number and try to persuade the housekeeper to tell him where he could contact Mrs Bennett, but in the end he had decided against it. He would wait a couple more days till she got back, then go and see her. And this time he would insist on answers.

When he left the park – partly from restlessness and partly to escape the irritating sound of the transistor radio which a young man had set down on the seat between them – he wandered along the teeming pavement of Oxford Street. And all the while the questions regarding

216

Luke's birth and death nagged at him. By the time he reached Oxford Circus he had convinced himself that somehow he had made a mistake or missed the relevant entry when consulting the registers at St Catherine's House. Luke's birth and death had to be noted there.

He reached St Catherine's House not long before it was due to close. He went at once to the Births section – it didn't seem quite as crowded as last time – took down the volume covering the letter H for the first quarter of 1982 and found the short section for Holman. To his disappointment he saw at once that it was the same page he had studied before; he had made no mistake. And Luke's birth registration was not there. He then checked the death register for the period, and got the same result.

Setting the volume back on the shelf he went to the information desk and got in line behind the five or six other people waiting there. When his turn came he told the female assistant of his unsuccessful searches.

'Are you certain you've got the right year and the right quarter?' She was in her forties, all matching accessories and cool efficiency.

'Yes, quite certain.'

'And there's no doubt about the spelling of the surname?'

'No doubt at all.'

'What's the month?' she asked.

'March.'

'Ah.' A slow nod. 'The *end* of March?'

'Yes. He was born on the 20th.'

'In that case,' she said, 'the entry might be in the following quarter. You're allowed sixty days to register a birth, so sometimes if a birth isn't registered at once and it occurs near the end of a quarter it will be in the register for the *following* quarter. Try April to June.' Quickly she

217

added, 'But you haven't got long; we'll be closing in a few minutes.' She smiled a mechanical smile at him, her attention already moving on to the woman who stood next in line.

With a feeling of relief Guy moved back to the Births registers. The number of researchers was thinning out. Pulling down the register covering H for April through June 1982, he flicked through the pages till he came to Holman. Swiftly his eyes moved down the entries. No Luke.

This was ridiculous. He couldn't believe it. It had to be there. He went down the list of first names again. Beth, Charles, Charles, Charlotte, Clive, Dawn, Diana, Diana, George, Helen, James, John, John, Jonathan, Petra, Samantha, Thomas, Tracie, Tracy, Wayne. But no Luke. The entry should have been there between Jonathan and Petra, but it was not. His eyes scanned the rest of the page for any penned note of an omission. There was none.

Consulting the Death register for the same quarter he got a similar result. Alice, Diana, Edward, Edward, Elizabeth, Florence, Frederick, George, Mary, Peter, Rachel, Rose, Stephen, Thomas, Violet, Walter, Walter. No Luke.

'Excuse me, sir, we're closing now.' The voice came from one of the uniformed assistants. Guy vaguely recalled having heard a bell ring. The other researchers were collecting up their bags, notebooks and pencils. He slipped the heavy register into its place on the shelf and joined the others moving out onto the street.

From a public call box he dialled Annie's number and, as he had anticipated, heard the ringing go unanswered. She was still not back from Bradford. Aimlessly, he bought an evening newspaper then went to a pub where

218

he sat reading and smoking over a couple of glasses of beer. Afterwards he ate a pizza then set off to walk back to the hotel.

When he approached the desk on his arrival the porter smiled at him and, with a flourish, held out his key. As Guy took it the man said:

'A lady phoned after you went out this morning, sir, and again this evening just after seven.'

A lady? Annie, calling from Bradford, Guy thought. 'Did she leave a name?' he asked. 'Or any message?'

'No, sir. But she seemed very anxious to speak to you. She said she'll phone you again first thing in the morning.'

Guy thanked him, said goodnight and went up to his room. He had no doubt that the calls had come from Annie. He wondered what the urgency was.

18

At eight-thirty the following morning Guy was just on the point of getting out of bed when the telephone rang. It would be Annie. He stretched out an arm, picked up the receiver. 'Hello?'

'Mr Holman?' A woman's voice.

'Yes. Who is this?'

'My name is Mrs Briars – though that might not mean anything to you. I think I only told you my first name – Nora. We met in a pub – The Four Sisters, in Dunstead, a village near Pangbourne in Berkshire. You'd just had an accident and I took a thorn out of your palm. Do you remember?'

He sat up in the bed. 'Of course – you're the lady who keeps cats and paints flowers.'

'That's right.' She gave a little laugh, but the sound was more nerves than amusement. Guy said, sounding more formal than he had intended:

'Well – what can I do for you . . .?'

A little forcefully she said, 'I need to see you.'

'Oh . . .? What about?'

'I can't tell you on the phone. Please – can we meet?'

'Well . . . What is it about?'

'Please, Mr Holman, don't ask me that now. I'll tell you everything when I see you. At the moment I can just tell you that I know something that – that is of the greatest importance to you. I have to see you. It's vital.'

'What – what's it about?' he said. Her urgency smacked of eccentricity.

220

'I'm coming over as a complete crackpot, I know I am,' she said. 'But if you'll only see me for five or ten minutes you'll realize I'm not.' She paused. 'Please?'

What could she tell him? She had taken a thorn out of his hand, that was all. He had told her almost nothing about himself. After a moment's hesitation he said, 'Look, I'm so busy, Mrs Briars, but if you could just tell me what it is . . .'

'Oh, listen,' she said. 'Just listen to me for a minute, will you?'

He smiled. 'Of course. I'm listening.'

'Well . . .' She paused as if marshalling her thoughts, then she said, 'When I took the thorn out of your palm I saw something there . . .'

'What d'you mean?'

'Well – for one thing I saw certain things in your past . . .'

'In my . . . Are you telling me you *read palms*? Is that what this is about? While you were taking out the thorn you were reading my palm, is that it?' He wanted to laugh.

There was a brief pause, then she said, 'When I looked into your palm I saw that you had lost two people whom you loved very much . . .'

For a moment her words took away his breath. 'Go on,' he said warily.

'I could also have told you,' she said, 'that one of them was your child – your son . . .' A moment of silence. 'I'm right – yes?'

'But – how can you know that?' he said hoarsely.

'And his death,' she went on, ' – it had something to do with the sea. Did it have some connection with the sea?'

Into Guy's brain came the sound of the waves on the beach – the only sound as he had bent over Davie's

221

twitching body. 'What are you doing?' he said. 'What is all this about?'

Now when she spoke she sounded near to tears. 'I'm just telling you that to show you that I *know*,' she said.

'You *know*? *What* do you know? Tell me.'

'In your hand. When I looked at your hand I could see so much. I could see all that – and more. Much more.'

Guy was silent for a moment, then: 'Go on, please.'

'And I'm talking about your future now. Not your past.'

Pause. 'Go on.'

'I saw something of your future. Right at the last. Just a glimpse . . .'

'Yes?'

'I – you still think I'm mad, don't you?'

'Mrs Briars, I don't know what I think. Please – go on.'

'It's just *that*. In your palm I saw a little of your future. I didn't get a chance to see more. There wasn't time. I need to see more to be able to tell you more, but the little I did see gave clear enough indication.'

'Indication of what?'

'I know how crazy it sounds, but – I could see that you are in great peril.'

'Peril . . .'

'I know what I'm saying, Mr Holman. Believe me – I could see it, so clearly. Could we meet? Please?'

'Well . . .' He was intrigued. He had never believed in clairvoyance – yet she had known about Davie's death . . .

Her voice came into his thoughts:

'Only for a few minutes, that's all. But I must see you – for your sake. I've debated and debated whether to get in touch with you. In the end I decided I had to – whatever you thought of me.'

222

He said nothing. Part of him urged him to say yes; another part told him that he should wish the woman goodbye and forget the whole thing . . .

'Are you there, Mr Holman?'

'Yes, I'm here. Tell me – why didn't you say something at the time?'

' – Well, as I said, there really wasn't time. And it wasn't the right place, if you know what I mean. I didn't know what to do. Anyway, I got from you the name of your hotel. So at least that gave me the chance to think about it and decide what to do.' A little silence, then she said, 'Well?'

'All right,' he said. 'When – and where?'

Relief sounded in her voice. 'Well – as soon as possible.'

'Are you calling from London?'

'No, from Dunstead. But I've got to come up to London sometime over the next couple of days. Could we meet tomorrow? Say, late morning?'

'All right. Whereabouts?'

'Well – d'you know some place where we could meet for coffee? Some place not too far from your hotel?'

'What about the coffee shop in Selfridge's? Would that be okay?'

'Oh, yes. I know Selfridge's all right. Shall we say eleven?'

'Eleven is fine.'

'Right, I'll see you then. And Mr Holman – ?'

'Yes?'

'You will be there, won't you? You won't forget?'

'I'll be there,' he said. 'I won't forget.'

Fifteen minutes after putting the receiver down the telephone rang again. It was Annie.

'Are you in London?' he asked.

'No, I'm still in Bradford. Did I get you out of bed?'

'Hell, no,' he said, 'you're way behind. I've already had one call this morning.'

'Oh, popular man.'

'I'll say. As a matter of fact I thought at first it was from you, but it was from that woman we met in Berkshire last Sunday.'

'Who?'

'After our run-in with that van. We met her in that little pub in Dunstead – The Four Sisters. You remember – she took the thorn out of my hand.'

'Oh, yes! Good God, what did she want?'

'You're not going to believe this, but she said she read something in my palm.' He laughed, and felt slightly disloyal for it. 'My future,' he added.

'Are you serious?' Annie's tone was incredulous. 'You're not really serious, are you?'

'Really. She says she saw something in my palm. Beware the one-eyed man with the limp – something like that.'

'A one-eyed man? With a limp?'

'I'm kidding. But she said she could see some kind of danger ahead for me. And like all good fortune-tellers she feels it incumbent upon her to give me a warning.'

'Are you making this up, Guy?'

'No, truly. There's danger ahead for me – or peril, in her words. She's going to tell me what it is.'

'How?'

'I've arranged to meet her tomorrow at eleven.'

'Oh, come on.'

'I know it's dumb, but I said I would, so I must.'

'How did she know where to get in touch with you? Oh, yes, you mentioned the name of your hotel, didn't you?'

224

'Yes, I think I did.'

'Where are you going to meet her? At her home? She lives close to the pub, didn't she say?'

'Did she? Anyway, she's coming into town. I'm meeting her in Selfridge's.'

'I don't believe this,' Annie chuckled. 'But do *you* believe it? You do, don't you? You must do.'

'Well, I don't know that I actually *believe* it. But I'm curious.' He paused. When he spoke again his jocular tone was gone. 'You know,' he said, 'she told me something about Davie. Something she had no way of knowing.'

'Really?'

'Yes. Who knows, maybe she does know what she's talking about. There might be something in it. I mean, just because it's outside my experience doesn't mean it doesn't exist. There are more things in heaven and earth, Horatio, than are dreamt of in your philosophy.'

'Yes, I'm sure. So you're really going.'

'Oh, yes.'

'Well – ' he could hear the smile in her voice, 'if you've got nothing better to do. Time must lie very heavy on your hands.'

He smiled. 'Is that my fault?'

'Oh, I see, it's *my* fault. I'm forcing you to spend your time indulging eccentric old women.'

Guy laughed. 'When are you coming back?'

'Tomorrow.'

'Good. Is your dad better?'

'Yes, much better, thanks. Poor old thing – quite knocked him sideways. Still, he seems to be going on all right now.'

'That's good. So – shall I see you tomorrow evening?'

'If you want to.'

225

'You know I do.'

'Good. Shall I expect you about seven – seven-thirty?'

'I'll be there.'

Since making the phone call to the young American, Guy Holman, Mrs Briars had felt a great sense of relief. As she had told him, she had debated whether or not to phone, but she had had no choice. Anyway, it was done now, and tomorrow they would meet. She would have to make an early start to get to Selfridge's on time. She had lied when she said she had to go to London. In fact it had been years since she had been there and she had no wish ever to go there again. Like most cities, it was not geared for someone of seventy-four. But she had wanted to make the meeting place convenient for him.

She thought about the coming meeting. She had no idea how much more she would be able to read in his hand. At first when she had looked into his palm she had seen only his past; only at the very last had she glimpsed his future. But by then it was too late; the young woman had arrived, the thorn had been removed and there had been no more time. She had seen enough, though, to know that there was something there. All she needed now was the opportunity to look deeper.

Sitting at the table she lifted the lid from the teapot, stirred the tea and poured it. As she sipped at it Carl and Jenny, the two tortoiseshells, came and looked up at her. 'You'll have to wait a minute,' she told them. 'It's too hot. Your turn will come.' From the kitchen came the familiar *tak* of the cat-flap falling back. The sound was repeated three times, followed by the sight of the cats moving silently into the room and gathering about her, sitting, waiting. They knew about time. Carl, Jenny, Tommy, Timmy, Lulu and Miss Muffet. She turned and

226

saw that the remaining two, Patty and Miss Puss, were sitting on the sofa. They could all be relied upon to be around at tea-time. Taking a digestive from the tin, she dipped it into the tea and took a bite.

At her feet Carl moved closer, looked up and made two feints at springing up, warning her to move her hands so as not impede him. She did so and he leapt softly onto her knee and settled in her lap. She drank over his purring head. If she had to have a favourite, then she supposed it would be Carl. Neutered as a kitten, and now placid and a little overweight, his whole existence was one long, shameless search for indulgence. He of them all could be relied upon to show never-ending affection and dependence. And it was nice to get *some* reward, some acknowledgement of one's presence and efforts. Not that the others didn't also show affection, but with them it was more clearly on their terms.

She ate most of the rest of the biscuit then held a tiny piece in her palm and put it close to Carl's mouth. He took it gently and then licked her palm clean; the feel of his tiny, rough tongue on her skin was the most delicious sensation.

She thought again of the American's palm. The lines on it had been unlike any that she had seen in any other hand. There had been signs in the life line that in other hands would have indicated a termination of life, but with him it had clearly not been so, for he had survived beyond those signalled times. There were also the signs she had seen regarding his future – a future that was very close; she might have been wrong about that but she did not think so. Anyway, they would meet tomorrow.

The thought suddenly occurred to her that he might not turn up, and she recalled that she had meant to give him her telephone number in case something happened to

227

prevent him keeping the appointment, but had forgotten. She looked over at the telephone. Perhaps she should call him now – or would he think she was just a terrible nuisance . . .? After a moment's deliberation she gently urged Carl off her lap, got up and moved to the phone.

She had just got to the telephone when it rang. She wondered who it could be; her son Alan had already phoned from Reading that day. As she reached out the ringing tone changed and took on an odd broken sound, as if there was some loose connection in the bell mechanism. She hesitated for a moment then picked up the receiver.

'Hello?'

'British Telecom here,' a man announced. 'We think you've got a fault on your line.'

'It was all right earlier on,' she said.

'Anyway, we'll put it right. Will you hang up, please?'

She did so, waited for a while and then turned to the table where she poured tea and milk into three saucers which she then placed on the carpet. At once the cats converged on them. Sitting down she continued drinking her own tea while they lapped at theirs.

The telephone rang again as she was finishing her second cup.

'Hello?'

'Hello,' the man said. 'We've traced the fault to your set. We'll have to send somebody round.'

'Oh – when? I have to go out first thing in the morning.'

'Don't worry – we'll send one of our engineers round now. Will you be in for the next hour?'

'Yes, I shall be here.'

'Good. We'll have somebody there within the hour.'

After she had replaced the receiver she lifted it again and found that the line was dead. She would have to wait till the engineer had been before she could ring the young American.

The thought suddenly came to her that when she eventually got to look more closely at his palm she might see nothing there. Perhaps she had been mistaken. Perhaps in those few moments she had allowed herself to believe what was not so. No; she could not accept that. She had seen signs of danger there, great danger – and not waiting for him here but in another country, and very soon. It was her duty to tell him, to warn him – though whether his fate could be changed was another question. If it was written in his hand then that was his fate; it told of what *would* be, not what *might* be. But there again, the lines in his hand were unlike any she had ever seen.

Less than half an hour later, as she was washing up the tea things, there came a ring at the door bell. She switched off her portable radio and went to the door. A smiling man in British Telecom uniform stood on the step. Behind him, at the gate, stood a van bearing the British Telecom logo.

'Mrs Briars?'

'Yes. Come in, please.'

She stepped aside and he entered the narrow hallway. He was a short man in his late thirties, thick-set and prematurely balding. Entering the sitting room he spotted the telephone and moved towards it. From his bag he extracted a screwdriver and other tools then glanced around and took in the cats who lazed on the sofa and the armchairs. 'Ah, a cat-lover,' he observed with a smile. 'How many have you got?'

'Eight.'

'Eight! Good Lord! Must cost you a fortune in Whiskas.'

She smiled. 'We manage.'

229

He gave his attention to the instrument. 'Yes,' he said, 'our repair time has improved enormously of late. And so it should, of course. We can't live without the telephone today, can we? It's so much a part of our lives – and a necessity for someone living alone, I should think.' He smiled over at Carl as he stretched on the sofa. 'Still, it doesn't look as if you're really alone, does it?'

She smiled. 'Oh, no, I'm not short of company.'

She hovered there for a moment then asked if he would like a cup of tea. 'It's no trouble,' she added.

'Well, that's very kind of you. Thank you. A nice cup of tea wouldn't come amiss at all.'

'Good. Milk and sugar?'

'Milk and one spoonful. Thank you.'

As she finished making the tea in the kitchen she heard his voice as he spoke into the phone: 'Will you call me back on this number, please?' Moments later the phone rang, he answered it and declared it to be in working order once again.

As she carried a tray into the sitting room and set it on the table he tapped the telephone and said, 'All okay now. You shouldn't have any more trouble with it.' She thanked him and began to pour the tea. He put his tools away then sat down and helped himself to sugar. As they drank he spoke about the weather and then of his wife and two daughters. 'We've got a cat too,' he said. 'A little black and white one. Not much more than a kitten, really. Pepé the girls call him. They love him.' He seemed a warm, kindly man, Mrs Briars thought, and when he got up and bent over Carl on the sofa she warmed to him even more.

'Now here's a prize one,' he said. 'What beautiful markings.'

'Yes, he *is* beautiful, isn't he?'

His hands moved towards the cat, then hesitated. 'May I pick him up?'

'Oh, do. He won't object.'

The man gathered Carl up in his arms. 'And wouldn't dream of scratching me, would you?' he murmured, bending his face close to the cat's. 'No, of course not.' He stood holding the cat, gently stroking him. Carl began to purr. 'He likes it,' the man said.

'Oh, yes, he likes it all right,' Mrs Briars said. 'He can take any amount of that.'

The man bent his head lower, murmuring, whispering into the cat's ear. Carl's ear flicked once or twice then he lay still, eyes half closed in an expression of bliss. 'What are you telling him,' chuckled Mrs Briars.

'Just what a beautiful creature he is.' The man spoke softly to the cat: 'And you *are* beautiful, aren't you?'

Moving back to the sofa he gently set the cat down. At once Carl curled up into a ball and closed his eyes again. The man moved then to each of the cats in turn, stroking them, murmuring to them little soft sounds which Mrs Briars could not catch. 'Oh, you're a cat-lover, too,' she said.

'They're such lovely creatures.'

His tea finished at last, Mrs Briars offered him more, but he politely refused it.

'It's very kind of you,' he said, 'but I must get on. I've got another call to make, so I mustn't leave it too late.'

He took up his bag, glanced briefly around to make sure that he had forgotten nothing, then touched the fingers of his right hand to his forelock in a little salute. 'Well, thank you again for the tea, Mrs Briars.' He nodded towards the telephone. 'You shouldn't have any more trouble, but if you do just give us a call and we'll put it right.'

'Thank you very much.' She followed him to the front door and waved him goodbye as he went through the gate. Such a nice man. Returning to the sitting room she picked up the tray of tea things and took it out to the kitchen. She would wash up in a minute; first of all she would telephone the young American.

As she entered the sitting room one of the cats sitting near the door reached out a hooked paw and raked her calf. She gave a little cry. 'Oh, Miss Puss! Why did you do that, you naughty girl.' Looking down at her leg she saw that it was bleeding. 'Oh, dear . . .' She moved to the sideboard, opened the right-hand door and took out a little tin containing gauze and lint and other first-aid items. 'Jump down, Tommy dear,' she said to the cat that sat in her chair, and with her free hand gently urged him down onto the carpet. To her shock and horror he responded by stretching up, arching his back and spitting at her. It was a ferocious sound, and quite terrifying, the cat's lips drawn back in a horrific semblance of a smile while a loud hissing issued from his gaping jaws.

In her surprise Mrs Briars dropped the tin and stepped back from the chair. 'What's come over you?' she said. 'I've never seen you like this before.'

More hissing, spitting sounds were coming at her, and turning she saw the tortoiseshell Jenny and the black and white Lulu standing on the table. They stood side by side, backs arched, all their spitting fury directed at her.

Suddenly there came a blood-chilling scream from behind her, and she whirled about just as Carl launched himself at her from the sofa-arm. He landed heavily on her upper breast, needle-sharp claws digging into her flesh and raking at her face. She reeled back, crying out, shrieking in pain and fear as the cat clung on, tearing at her in a spitting paroxysm of hate. As she fell, partly on

232

the carpet, partly on the tiled fire surround, the other cats began to leap upon her. For long, long minutes she fought, rending the air with screams while she tried to fight them off and get up. But the power was theirs, and they covered her writhing, squirming body like a single animal, an animal with a patterned coat of different colours. Splashes of blood flecked the carpet, the fireplace, the splashes growing larger. Her screams eventually became moans. At last she lay silent and still.

19

Guy was in Selfridge's coffee shop by ten-fifty the next morning. The place was fairly crowded; nevertheless he managed to find a table from which he could watch the door. Mrs Briars should be arriving any minute.

He realized that for all his flip comments to Annie he was anxious to see the woman. He had not the slightest idea what she had to tell him, but he could not get out of his mind the fact that she had known about Davie.

Amid the chink of china and the chatter of the other customers he drank coffee, ate a Danish pastry and kept his eyes on the entrance. And as he sat there he found his thoughts returning inevitably to the preoccupation that lay at the back of his mind, once again dragging it out and poring over it. Luke . . . There were so many unanswered questions about him – and questions which, he was sure, Mrs Bennett could answer if she chose. She would, he realized, be back at The Willows by now. He could talk to her again; demand the answers to his questions . . .

When eleven-thirty came without a sign of Mrs Briars he left the café and from a public telephone dialled the hotel to inquire whether she had called with any message. No, he was told, no one had phoned. He could not understand it; she had seemed so anxious for them to meet. Either something had happened to prevent her getting there or the whole thing had been some kind of hoax. No, he thought, not the latter . . . Returning to the café he stood in the entrance and scanned the tables. She had not arrived in his absence. He turned away. He would probably hear from her later . . .

Emerging onto the pavement he came to a brief stop while the pedestrians streamed by him. And now, he decided, he would see Mrs Bennett. Swiftly dismissing the idea of telephoning to arrange a meeting – she would refuse to talk to him, he was certain – he turned and started off for Paddington Station.

He reached Forham Green just after three o'clock and made his way at once to The Willows. His ring at the bell was answered by the cleaning woman and he saw wariness come into her face as she recognized him.

He smiled at her. 'Is Mrs Bennett at home?'

'No, I'm afraid she's not.'

'Can you tell me what time she'll be back . . .?'

'She won't be – not yet.' She was giving nothing away.

'Oh – I understood she was returning yesterday.'

'Yes, but – she changed her plans. She won't be back yet.'

He paused. 'Can you tell me where I can get in touch with her?'

' – No, I'm sorry . . .' She moved the door an inch, narrowing the gap.

'It's very important that I see her.'

' – I'm sorry but I've got instructions not to tell anybody . . .'

Yes, Guy thought, instructions meant specifically with himself in mind. He sighed, acknowledging defeat. 'Well – thanks anyway.'

When he got to the centre of the village he stopped at a pub to eat a couple of sausages and a chicken sandwich with a glass of lager; he had had nothing since the coffee and pastry at Selfridge's that morning. As he sat there he

235

wondered at Mrs Bennett's instructions to her cleaning woman not to divulge her whereabouts. Obviously she was anxious to avoid him – and she probably thought she wouldn't need to avoid him for long, for he would soon be going back to America.

Had she gone away with that purpose in mind – simply to keep out of his way? If so, where had she gone?

Then an answer came to him. Marianne. Of course – she had probably gone to stay with Marianne.

Marianne and her family lived in a detached red-brick Victorian house in a tree-lined street on the outskirts of Bath. By taxi from the railway station it took less than twenty minutes to get there. Asking the taxi driver to wait while he checked whether anyone was in, he opened the gate, went to the front door and rang the bell. There was no answer. He rang again, waited another half-minute then turned away. As he moved to the cab he noticed three figures moving towards him along the pavement – a girl in her early teens and two young boys. He recognized the shorter of the two boys. As they drew nearer he heard the girl say, 'You'll be all right now, then?' 'Yes, of course,' the shorter boy replied. The girl and the other boy turned and started across the street, the boys calling out to one another: 'See you, Alastair.' 'Yes, see you, John.' Standing beside the taxi, Guy waited until the smaller boy drew near the gate and then spoke.

'Hello, John.'

The boy came to a halt, looked curiously up at him through the round lenses of his spectacles, then, recognition dawning, gave a nod. 'Oh, hello.'

Guy moved towards him. 'How are you?'

'Very well, thank you.' The boy gave a shy smile and nodded. He was wearing shirt, sweater, jeans and sneakers.

236

'Do you remember me?' Guy asked.

'Yes.'

'I came to call on your grandmother a little while ago. In Forham Green.'

'I know. I remember. Cressie and I were there.' The boy blinked at him, shifted his weight from one foot to the other and brushed back a heavy lock of dark hair from his forehead. As Guy looked at him he became aware that there was something a little odd about the boy's eyes. And then it suddenly came to him that the boy was blind in his right eye; his right eye was false.

'I've just come from Forham Green now,' Guy said. 'I wanted to see your grandmother.'

'She's away.'

'Yes, so I was told. I thought she might be here.'

'No. She went up to Scotland.'

'Ah.' Guy nodded. 'I thought she was getting back yesterday.'

'She was, but now she's not coming back till next week.'

'D'you know when?'

'Next Wednesday, she said. She sent me a postcard.' This last with a little expression of pleasure. 'She went with her friend Mr Rossi.'

'Ah, yes.' Mr Rossi. Mrs Bennett's Italian neighbour; with a similar interest in wire-haired terriers.

'They went to Edinburgh.'

Mrs Bennett was getting about a bit. Guy pointed a thumb towards the house. 'I rang the bell but there was nobody in.'

'No, they've gone to Cressie's school. She's playing a tennis match. They should be back soon. I've been to have tea with Alastair, my friend.'

Guy smiled. 'You didn't want to watch the tennis match?'

237

'Not really. I'm not really interested. I can't play, you see. I'd like to, but I'd never be any good.'

'Perhaps you just need to practise.'

'No, it's not that. You see, I can't see the depth of things. I can't see three dimensions, and to play well you need to be able to see three dimensions.'

Three dimensions. The words had come off the boy's tongue with the facility of usage. Guy nodded dumbly, silenced by his own stupidity.

After a moment Guy said, 'How did it happen – your eye . . .?'

'With a stick. Oh, years ago. We were playing – one of my friends and me. It wasn't Clive's fault really. It hurt a lot at the time, but I can't remember that much about it now.' He grinned suddenly, showing very white, even teeth. 'Mummy was more upset about it than I was.' He gave a little laugh.

A little silence fell. The boy put his hand in his pocket and drew out a latchkey on a piece of string. He held it out on his palm. 'My key,' he said with the faintest note of pride. 'I can let myself in. I've got my own key.'

'So you have.' Guy smiled at him. 'How old are you, John?' he asked.

'I was seven last month. April the 8th.'

Not much younger than Luke would be, Guy thought. The boy said, a slightly worried look on his face: 'I've got to go straight in.'

The precautions of the time. 'Oh, yes,' Guy said, 'of course you must.'

'Well . . .' the boy turned, 'cheerio, then.'

'Cheerio.'

Guy watched as he ran up the path to the house, fumbled with his key at the lock and opened the door. In the doorway the boy turned and waved. 'See you.'

238

Guy waved back. 'See you.'

He watched the door close, then, moving to the cab he paid off the driver and watched as the vehicle took off down the street. As it disappeared from view he settled himself to wait for Marianne's return.

Almost fifteen minutes went by and then at last Marianne's white Renault approached along the street, pulled into the drive and stopped in front of the closed garage. Marianne got out followed by three children – Cressida, carrying a tennis racquet, and an older boy of about eleven and a younger girl of five or six.

Frowning slightly at Guy, Marianne moved to the front door and opened it. 'You go inside now, you children. I'll be there in a minute.' At her words the children ceased their curious appraisal of him and went indoors. Marianne moved back to Guy where he stood just inside the drive's entrance.

'Well, I must say I'm surprised to see you here, Guy. I thought you'd have been back in New York by now.'

He shook his head. 'I'm not going for a few days yet. I came over thinking maybe your mother was here.'

'She's up in Scotland.'

'Yes, I know that now. John told me.'

'John? Is he back?'

'Yes, a couple of minutes ago. We had quite a little chat.'

'Oh? What did you two have to talk about?'

'Oh, nothing of any importance.' A little silence fell. He waited for her to invite him inside but she did not. As he stood there he thought he could see tension in her body and her face, and he was reminded suddenly of Sylvie as she had stood beside Luke's grave anxious to be gone.

'Look,' Marianne said, 'I'd ask you in but I'm afraid I

239

can't just now. I've got to feed the children and then go out. I'm very sorry . . .'

'That's okay.'

She half turned, winding up for goodbye. Guy said:

'I'd like to ask you something, though . . .'

'Oh?' There was an applied note of surprise in her voice.

'I went to St Catherine's House,' he said, 'and I – '

She broke in: 'Where? You went where?'

'St Catherine's House, in London – where they keep all records of births, marriages and deaths.'

'Yes . . .?'

'Neither Luke's birth nor death is registered there.'

She shook her head, flustered. 'But – they must be.'

'They're not. I checked and re-checked.'

She hitched her shoulders, sighed. 'Well – I don't know.'

'I don't know either. That's why I wanted to see your mother. I thought maybe she could enlighten me.'

She did not answer.

'I guess you can't tell me anything,' he said.

'No, I can't. I'm sorry. Oh, it's got to be there somewhere.'

'It's not. I checked very carefully. They told me he has to be registered by law.'

'Well, yes . . .' She shook her head again. 'I don't understand. I don't know why it should be.'

'It's beyond me,' Guy said. 'First of all I find that Sylvie wasn't buried with Luke but in a different grave – a different churchyard. And now I find that his birth and death haven't been registered.'

'Guy,' Marianne said, 'it's got to be there somewhere in the records. It must be. You obviously weren't looking in the right place.' She paused. 'Honestly, look, don't you

240

think perhaps you're getting a bit – obsessive about all this? Leave it, Guy. Forget it. You'll drive yourself crazy if you keep on like this.'

'If I could get a few answers to some simple questions maybe I *could* forget it.'

'Look,' she said, 'I have to go inside . . .' She turned away. How different she was from their last meeting; now she seemed so on edge, so evasive. 'I can't help you. I'm sorry.'

'Marianne – '

But she kept on going, moving towards the house. At the front door she turned back to him. 'Guy, I'm sorry. I wish I could help you but I can't. I don't know anything. Believe me.'

Next moment she was gone. He stood there watching as the front door closed behind her.

When Guy got to the railway station he called Annie's number. She answered almost at once.

'Ah, good, you're back,' he said with relief.

'I've been back for ages,' she replied. 'Where are you?'

'I'm in Bath.'

'Bath! What are you doing there?'

'Oh – well, I'll tell you later. How's your dad? Is he okay?'

'Yes, he's getting on fine now. He hopes to be discharged in a few days.'

'That's good.'

'What are you doing now?'

'Coming back to London.'

'Shall I see you?'

'That's what I'm hoping.'

'Good. You haven't had dinner, have you?'

'No.'

'Then don't – if you can hold on. We'll go out and eat when you get here. We'll find a table somewhere. And I'm paying. Just get here as soon as you can.'

It was after nine by the time Guy arrived at Annie's flat. In her car they left at once in search of somewhere to eat. Eventually, after some driving around, they found a table at a small Italian restaurant. Its rather too-bright lighting did little for its ambience, but it would do.

As they waited for the menus Annie said:

'Tell me – how did it go this morning?'

'How did what go?'

'My God, it must have been a really impressive meeting. Your date with the old girl, the clairvoyant, remember?'

'Oh, yes.'

'Oh, yes! You were going to meet her at Selfridge's, and she was going to reveal all.'

'Yeh, well, she didn't show up.'

'After all that, and being so insistent?'

'I waited quite a while but there was no sign of her.'

'You're sure you got the right time and the right place?'

'Of course.'

'Well – maybe you'll hear from her again.'

'Maybe she'll call me.'

'I wonder what she wanted to tell you,' Annie said.

Guy shrugged. 'Perhaps we'll never know.'

As they ate the first course – melon and some rather indifferent *prosciutto* – Annie asked him what he had been doing in Bath. He hesitated before he answered.

'I was looking for Sylvie's mother.'

'What do you mean – looking for Sylvie's mother?'

'I thought she might be with her other daughter – Marianne.'

242

'And was she?'

'No. Apparently she's up in Scotland on vacation.'

'And you went all that way on the off-chance of seeing her?'

'Yes, but – oh, it's a long story.'

She smiled. 'I'm not in a hurry.'

He said nothing.

'Well,' she shrugged, 'if you don't want to tell me that's okay.'

A little silence fell between them. Guy poured more wine, the waiter took away their plates and brought the pasta and salad they had ordered.

In spite of the fact that Guy had not eaten in some time he was unable to summon up much enthusiasm for the food before him.

'You're not really enjoying it, are you?' Annie said.

'I guess I'm just not that hungry.'

He picked at a few more mouthfuls, then said:

'My going to Forham Green today, and then to Bath . . .'

Annie said quickly: 'You don't have to tell me anything you don't want to.'

'No, I want to.'

She said nothing. He hesitated, wondering where to begin, for he knew that she would have to hear the full story. Then, with the food all but forgotten before him he began, starting by referring again to his estrangement from Sylvie during the last years of her life, of his efforts to win her back, and then of her death. He went on to speak of his bewilderment at the fact that she and Luke had been buried in separate graves, and then, haltingly, of Mrs Bennett's revelation to him that Luke was not his son. Through it all Annie listened in silence, her expression a mixture of sympathy and consternation. He ended by telling her of his consultation of the birth and death registers at St Catherine's House when he had searched for some clue as to the identity of Luke's father.

'And he's not registered,' he added with a shake of his head. 'Neither his birth nor his death. It's as if he never existed.'

Annie sat gazing at him. 'But Guy,' she said, 'what purpose will it serve – to get answers? Are you going to be any better off once you've got them?'

'I don't know. Probably not.'

She shook her head. 'All this – this chasing around you're doing. You're just torturing yourself. Why are you doing it?'

'You sound like Sylvie's sister Marianne,' he said. Shrugging, he added, 'I just – need to know, I guess.' With sudden, depressing clarity he saw the whole trip, the whole confused thing as some kind of wild goose chase. But it did not change anything. 'I can't help it,' he said. 'I keep thinking about it. I've got to find out. I've got to know.'

'And will you be happy then?'

'Oh, I wouldn't expect that. It's just – just not knowing, that's all.'

She reached across the table and laid her hand on his. 'I hate to see you doing this to yourself.'

He said nothing.

'You're supposed to be on holiday,' she added. 'You should be having some fun, not running around torturing yourself with all these questions. What with this on top of that dog bite and all your worry over that – you're going to drive yourself crazy.' She paused. 'Maybe you need to get away, right away – where you *can't* keep pursuing it all.'

'Maybe.' He didn't want to discuss it any further. She

244

didn't understand the compulsion he felt. But who could? He himself was at a loss.

'Come on,' Annie said. 'Let's pay up and go.' She signalled to the waiter and asked for the bill, then, looking at her watch, she said to Guy, 'It's getting late. Why don't you stay over tonight?'

'You've got school in the morning, haven't you?'

'I can go in late. I'll phone in.'

'Well – if you're sure.'

'I'm sure.'

When the bill came she took her change purse from her bag and began to sort out money. Guy took out his wallet. 'No,' Annie said, 'I told you this is on me. I'm just sorry it's been so disappointing.'

'Please – let me get it.'

'*No*,' she said firmly. 'It's mine.'

Ignoring her, he opened his wallet and extracted some notes. Annie responded by reaching across the table and snatching up both notes and wallet. Holding them out of his reach, she said, 'I said no.' Counting out notes and coins from her purse she laid them on the bill. 'My God, you can be difficult,' she added as she picked up Guy's money. Opening his wallet she slipped the notes inside. As she did so her eye lighted on the little photograph of Sylvie framed in its plastic window. Her movements halted. She stared at the picture. Guy watched her, his heart sinking.

'So this is Sylvie,' she said softly.

He nodded.

She added, without raising her eyes, 'You said you didn't have a photograph of her with you.'

He nodded. 'Yes – I know.'

She looked at him now. 'Why did you say that?'

245

He spread his hands in a little gesture of helplessness. 'I don't know. It was stupid of me.'

'Why did you lie?'

' – I don't know.'

'Of course you know. You must know.'

'Annie – ' He reached out a hand for the wallet. 'I'm sorry.'

She ignored his outstretched hand, her eyes once again on Sylvie's face. Guy withdrew his hand, sat there helplessly. After a few moments Annie gave a nod.

'I know why,' she said.

Silence between them. Annie carefully closed the wallet and held it out. Guy took it, put it in his inside jacket pocket.

With a bitter little smile Annie said: 'No wonder you didn't want to show me her photograph. She looks just like me. Or rather *I* look just like *her*.'

'Annie . . .'

'It's all right,' she said with a little shake of her head, 'you don't have to explain.'

All at once she was getting up from her seat, picking up her bag. Guy got up facing her. As he did so she raised her hand, palm out.

'No, please. Don't come with me.'

'But . . .'

'No.' Her voice was firm. There was a look of hurt on her face. 'Oh,' she said, shaking her head, 'I wish I'd seen that photograph at the start.'

'Wait a minute.' He moved to stand before her. Her voice controlled, she said evenly:

'There are people looking at us. Don't make a scene. I'm going. Please don't come with me.'

'But – when shall I see you?'

She did not answer. He stood there helplessly as she

246

walked past him, took her coat from the waiter and walked out into the night.

Picking up his own coat Guy followed her out onto the street. She was there ahead of him, moving to her car. He started towards her, but he was too late; she was inside and the car was moving off. For some moments he stood there, deliberating whether to follow her to her apartment. No, now was not the time. He would try to see her tomorrow. He turned and started off along the street.

After walking for some distance he stopped to get his bearings and light a cigarette. He had been walking without direction. He looked about him. There were very few people about; he did not recognize the street and he had no idea in which direction lay the nearest tube station – though it was probably too late for a train anyway. He must look for a taxi. Ahead of him at the end of the street he saw traffic going by. He set off towards it.

With the sound of the busy traffic on the road ahead he was not at first aware of the car that approached along the street behind him. Then all at once his senses told him that the sound was too loud, too close, and he turned and the large, black car was suddenly right there, mounting the pavement, almost upon him. The next moment hands were grasping his shoulders and he was being violently thrown aside. He fell against the wall of a house, the impact knocking the breath from his body. As he sat up he saw the car swiftly turn the corner at the end of the street and disappear from sight.

There was a man bending over him, the man who had saved him. Gasping for breath, Guy looked up into the man's bearded face. He tried to speak but he was so shocked and shaken that no words would come.

'Are you all right?' the man asked. He spoke with a Scots accent. 'Are you hurt?'

247

Guy shook his head. 'I'm all right, I think . . .' Unsteadily, with the man assisting, he got to his feet. He stood there, the man's hand still under his elbow, breath rasping from his open mouth. He was aware that he had bruised his right hip and elbow. 'He – he almost ran me down,' he said. 'He almost killed me.'

The man shook his head. 'Drunks,' he said. 'They shouldn't be allowed on the roads.' The light of a nearby lamp glinted on the gold ring in his ear. 'Are you going to be okay?' he asked.

'Yes, I'll be fine now. I'm just a little shaken, that's all.' Guy shook his head in relief. 'You saved me,' he added. 'I don't know where you sprang from but you saved me. If it hadn't been for you I'd have had it.'

The man smiled showing wide-spaced front teeth. 'Well, I'm just glad that I was able to help. Now,' he turned Guy in the direction of the main street, 'let's go and find you a taxi.'

At the end of the street the stranger hailed a cab and held the door open while Guy got in. Seconds later when Guy turned to thank him the man had gone.

20

Guy dreamed that night that he was in some vast, cavernous hall searching through endless registers. For what, though, he did not know. And always the answer he sought stayed out of reach, promised in the next list of names, the next volume. And so he went on, from one to the other, his goal continuing to elude him.

He awoke later than usual and at once thought of Annie and the look on her face when she had seen Sylvie's photograph. He must talk to her. When he dialled her number, however, there was no answer. Either she had gone to school or she was not answering her phone.

Soaping himself under the shower the bruises on his elbow and hip reminded him again of the incident with the car. For the second time in days he had come close to death, and on both occasions an automobile had been involved. For a fleeting moment he was almost tempted to play with the terrifying thought that someone was out to kill him, but he knew that such a notion was madness; who would wish for such a thing? – and for what reason? – he had no enemies.

Later he set out from the hotel, walking in no particular direction, killing time. There was a restlessness about him that was greater than any he had known since arriving in the town. It was partly to do with Annie, but it was more particularly to do with Luke. There was something that hovered at the back of his mind, like some half-forgotten tune that refused to be pinned down. The thought went through his mind that it was the kind of phenomenon experienced by detectives in novels, a puzzle eventually resolved with some flash of insight that suddenly made everything crystal clear. But that was in fiction; this was reality. Irritably he told himself to leave it alone; stop chasing it and it would come. But his admonitions were only effective for the briefest periods, and he would find himself once again searching, trying to grasp what he could not see, probing at it like a tongue probing a broken tooth.

On the way along Oxford Street he stopped at a branch of the HMV record stores and spent a while sorting through record albums and cassettes. But there was nothing there that he wanted enough to have to carry around and he left empty-handed. In the same way he window-shopped at several fashionable clothing stores, but always his lack of any real interest stopped him short of commitment.

At twelve-thirty he was wandering about the crowded stalls, boutiques and cafés of Covent Garden. After stopping long enough to buy a cheeseburger and a cup of coffee and to watch a group of street-entertainers go through their act he went on his way again.

An hour later, still wandering, he found himself in a quiet little backwater of a street, away from the grind of the traffic and the crowds. Stopping before a small church he stood looking at its façade for a moment then went along the path and up the few shallow steps to the porch. The door opened easily under his touch. Entering, he saw that there were three people inside, sitting apart from each other. Quietly he slipped into a pew near the rear and sat down.

The people in front of him sat with bowed heads, in prayer or contemplation. After the hustle and bustle outside the silence and the peace were almost a miracle.

He himself had no thought of prayer, and looking at the three bent heads he wondered how anyone could believe that any kind of prayer, be it silent or voiced aloud, could ever make a difference. With all the prayers that had been prayed had a single one ever reached out beyond the one who prayed?

Yet the atmosphere was soothing, the place was cool and comforting. It had the same air, the same smell about it as St Peter's in Forham Green, the only other English church he had been in. He let his eyes wander around the walls, taking in the plaques set in memory of the dead – long-forgotten victims of war, and beneficiaries of the church. On the southern side the bright sun streamed through stained-glass windows, throwing the brilliant colours of St George and the Dragon and St Francis of Assisi in soft, muted projection onto the pews and the wide flags of the aisle. There were flowers at the altar – irises and tulips and narcissi.

The time crept by. One by one the three worshippers got up and left. And still he sat there. There was nowhere else he wanted to go, nothing else he wanted to do. He did not want to walk any further, and neither did he wish to return and sit in his room. Closing his eyes, he briefly tipped back his head and tried again to catch that something that danced like a butterfly in his brain. Still it eluded him.

After a while he felt an ache starting up in his head, at the site of his accident scar. He closed his eyes more tightly as the pain increased. He had been free of the headaches for so many days now that he had almost forgotten how they could strike so swiftly, so completely without warning.

Eyes closed, he sat there while the minutes went by and the pain throbbed in his head. He had brought no pills with him and he could only wait for it to pass. It felt as if the pain were centred on a single line, stretching from his hairline at the front to somewhere low at the base of his skull, as if his brain was throbbing with some frenetic energy. Before his clenched eyelids dazzling shapes danced like flashing neon lights and electrical currents. At one point through the fog he was vaguely aware of softly approaching footsteps that slowed and moved on again. He did not open his eyes.

After what seemed an age he felt the pain slowly begin to subside. As it lessened he opened his eyes. He must get away, back to his hotel room. Gripping the back of the pew in front of him he slowly got to his feet. He stood for a few moments holding on, then, with an effort, directed his unsteady feet into the aisle. Looking neither to left nor right he headed for the door. He got to it; turned the handle.

Brilliant sunlight struck him as he emerged from the porch, dazzling his already dazzled eyes so that for a second he staggered. He gathered himself, mentally holding on, while the pain rushed back with renewed violence. He forced himself to move on but as he walked slowly down the three shallow steps to the path he knew he was not going to make it. With the realization he lurched towards a bench beside the path and sat down.

Eyes clenched tight he sat gripping the edge of the seat while the pain came and went in waves. It had been so long since he had suffered such an overwhelming attack. Above the pounding in his head he imagined hearing a voice. The voice came again.

'Are you all right, sir . . .?'

Guy opened his eyes. A man was bending to him. Dark-brown face, black robe, snow-white collar. Guy did not speak. The priest spoke again.

252

'I saw you inside – in the church. I thought at the time that you appeared to be in some – trouble. Can I do anything to help?'

Guy bent his head, raised a hand to his forehead. 'It will pass,' he managed to say.

'You're in pain, are you?'

Guy nodded. 'Some,' he muttered.

'Can I get you some water? Perhaps some aspirin. Would that help?'

Aspirin. Like attacking an oak with a penknife. Better, though, than nothing. 'Thank you.'

The man went away, and returned after a short while and handed Guy a glass of water. 'Paracetamol,' he said as he opened a small packet. 'Is that okay?'

'Anything.'

'How many would you like? Two?'

'Give me four.'

The man's dark face was impassive as he extracted the tablets and held them out on his pink palm. Guy nodded his thanks, took them and swallowed them, washing them down with some of the water.

'Would you like to come back inside for a minute?' the man asked. 'Come and rest for a while.'

'No, I'll be all right, thank you.'

'You'll be much more comfortable.'

'Well . . . Okay – thank you.'

Guy got to his feet, and together he and the priest went into the church. They walked down the aisle and into the vestry. Gesturing to Guy to sit in what was clearly the more comfortable of the two armchairs there, the priest said, 'I'll make some tea. Would you like some?'

'Thank you – but I'm beginning to feel better now. I don't want to take up your time.'

'It's what time is for.' The man switched on an electric

kettle, began to arrange tea cups, milk and sugar. Guy looked around him. The room was softly carpeted. Books filled shelves on one wall. There was a rather worn globe, a desk with papers and files on it. Framed photographs stood on the desk showing smiling black faces. A few pictures hung on the walls; all religious subjects; the traditional milquetoast Jesus Christ shown in various set pieces.

Guy said, 'I'm putting you to so much trouble.'

'Not at all. Listen, any excuse for a cup of tea.' The man smiled at Guy as he switched off the boiling kettle, his teeth very white in his dark face. He had a slight accent; there was a faint West Indian softness in his pronunciation.

'Do you take milk and sugar?' asked the priest.

'Milk but no sugar, please.'

The steaming cup was placed beside Guy on a small table, then the man held out a tin of biscuits.

'Would you like a biscuit?'

Guy smiled. 'No, thank you; the tea will be just fine.'

The priest took the other armchair. He made no attempt to engage Guy in conversation but just sat there in silence, drinking his tea.

Sipping his own tea, which was delicious, Guy felt himself beginning to relax, while at the same time he could feel the pain draining slowly away. Glancing up, he caught the eye of the young priest. The black man smiled and said:

'How are you feeling now?'

'Better. Much better, thank you. It's beginning to go now.'

'Do you get them frequently – headaches like that?'

'Not as much as I used to.' Guy touched fingertips to his forehead, adding, 'I had an accident a year ago. I've

254

got the headaches from time to time ever since. I have pills I can take, but I didn't bring any out with me today.'

'You'll know better in future, yes?' This with a smile.

'I guess I shall.'

'Is there something in particular that brings your headaches on? I mean – have you been worrying about anything?'

When Guy didn't answer at once the man added, 'I don't wish to pry.'

'Oh, that's all right.' Guy nodded. 'Yes, I guess you could say I've been worrying. To a degree, anyway.'

'If you want to talk about it I'd be glad to listen.'

'No, it's okay. But thanks anyway. I'll get it sorted out. It's just a matter of time now.' Guy took a sip at his tea then said: 'I feel a fraud, sitting here.'

'A fraud? In what way?'

'Well . . . I've never been one for going to church.'

'D'you mean you've never been one for going to church, or do you mean that you're not a believer?'

'The second, I guess. Does it bother you?'

'No. But it saddens me a little. Though tell me,' the priest added, 'what were you doing in church if it has no meaning for you?'

'I don't know.' A shrug. 'I needed a rest, I guess.'

The priest nodded. After a moment he asked, 'You're American, are you?'

'Yes. I'm here on vacation.'

'Did you come alone – or with family . . .?'

'I have no family. I was married. My wife died.'

'I'm so sorry to hear that.'

Guy nodded, avoiding the sympathy in his eyes. The priest added:

'You know – perhaps you didn't just happen to wander in here today.'

255

'Into the church, you mean?'

'Yes.'

'You think I might have been led here? By God?'

'D'you think it's impossible?'

Guy sighed, hesitated, then said: 'Well, I do really – yes. I can't accept that we're all puppets – that we're all put on earth solely to do God's will. I mean – what would be the point of it?'

'Do you think God has no power over man?'

'Oh,' Guy said, 'you don't really want to know what I think.'

'Tell me, please. I'm interested. Do you think man has no kind of direction at all?'

'I don't know. I guess it depends on what you mean by direction. I believe every man has his fate, a destiny to fulfil – but that's just through the laws of cause and effect.'

'Did you *ever* believe in God?' the man said.

'I don't think so. I don't know any more. I certainly don't now – and I can't imagine that I ever shall.'

'How can you be so sure?'

Guy hesitated then said, 'To tell you the truth, I don't think Christianity's got a case.' He looked at the other, trying to gauge his reaction. The young priest's eyes remained steady upon him. Guy added: 'Oh, there's no doubt that Christ lived, but I don't believe there's anything divine about him. I'm quite sure he was a good man, a truly good man – his teachings show that clearly enough. But he was *that* – a *man*, nothing else. Not divine, not the son of God, not the embodiment of God. Just a good man.' He shook his head. 'You don't want to hear this.'

'Go on.'

'Well – I just can't accept that there's a God up there and that he sent his son down to earth to save us. I mean

– look around you. If Christ *was* divine and he *did* die on the cross for our salvation then it didn't work, did it? Man is no different, is he? People are still killing each other. They still lie and cheat and steal. Christ's coming hasn't changed a thing – except that now so much of the evil is done in his name.'

'You seem to have it all worked out.'

'I wish I did,' Guy said. 'I'm quite sure that Christ's divinity is something invented by man. Man's always needed *something* to believe in, and for the past two thousand years it's been Christ. You only have to look at the things that have been done in the name of Christianity to see that they all stem from the *desires of man*, not from the teachings of Christ.'

'But you don't dismiss the teachings of Christ, do you?'

'No, it's not Christ's teachings I quarrel with. I'm sure he was a truly good man. And if more of his Christians obeyed his teachings the world would be a better place.'

'But cannot you accept that if God – Christ – is good, and there is a belief in that goodness, then that in itself is a manifestation of him?'

'No, I can't. We're taught that God is good, and that he governs the earth, but as I said – look at what a mess it's in. If God is all-powerful then he must just turn a blind eye to what's going on. You ask a believer how it could happen and he'll tell you "God works in a mysterious way". That's supposed to be an answer? That's supposed to explain why one race enslaves another? Why millions of Jews and gypsies and homosexuals died in gas chambers? Why Palestinian children are being shot? Why villagers in Iraq are murdered with poison gas?'

'But you take no account of *evil*.'

'Evil? How can I *not* take account of it? How can anybody miss it? It's all around us.'

257

'I mean evil as a *force* – a real force.'

Guy shook his head. 'You don't mean that, do you?'

'Of course I do. Just as God-Christ is a force for good, so the Devil is a force for evil.'

'Oh, I see – like some warring factions, right?'

'Well – if you like.'

'No, what *you* like.'

'Yes. I believe it to be so. I believe there is a power, another side to the coin. There has to be. A dark power struggling for supremacy – in which evil is seen as good, and good, evil. Even at this moment.'

'I couldn't accept that.'

'Why not?'

'It's too – too *neat*. It's that ready answer to explain it all. It doesn't really explain anything to me. Not a sparrow falls but God doesn't know about it, right? And if that doesn't explain it then the concept of Satan will.' Guy's voice rose with intensity. 'I accidentally killed my son, whom I loved. I lost the love of my wife – and she died. I lost, too, in a way, another son. Explain to me in the name of your god why those things happened, because for the life of me I can't think of a reason.'

There was silence in the room. Guy became aware, for the first time, of a ticking clock. The seconds going by, the heartbeats of life sounding, passing. After a few moments the young priest leaned forward, reached out and laid a dark hand on his arm. A brief pressure and the touch was gone. 'How can anyone believe in God, love God,' he said sadly, 'if he has no belief in life, no love for life.' It was not a question. 'I think perhaps I understand,' he added.

'I wish *I* did.' Guy bent his head and wept.

The priest said nothing, but watched in pain. When Guy's tears had ceased the priest said:

258

'So much of what you said is true. I know that much of what are regarded as the teachings of Christ are in fact the teachings of men – and usually a few men, men of power. But that doesn't stop *me* from trying to find that *real* Truth. And I know it's there. And it's there in God, in Christ.'

Guy sat silently, head bowed, the tears drying on his cheeks.

'And if you are denied happiness now,' the priest went on, 'it won't always be so. I know I'm right – there will come a time when you will be happy. I know it.'

Without raising his head Guy said dully, 'The Afterlife, yes?'

'Certainly then, yes.'

Guy shook his head. 'It's all part of the same package.'

'If you like. But can you look around you at this world, at the miracle of this world, and deny the possibility of there being an equal miracle, *another* world? Look at the opening of a flower, a chick coming out of its shell – all the living creatures whose existences fit like jigsaw pieces one into the other. Who could ever conceive of such an incredible miracle? And why should it be the *only* miracle?' He paused. 'You lost your wife, your sons, but does that mean you've lost them for ever?'

Guy raised his head, his bruised eyes gazing at the other. 'Oh, God,' he said, 'I wish I could believe. I would give anything to have your belief, to be sure that it was not the end.'

'Try.'

'I wouldn't know how.'

'Do you really think that your spirit – that essence that is you – dies with the body? No. It's not confined by the flesh. And released, it must go soaring – like a bird.'

Guy turned his head from the man's gaze and got slowly

259

to his feet. 'It's time I went.' The priest looked at his watch and also rose. 'I must get off too. I'm due at the hospital.' He gave a melancholy shake of his head. 'One of my parishioners has Aids. It's very sad. But he has great courage.'

In the church porch Guy offered his hand; the priest shook it.

'Will you be all right?' the priest said. He still clasped Guy's hand.

'Yes, thank you. I guess I'll work it out.' Guy shrugged. 'I don't know what to say.'

A moment of silence. 'I failed you,' the priest said.

'No – not you. Not you.'

'But I meant it – what I said. And I believe it. There is more than this – here, now. I know it. Your wife . . .' He pressed Guy's hand, released it. 'Love is such a power. It is the greatest power of all.'

Sylvie . . . David. 'If I could believe it,' Guy said, 'that one day we'd be together again.'

'You will,' the priest said. 'Believe it. Oh, believe it. One day you shall be.'

The light was changing as Guy walked along the street. Lifting his head he saw that dark clouds had gathered, while on his upturned face he felt one or two spots of rain. Moments later the rain was falling heavily.

Quickly he moved beneath the cover offered by a nearby doorway where an old woman already stood taking shelter. They stood side by side watching as the rain came down, bouncing off the flags of the pavement. Most of the other pedestrians had been driven off the streets while those remaining ran for cover. In minutes the gutters were awash and passing cars were throwing up sheets of spray as they sped by. A brilliant flash of lightning lit up the scene, causing the old woman to start back in alarm. Seconds later came the distant crack and rumble of thunder.

Then, as suddenly as it had begun, the rain ceased. The clouds passed and the sun came out and the pavements once again rang with the feet of the pedestrians. From the doorway Guy turned and walked towards a busy road junction up ahead. As he drew nearer he recognized it: Holborn; it was close to St Catherine's House. And in the middle of the wet pavement he came to a halt. He had suddenly realized what it was that had been tantalizing him, that thought that he had been unable to grasp.

Starting off again he crossed the street and walked on. His steps were hurried now. Reaching the station he turned the corner into Kingsway and strode on. At the foot of Kingsway he moved to the entrance of St Catherine's House and went in.

Inside he did not hesitate. He knew exactly where to go. When he had found the register he opened it before him, stood gazing down at it for a moment and then, with his pen, wrote down the details of the entry on a restaurant receipt that he had found in his pocket. He felt slightly breathless, and he was aware of the beating of his heart.

After making inquiries he filled out a requisition form and joined one of the lines at the counter. A few minutes later he had paid over the required fee and was given a receipt. The certificate would be ready for collection on Tuesday after three o'clock, the clerk told him.

Out on the street again he walked for a few yards then stopped. He took a deep breath, trying to calm the pounding of his heart. 'If it could be,' he said aloud. 'If it could be.'

261

21

Back at the hotel Guy tried calling Annie's number. No answer. He tried again later in the evening, but without success. As soon as he had breakfasted the next morning, he dialled her number again. As before the phone went on ringing. He tried again just after ten o'clock. This time, to his immeasurable relief, she answered.

'Annie,' he said.

'Oh – hello, Guy . . .'

'I've been trying to call you.'

'I went out to do some early shopping.'

'I want to see you.'

A little pause. 'Why . . .?'

'Oh – listen, we can't talk on the phone. Can I come over?'

She hesitated. He added quickly, 'I'm coming over, okay?'

'Yes . . . okay.'

She made coffee and in an awkward silence they sat facing one another. She said into the quiet:

'I don't know why you came back, Guy.'

'I had to. Of course I had to.'

She said nothing.

'Don't shut me out, Annie,' he said. 'Please.'

'I don't want to shut you out. I just – don't know what you want.' She shook her head, raised her eyes to his. 'No, that's not true. I *do* know what you want – but what you want is nothing to do with me. You've got no interest

262

in *me*. I realized that last night. I thought you were fond of me – genuinely fond. It wasn't me, though.'

'Oh, Annie – '

'You know it's true. When I saw Sylvie's photograph I suddenly realized. But I'm not her. I'm *me*. I can't be her for you.' She shook her head. 'Oh, listen, I know you're only here on holiday. I know you'll be going back to New York soon. I hadn't lost sight of those things. As much as I – I liked you I still tried to be realistic, to face the facts. I knew that things were generally – well – against us as regards anything more permanent. But I thought – what the hell – it's good, and it will be good for as long as it lasts, for the time you're here. I won't make any demands, I thought. I'll just take each day as it comes, and enjoy them, and be glad of them; and when it's over, and you go away, I'll know that at least we both got something out of it all, these few weeks. And I wouldn't be sorry, because at least we were honest with each other.' She sighed. 'Then, when I saw Sylvie's photograph, I realized that for you it was all a sham. You were playing some kind of game.'

'Annie . . .'

'It's true. You weren't interested in me at all. God knows what it was all for but . . . What were you trying to do? Bring your wife back through me? Did you think that through me you could have some kind of second chance?'

He said nothing. She went on:

'I couldn't believe it when I saw her photograph. For a second it was almost like looking at a picture of myself. Then it hit me, and I realized what it meant. What did you think I was going to do? – give you another chance to save your marriage? I'm *me*, Guy; Annie. I'm not Sylvie.

263

And no amount of wishing on your part is going to make it so.'

Silence in the room for a few moments, then Guy said lamely:

'I don't know what to say.'

'It's true, isn't it? We're here together because I look like Sylvie.'

He sighed, briefly closed his eyes. 'Can you forgive me?'

She nodded. 'Yes, of course I can forgive you. But it doesn't change anything, does it? Guy, I think I can understand what you've been going through. I don't know the *full* story with you and Sylvie but I know enough from what you've told me to realize that you're going through some kind of – torment. And I'm so sorry for you. But I don't think I can help you. I wish I could.' She looked into his eyes. Her own were swimming with tears. 'Oh, Guy,' she said softly, 'Sylvie is dead. I know how hard it must be for you to accept that, but she's dead, and whatever you think, whatever you try to do, nothing is going to change that. Nothing will bring her back.'

'I know.' Every word she had spoken was the truth. The past was past, and he must face up to it or never know a moment's peace. He was silent for a moment then he said: 'It's true: when I saw you first I was drawn to you because you looked so like her – Sylvie. I can't pretend otherwise. My God – it was as if she was standing there. I couldn't believe it. And I suppose, subconsciously, I did want you to be her, in a way. It's insane, I know, but . . .' He shook his head. 'I'm sorry. Believe me, I'm so sorry.'

She gave a little shrug, sighed. 'Anyway – it's over now.'

'Oh – oh, listen,' he said, 'it doesn't have to be, does it?'

'What are you saying?'

'Oh – listen – I know my reasons were all wrong at the start, but they're not now. I'm here now because of *you*. It's nothing to do with Sylvie. Not now.'

She eyed him steadily. 'Do you mean that?'

'Yes. Oh, don't say it's over. I'm sorry I hurt you, but I'll make it up to you.'

'Guy, you don't have to make anything up to me. And I wouldn't want you to think you did. Whatever you do for me has to be because you *want* to, because of what I am – not because of who you want me to be or because of some sense of guilt you're feeling.'

'I know. But it's because of you that I'm here. Not for any other reason. Let's start again – for the little time we have left together. Let's give it a chance. Give me a chance.'

'Is that really what you want?' she said.

'Yes, so much.'

She was silent for a moment, then she said: 'Well, it would be good to salvage something. And if it's really what you want.'

'And if you want it too.'

'Oh, I haven't been in any doubt,' she said. 'D'you think we could?'

'I know we could. Just – give it a chance.'

She nodded, tears welling in her eyes again. 'We'll take each day as it comes,' she said. 'And if at the end there is nothing, then so be it. But if there is, then we'll have something to be glad about.'

'Yes, oh, yes.'

He moved to her, crouched at her side and wrapped his arms around her. 'We'll do nice things,' he said. 'And we'll be together.'

'Yes.' Her own arms moved, held him, a haven in the

265

storm of his confusion; he knew a sense of beginning to feel safe again. He must not jeopardize that.

'What shall we do?' she said, breaking from him, smiling into his eyes. 'Tell me what we shall do.'

'We'll do whatever you want to do.'

'Yes. We could go away somewhere.'

'Can you get time off school?'

'That's the beauty of supply teaching. Anyway, I've already had so much time off, what with my father and everything. A little more's not going to make much difference.'

'Good. Then we'll go away somewhere. Where shall we go?'

'Oh – somewhere away from here, away from London. We could go to the Continent. Go to Paris, or Rome, or Barcelona or – oh, I don't care.'

He grinned. 'We'll think of something. When shall we go?'

'Well – perhaps towards the end of next week. We could go for a long weekend.'

'It sounds good.'

Raising a plump hand to touch at his silver hair, Rawlinson said, 'We've had your reports on how you've manipulated him, kept him dancing. Did he, then, agree quite readily?'

'Yes,' she said, 'he agreed at once. It all worked out very well. Surprisingly so. But he was very eager to please me by then.'

That evening of Monday, May the 8th, the group sat around a table in a tall house on the north side of Clapham Common. With all eyes upon her, Annie sat facing Rawlinson as he sat in his chair at the head of the table.

'You're fortunate it's worked out well,' Rawlinson said.

266

'For I understand you've left him to his own devices for considerable periods since you met.'

She nodded reluctantly. 'Yes.'

'Quite. When your instructions were to remain with him as much as possible.'

She did not answer.

'Well?' Rawlinson said.

'Yes. But – I was afraid.'

'Afraid?' Rawlinson said.

'For my safety. I know there have been two attempts on his life. When the first one happened I was with him. I was almost killed as well.' She shook her head in distress. 'I'm sorry, but I panicked. I was afraid I'd be killed too. So – I invented a sick father.'

Rawlinson gazed at her in contempt for a moment then said, 'How is your relationship with Holman now?'

She hesitated. 'It's very good. It all seems to be working out.'

'You don't seem to be that certain.'

'Well . . .'

'Is he in love with you? Or falling in love with you?' The word love did not come easily from his pursed mouth.

She hitched her shoulders slightly. 'Well, going by what I understand of love, it's hard to say. I believe he *thinks* he is.'

'Go on.'

'I know that I was chosen because I look so much like his dead wife, and at the start it worked out perfectly. I'm not sure, though, that it will continue to work for us.'

'What do you mean?'

'Well – he's so obsessed with his family. He's tormented by questions about them, and while that's going on he needs someone to hold on to. At present that someone is

267

me. But if his problems get sorted out I don't know what will happen.'

'You mean he might find that he has no real need of you.'

'It's possible.'

Rawlinson nodded. 'When did the conversation about going to the Continent take place between you?'

'On Saturday. Late Saturday morning.'

'And what's happened since?'

'We spent that evening and night together, and all the next day.'

'Have you seen him today?'

' – No, I said I had to work.'

'Judging by your tone,' Rawlinson said, 'one might infer that you find your assignment not altogether to your taste.'

'I don't,' she said quickly. She shook her head. 'Well, it's been, shall we say, difficult.'

'Meaning you don't care for the man.'

'I despise him.'

Rawlinson nodded; the information was only of passing interest. 'What is he like?' he asked.

'Very moral. A great capacity for affection and love. Obsessional. Full of preoccupations.' She shook her head in dismissal.

'Is he fit?'

'Fit, sir?'

'His encounter with the rabid dog. He's showing no ill effects?'

'Oh, no, none at all.'

'Good. When do you intend going to Italy?'

'On Thursday. But he doesn't know it's to be Italy yet. We'll decide on that tomorrow.'

Rawlinson allowed himself a flicker of a smile. 'And how do you intend to spend the time till then?'

'I've told him that I have to work in the days, but that we can meet in the evenings.' She paused. 'I don't want to spend any more time with him than is necessary.'

'Young woman,' Rawlinson said, 'you don't seem to be aware of the significance of the information that you yourself have put before us. This man must not be left on his own for long periods. You've already told us how obsessional he is, how preoccupied with his domestic troubles. Leave him alone again for too long when he's like this and you could lose him. I suggest you make yourself free. He must be got to Italy by Friday evening at all costs.'

When she had been dismissed and had left the room, the bearded Scotsman, Campbell, said to Rawlinson: 'Does everything rest with her?'

'Thankfully, no,' said Rawlinson. 'Though she doesn't know that. We've taken other measures. We'll get him there by some means or other.'

From a public call box in the street Annie tried to phone Guy at his hotel. There was no answer. Trying again on her return to Hammersmith she found him in and on the point of going to bed. She was calling, she told him, to say that she was not going to school the next day.

'Why not?' he asked.

'I thought to hell with it. You're only going to be here for a little while longer – so let's make the most of the time left. Are you glad? Tell me you're glad.'

'Of course I'm glad. But they're gonna fire you if you're not careful.'

'Don't worry about that. Anyway, I've already told

269

them. So – tomorrow is ours. All day. Unless you've already made plans.'

'No, I've made no plans.'

'Shall we meet, then?'

'Yes, of course.'

'We'll drive out somewhere, shall we? Into the country again.'

'Great.'

'I'll try and think of somewhere nice. I'll call you first thing in the morning.'

'Okay.'

'Okay.'

'Well – goodnight.'

'Goodnight, Guy.'

With Annie's flat situated so close to the M4 motorway they drove west again, after an hour turning off the main highway onto secondary roads. They ended up at Hungerford where they stopped at a pub for lunch and afterwards browsed among some antique shops. They bought ice-creams and then left the little town and walked into the surrounding fields where in the hedgerows the hawthorn was in blossom and dog roses twined among the brambles. At the top of a green hill they sat on the grass in the shade of a flowering chestnut tree. Guy sat looking down the hillside to the town. 'What are you thinking about?' Annie asked.

He turned to her, smiling. 'Nothing much.'

'Nothing much,' she repeated. 'A likely story.'

'I was thinking how peaceful it is here,' he lied. 'How beautiful the English countryside is.'

'It is, isn't it?' She paused. 'Are we still set for Thursday?'

'Thursday?'

270

'Come on, wake up.' She reached out, ran a hand through his hair. 'We're taking a trip somewhere – or had you forgotten?'

'Of course not. Have you decided yet where you'd like to go? Which is it to be? France? Italy? Spain?'

'I'd really like to go to Italy,' she said.

'Great. Whereabouts? You mentioned Rome.'

'Yes, I know, but – I think I'd like to go to Milan.'

'Okay, fine,' he said.

'Good.' She grinned, leaned over and kissed him on the cheek. 'So – shall I go ahead and make the arrangements?'

'Yes, sure – if you don't mind.'

'Of course I don't mind.'

He took out his cigarettes and lit one. Putting them back in his pocket his fingers touched paper. Drawing it out he saw that it was the receipt from St Catherine's House. The certificate he had requisitioned would be available at three o'clock that day. He looked at his watch. Three-twenty.

'Have you got an appointment?' Annie said.

'What? No.'

Since making up the rift with Annie on Saturday he had refused to allow himself to dwell on any of the questions that had previously plagued him. When they had surfaced in his mind from time to time he had thrust them aside. Annie was right when she said that he had to accept what was past and get on with the present, with life. Sylvie was dead, David was dead. Luke was dead too; though Luke had never been his. He looked at the slip of paper held between his fingers. It was another symbol of his inability to give up the past, of that obsession that had led him to indulge in the wildest fantasies and hopes, of imaginings that had no place in reality.

271

'What's that?' Annie asked, gesturing at the slip of paper.

'Nothing. Nothing of importance.' He hesitated a moment then tore the receipt into tiny pieces, then tossed them into the breeze. They fell like snow into the grass.

'Litterbug,' Annie reprimanded.

'I know.' He reached out, drew her down and kissed her. 'Oh, Annie . . .' The fragments of paper were like stars about the spreading halo of her hair. He bent, kissed her again. This is what is real, he said to himself. This is what is real.

Guy spent the night with Annie and parted from her just before nine the next morning. Arriving at his hotel he changed his clothes then rang the Aldwych Theatre to reserve seats for that evening's performance of *The Black Prince* which Annie, an Iris Murdoch admirer, wanted to see. The booking made, he set off to pick up the tickets. Annie, who in the meantime was to make the arrangements for their trip, was to meet him outside the theatre at twelve o'clock; they would then have a leisurely lunch and do a little shopping before the performance.

Emerging from the theatre foyer with ten minutes to spare, Guy stood waiting beside the theatre entrance for a few moments and then turned and wandered away along the pavement.

His footsteps took him along the curve of the street until, just a few yards further along, he came to the junction with Kingsway. On the opposite side of the street stood St Catherine's House. For a minute he stood gazing across the traffic at the building, while at the roadside the pedestrian lights flicked from red to green. Then, suddenly, when the light became green again, he was joining the throng and moving forward.

272

Inside the building he joined the line at the information counter. There were three people before him and he waited with growing impatience as they made their various inquiries. At last it was his turn. Facing the same woman he had spoken to before, he told her that he was due to pick up a certificate but that he had lost his receipt. It was no problem, she said; he should go back to the till where he had paid his fee and give the clerk the details of the requisition. When he had his receipt number, she added, he could be given the certificate.

He thanked her. After lining up at the till at the rear of the room he gave the clerk the name and date on the requisitioned certificate and the clerk shuffled through a stack of forms and eventually found the one that Guy had completed. He copied from it a number onto a scrap of paper and pushed it across the counter. 'Your receipt number,' he said. 'Hand it in at the front desk.'

Guy moved back to the front of the building and joined another line. As he waited he looked at his watch and saw that it was ten minutes past twelve. Annie would be waiting for him. It couldn't be helped. He was so close now, and he had to know. When his turn came he gave the receipt number to a young male clerk and a few seconds later the clerk was handing him a rectangular piece of paper. Guy thanked him and moved away.

Standing to the side, out of the way of the traffic of the other researchers, Guy unfolded the certificate and gazed at it for long seconds while his heartbeat quickened and his palms grew damp. Then, folding the paper and putting it into his inside jacket pocket, he left the building.

As he hurried along the street he saw Annie standing outside the theatre. She turned, saw him and smiled. As he got to her side she said, 'I was beginning to think I'd been stood up. I've been expecting the police to ask me to move on.'

'I'm sorry,' he said. His voice sounded a little hoarse, and he was slightly breathless.

'Are you okay?' she said, looking at him, studying him.

'Yes, I'm fine.'

'Good.' She slipped an arm through his. 'Did you get the tickets?'

'What? Yes.'

'Great. And you'll be glad to know that I've been doing my part at the travel agent's. We leave – '

'Listen,' he broke in, 'I've got to go somewhere. I'm sorry . . .'

'What? What d'you mean?'

'I have to go somewhere. Now.'

'*Now?*'

'Yes. I'm sorry.'

She withdrew her arm. 'Well – okay. I'll wait. Where have you got to go? How long will you be?'

'No, I – it'll take me a while – a few hours.'

She frowned. 'Guy, what are you saying? I don't understand.'

'I've got to leave. Now.'

'Leave? What d'you mean – leave? I don't get it.'

'I'm sorry. I have to go somewhere. Something's come up.'

'Something urgent.'

'Yes.'

'Well – what time will you be back?'

' – I don't know.'

'But what about the theatre? We've got tickets for the theatre . . .'

'Well – I'll try to be back in time. I'll call you a little later.'

274

'You'll *try* to be back?' She looked frowning into his face. 'Would you mind telling me what this is all about?'

' – I'm sorry. I'll tell you later on.' He was backing away. 'I'll tell you all about it when I get back to town.'

'You're going out of London?'

'Yes. Please – don't ask me any more now. I've got to get to the tube. I'm sorry. Forgive me.'

Turning, he walked quickly away. Some yards further on he paused in his step and looked back. She was standing there, gazing after him. He turned away again, thrust from his mind her look of bewilderment and consternation, and strode on.

He arrived at The Willows just on three-forty-five. And he saw at once that Mrs Bennett was back; her blue Ford Cortina was standing in front of the garage. There was a second car there too: Marianne's white Renault.

Striding across the forecourt he rang the door bell. At once came the yapping of Mrs Bennett's terrier. Then the sound abruptly ceased and the door was opening and Marianne was standing there.

She frowned. 'Guy . . .'

'Hello, Marianne. I've come to see your mother. May I come in?'

She was clearly uncertain how to respond, but she stood back and he walked past her into the hall. As she closed the door behind him he heard Mrs Bennett's voice from the kitchen – 'Who is that, Marianne?' – and a moment later she had come into the doorway.

'What do you want?' she said. From behind her skirts the terrier nosed forward, sniffed at Guy's leg then retreated again.

'I want to talk to you.'

'I'm sorry, but I've got nothing to say to you.' It was

275

not only anger he could see in her eyes; there was fear there also. It had been there the last time, too, but he had not then recognized it for what it was.

'I don't think you have much choice,' he said.

'Oh, really? We'll see about that.' She drew herself up. 'D'you realize you're trespassing?'

'Oh,' he said, 'meaning that you'll call the police and have me removed?'

'If I wish. I hope it won't be necessary.'

He stood there with Mrs Bennett facing him from the kitchen doorway; Marianne was at his back, near the front door. In the silence he could hear his breathing. 'Mrs Bennett,' he said, 'you know very well you wouldn't dream of involving anyone else in this, let alone the police.'

'And what is that supposed to mean?' Her tone was sharp, but she could not hide the note of doubt in her voice. He gazed at her for a moment then reached into his jacket pocket.

'I have here,' he said, 'a copy of my son's birth certificate.'

He unfolded it, held it out towards her. She lowered her eyes to it for only a second then raised them again to his. There was alarm and panic in them now.

'Now,' he said, 'perhaps we can go and sit down.'

She hesitated for a moment then turned and led the way into the front sitting room. He followed, watching as she moved to the window and stood with lowered eyes. Marianne came behind them and stood near the door, looking from one to the other. A little silence went by then Guy said to Mrs Bennett:

'You told me that my son was not my son. You told me that Sylvie had deceived me, that she had had a love affair with someone else; had borne another man's child. When you told me that you took away the little I had left. In that single afternoon you took from me my wife and my son.' He shook his head. 'I don't think I can ever forgive you for that.'

She said nothing, just stood with her hands clasping and unclasping at her breast. He went on:

'I couldn't stop thinking about Sylvie – and her love affair with the guy – whoever he was. You said she never told you who he was. Of course she didn't. He never existed, did he? – not for a moment. You made him up.'

Silence in the room. He opened his clenched hands, wiped his damp palms on the thighs of his cords. 'And little Luke, too,' he said. 'No wonder I couldn't find any record of him in the birth or death registers. There never was any Luke Holman. I don't know whose son that little boy in the churchyard was, but he was not mine.'

Mrs Bennett's eyes were closed tight in anguish. Turning briefly, Guy looked at Marianne. She returned his gaze only for a second and then lowered her eyes. When he looked back at Mrs Bennett she was leaning forward slightly, body tense, gazing at something outside. He took a step forward. Looking past her, past the monkey puzzle tree in the centre of the forecourt, he saw the small boy sitting astride the gate.

'There he is now,' Guy said. 'There's my son.'

Part Four

'Tis all a Chequer-board of Nights and Days
Where Destiny with Men for Pieces plays:
Hither and thither moves, and mates, and slays,
And one by one back in the Closet lays.

> The Rubaiyat of Omar Khayyam –
> Edward Fitzgerald

22

John looked as if he was talking to himself, or, rather, to an imaginary friend. Guy watched as the boy gesticulated, a hand raised in admonition, and felt himself engulfed in a rush of emotion that set his heart pounding again and made his knees weak. He wanted to rush outside, run to the boy and wrap him in his arms. After a few moments of silence he said:

'Does he live here with you?'

'Yes,' Mrs Bennett said; then: 'Except if I have to go away. Then he stays with Marianne and her children. But that isn't often.'

'Not like recently,' Guy said. 'But before I turned up you didn't have anybody to avoid, did you?'

She ignored this. 'He's just back from school,' she said. Then with agitation in her voice she added: 'He'll be coming in any second. Please – don't say anything in front of him.'

'Of course not.' After a moment Guy added, 'I would have gone back to New York without ever knowing. I would never have known that my son was alive. You let me believe – you *led* me to believe – that he was Marianne's boy. I saw him here in your garden, and again in Bath the other day – and I never dreamed.' He glanced across at Marianne at this. She avoided his eyes. Mrs Bennett moved to an armchair and sat. Guy watched her. Her face was pale; her hands gripped the chair-arms, the knuckles white. Marianne said to her:

'Would you like some water or something?'

'Please.' She gave a faint nod.

As Marianne slipped from the room Guy sat down on a chair. In his sightline, beyond Mrs Bennett's bowed head, John remained near the gate, now crouching at the edge of the herbaceous border. After a while he straightened and started across the forecourt towards the house. 'He's coming in,' Guy said.

'Please,' said Mrs Bennett, 'don't say anything yet.'

'I won't. I told you I won't.'

He waited, expecting at any moment that John would come into the room, but he did not. When the door opened some minutes later it was Marianne, bearing a tray with three cups and saucers.

'I made some tea,' she said. As she poured it she added, 'I gave John a glass of milk and a piece of cake and told him we're talking. He's gone into the back garden.' She handed the tea around. Guy set his cup and saucer on a small side table. Marianne took a chair near the window, not far from her mother. She took a sip from her cup then said to Guy:

'How did you know about John? How did you find out?'

'It was purely by chance,' he said. 'I had searched for the name Luke Holman in the registers – the birth and the death registers – and of course I couldn't find it. Later, something came into my mind. There was something about one of the other entries in the birth register for the second quarter of the year. I couldn't think what it was, but then suddenly it came to me. Each name entered in the register has beside it the district where the birth was registered. And I recalled that one of the births in the register I'd looked at rang a bell. It was because of the registration district, I realized. It was familiar to me.' He smoothed out the certificate on his knee and read:

'"Registration district: Warminster."' He looked up. 'Of course it rang a bell – though I didn't know why at the time. I should have. The same place is written on our marriage certificate. When I remembered it I went back and looked again. And then I saw that it was a *John* Holman who had been registered in that district. And I thought – well – *could* it *be* . . .? So I ordered a copy of the certificate. I picked it up today.' He gave a breathless, nervous little laugh. 'I could hardly believe it. I read it and – there it was.' With his finger he traced the words on the paper: '"When and where born: 8th of April 1982, Warminster Maternity Hospital; Name if any: John Guy; Sex: boy; Name, and surname of father: Guy Edward Holman; Name, surname, and maiden surname of mother: Sylvie Julia Holman formerly Bennett; Occupation of father: Teacher."' He looked at Mrs Bennett, then at Marianne. 'There he was – my son. I couldn't believe it. I can still hardly believe it.' There was a little silence, then he said, directing his words at Mrs Bennett:

'You and Sylvie – you hid from me the fact of his existence.'

She did not answer. Guy added:

'And just so that you could keep him here.'

Under his accusing glance Mrs Bennett set down her cup, in the process spilling tea into the saucer. 'Why did you have to come back?' she said. 'Why couldn't you have stayed away?'

He turned, looked at Marianne. Catching his eye she gave a groan and said:

'This has been a nightmare, I don't mind telling you. A nightmare – and going on for seven years. Well – it's time it was finished.'

'How did it start?' Guy said.

283

Marianne looked across at her mother for a moment as if waiting for her to speak, then said:

'When Sylvie came back from New York she was in a terrible state. Mother phoned me that evening to say that Sylvie had turned up and I came over here straightaway. Sylvie told me she'd left you, and that she couldn't go back. She'd worked herself up almost into a state of hysteria. She was always far more highly strung than I, but even so I'd never seen her like that before.' She paused. 'Of course, it wasn't long before you arrived and tried to persuade her to go back to New York with you.'

'Which she would have done,' Guy said, 'if she hadn't been persuaded otherwise.' He looked at Mrs Bennett as he spoke, but she ignored his words. He added:

'If we'd been left alone to get on with our lives we would have worked it all out. Particularly with Sylvie finding she was pregnant again.'

He pictured Sylvie as she had been that September day when he had come back to England to see her and they had walked in the orchard.

'I was aware of a difference in her as soon as I arrived,' he said, ' – both in her appearance and in her state of mind. She looked so well, but also there was a – a calm about her, a kind of – quiet happiness. And then of course I learned the reason for it.' Seeing Sylvie in the orchard, the tears of happiness in her eyes, hearing her little laugh as she had told him that she was pregnant, he said, 'It was marvellous. In that moment I really thought that everything was going to be all right. I loved her, and I was so sure that I could make her love me again.'

'Love,' Mrs Bennett said, raising her head. 'What do you know of love.'

Turning from the cold contempt in her eyes he said to Marianne:

284

'I did love her. *You* know that, don't you?'

'Yes,' she said. 'Sylvie knew it too.'

'Did she?' He wanted to hear it again, to know it. 'Did she?'

'Oh, yes.'

'It could have worked out,' he said sadly. 'A new baby – all that promise. It could have worked out.' He looked back at Mrs Bennett. 'But you persuaded her to stay and have the baby here.'

Marianne said quickly, 'I don't think she took much persuading, Guy, to be honest. She'd found a sort of – peace here; she was happier, and just beginning to get herself together, starting to come to terms with David's death. And of course New York was associated with the greatest unhappiness for her. It's not really so surprising that she decided to stay till the baby was born, is it?'

'I don't know,' he said. 'I only know I wanted her back with me.'

Mrs Bennett said: 'You wanted her, but you never cared what *she* wanted – what she needed. Living in that place, with you working for your degree every evening – are you surprised she was so unhappy?'

The fact that there was so much truth in her words did not make Guy feel any warmer towards the woman. 'You don't understand,' he said harshly.

'I understand that she was unhappy,' she said. 'That's what I understand. She was so unhappy that she couldn't bear to stay with you another minute.'

'Mother,' Marianne said, frowning, ' – please.'

'Well,' Mrs Bennett said, 'he comes here with that look of self-righteousness. You'd think he had nothing to do with it all, that he was always the one who was wronged.' She looked at Guy. 'And now you're going to sit in judgement of us, is that it?'

285

'I came here because of my son,' he said, adding: 'My son who I thought was dead – and who I thought was not even mine.' He paused. 'Didn't it matter to you how you impugned Sylvie's memory? Telling me that she'd had an adulterous affair with someone in New York? How could you do that, tell such lies about your own daughter? Is that an example of the love you felt for her?'

She said sharply: '*Our* relationship has nothing to do with you. I just wish she'd never met you, never married you. I knew it would be a disaster.'

'You mean you *wanted* it to be a disaster. Well, my God, you worked hard enough to ensure that it was.'

'I wanted the best for Sylvie, that's all I wanted,' she said.

'Keep telling yourself that,' Guy said contemptuously. 'You didn't want Sylvie to go to anyone. You wanted to keep her to yourself, always. And you managed to do it in the end. Even though it meant lying – telling me that my son died soon after his birth – and that he wasn't *my* son anyway.' He paused as a sudden thought came to him. 'Does he know anything about me? Is he aware that he has a father?'

Mrs Bennett did not answer.

'Is he?' he said.

Almost in a whisper, avoiding his eyes, she said, 'We never spoke about you.'

'But he must have asked questions. It's only natural that he'd want to know, that he'd be curious.'

'Yes – well, he was led to understand that you left before he was born.'

'Great,' he said bitterly, 'he must have very fond thoughts about his father.'

'I don't believe he ever thinks about it. He only rarely

286

mentions his father. He thinks no one knows where you are, or what happened to you.'

'It gets better.' Guy looked at her with undisguised hostility. 'Does he know *any*thing about his father? His name? His job?'

Mrs Bennett nodded. 'He knows your name. I don't know what else Sylvie might have told him. She'd want to avoid the subject.'

'I'm not surprised.'

He got up from the chair, stood there for a moment then turned and started across the room.

'Where are you going?' asked Mrs Bennett, sudden alarm flashing in her eyes.

'To see John. To see my son.' In the doorway he turned back and added, 'We'll go on with this later. I want to see him for a minute.'

Leaving the house he went down the rear garden path. He couldn't see John at first, but after a minute he found him kneeling over a patch of dry earth at the side of the vegetable garden. The terrier was with him and as Guy approached the dog ran to him, stopped before him and gave a couple of half-hearted yaps. The boy looked around. 'Come here,' he said to the dog. 'He's a friend, not a foe.' The dog gave another uncertain yap, then subsided and went off snuffling among the currant bushes. John smiled up at Guy. 'Hello,' he said. His hands were dusty with earth.

Guy nodded and smiled back. 'Hi.'

'I didn't know that was you indoors. Aunt Marianne said there was a visitor, but I didn't know it was you.' As he moved his head the sun glinted off his spectacles' lenses.

'What are you doing?' Guy asked.

'Oh – nothing much. Just digging.' The boy bent his

287

head and began hooking at the earth with a piece of wood. As Guy watched he saw something white revealed in the soil. John nodded. 'Still here all right.' He dug in with his fingers and lifted out a plastic shopping bag. From inside the bag he brought out a tin.

'You buried it?' Guy said.

'Yes.' The boy looked up at him for a second – an appraising glance – then said: 'For safety.' He pulled the lid off the tin and checked the contents. Another moment of silent appraisal then he held out the tin for Guy's inspection. Guy crouched and peered into the tin. 'This,' said the boy, pointing to a piece of stone, 'is a fossil. Of something.' Guy could make out a shape on the surface of the stone. 'I don't know what, though,' John said. He held up another piece – 'This is an arrowhead' – put it back, then gently picked up a small blue egg. 'A robin's egg.'

'How do you know it's a robin's egg?'

'I've got books. Besides, I watched them nesting. When the chicks had flown I climbed up and this egg was still there. I waited but the mother never came back. I suppose she knew it was no good. So after a while I took the egg.' He looked at Guy. 'It wouldn't have been any good, would it?'

'No, I wouldn't have thought so.'

'That's what I thought.' John put the egg back into the tin among the other bits and pieces.

'Why did you dig it up?' Guy asked.

'I've got a couple more things to put in it.' The boy took from beside his shoe two brightly coloured glass marbles. He held them up for Guy to see then laid them in the tin and pressed down the lid. After wrapping the tin in the plastic bag he put the package back in the hole.

288

'You're American, aren't you?' he said as he began to push the earth back into place.

'Yes, that's right.'

'I could tell.' When the soil was in place he smoothed it over with the piece of wood. 'My father was American,' he said, concentrating on his work.

' – Oh? Really?'

'Yes. I've never seen him, though.' He stood up and began to press down on the soil with his shoe. 'Where in America do you live?'

'New York.' Guy straightened beside him.

'I'd like to go there one day. I expect I shall, when I'm older. Is it a nice place?'

Guy smiled. 'It can be.'

A nod. 'Yes, I'd like to go there.'

'This is nice, though. Forham Green.'

'Oh, yes, it's fine. Have you ever been to Scotland?'

'No, I haven't.'

'Gramma's just been up to Scotland. I told you, didn't I? The other day. I'd like to have gone with her, but I had to go to school.'

'In Bath, yes? You stayed in Bath with your aunt and went to school there.'

'Yes. I went with Cressie, to her school, just for a week.'

'Did you like that?'

'Oh – it was okay. I've done it before. I prefer my own school, though.'

The boy removed his spectacles, took a slightly grubby handkerchief from his pocket and began to clean the lenses. 'Let me do it,' Guy said. He took the handkerchief and the spectacles. Laughing, he said, 'God knows how you manage to see anything through them! They're so smeared up.'

289

John laughed. Guy breathed on the lenses while the boy watched him. He looked so vulnerable without his spectacles, and the sight of the exposed false right eye made Guy's throat constrict. He could see now how like Sylvie he was. And like himself, too; he could see himself in the boy's face.

'There you go,' he said, handing over the newly cleaned spectacles. He watched as John put them on, hooking them over his ears. 'How's that?'

'Good. Much better, thanks.' John smiled up at him for a moment, then said, 'Hey – would you like to see the girls?'

'The girls? Who are they?'

'*Ah*, you don't know, do you? I'll show you.'

John turned and led the way on down the garden path till they came to a little uncultivated patch near the orchard gate. He pointed to a small chicken coop and run beside the hedge. 'There they are.'

'Ah, they're chickens.' Guy followed the boy to the run and they stood side by side looking at the hens that strutted and pecked inside. There were five of them, varying in size, shape and plumage. 'Are they yours?' asked Guy.

'Yes. Well, they were Mummy's and mine. We kept them together.' He pointed to one of them, a rather elegant-looking bird with a fluffy pompon and feathery leggings. 'That's Tracy. I got her on my birthday last year. Mummy said she looks like one of the Queen Mother's hats. She does, doesn't she?'

Guy grinned. 'If you say so.'

'Yes, she does.' John pointed to the others, one by one. 'That's Florence, that's Enid, that's Christine, and that's Pearl. We used to have lots more at one time, but the fox got them.'

'Oh, really?'

'Yes. The vixen used to come down from the hill – ' John gestured off, 'and get into the coop. She got them all gradually – Sally and Rennett, and Constance, and Mary and Martha, and Louisa and Doreen, and Cilla and Fergie and Lady Di, and the rooster, Cecil.' He turned, looked up at Guy. 'What's your name?'

The question took Guy by surprise, and he realized he could not answer truthfully. After a moment he said: 'I've got the same name as you – John.'

The boy grinned in delighted surprise. 'Have you really?' Then he added, 'But it's a common name, isn't it?'

'Fairly common, yes.'

John nodded, then turned back to the chicken coop. 'The fox didn't get all the chickens at the same time. Usually she just used to take one or two, though one time she killed four.' He gave a little sigh. 'Mummy said the fox treated it like a McDonald's take-away. She said every time the fox got peckish she'd pop in for a snack.' He laughed, the sound ringing out in the quiet afternoon. 'She was always peckish, that fox. And of course, being chickens they couldn't fight back. Though Martha put up a fight. She wasn't killed; she was injured. We nursed her, Mummy and I, but she died a couple of days later. Mummy told a man in the village about it and he said he'd shoot the fox, but Mummy told him no, he mustn't. She said the vixen was only doing what she had to do.' He tapped the top of the run. 'Course, this is all stronger now, and the fox can't get in any more.'

'That's good.'

'Yes. Gramma doesn't like them that much, I know, but she lets me keep them.'

'Do they lay eggs?'

291

'Oh, yes! Not every day, but often. Though some of the eggs are quite small – smaller than those you get from the supermarket. Come with me.' He reached out for Guy's hand, but his small fingers caught only Guy's thumb, and in this way Guy let himself be led round to the back of the coop. There John released him, loosed a hook fastening in the side and lifted a flap, revealing a row of nesting boxes. One of the boxes had a single egg lying in the straw. He reached in and drew it out.

'It's still warm. Here.'

He put the egg gently into Guy's palm.

'It is small, isn't it?' Guy said.

'Yes, but they taste good. Very good. We sometimes have them for breakfast. Course, it depends on which hen the egg is from.'

'Is there a difference?'

'Oh, yes. We used to think so, anyway. I liked them best from Tracy and Martha.' He bent, peering at the egg in Guy's hand. 'That one's very small. I should think that's from Pearl or Florence. You can't always tell.' He raised his head, looking into Guy's face. 'The best eggs of all came from Cecil.'

Guy started to say, 'But I thought – ' then stopped, realizing that he was being kidded. John gave a little hoot and said, 'I almost caught you there, didn't I?' He laughed. 'I was joking.' He carefully lowered the wooden flap, secured the hook in place. 'If I get another one I shall call her Samantha. There's a girl in my class called Samantha.'

'Is she your girl friend?'

John gave him a withering look, then smiled. 'Of course not. But it's a nice name.' He was still for a moment, then he said: 'My mother's name was Sylvie. That's a nice name, isn't it?'

292

'It's a very nice name.' Guy saw the smile that was only just there.

'She died. Did you know that?'

' – Yes.'

'She died last year.' A pause. 'I'm getting used to it now.'

'Are you?'

'Well – I try to. You do – after a while.'

' – Do you think about her much?'

'Oh, yes, a lot. But I won't, as time passes. So Gramma said. She told me that it will get better. "Everything passes," she says. Does it?'

' – Yes,' Guy said, standing there with the smooth, warm egg in his hand, looking down into the earnest face of his son. 'Yes, it must do.'

'That's what Gramma said.'

They stood in silence while the chickens clucked and scratched in the straw and the wood pigeons cooed in the trees. Guy said, holding out the egg, 'Will you have this for breakfast?'

John turned, coming out of a brief reverie. 'It's for *you* – for *your* breakfast.'

'Oh.'

'Don't you want it?'

'Oh – yes! Yes, I do. Thank you very much.'

'You could have it boiled, or scrambled. Scrambled is nice. We'll get something to wrap it in so it won't break.' He turned, began to move away. 'Stay here.'

Guy watched him as he ran up the path towards the house. After a few minutes he was back carrying a half-sheet of newspaper and a brown paper bag. 'Aunt Marianne says my tea's ready. I shall have to go in in a minute.' He took the egg from Guy, wrapped it carefully in the newspaper and put it into the bag. 'This will be all

293

right if you're careful.' He handed the bag to Guy. 'Don't break it, will you? – or you won't have an egg for breakfast in the morning.'

'I won't break it.'

Over the boy's head Guy saw Marianne standing some yards away on the path. John followed his eyes and nodded. 'Oh, here's Aunt Marianne. I'd better go indoors and have my tea. I'll see you later – John.' He laughed on the last word.

'Yes – see you later, John.'

The boy ran past Marianne and headed back up the path to the house. Marianne came towards Guy, stopped a few feet away. 'He's a great little fellow, isn't he?' she said.

'Yes.'

'I noticed he called you John . . .'

Guy shrugged. 'He asked me my name. I had to think of something.'

She nodded. 'You didn't say anything about any of this.' Half statement, half question.

'No, of course not.' He added: 'Not yet.' There was a little silence and he went on:

'When we met and talked the other day in Bath he told me how he lost his eye.'

She gave a little shudder. 'That was terrible. Really terrible. Sylvie was in an awful state.'

Silence fell between them. Into the quiet came the sound of the chickens as they clucked and scratched in the straw.

Marianne sighed. 'I wish it could all be undone, but it can't.'

Guy said nothing.

'Do you hate us?' she said.

'No. I don't know what I feel. The only thing I know is that I'm just so happy – to find him.'

'I'm sure.'

'To be thinking all these years that my son had died – and now to find out he's alive. I can't tell you what it feels like.' He paused. 'But then I start thinking how I've been denied this knowledge till now. I might never have known.'

'Guy – I'm so sorry.'

'Whose idea was it? Your mother's?'

She didn't answer.

'Well,' he said, 'I should think it would have to come from her.'

'Ah,' she said quickly, 'but you don't understand.'

'No, I don't.' He paused. 'How did it happen?'

She sighed. 'I told you what a state Sylvie was in when she came back from New York that time. And she was. But gradually she began to pick up a little, and then, of course, she discovered she was pregnant. Well, you can imagine what that did for her – after losing David . . .'

Guy winced as memory came rushing in – and *thwuck* goes the head of the club, followed by a little squeak from David as he falls into the sand.

'It was the most wonderful thing for her,' Marianne said. 'And whatever her intentions might have been I think that once she found she was pregnant she became more and more reluctant to return to New York. Having found some kind of – peace here. Not feeling threatened here. This place had only good, positive associations – whereas New York only held bad memories for her. So when Mother suggested that she stay on longer, till the new baby was born, I think she grasped at the idea. Then, of course, once John was born she had to face up to the situation again. And she dreaded it – leaving here and

295

taking her new baby and going back to the life she'd left. I think she feared that something could happen to John as it had happened to David. She just couldn't get it out of her mind. It didn't matter how much one told her that what happened to David had been just a freak accident. She'd agree, on the surface, but you couldn't really convince her – underneath. Yet at the same time she didn't really see how she could avoid it – going back to New York, I mean. And she dreaded it.' She paused. 'Don't think too badly of her.'

'I don't know what to think.' He shook his head. 'One part of me tells me I should hate her, for taking my son away from me, but – '

'No, please,' Marianne said. 'Don't hate her.'

'I don't. I can't.'

'And of course you were right – it was so much my mother's doing. But I think where she was concerned – well – she'd lost Sylvie once, and now Sylvie was back, and she didn't want to lose her again. Added to which, of course, she was so glad, so happy about the baby. Having lost her own son I think she almost saw John as partly her own.' She breathed a deep sigh. 'I don't know when it was decided. I didn't know about it till it was done. Eventually it came out, of course, and I learned that you'd been told that the baby had died soon after his birth. I couldn't believe it. I couldn't believe they could do such a thing.'

'Couldn't you have done anything?'

'I tried. I talked to Sylvie and tried to make her see what she had done, and gradually it came to her, and she said she would talk to you, or write to you, and explain, and try to put it right. But she was afraid. How could she admit it? – something like that? So she kept putting it off, and then in the end it was too late. Too much time had gone by. And I think she just – tried to put it out of her mind. No one else knew about it. Just the three of us. Not even my husband. It was a terrible weight on my mind. I hated having to keep such a secret. On various occasions I tried to persuade her to get in touch with you, and tell you. She always said she would, but she never did. In the end the very mention of it got her so upset. It took its toll of her, though. Oh – she so dreaded the thought of your finding out.'

'That's why she would never see me here in Forham Green,' Guy said. 'On those occasions when I came to England she'd only agree to meet me in London.'

'Yes, I knew about that. Of course, the thing that kept her going was John. He was growing up in the country, and safe. She loved him so much. And although she was tormented by her deception of you she was so happy in having him.'

With Marianne's words Guy remembered that he had seen that happiness in Sylvie's face. Once when they had met in London. He had thought that perhaps she had a lover. But it was not the happiness that came from having a lover; it was her happiness in her son.

'Once,' said Sylvie, 'when John was about four, I think she'd really made up her mind to tell you about it. It was very difficult for her but she'd finally made up her mind that she couldn't continue with it. But then John had his accident and lost his eye. That stopped her. I think from then on she wouldn't allow herself to think about it. Certainly she refused to discuss it with me any more. So – the whole pretence went on.'

'Whose was the grave I was taken to see?' Guy asked. 'The baby named Luke. There's no surname on his stone.'

'He was a baby born to a couple from Australia who were staying in the village. I heard afterwards that they

297

went back to Australia and were killed not long afterwards in a fire.'

So that accounted for the grave remaining untended. Guy thought of how he had wept at the graveside, and how anxious Sylvie had seemed to get away. Now he knew why. She hadn't wanted anyone to see her laying flowers on the grave, mourning a stranger's child.

'I don't know when she got the idea to pretend it was her own child's grave,' she said, 'or whether it came from her or from Mother. I suppose one of them saw it there, and realized that the dates were so close . . .'

He stood in silence for a moment, thinking about the deceit, then he said:

'You could have told me earlier. Sylvie's dead. She couldn't be hurt by my finding out the truth.'

'I couldn't. So much of it was my mother's doing, and as much as I disapproved of what she had done I couldn't expose her. And I thought – well, John *is happy* as he is – he really is – and you would be returning to America any day. I suppose I – I just decided to let it all alone.' She shrugged. 'And I suppose in doing so I'm as guilty as my mother and Sylvie.' She looked at him for long seconds. 'What are you going to do?'

He sighed. 'I don't know. It'll take a while for all this to sink in. And I'm not sure what I should do for the best. I know one thing, though: I want him. He's my son and I want him with me.'

'Of course.'

'Though I suppose,' he said, 'that your mother will argue that this is the only life he's ever known. That this is his home.'

She lowered her glance. 'He does have a good life here. He's a very happy little boy.'

'Yes, I can see that.'

298

'And Mother – she's been a good mother to him since Sylvie died – whatever else she's done.'

'I don't doubt it. But he's *my son*. He's all I've got in the world. I want him with me. He belongs with me. All right, so he's happy here – but he could be happy with me, too. I could make a good life for him. He'd adjust and settle down.'

'I'm sure he would – in time.'

'Besides – your mother's getting old. She's not going to live for ever. What was to happen to him when she died?'

'We thought – he'd come and live with us – me and the children.'

'Great. And all the time his father is alive, and not knowing. And there's another thing – do you think you could keep a secret like that for ever? When he grows up he'll ask more questions. About his father for a start. What did you plan to tell him when he started to ask for chapter and verse? Or hadn't you thought that far ahead?'

She gave no answer. After a moment he said, turning, looking off towards the house, 'I must go in and see your mother.'

She stood aside. He went past her and up the path to the house. In the front sitting room he found Mrs Bennett still sitting in her chair. She did not look up as he stopped before her. He still held the bag containing the egg.

'Where's John?' he asked.

'Up in his room.'

'I know all about everything now,' he said. 'Marianne's told me everything.' He paused, looking at her with contempt. 'How could you have done it?'

She did not answer; just studied her hands in her lap.

'I know one thing,' he said, ' – Sylvie would never have done it if it weren't for you. Did you get some pleasure

299

from it, knowing how you were depriving me? Cheating me?'

'No,' she said, and her voice had lost its arrogance. 'That was never a part of it. I had no feeling for you, but that was never a part of it.'

He stood looking down at her. Her former spiritedness seemed to have gone. Now she merely appeared pathetic. After a while he said:

'Why didn't anyone tell me that Sylvie was so sick – that she was dying?'

She did not answer.

'When she was sick,' he said, 'did she – did she speak of me at all?'

Now she spoke. 'Why should she?' she said. 'She'd managed perfectly well without you for years.' Anger rose in her voice. 'Why should any of us ever give a thought to you? You only ever thought about yourself.' Her eyes were blazing. He had thought that the fight had gone out of her; he had been wrong.

She got up from her chair and stood before him. 'And now, I suppose you've come to tell me that you're going to take John away. Is that it? You're going to uproot him from all he's ever known and loved. You're going to do to him what you did to my daughter.' Her lip curled while tears sprang to her eyes and rolled down her cheeks. 'Have you no thought of anyone but yourself and what makes *you* happy?' She took a step towards him. 'Is that what you're going to do? Take him away?' She gazed at him, her mouth opening in a cry of anguish. 'You bastard!' she cried, and came forward, striking out at him. He stepped back, raising his hands to ward off her blows. As he did so one of her own flailing hands struck the paper bag and knocked it from his grasp.

Her attack ended as suddenly as it had begun. He

300

crouched and picked up the bag. He could feel through the paper that the egg was broken. He thought again of how John had put the egg into his hand – 'It's still warm'; he could have wept.

He straightened, breathing heavily. As he stood there he thought of John digging up his secret treasure tin from the earth; thought of him standing beside the chicken coop. And through the pain in his heart he realized that John was happy. He was happy. Such a conclusion was inescapable.

He turned and looked at Mrs Bennett. She was standing glaring at him, the tears of anger and frustration glistening on her cheeks. As he took a breath to speak she said:

'So, take him away. Take him away from everything he's known. It doesn't matter to you that he'll be living with a stranger, in a strange country.' She paused and added: 'You've already killed one son, and wrecked the life of your wife; why should it matter what else you do.'

He stared at her, his mouth still open for the delivery of unspoken words. Then, turning from her hatred, he moved towards the door. Marianne stood in the doorway. How long she had been there he did not know. Gazing apprehensively into his face she stepped aside. In the doorway he turned and looked back at Mrs Bennett.

'I'll be back for him tomorrow,' he said through gritted teeth. 'I'll call you and let you know when I'll be arriving. Have his things ready.'

Without looking back again he strode into the hall, opened the front door and went from the house.

On the way to the bus stop he dropped the dripping paper bag into a waste bin.

23

At Trowbridge Station Guy checked on the time of the next train to Bath for his connection to Paddington, then hurried to a phone box and dialled Annie's number. She answered at once.

'Well, nice to hear from you,' she said coolly.

'Annie, forgive me,' he said. 'I'm terribly sorry for running out on you like that. But I had no choice.'

'No choice?'

'No. I – I'll explain when I see you.'

'Where are you?' she said. 'I've been sitting here waiting for you to phone.'

'I'm at Trowbridge Station.'

'Trowbridge?' She groaned, then added, 'Well, I hope you're not still thinking of going to the theatre.'

'No, I'd never get back in time. I'm sorry about that too.'

'I'm sure you are.'

'No, listen – I'll tell you everything when I see you. But I had to come down here and see Mrs Bennett.'

'Oh, Guy . . .' There was weariness and resignation in her voice.

'No, truly,' he said. 'And I have some wonderful news. Something incredible's happened.'

'Really?' She was silent for a moment. 'What is it? What's happened?'

'I can't tell you now; my train's due to leave in a few minutes. I'll call you when I get back to the hotel.'

'You mean that?'

'Yes, of course.'

'Okay, I'll see you then.' She paused. 'I can't wait to hear your news.' A little laugh. 'And after running away from me like that it had better be good.'

'It is,' he said. 'Believe me, it is.'

On the train as the miles sped by he sat thinking more and more of his confrontation with Mrs Bennett. And, calmer now, he began to regret his outburst in which he had told her that tomorrow he would come and take John away with him.

He had said it for the simple reason that she had hurt him. *You've already killed one son, and wrecked the life of your wife* . . . She had known exactly *how* to hurt him, and so, striking back, he had used the only weapon to hand – John.

He knew in reality, though, that he could not possibly do as he had said he would – take John away so soon. For a start, what could he do with the boy? Where would John sleep? On some cot in the hotel room? And what would they do for food? – go out to cafés for every single bite? And, having brought John back to the hotel, how long would it have to be for? He, Guy, certainly couldn't take him at once to New York. There would have to be documentation processed. There were legal formalities that would have to be gone through. Such procedures might take a very long time, and he couldn't keep him at the hotel indefinitely. And besides, how could he just uproot the child from one country and transplant him in another. And any attempt to do so would brand him as irresponsible in the eyes of the authorities – which was what he must avoid at all costs.

Most important of all, though – what would be the effect on John himself? What might it do to a small,

303

vulnerable child of seven – to take him from a secure, happy environment and subject him to a period of the greatest insecurity, removed from everything and everyone he knew, surrounded only by strangeness and strangers?

Guy knew that he would never attempt such a thing. He would go back to Forham Green, yes, but not to take John away. Not yet, anyway. No – he and Mrs Bennett would have to sit down and talk the whole thing over. He wanted John with him – he was never in any doubt about that – but in whatever action he took John himself must be the prime consideration. The boy would go through enough upheaval as it was when the time came, so every possible effort must be made to keep that upheaval to a minimum . . .

By the time the train pulled into Paddington he had made up his mind what to do.

As he emerged from the platform he was surprised to find Annie standing waiting for him.

She came towards him; kissed him.

'What are you doing here?' he asked.

She nodded. 'That's a nice greeting. Whatever happened to: "What a nice surprise"?' She smiled. 'But I should have thought it was obvious, anyway. I'm meeting you. Aren't you pleased?'

Uncertainly he smiled back. 'Yes, of course. I just wasn't expecting to see you here, that's all.'

'Well,' she said, 'I decided I couldn't wait till you got back to your hotel and phoned me. So I found out the times of the trains and worked out which one you'd be on. Wasn't that enterprising?'

'Very enterprising.'

She linked an arm through his. 'I've got the car outside.

Would you like to come back to Hammersmith? Then you can tell me all this wonderful news.'

He hesitated in his step, feeling strangely disorientated. 'Listen – would you mind if I don't come back tonight?'

'Oh – okay.' She released his arm, gave a little smile. 'I just thought you'd like to, that's all.'

'Please – don't misunderstand me. It's just that I – I think I need to be on my own tonight. I've got some telephone calls to make and – '

'It's all right. Whatever you want.'

They stood there with the other pedestrians milling about them. 'Well,' Annie said, 'what happens now . . .?'

For the moment Guy wanted only to get back to his hotel. But that would have to wait for a while. 'Let's go and get a drink somewhere,' he suggested.

'Okay.'

In the station pub Annie commandeered a vacant table while Guy brought beers from the bar. He set them on the table and sat down. After looking at Annie in silence for a moment he said:

'Annie, I found my son.'

And with his words the wonder of it came over him again, almost overwhelming him.

Annie looked at him wide-eyed. 'What . . .?'

Struggling for control of his emotions he took a deep breath and said, 'My younger son – he's *alive*. He didn't die when he was a baby as I thought. He's alive. I've met him, and talked to him. And, Annie – he's mine. *Mine*. Not some other man's child. And – oh, Annie – ' and here the tears shone in his eyes, 'he's the greatest little fellow you could meet.'

Shaking her head she said, 'I don't understand what you're saying. Tell me.'

After a little hesitation he began to tell her about his

305

discovery, starting with the entries in the registers, and the obtaining of the copy of John's birth certificate. 'Here,' he said, ' – look.' He took the certificate from his pocket, unfolded it and laid it before her on the table. He watched her face as she studied it.

'His name is John,' she said, ' – not Luke.'

'Yes. His name is John.'

She handed the certificate back to him. 'Well, I can't say I'm that surprised now at your dashing off the way you did.' She laid a hand over his, pressed his fingers. 'Oh, Guy, it's wonderful news. I'm so happy for you! What a marvellous, marvellous thing.'

'Yes.' He looked again at the words on the certificate – he could never read them enough.

'So,' Annie said, 'what happened when you went to Forham Green? Tell me about it.'

He folded the certificate, put it back in his pocket, then told of his meeting with Marianne and Mrs Bennett, of what he had learned. He told also of his meeting with John in the garden. 'But at the end I screwed it up,' he said.

'What do you mean, you screwed it up?'

'In a fit of anger I told Mrs Bennett that I'm going back there tomorrow to take John away – to take him back to the States with me.'

'But – you couldn't do it just like that, could you?'

'No, of course not.' He shook his head. 'And I wouldn't want to. But – ' he sighed with dismay, 'she stung me; she got me where it really hurt. Something she said and . . . Well, I guess I just wanted to get back at her. So – I said that I'd be returning tomorrow to take John away. Oh, God,' he shook his head, 'it was really dumb. I can't stop thinking about it.'

They sat unaware of the clamour of the voices around

them, the thudding bass from the juke box. Annie said after a moment:

'What are you going to do?'

'I'm not sure.' He shrugged. 'I only know I've got to try to do it properly – do it the right way. And for a start I realize that it can't be hurried. It'll take time, I know that. And John's got to be considered above everything and everyone else. I've got to make sure that he doesn't suffer; I've got to be sure that he's going to be happy.'

Absently he drank from his beer glass. 'For a start we've got to get to know each other. That's so important. I want him to like me. He's got to like me.' He sighed. 'This is so important and I've got to do it right. It's as if I've been given a second chance for happiness. I know that sounds dumb, but I mean it. I mustn't screw it up again. I've got to think it out carefully. We must spend time with each other. Here *and* in the States. But here first. Later, when he's at ease with me he can come out for a vacation. I've been thinking about it on the train. And at some time he's got to know who I am, that I'm his father. But only when the time is right. Not at once, maybe, but later . . .' He nodded. 'If I do it properly it'll be okay, I know it will.'

'Of course,' Annie said.

'Yes. And I'll give him a good life. But I won't try to cut him off from his grandmother. He loves her. And she loves him – and even after what she did to me I have to admit that she's done a good job in helping to bring him up. I have to hand her that. He's such a bright, spunky little guy. He's a son any father would be proud of.'

They sat in silence for a moment, then Annie said:

'So – what's your next move going to be?'

'I've been thinking about that. I'll have to telephone Mrs Bennett – this evening or in the morning – and tell

307

her that I was hasty, too hasty – that I didn't mean what I said. We'll make arrangements to meet, to talk about the best way to proceed, for all our sakes. I've got to consider her feelings as well in this. I can't forgive her for what she did to me – but I don't want to hurt her more than she's going to be hurt already. Because in the end there's no doubt that she's the one who's going to suffer. I don't want to make it worse for her than I have to. I'll tell her that she can still see him, that he can come and visit her. She won't lose him altogether. But I want him to be with me, to live with me. And she'll have to accept that.'

'What if she doesn't?' Annie asked.

'She doesn't have any choice. He's *my* son, and she kept him from me by deception. Listen, I don't think she'd want to get up in a court of law and admit to what she did.'

'So when d'you think you'll go and see her?'

'As soon as I can. Tomorrow or – ' He came to a halt. 'Oh, God, Annie – I forgot. Our trip to Milan.'

She gave a little smile, shrugged.

'You've been looking forward to it, haven't you?' he said.

'Very much.'

'And you got the airplane tickets . . .'

'This morning, yes.' She opened her purse, took out the tickets and dropped them onto the table. Turning her head, she said into the air in a mock announcement: 'Anybody like a couple of tickets to Milan?' Turning back to Guy she pressed his hand. 'It doesn't matter, believe me. If you want to go and see about your son, then that's what you must do.'

He glanced briefly at the tickets. 'Milan. That's where Leonardo's fresco of his "Last Supper" is, am I right?'

'In the church of *Santa Maria Delle Grazie*. I've always

308

wanted to see it. Still, it's lasted nearly five hundred years, so I'm sure it'll last a while longer.'

He smiled at her, steeped in guilt. After a moment he said: 'I don't have to go and see Mrs Bennett tomorrow.'

'Well – that's up to you,' Annie said.

'What time is the flight?'

She looked at the tickets. '18.45 from Heathrow. It would get us in just before nine o'clock.'

'And what about a hotel?'

'I picked up a list of hotels this morning from the Italian Tourist Board. I thought we'd just phone a few of them. We'd easily find something.'

'Okay.' He nodded. 'We'll go as we planned.'

'Guy, are you sure?'

'I'm positive. I'll call Mrs Bennett when I get back to the hotel. At least she'll be relieved to know that I'm not going to rush in and snatch John away. When did you think we'd come back? Sunday?'

'Yes. I've got to get back to school.'

'Well, if we come back on Sunday I could go to Forham Green the next day. It won't make any difference. In fact it might be better like that. She'll have a couple of days to think things over, to get used to the idea of it all. Then, on Monday she and I can meet – and also I'll have a chance to spend a little more time with John.' He smiled at her. 'We'll have our trip after all.'

'Oh – terrific.'

'Yes, and we'll have a good time.' He leaned across the table and kissed her on the mouth. 'And I can relax, too. It's all coming right for me, at last.'

'Hello?' Annie said. ' – Mr Rawlinson?' She was telephoning from a call box at Paddington Station. She had just

309

watched the American walk away towards the Underground.

'Yes,' Rawlinson said impatiently. 'Who is this? Milburn?'

She heard the disdain in his voice and pictured his pink, pursed mouth. 'Yes, sir.'

'Well?'

'It was difficult, but we'll be there. I'll have him there.'

'Good. Will you travel straight to Milan?'

'Yes, we're flying from Heathrow tomorrow evening. He's going to meet me there.'

'You're sure of that? Can you depend on him? Wouldn't you have done better to stick with him from now on?'

'It's not possible. There's some domestic problem he's involved with. But don't worry. We've got round that. I'll have him in the piazza dei Fiori at the required time.'

'You'd better. You sound remarkably sanguine – in spite of the fact that the man's a law unto himself. Have you made the flight reservations?'

'Oh, yes, I bought the plane tickets two weeks ago.'

'Fine,' he said grudgingly. 'Well – keep me informed.'

'I will.'

'And Milburn . . .?'

'Yes, sir?'

'Watch your back.'

Riding back to Bayswater on the tube, Guy thought over what he would say to Mrs Bennett. As soon as he was in his hotel room he tried to call her. There was no answer.

As he sat beside the telephone he realized he was hungry; he had not eaten in hours. Putting his coat back on he hurried from the hotel and made his way to a café where he ordered a steak, French fries and salad. As soon

310

as he had eaten he hurried back to the hotel. He could not rest until he had talked to Mrs Bennett.

Still no answer to his ringing.

Sitting on the bed he thought once more of his visit to The Willows that day. How could Sylvie have done to him what she had done? 'Don't think too badly of her, Guy,' Marianne had said. Easy to say. Sylvie – she had stolen from him his surviving son. He could see her again now as she led him to the little grave of Luke and went through the charade of placing flowers upon it. He saw himself standing at the graveside, shedding tears over a stranger's child. And all the time his own son had been alive and well. What did it matter if she had carried out her actions with regret? She had nonetheless gone ahead with them. And where he himself was concerned she had carried her secret with her to her grave. Had he not found the truth through the birth register he would never have known.

He felt overwhelmed with a sudden wave of bitterness towards her. He had been responsible for the death of Davie – he could never escape that knowledge – but it had been an accident. What Sylvie had done she had done wilfully, calculatingly. After Davie's death there had only been Sylvie in his life. But she had gone away. Then, when John was born she, through deception, had taken him too. And in doing so she had deprived Guy of all that he had left. Then, to keep him from suspecting the truth she had kept him at arm's length for the rest of her life.

'I can never forgive you for what you've done, Sylvie,' he muttered into the still room.

Growing increasingly tense with the passing time, he called the number of The Willows every fifteen minutes. It was after midnight when he gave up.

311

24

After an almost sleepless night Guy was already awake when his wake-up call came at seven-thirty the next morning. As he smoked a cigarette and drank the coffee that was brought to his room he tried calling Mrs Bennett again. Still no answer. He tried again ten minutes later with the same result. By the time he had showered and dressed it was eight-twenty-five. Without hope of success he tried the Forham Green number again. As before he heard the ringing tone go unanswered.

His decision was made. He put on his jacket and picked up his raincoat. As he reached the door he was brought to a halt by the thought of the trip to Milan. He hesitated. That would be all right, though; if necessary he could travel to the airport from Trowbridge. Moving to his case he unlocked it and took out his passport.

With the usual change at Bath, the nine-fifty from Paddington got him to Trowbridge just on noon. Finding no taxi immediately available he went to the bus stop and found a bus about to leave. Thirty-five minutes later he was standing at the front door of The Willows, ringing the bell.

There was no answer. He rang again. Still no answer. And no barking of the dog either. After a minute he walked round to the rear of the house. There were no signs of life in evidence and he got no response to his rap on the back door. He tried the door. Locked. After standing there for a few moments he moved to a little seat at the side of the yard and sat down to wait. Where could

312

they be? There was fear in his mind, a fear that he had refused to face but which had been growing ever since last night when he had got no answer to his repeated attempts to call Mrs Bennett. Now that fear was like a lead weight.

Twenty-five minutes and two cigarettes later he got up and walked back round to the front again. Glancing over to the garage he saw that its door was closed. He went over to it and, finding it unlocked, swung the door up. To his surprise he saw that Mrs Bennett's blue Ford was inside. Where could she have gone without a car? Had Marianne taken her and John to Bath?

He closed the garage door and stood there wondering what to do. After a moment or two he was striding off across the forecourt and out onto the road.

As he approached the centre of the village he saw a telephone kiosk ahead of him. He went inside, consulted his address book and dialled Marianne's number. No answer. But of course, she would be at school, teaching. He let it ring for a while then replaced the receiver.

Returning to The Willows he moved around the house, going from window to window, peering in. As far as he could see everything looked as usual. Going back to the bench he smoked another cigarette, sitting there while the minutes passed and his fears grew. Without hope he got up and tried the handle of the back door again, then he moved to the rear windows to see whether one might allow him entry. They all appeared to be locked.

He did not know what to do. Dismissing the notion that Mrs Bennett was in the house all the time and was refusing to answer the telephone or the door bell he moved around the side of the house again. And suddenly he came to a stop. There was a key. Or there *had been* a key. He remembered clearly an occasion when he and Sylvie had been returning to the house and she found she had

313

forgotten her front-door key. When a ringing at the door had got no response she had immediately gone to the shed in the back yard and come back with a key to the rear door. It was always kept there, she had remarked, and had been since they were small children.

Turning abruptly, Guy went into the back yard and walked the short distance down the garden path to the little potting shed. The door was unlocked and he went in, and in the gloom stood and looked around him at the rows of gardening tools, boxes and tins. A search along the shelves and in the drawers of a small, ramshackle table revealed nothing. Then, raising his eyes, he saw the low beams that crossed above his head. He reached up, his fingers feeling the dust that had long gathered there undisturbed. Another two or three seconds and his searching fingers felt the shape of a key. In moments he was back at the rear door of the house and turning the key in the lock.

On the kitchen table he found two used breakfast mugs – one of them bearing a picture of Winnie the Pooh – and plates and dishes bearing the remains of cereal and a half-eaten slice of toast. Moving on, he looked into the other downstairs rooms then moved to the foot of the stairs. He stood there for a moment, his hand on the newel post, then started up. Upstairs, the first room he entered was at the back: John's room. He stood in the centre of the room and looked around him. There were shelves of books; old picture books from the boy's earlier childhood, and more recent ones – books on nature, and birds, and animals, and locomotives. Some of the shelf space was taken up with little metal models of cars. The single bed was unmade, the pillow flattened and the cover thrown back just as the boy might have got out of it. A worn teddy bear lay at the side of the bed against the wall.

Returning to the landing, Guy stopped at the next door. Sylvie's room. Pushing open the door he went in. It was just as he remembered it from those few occasions when they had slept here, after their marriage. On shelves stood Sylvie's books and a few pieces of china and porcelain she had collected over the years. On the walls hung the prints she had loved. All things she had chosen to leave behind in England rather than take to America with her. Backing out of the room, he closed the door, softly – as if fearful of waking ghosts – and moved along the landing towards the front of the house.

In the bedroom that was Mrs Bennett's he found her bed unmade, and on it various folded clothes – a couple of skirts and some underwear. The top drawer in the chest of drawers was open, exposing its contents of neatly folded blouses and sweaters. Back out on the landing he noticed that a cupboard door was ajar. It was an airing cupboard, its shelves laden with sheets and clothing, some of the latter having been replaced untidily. He took down one of the items and found it to be one of John's shirts. He held it in his hands for a moment then carefully folded it and replaced it on the pile.

As he closed the cupboard door he was only too aware of the significance of it all. It only confirmed his fears. Mrs Bennett had taken John and gone away.

With a groan of anguish he leaned back against the airing cupboard door, his hands hanging helplessly at his sides. Why had she done it? Though the answer was clear: she was trying to prevent him from taking John away. But it was madness. She must know that she couldn't avoid him for ever. Eventually she would have to give John up. In the meantime she was only making the situation worse.

And where had she gone? To Marianne's? Was she

315

sitting there now in Marianne's house ignoring the telephone when it rang? No, she would realize that that would be the first place he would look. Then where? He realized only too well that he didn't know enough about her to have any idea where to start looking.

He stood there wondering what to do next. After a minute or two he set to work.

He proceeded methodically, starting in Mrs Bennett's bedroom. Beginning to the right of the door he worked his way around the room, searching for any clue that would give some idea as to her whereabouts. He took down the dozen or so books – romances and biographies – wedged between bookends on a small bureau, and riffled through their pages. He looked through the drawer and cupboard of the bureau itself, and found them to contain only sewing tools and materials. He looked into her wardrobe and in each drawer of her chest of drawers. He looked in the drawers of the two small bedside cabinets, feeling a momentary flush of guilt as he briefly shuffled through her patent medicines and bottles of pills. No part of his search revealed anything of the least interest.

The unused bedroom immediately next door also revealed nothing. He did not search either John's or Sylvie's rooms, but merely stood in their doorways for a moment before turning away. He wouldn't bother yet with the bathroom.

Downstairs he went first into the room which Mrs Bennett used as a study. Facing over the forecourt, it was a small room with bookshelves and, over by the window, a desk with blotter, pens and pencils, and little stacks of papers – each stack held in place by a paperweight. The desk seemed the obvious place to begin and he set to work at once, first going methodically through the papers

316

on the desk. Two of the piles consisted of nothing but receipts. A third were recipes, scribbled down in pencil and waiting to be transferred to the notebook on which they lay. A fourth consisted of several birthday cards, all inscribed to her. She had obviously had a birthday recently. There was a card from Marianne and her children; another from John; one from some women's group in the village, and another whose signature Guy could just make out as *Alberto*. After a moment he recalled that Alberto was her Italian friend who bred the terriers. He put the cards back and picked up the fifth stack of papers. Bills and more receipts.

He turned then to the little pad beside the telephone. On the top was written 'Pale primrose for walls? Poss buttermilk? White woodwork?' He put the pad back and looked at the blotter (and how many people kept blotters on their desks today? he wondered) and saw that she was not a doodler (too controlled?); the blotting paper only bore the undecipherable, mirrored blottings of her penned writings. The only remaining item on the desk was a diary. He opened it but was disappointed to find that she only used it for noting down appointments: 'Dentist 3.15.' 'Plumber 10.00.' He closed it and turned his attention to the drawers below.

The top drawer on the left held pencils, erasers, pins and other odd stationery accessories; she was so neat: a place for everything and everything in its place. The second drawer held stationery, writing paper and envelopes, a packet of carbon paper, a paper bag containing half-a-dozen birthday cards and a box half-full of Christmas cards. In the bottom, last, drawer he saw two brown, leather-bound volumes. He drew them out. They were photograph albums. One of them contained photographs of an older time, with some of the photos in sepia

317

– men and women in late-Victorian, Edwardian, and First World War dress. Many of the men were in uniform, nearly all solemn-looking, stiffly posed and gazing out at the camera. He closed the album and put it on the desk.

The other album held more recent pictures. There was Sylvie's father as a good-looking young man who bore a strong resemblance to Sylvie; there was Sylvie's mother and father on their wedding day, Sylvie's father standing tall and proud and Mrs Bennett very pretty in her late-forties wedding dress. Guy had never imagined her as a young woman. There were numerous other photographs: Marianne, Sylvie and their brother Jonathan as small children; pictures of Marianne and Sylvie growing up, showing them in their teens and early twenties. There were later studies: Marianne with her husband on their wedding day; Marianne with her husband on the lawn of their house in Bath; Marianne and two of her children in the garden of The Willows; Sylvie on her wedding day, standing in her white dress at the gate of The Willows; Sylvie and himself, Guy, on the steps of the church. The last photograph in the book was of Sylvie and John standing beside the chicken coop in the back garden. And in it Sylvie, smiling gravely, looks out at the photographer, while beside her John stands with his head thrown back, his mouth open in laughter, the sunlight shining on the lenses of his spectacles.

Guy looked down at the picture for long moments and then closed the book.

As he bent to put the albums back in the drawer he saw towards the back, in the shadows, a little pile of envelopes. He drew them out. They were letters, in their envelopes. He looked at the top one. An air mail envelope, addressed to Mrs Bennett in Sylvie's round hand. Sylvie had written it from New York, and, going by the

318

post-marked date, a couple of months after Davie's death. Was it full of the outpourings of her heart? Expressions of her unhappiness? For a moment he was tempted to read the letter inside, but he could not bring himself to. Not only could he not bear to be faced with new evidence of Sylvie's unhappiness, but he also knew that he would never forgive himself for invading her privacy.

Swiftly he went through the stack looking at the addresses on the envelopes – all air mail, and all addressed by Sylvie to her mother. All except the last one. And seeing it his movements came to an abrupt halt. Like the others it was also written by Sylvie. But it was addressed to *him*. And, further, it was unstamped and unopened.

Putting the other letters aside he stared at the envelope in his hand then tore it along the top and took out the letter. He unfolded it and smoothed it out. It was dated 2nd July. Just days before Sylvie's death. For a moment her words swam before his eyes. He leaned back against the desk and began to read what she had written:

My dear Guy,
This is my fourth letter to you in the past month. I have waited and hoped every day for some response to the three earlier ones, but so far there has been nothing. Well, after my revelations in the first perhaps I'm being unrealistic in expecting anything else. I know I've caused you the greatest hurt possible but I'm hoping, praying, even now, that it's not too late to repair in some small measure the terrible wrong I've done you. I won't go into it again now; there's no point; I can't add anything to what I wrote before, but I do ask you to believe me.

All I can say, again, is that I never looked beyond those moments of my own unhappiness. I never seemed to be able to. All my actions seemed to be governed by my desperation.

And believe me, Guy, I realized only too soon that I had done the most terrible thing. But all I can say is that it was not really *me*. Later, when I was calmer, I looked at myself and my actions, and it was like looking at the acts committed by some

319

stranger. I don't know – I suppose she was in some way the product of the unhappiness I felt following Davie's death. I don't know what happened to me. Perhaps I had some kind of breakdown. I just know I could not even begin to cope. I don't think I'm trying to excuse myself – I don't think anything could do that. But I do want to try to make you understand – if it's possible.

Sometimes, lying here in my bed, I see myself as we were when we met, when we married, and when I went off with you to New York. Oh, Lord, that was such a time of hope for me. Oh, I was afraid, yes, but even so it never occurred to me for a moment that it would all go so wrong. Yet now, looking back, I sometimes feel that had we been left to ourselves we might have got through it all, and made it work.

'We could,' he murmured. 'We could have got through it.' He stood there in the little room with his eyes shut tight, leaning back against Mrs Bennett's desk, the faint sound of birdsong drifting into the quiet. After a moment he opened his eyes and went back to the letter.

But of course it's too late now. It may even be too late for me to write these words that I'm writing. Perhaps, like those written before, they'll have no meaning for you; they won't touch you. I don't know; I can only hope.

I want you to believe one thing, though. I never stopped loving you. Never. And deceiving you, hurting you as I have done, has made me more miserable than you could imagine. I soon discovered that no real happiness could come from what I did. It tormented me. Perhaps if I had hated you it would have been easier, but I didn't. Underneath all the pain of my homesickness and the loss of Davie I loved you, and as a result these last years have been a nightmare. My only happiness has been in seeing our son happy, and in trying to give him the love and affection he needs. For he does need it so. As you can imagine, his accident has brought him a certain amount of unhappiness (not least in that other children can sometimes be cruel) but it is wonderful to see how well he tries to rise above it. And I feel, I suppose, that with his particular disability, any

320

security he finds in his early life will help to set him in good stead for when he is older.

Guy, I was so afraid to tell you what I had done – though I knew I would have to tell you in time. But the time went by, and I kept putting off the moment, and all the while we were growing further and further apart, till in the end I tried to blot the whole thing out of my mind.

Once again he closed his eyes in anguish. Oh, Sylvie, you should have told me. I would have understood. I would not have blamed you. It was not your fault. I was blind – for so long. I knew you were not happy, that you had no peace, but I always saw our real happiness and peace just around the corner. I didn't realize that you needed it *then* if you were to survive. I tried to tell myself that you were stronger than you were; it was not your fault that you were not.

He opened his eyes, gazing at the letter again, the words splintered beyond his tears.

My mother knows that I have written to you. And I have told her that she must be prepared for the fact that you will come and take John away. She says little about it, but I think she is slowly becoming resigned to the idea. Well, there is no other way. He is your son, and he must be with you. He belongs with you. And you will love him, Guy, I know that. And I hope that in knowing him and loving him you will somehow find it in your heart to forgive me.

I must tell you again: I never stopped loving you. Through it all I loved you, and I hated myself for what I had done and what I was doing.

I am writing now, at this particular time, because I know there is not much time left for me. I have debated whether to try phoning you myself, but since my mother's recent attempt and your refusal to speak to her I can't see that it would do much good. So, being always a coward I fall back on trying to put it all into a letter; at least that way I can choose my words

321

and at the same time I don't have to risk hearing disgust and hatred in your voice. Though I shall not write again.

John knows very little about you, simply because I have not known what to tell him for the best. I have decided to enlighten him no further until I hear from you. I'll keep waiting. Don't forget – it is his happiness that is at stake now. It is too late for mine.

Sylvie

Beneath her signature she had written two verses:

The cost of love is grief, but have no fear,
For all who love can hold some comfort near,
Remembering that love is like the soul,
And cannot die, but lives for ever whole.
Beyond the spheres of science or of charm
It shines, untouched by common hurt or harm.
And though the fabric of our mortal lives we rend,
True love, begun, can never know an end.

So he who loves must know within his heart
That though two loving souls are made to part,
That parting lasts no longer than a sigh
In God's great scheme; and, by and by,
A gentle waking, free of hurt and pain.
And we shall stir, and rise, and meet again.
Then, side by side, and ever it shall be,
In Paradise we'll live, for all eternity.

He stood for some moments without moving. His heart was full, his throat so constricted that it hurt him to swallow. Throughout it all she had loved him.

He read the letter through again. So Sylvie had asked her mother to telephone him. But Mrs Bennett had never done so; yet she had told Sylvie that she had tried.

Carefully he folded the letter and put it back in the envelope. According to Sylvie this was the fourth letter she had written in a month. Stooping, he looked into the drawer. There were no others there. Only Mrs Bennett would know what had become of the other three. She had probably destroyed them. This one she had put away, perhaps intending to destroy it at a later time. But then Sylvie had died, and the letter had been forgotten. It didn't matter so much about the others, though; this one was enough to tell him all he needed to know.

'Where is he now?' Paxton asked.

Crane shook his head. 'We don't know. All we know is that he's due to take a flight for Italy – Milan – this evening, leaving London Heathrow at 18.45. It's getting more and more difficult to predict his moves. We're lucky if we can keep just a few paces behind him.'

'When was this learned?' asked Hughes. 'About his flying to Milan?'

'Just an hour ago. Minutes before you were summoned.'

The hastily convened meeting was taking place in a rather shabby hotel room near Charing Cross Station. The members were grouped around the table facing Crane who sat at its head.

'It doesn't give us much time, does it?' Hughes said.

'No,' Crane agreed, one hand ruminatively rubbing his angular chin. 'But if we move quickly there'll be time enough.'

'Time for what?'

'To stop him – if it's possible.'

'He looks to be pretty much unstoppable,' said Levin. 'Neither of the two attempts on his life worked out.'

'Right.' Crane nodded. 'And we don't know why. Either he's got something going for him – which we don't know about – or else it's just fate playing against us. *His* fate – whatever line that might be taking.'

323

Mrs Haddon put a peppermint into her mouth. 'You mean,' she said, 'that he will only die when the time is right? No matter what we try to effect?'

'It could be.'

'Shame about that rabies treatment he got,' Levin said. 'If it hadn't been for that he'd have stopped being a problem. Today's the eleventh. He was supposed to die of rabies today, wasn't he?'

'Yes, he was,' said Crane. He sighed. 'Still, it's no good sitting here discussing what might have been. He had the necessary treatment and as far as we know he's in good health. No – we've got to consider our next move – which has to be soon.'

Mrs Hughes opened her mouth to speak, but Crane went on, holding up a hand:

'Let me just tell you all that we have made one important discovery.' He paused. 'We do know now that the girl, Ann Milburn, is a major tool in the opposing operation. It's she with whom he's due to fly to Milan. Obviously she managed to persuade him to accompany her.'

Levin leaned forward. 'Would he go without her?'

'We don't know,' said Crane. 'I doubt it.'

'In which case,' said Levin, 'perhaps we can stop him through the girl.'

25

It was after half-past two when he left The Willows and set off for the station. He must call Annie, he told himself as he hurried through the narrow streets of Forham Green. He was to meet her at the airport at five-fifteen so he must catch her before she started out; explain to her what had happened. He couldn't think now of going to Milan. It was out of the question. She would be very disappointed, he knew, but she would understand.

Reaching the telephone kiosk he had used earlier he found that it was occupied. He hesitated for a minute then hurried on. He couldn't wait; he would call from Trowbridge Station. When he eventually got to the station, however, the train to Bath was already in, and he bought his ticket and got on board just in time. He would telephone Annie from Marianne's house.

Arriving at Bath he got a taxi to Marianne's house, and on arrival saw at once, and with great relief, that her white Renault was parked in front of the garage.

Asking the taxi driver to wait until he was quite sure somebody was in, he rang the bell. A few moments later the door was opening and Marianne was there. She nodded and gave a melancholy smile. 'Hello, Guy.' She did not, he thought, appear over-surprised to see him.

'Marianne,' he said, 'I have to talk to you.'

Without hesitation she nodded. 'Come in.'

'Hang on – I must pay off my taxi.'

While Marianne stood waiting in the doorway he

turned, went out to the cab and paid the driver. Returning to the front door he stepped past Marianne into the hall.

'I haven't long got in with the children,' she said as she shut the door behind him. 'They're having their tea right now.' From behind a closed door at the end of the hall he could hear the chatter of children's voices. Marianne opened the door to the front room. 'Go on in here. I'll check on the children, then we can talk.' While she moved away he went into the room. Bright with the afternoon sun, it faced out across the front lawn to the street. The furniture – overstuffed sofa and armchairs, upright grandfather chair and piano – appeared worn and well-used. There were open magazines and comics beside the books on the coffee table, and a half-completed jigsaw puzzle on a tray on the carpet before the fireplace.

Marianne came back into the room. 'Maybe they'll be quiet for a few minutes.' She waved to one of the armchairs. 'Sit down. Excuse the mess, but it's impossible to keep things tidy with children around. Something has to give.' She looked slightly harassed. 'Can I get you a cup of tea or something?'

'No, thank you.' He remained standing. 'You know why I've come, don't you?'

She said at once, 'I can guess – and I'm sorry but I just can't help you, Guy.'

'Listen, I have to know where your mother is – where she went with John.'

'I don't know,' she said.

'You don't? Oh, c'mon, you must know. She'd be bound to tell you.'

'Well, she didn't.'

'I – I can't believe it.'

'It's the truth.'

He sighed. 'I started calling her from London last night

326

but got no answer. So I got the train down and found that they'd gone. Marianne, please – tell me where they are.'

'I don't know,' she said. 'I wish I did. She phoned me. After I got back yesterday. She was terribly upset. You can't imagine the state she was in. She just couldn't face it – the idea that you were coming back today to take John away with you.'

'I'd thought about that,' Guy said. 'I realized very soon after I left you both that I couldn't do it like that. I knew I'd been hasty. That was one thing I wanted to talk to her about. To tell her that I realized we'd have to have discussions about it all, and do it the right way. For John's sake if no one else's.'

She looked at him, studying him in silence for a second, then she said:

'She phoned me and told me she was leaving.'

'She did?'

'She was taking John and leaving, she said. She wouldn't say where. I asked her but she wouldn't say.'

He felt totally helpless. 'But she must know it won't achieve anything. I shall find him – she must realize that. She can't just keep running with him. She must be aware of that.'

'God, I don't know,' Marianne sighed. 'She wasn't thinking straight – that much I *do* know. I suppose she – she just had it in her head that if she took John away for a while you might – well – just give up and go back to America without him.'

Guy snorted. 'Christ! How could she imagine such a thing even for a minute! I won't give up. He's my son and I intend to have him. I'm his father, and his rightful place is with me.'

'I know that, and I told her. But the state she was in there was no getting through to her.' She hesitated for a

327

moment then came towards him. 'Wait, Guy. Why don't you just wait.'

'Wait? What for?'

'She'll come back. She must before long. She can't just stay away indefinitely.'

'Where do you think she could have gone? You must have some idea. What about her friends?'

She shook her head. 'I can't think of anyone she could just go and stay with – not like that, just at the drop of a hat.'

'I shall get the police in on this,' he said grimly. 'They'll find her.'

'Oh, no, please!' She put a hand on his arm. 'Don't do that. You'll blow it up into some great scandal. It'll only make it worse – for everybody.'

'I don't see how it could be any worse. For God's sake, Marianne, aren't you aware of what's happened? She's taken my son and run away with him, and I have no idea where they've gone.' He moved aimlessly to the window; stood gazing out. 'I can't believe this is happening,' he said. After a moment he turned back to her. 'What time did she call you and say she was going?'

'I should think about half-past six. Something like that.'

'And she didn't tell you any more than that?'

' – No.'

'Did you try to stop her?'

'Yes, of course I did. But she wouldn't listen to me. She didn't want to hear.'

'You could have stopped her,' he said.

'I tried. Believe me, I tried. After I'd talked to her I thought I'd drive over there. Try to get her to see some sense. I went out and called Arthur – he's my oldest boy – and told him to look after Cressie and Jane and Peter.

328

Then I went to phone her back to say I was coming over. There was no answer. She'd already gone.'

'And leaving her car,' he said. 'I guess she got a taxi.' He paused. 'Have you heard from her since?'

'This morning. A phone call. She didn't say where she was calling from, but she said they were both okay. I was not to worry.'

'Not to worry,' he repeated. 'Not to worry.'

'Listen, Guy – I don't think she really knows what she's doing at the moment.'

'But you just said she's hoping I'll go back to the States without John.'

'Yes, I know, but – yes, I think that that *is* partly on her mind, but I also think she just – wanted to get away for a while. Somewhere alone with John. So that she could have time to think. I'm quite sure that she'll be back soon. She'll be on the phone to say she's coming home, I'm sure of it.'

'I wish *I* could be that sure.' He let out a groan. 'I don't know – I just – I have this awful feeling that I'm never going to see him again.'

'Oh, no – don't talk like that.'

'I can't help it. Anything could happen to him. And it could happen without any of us knowing.'

'Just wait,' she said. 'Wait and they'll be back. I know they will.'

'Wait,' he repeated, turning back to the window. 'Easy for you to say.'

As he stood there he felt a pressure starting to build up in his head. Beginning at the site of his scar it was creeping slowly back through the interior of his skull. He reached out, gripping the window ledge, closing his eyes tight against the threatened onslaught.

'Are you all right?' Marianne said behind him, her

voice filtering through the waves of his pain. He gave a little shake of his head, a movement that sent searing sparks of agony shooting through his brain. 'It'll pass in a while,' he muttered.

He was aware of her hand upon his arm, gently urging him, guiding him. Feeling a slight pressure against the backs of his knees he sank down into an armchair. Minutes went by while he was aware of nothing but the pain in his head; then he heard Marianne's voice:

'Here – take these . . .'

Through heavy eyelids he saw her bending to him. She dropped three tablets into his palm and put a glass of water into his other hand. He put the tablets in his mouth, crushed them and chewed them, then washed them down with the water. The acid taste lingered sharp on his tongue.

'Lie back,' Marianne said, and he did so, letting himself go, giving himself up to the throbbing pain that tore at the inside of his skull.

Marianne laid a rug over him. 'Would you like me to call a doctor?' she asked.

'No, I'll be okay,' he said. 'There's no need to worry. I get them – these headaches – since my accident. They pass.'

His body seemed to be without strength; his legs might have belonged to someone else; his head was unbelievably heavy on his neck. But it was warm under the rug, and he could feel the pain beginning to diminish. He closed his eyes, letting the comfort wash over him; take him where it would.

He slept.

And he dreamed. And in his dream he was with John. They were in the garden at The Willows, standing beside the chicken coop. The sun is shining down, warm and brilliant. He watches as John lifts the wooden flap to reveal the nesting boxes. The boy reaches in and takes from a nest a single egg which he places, warm, smooth and perfect, into Guy's waiting palm. And there is still another egg to be taken from the nest, and another, and another. No matter how many are plucked there are always others there. And one by one they are placed in Guy's hand, and he smiles into the boy's upturned face. And he takes them all, the warm eggs, though he still holds only the one, the first. And John *whoops* in a sudden little expression of joy, and the egg is suddenly in a brown paper bag and Guy's thumb is tightly enclosed in John's small fingers. They move together through the garden, through the orchard, and John points to a patch of sun-dappled shade where foxes play. Sylvie calls to them, calls their names and comes towards them through the apple trees. John runs to her and she bends and kisses him, then lifts her face and smiles at Guy over the boy's head. And suddenly it is not Sylvie who stands there, but Mrs Bennett. And she takes John's hand and leads him away. Guy calls after them but they go on, their forms diminishing among the trees. Just before they move out of sight John stops, turns to him, lifting his hand, reaching out, mouth opening in an unheard cry. And behind the right lens of his spectacles the eye socket turns red and the blood runs down his cheek. A second later he and the woman disappear from view. Guy shouts after them and tries to follow but cannot; his leaden feet are unable to make any but the slowest, most torturous progress. When at last he reaches the edge of the forest that was once the orchard the pair are nowhere in sight. He kneels on the pavement, presses his hands to his eyes and weeps.

'Are you all right?' Marianne's voice. 'You were shouting out in your sleep.'

331

He opened his eyes and lay looking into the dim interior of the room. Marianne moved into the line of his vision. 'I was dreaming,' he said. He realized that his feet were resting on a footstool. From the next room came the murmur of a television set. The thoughts in his head seemed to have no direction. His mind was a shifting kaleidoscope of conflicting images. John, Mrs Bennett, Sylvie.

He became aware that Marianne was speaking to him. He turned his eyes to her. 'I'm sorry?'

'I said, you were asleep quite a while. You must have needed it.'

He did not answer. She studied him for a moment. 'Would you like some coffee? Some tea? I could have brought you something earlier but I thought it was better to let you sleep.'

He nodded. 'Some coffee would be good. Black. Thanks.'

'I'll get it.'

She went out of the room, leaving him in the quiet. He felt lost, in a state of limbo. He lowered his feet to the floor; sat up. Remembering Sylvie's letter he drew it from his pocket, took it from its envelope and read it through again. *I must tell you again: I never stopped loving you.* Sylvie . . . How was it possible that something that had begun with so much promise could end in so much unhappiness and loss? And with the thought Sylvie, a young, untroubled Sylvie, smiles into his eyes, one hand lifted to her hair, while the other holds the dandelion artlessly to her cheek. And then suddenly *thwuck* goes the head of the club, and he sees Davie writhing in the sand. He pushed the image away. Think of Sylvie. *I must tell you again: I never stopped loving you.* Oh, Sylvie, he thought, it was always you . . .

The thought of Annie suddenly came into his head. He was supposed to be meeting her at the airport. She would be waiting for him. He drew his arm out from beneath the blanket and looked at his watch. Six-forty. The flight was due for take-off in five minutes. He started to move then sat back again. It was too late to do anything about it now.

He sighed. He had let Annie down so badly. And suddenly with his regret came an awareness, like light in a darkened room, that what he had felt for Annie had not been real. It was true what she had feared: he had been drawn to her for her physical likeness to Sylvie. For no other reason. Finding her he had used her, used her in some insane attempt to resurrect his past, to make that past right again, to put right his mistakes – as if it could ever be done. But Annie was not Sylvie. And knowing it, realizing it, at last, he knew also that she had nothing for him. She had never had – except in his wretched, groping mind, that part of his mind that had refused to accept what was real, what was the truth. Sylvie was dead; that was the truth. Her living was a part of his past, living now only in his memory. And Annie, she had no part in his present. The game he had played, in which by striving to win he could only lose, was over.

When he got back to London, when this was all over and he had got John back, he would see Annie. And he would explain to her. Try to make her understand . . .

333

26

Annie had arrived at Heathrow just after five o'clock, ready to meet the American at the appointed time. Reaching the lounge she went straight to a telephone and dialled Rawlinson's number. When he came on the line she said:

'Milburn, sir. I'm just reporting in. I've arrived at Heathrow.'

'Is Holman there yet?'

'I'm just about to go to the Meeting Point. We've arranged to meet there at five-fifteen.'

'Fine. Just make sure you get him on that plane.' His tone was clipped.

'I will.'

There was no sign of Holman when she got to the Meeting Point, but she was not concerned; there was still plenty of time. She set herself to wait – at the same time telling herself to relax; she always had a sense of unease in the midst of a crowd, and now it was particularly strong.

As she stood there, her strapped overnight bag over her shoulder, the teeming throng moved and swirled about her like water eddying in the current of a river. And always she kept a watchful eye on the faces that passed, ever alert for those eyes that showed interest, and possibly posed a threat.

At one point a smartly dressed young man sidled towards her and came to stop a yard from her side, there taking out his wallet and going through its contents. He turned, took a step towards her.

'Excuse me,' he said pleasantly, 'but do you possibly have change for the telephone?'

She took a half-step away, at the same time turning to him, and said quietly but crisply:

'Go fuck yourself.'

He blinked at her. 'What? I just asked if you – '

'I know what you just asked,' she said. Her smile was brittle. 'And no, I haven't got any change. What I have got is a strong right foot, and if you don't move from here in three seconds you're going to get it right in the balls.'

He left without a further word.

She checked her watch, saw the seconds ticking by. Hurry up, damn you. Her palms were slightly damp. She loathed being placed in this vulnerable position. She wouldn't begin to relax until she and Holman were sitting on the plane.

Her anxiety grew. Supposing he didn't turn up . . . Suppose something had happened . . . She was losing him, she knew. She had become more and more certain of it since their meeting last night when he had told her about his son. He had been slipping away from her so swiftly over the past couple of days, and in the end she had been powerless to stop it. His dead wife and son – he was obsessed with them. And now there was this other child, his living son. How could she get past that preoccupation? She thought of how he had turned down her suggestion that he stay the night with her in Hammersmith, how he had gone off alone to his hotel . . . Please, she silently prayed, let him come. Just give me one more day with him. Let him come.

She looked over to the desk where messages were accepted from, and given to, the travellers. If Holman

335

was going to be late he would surely send a message. She checked her watch again. Five-seventeen. Another minute and her anxiety drove her over to the counter where a blonde female official was just taking over from a red-headed one. She waited while the switch was completed and then said, as the pretty, well-groomed, young blonde woman turned and smiled at her:

'Would you check, please, whether there's any message for me?'

'Certainly. What name, please?'

'Milburn. Ann Milburn. I'm expecting to meet a Mr Guy Holman.'

The young woman shuffled through papers and shook her head. 'No, I'm sorry, there's nothing so far.'

Annie thanked her and moved back to resume her position of waiting. The minutes went by, and still there was no sign of him.

'Miss Milburn . . .?'

She started slightly and took a half-step backwards. But it was only the uniformed young woman from the desk.

'It is Miss Ann Milburn, isn't it?' said the blonde girl. 'You were at the desk just now, making an inquiry . . .?'

'Yes.' Annie nodded, relaxing again.

'Something just came through for you,' the other said. 'If you'd care to come over to the desk.'

Annie followed her to the high counter, waiting as the young woman went behind it. 'From a Mr Holman,' the girl read. 'That is the party you were asking about, isn't it?'

'Yes. What is it?' Annie leaned forward, making no attempt to hide her impatience. 'What's the message?'

The young woman placed a notepad on the counter, but with its head outwards so that Annie was unable to read it. With a loud sigh of impatience Annie moved to swivel it around towards her. As she did so the blonde girl also reached towards the pad. Their hands collided and the pen in the young woman's hand jabbed sharply and forcefully into the flesh between Annie's thumb and forefinger. Annie gave out a loud gasp at the sudden pain while the other girl recoiled, one hand to her mouth.

'Oh, dear! Oh, I'm *so* sorry.'

The blonde girl's face was a mixture of horror, sympathy and contrition. Annie looked at the bead of blood that was swiftly growing on the back of her hand. Then she lifted her eyes to the face of the blonde girl. Their eyes met, and in that second she knew.

For a moment she was held transfixed by the blue eyes that held her own, eyes whose expression did not mirror the concern on the girl's brow. The eyes were cool and dispassionate. And yet not totally; they did not quite conceal the faint gleam of triumph that shone.

In that same moment Annie knew that the message on the pad would be meaningless. She lowered her eyes to it and saw written there: 'If I'm a few minutes late be patient. Guy.' A message that had not been worth sending. It had not come from him. It had been a mere pretence. It was the final confirmation.

'Thank you.' She pushed the notepad away. The young blonde girl glanced down at the swelling ruby of blood on Annie's hand. Shaking her head she said apologetically: 'I'm awfully sorry about that, Madam. Can I get you a Bandaid or something?'

Annie shook her head. 'No,' she said; and now on her lips was the faintest hint of a smile. No Bandaid would bring any good to her. For her the scenario was coming to a close. It was the irony of the situation that made her smile. They had caught her by means of her own anxiety.

She was aware that she felt strangely calm. She gave a

337

little nod of acknowledgement to the young woman – the airport official who was no airport official – and turned away. Moving back across the floor she took up once more her position of waiting. The blood had run down her hand in a fine stream onto her forefinger. She took a tissue from her bag and wiped the blood away. At once it rose again, forming a perfect bead. She pressed the tissue to it and looked over to the counter. She was not surprised to see that the red-haired girl was back in her place, and that of the blonde girl there was no sign.

While the travellers moved about her Annie remained at her post, eyes scanning the faces of the people for some sign of the American. Not that his arrival now would do any good. She knew that she would never get on the plane even if he did turn up. She would never get him to Milan. She wondered what Rawlinson would say when he learned that she had failed. He, the highest of the superiors she knew, had always intimidated her; she had always feared their meetings. She was not afraid of him now. He could do nothing to her now.

Tossing the blood-stained tissue aside (the bleeding seemed to have stopped now), she took a phone card from her purse and made her way towards a call box. As she reached it she was aware of a strange, cold sensation creeping up her arm to her shoulder. It did not surprise her that it was happening; she had expected something; it was the nature of the sensation that she had not been able to predict.

As she reached out to insert the card in the slot the feeling in her arm became a searing pain, turning from ice-cold to a white-hot burning that brought her up short and made her gasp. And then the pain was shooting, spreading into her chest, making her cry out. A moment later she was aware of a numbness surging through her

338

limbs. The card fell from her fingers and she staggered, falling against the metal wall of the call box. Unheeded, her bag slipped from her shoulder, slid down her arm and fell onto the carpet. The people around her, seeing her, murmured that she was fainting, and moved towards her, to help her. She was beyond help. Eyes rolling up in their sockets, she clutched without strength at the call box wall while the burning pain engulfed her body. A great stab of fire wrenched at her heart, her knees buckled and she fell heavily to the floor. By the time the first of the concerned travellers reached her side and bent over her she was dead.

'She's dead,' said the blonde girl. She had changed out of the uniform back into her blue jeans, sweater and trainers. From the telephone kiosk where she stood she could see the crowd gathered, see the ambulance crew pushing a way through the throng.

'Did it go smoothly?' Crane asked.

'Like honey. I didn't even need to put out a call for her. She herself set the whole thing up by coming to the desk in the first place. I never thought it would be so easy.'

'You've done well,' Crane said. 'Extremely well.'

'Thank you.'

'What about Holman? Has there been any sign of him yet?'

'Not as far as I know. But a watch is being kept in case he should still turn up – to intercept him if necessary. I doubt he'll be here now, though. The flight's due to take off at any second.'

Crane thanked her again for her work and hung up. Turning to the others he said:

'The girl is dead.'

'And what about Holman?' said Paxton. 'I gather from your conversation that he hasn't shown up at the airport.'

'No, he hasn't.'

'Where is he?' asked Levin.

Crane sighed. 'We don't know. We lost all track of him a few hours back. All we know is that he's still in England.'

There was a little silence, then Hughes said, 'Why didn't he show up at the airport? He must have had a pretty damn good reason. After all, he didn't know the girl was dead.'

'Maybe he's ill,' said Levin.

'You mean from rabies?' said Crane. 'No, that's all finished with. As far as we know he's still in perfect health. There's some other reason he didn't get there.'

'But he might still go to Italy, even now,' said Haddon.

'Why should he?' Crane said. 'He was only going because of the girl – and now that she's out of the picture he'll have no reason to go on his own.' He ran a hand distractedly through his hair. 'Of course, if we could keep tabs on him the way we could with any other individual it would make it all so much easier.'

'If we could keep tabs on him,' said Haddon, 'we wouldn't have this problem in the first place.'

'So,' said Hughes, 'what happens now?'

'I wish I knew,' said Crane. 'There's very little time left now, and we can only hope he stays put in England for the next twenty-four hours.'

'And if he shouldn't?' said Hughes.

'All exits are being watched – ports and airports – just in case. Every available agent is being used, and each one of us will have to take our turn. I don't think he'll go now, but we can't take any chances.'

* * *

340

Marianne had made coffee, and sandwiches of ham, cheese and salad. Guy realized he was hungry. Marianne sat without speaking as he ate. When he had finished she said:

'What are you going to do now?'

He set the mug down on the coffee table. 'You still think I should wait, yes?'

'I know they'll be back.'

'But when?'

She didn't answer. He shook his head. 'I can't depend on that. But at the same time I can't see anything else I can do. If I don't know where they are . . .' His words trailed off in hopelessness.

He became aware that Marianne's eyes were focused on the letter lying on the chair-arm. He picked it up.

'It's from Sylvie,' he said. 'The last letter she ever wrote to me. It was in a drawer in your mother's desk. I found a key and got into the house. I searched all through, trying to find some clue as to where they'd gone. There was nothing, though. Except this.' He looked down at the envelope, at his name written in Sylvie's hand. 'She loved me,' he said. 'I thought she hated me, but she loved me.' He put the letter in his pocket and leaned forward, burying his face in his hands; beyond tears.

Minutes went by, then Marianne said, 'I know where they are now.'

He raised his head, staring at her. 'You know . . .?'

'Yes. I got a phone call. While you were asleep. I wasn't going to tell you, but – '

'Oh – Marianne . . .' He was throwing aside the rug, starting up from the chair. 'Where are they? Tell me.'

'You can't go tonight, anyway. They've left the country.'

'What?'

341

'They took John to Italy.'

'Italy?' He was standing before her now. '*They* took John? Who are *they*?'

'She and her friend Alberto Rossi. They've taken John to Milan.'

Rawlinson gave a final nod of approval, replaced the telephone receiver and turned to face the other members of the small assembly.

'You'll be relieved to know that everything is going to plan,' he said. 'Agent Rossi has reported that he is in Milan with the child and the child's grandmother. It should only be a matter of time now before Holman follows.'

'The contingency measures you spoke of,' said one of the members.

'Correct,' Rawlinson said. 'I told you it would be through love that we'd get him. And we shall.'

'And Agent Milburn?' said another member.

'Milburn is dead.' Rawlinson spoke dismissively. 'But she was expendable. As indeed we all are.' He dismissed the girl with an impatient wave of his hand. 'She's unimportant now. Rossi has achieved what she couldn't. Everything will be all right now.'

'Mr Rossi,' said Guy. 'Her Italian friend.'

'Yes,' said Marianne. 'I hadn't dreamed. When I found she'd gone I phoned him – Alberto – to ask if he'd heard from her, but I got no answer. I never imagined for a moment that he might be with her.'

She got up and left the room while he stood thinking over her words. Mrs Bennett, Rossi and John – gone to Milan. Astonishingly where he himself had planned to go. And if he had not found that John had gone from the

342

house he would at that moment be on his way there with Annie.

When Marianne came back a minute later she was holding a little notepad. She tore off the top page and held it out to him. He took it. On it she had written an address of a villa on the via Soperga.

'The home of Alberto's sister,' Marianne said, 'so he told me.'

'Rossi did?'

'Yes, it was he who phoned. He said he knew I'd be worried.'

'Why are you giving me this address?' Guy said.

'Because – it's already gone too far. I've tried to protect her, but there has to be an end to it sometime. And I know what you're going through. What you've been through.' She paused. 'Will you go there?'

'Of course. As soon as I can.'

'What will you do when you find them?'

' – I don't know. I'll have to think about that. But it will be in John's best interests. I won't lose sight of that.' Nervously he pressed his hands together. 'I must call the airlines.'

Marianne's son Arthur was watching television in the rear sitting room so Guy used the telephone extension in the kitchen. On calling the airlines he found that the first available seat was on an Alitalia flight leaving Heathrow at four-twenty the following afternoon. It meant almost a whole day's delay, but there was nothing to be done about it. Without hesitation he made a reservation, paying for it with a credit card. As he put down the receiver Marianne said:

'What will you do? Stay over in Bath and travel to Heathrow tomorrow afternoon?'

He nodded. 'Yes, I think so. I've got my passport with me. Can you recommend a hotel in Bath?'

'No, but there are so many. Come on – I'll drive you into the centre.'

'Are you sure? I'd be very grateful.'

'Just let me get my keys. Arthur will keep an eye on the others.'

Marianne returned a minute or so later and they went out to the car together. She drove him to a small hotel near the centre of the city. He went inside, checked that they had a room available, then returned to Marianne where she waited in the car. He was all set, he said.

'Good.' She held out her hand and he reached through the window and briefly pressed it.

'Thanks, Marianne.'

'Good luck. I hope you find them.'

'Thank you.'

'And – don't be too hard on her, will you?'

'I won't.'

27

Once again Paxton surveyed the travellers who lined up at the check-in desk, observing them as they edged slowly forward, one by one checking their tickets, their luggage.

He glanced at his watch. Ten minutes past three. In a little less than an hour Mary Hughes would come to relieve him from his watch. He looked forward to the respite. He had been watching now for just over two hours.

While Paxton watched the Alitalia check-in desk at Heathrow other agents were at Gatwick and Manchester covering the alternative flights to Milan. The next one from Heathrow was the AZ 267, departure time 16.20. If Holman planned to catch it he would have to be checking in very soon. But there again, Paxton mused, Holman might have no intention of travelling.

From the line of air-travellers his gaze moved on, sweeping over the people who swarmed about the terminal building. Back and forth his eyes darted, searching for Holman's face among the throng. And not only for *Holman's* face. Just as he was there to prevent Holman going to Italy, so, he knew, there were others who would stop at nothing to ensure that Holman travelled unhindered. Paxton knew it was a safe bet that just as he stood there watching so he himself was being watched. With this awareness constantly at the forefront of his mind, he did what he could to stand somewhat apart from the other travellers, his back close against the wall of a rectangular pillar.

Paxton had his work cut out, and knew it. He would have no difficulty spotting Holman, but identifying the enemy was a different matter. It meant constant vigilance, unflagging concentration. The enemy could be anyone – the distinguished-looking elderly man who stood beside his luggage-laden trolley, either of the two young lovers who appeared to be so absorbed in one another, the punk with the purple hair who leaned against a pillar, drinking from a can of lager; the airport official who bent over one of the counters, writing; the skiers, the young black soldier . . . Paxton stood watching as the people came and went, some quietly, without fuss; others loud and raucous; nervous travellers, calm travellers. His gaze moved on, shifting from one to another.

Observing a female uniformed airline representative go by there came into his mind the thought of the enemy agent, the girl, who had died just yards from where he stood. In *her* case his people had used the ploy of impersonating an airport official. And, apparently, for all that the girl must have been very much on the alert, it had worked. She had, in the end, been careless, less than vigilant. It only needed a moment. He, though, he comforted himself, was almost certainly more experienced than the girl had been. He wouldn't make the mistakes that she had made.

Even so, it was all too easy to relax concentration. With the thought his eyes once again swept over the moving faces around him; at the same time he adjusted the shoulder strap of his travel bag and dipped his right hand into it, fingers immediately locating and gripping the hypodermic fixed in the base. A little pressure at the right moment, and the needle would shoot out through the small opening in the bag's side and discharge its poison. The needle would easily penetrate ordinary clothing. All

Paxton had to do once Holman showed up was get next to him. A sharp sting was all Holman would feel. Then the pain would swiftly wear off and he would go on his way unsuspecting. Unlike the venom used on the girl, the poison given to Holman would take a couple of hours to have its effect. He would die in mid-flight to Milan.

Attracted by a commotion, Paxton looked over to a nearby check-in desk and saw a short stout man raising a fuss at some confusion over his ticket. In front of the Alitalia desk a young woman's suitcase had burst, and she crouched over it, red in the face and desperately trying to stuff back inside it a scattering of underwear and cosmetics. A small boy dressed like a cowboy was painfully jabbing his toy six-shooter into a small girl who sat on a luggage trolley while the girl, wailing, stretched out her arms for her mother's protection. Two nuns had now joined the line at the Alitalia desk, followed by a girl and an old woman with a walking stick. The purple-haired punk was now on his second can of lager, leaving the empty can discarded at his feet. The well-dressed elderly man looked at his watch, glanced anxiously about him and sighed. Me, too, Paxton thought. Me, too. And still no sign of Holman.

Eyes constantly moving, observing, Paxton's gaze came back to rest on the uniformed man who stood writing at one of the counters. The man had been standing there for several minutes now, seemingly uninvolved with what was going on around him. Paxton focused his gaze upon the bent head of the man. And as he did so the man lifted his face and caught Paxton's eyes. Their glances held for a fraction of a second and then the uniformed man again lowered his gaze to the sheet of paper before him. But that split second was long enough. In that brief moment Paxton knew. He was looking at his would-be assassin.

'*Bang! bang . . .!*'

Momentarily distracted by the little boy in the wide-brimmed stetson, Paxton saw that the child had pulled his bandanna up over his mouth and, looking like a miniature bank robber in an old western movie, was now attacking the well-dressed old man who waited nearby. Paxton saw the man's mouth open in quiet reproval of the boy. The boy took no notice but shot him again, jabbing the pistol muzzle within an inch of the man's stomach, making him flinch. A few yards away the young woman had gathered up her belongings and was now trying to fasten the suitcase, the purple-haired punk continued to drink his lager, and the nuns stood silent and calm in the midst of the noise and the movement. Suddenly aware of his brief lack of concentration, Paxton's glance moved back to the uniformed man with the clipboard.

On the counter top at the man's side lay an airline bag. Paxton's eye and mind took it in; he was certain that it must contain the intended means of his, Paxton's, death. What would it be? The same means that he planned to employ with Holman – poison injected during a minor collision? Probably. It would be easily done; such trivial collisions happened all the time in a place like this in which the pedestrian traffic was so heavy. The poison would, Paxton knew, be different from the one he was carrying. Whereas the one in his bag would ensure Holman's death in approximately two hours, the one intended for himself would be so fast-acting that he would be prevented from even getting to Holman's side.

Paxton's eyes flicked nervously from the man at the counter to the faces of the travellers, searching for Holman. His heart was thudding. He knew that the moment he saw Holman he would have to act. There would be no time for delay. His gaze moved back to the

348

man at the counter, and once again he found the man's eyes upon him.

Gaze flicking away, Paxton once again briefly took in the punk who stood drinking his lager, the little cowboy who now jabbed his pistol at the nuns while they flinched and shrank away in distress, the young woman who seemed unable to fasten her suitcase and now stood looking about her with a helpless expression on her face. Turning from them all, Paxton glanced across the terminal floor and saw in the distance the tall figure of Holman approaching through the crowd.

Immediately Paxton flicked his gaze back to the man at the counter. He had straightened, seemingly casually, but Paxton could see clearly the tension in his stance. Keeping the man in sight from the corner of his eye, Paxton stepped forward. He himself was suddenly so tense, so nervous that his hand inside the shoulder bag was slick with sweat. His eyes moved back and forth, flicking from the approaching figure of Holman to the uniformed man at the counter. Now the man had picked up his airline bag and was adjusting it over his right shoulder.

Paxton took another step forward. He must do it now; go towards Holman and meet him in the crowd, get to him before he reached the check-in line. If he waited any longer it might be too late. Glancing back at the man he was startled to see that he was now only six or seven yards away. Breathing harshly through his mouth, his heart hammering, Paxton started off. A second later he came to an abrupt halt. Holman was no longer in sight.

Where could he have gone to? Paxton stood peering anxiously about him. He couldn't have gone far. He had probably just stopped off at the men's room, or gone to pick up a newspaper. Standing, waiting, eyes searching, Paxton felt naked in his exposure. A wave of panic struck

349

at him. Taking a couple of steps away, he increased the distance between himself and the watching man and stood turning his head back and forth – back to the man, forward again to seek out Holman.

'*Bang! bang! bang!*' Six-gun waving, the little boy shot an old woman in a wheelchair then darted to the uniformed man and shot him twice, '*bang! bang!*' The man lashed out at him in a gesture of furious exasperation and with a yell the boy ran for cover behind Paxton's long legs. In the same moment the uniformed man stepped forward again in Paxton's direction.

'*Bang!*'

The sharp yell came from behind Paxton's back, and in the same moment he felt the gun jab him in his right calf, a sharp, searing sting like the insertion of a red-hot needle. And in that second he knew. Gasping from the sharp pain he bent to rub his leg, at the same time half turning to face his attacker, his assassin. And as he did so the little cowboy lifted the pistol in his stubby-fingered hand and jabbed at him again. Lightning-fast, the needle entered Paxton's neck, a full inch, just above his collar. '*Bang!*' As Paxton reached up to clutch at his throat the child who was not a child raised his head, and for the first time Paxton saw his eyes. Earlier hidden by the wide brim of the too-large hat, the old eyes gazed up at him above the line of the red and white bandanna. The eyes glittered in triumph. Next moment the little cowboy was giving a *whoop* and charging off into the crowd.

Turning on the spot, Paxton noticed that the harassed mother-figure and the little girl were walking away in a different direction, vanishing from sight in the crowd. The uniformed man remained. To ensure, of course, that all continued to go well, to plan. Having moved back to the counter, he watched covertly, dispassionately, as the poison took effect.

And Paxton was right about the poison. In fact it worked faster even than he had imagined. He barely had time to realize it, though; he was already beginning to feel its power. He opened his mouth and groaned. He stumbled, his heart wrenched in a sudden seizure of the most excruciating pain, a pain like none he had ever experienced before. He fought against it, briefly, and through his agony he straightened – and saw as if through a fog the approaching figure of Holman. Perhaps even now . . . But his fingers, limp as rags, could not find their way inside the bag.

He was still groping for the syringe when his knees buckled and he dropped to the floor like a felled tree.

'My God!' cried out the uniformed man, 'this man is ill. Somebody send for an ambulance.'

On leaving the currency exchange bureau where he had stopped off to exchange some dollars for lire, Guy headed again for the Alitalia check-in desk. As he drew near he saw a commotion there, a crowd forming around someone on the floor. Peering over the heads as he went by he saw the figure of a tall black man lying sprawled. He had a brief glimpse of the man's face, eyes open and rolled back in his head. Distressed at the sight, he averted his gaze and moved on.

351

28

The flight to Milan was made in good time. The plane touched down at Linate Airport at 19.12 local time, and twenty-five minutes later, having no luggage to wait around for, Guy was sitting in a cab bound for the city centre.

The via Soperga, he learned from the driver, was situated near the central station. On arrival outside number twenty-seven he got out and, in his careful, limited Italian, asked the driver to wait.

The ground floor of the house was taken up by a shop devoted to film and video accessories. Beside it was a door with a bell marked with the name *Natoli*. Guy pressed the button. He stood waiting, his heart bumping, and after some moments the door was opening and a middle-aged, rather pretty, dark-haired woman was standing before him. She looked at him inquiringly.

'*Si?*'

'*Buona sera, signora.*'

She nodded, her expression guarded. '*Buona sera.*'

He hesitated, then: '*Parla Inglese, signora?*'

'A little,' she replied in her strongly accented English.

Relieved, he said in a mixture of Italian and English that he was looking for Signor Rossi and the English signora. She nodded. Signor Rossi, she said, was her brother, but he and the *signora inglese* were not there. They had been there, but they had left.

His heart sank. He was about to ask: And what of the

352

child, the little English boy, when she added, without hesitation:

'*Anche il piccolo ragazzo inglese.*'

And the little English boy too. He nodded his understanding, then asked whether she expected them back.

She shook her head, no. They had arrived yesterday, but now they had gone, into the city centre. Where they would be going afterwards, she didn't know; though it would be to a hotel somewhere in the city, she understood. Her brother would be getting in touch with her later.

Inwardly, Guy groaned. They might go anywhere; he might never find them. Did she know where in the city centre they were heading for? he asked.

She hesitated for a moment in thought, then said: '*Si, certo. Alla Scala.*'

'*La Scala?*'

'*Si. Il teatro. Sono andati a comprari biglietti per l'opera.*'

Of course – La Scala – the opera house. They had gone there to buy tickets for the opera.

'*Quando – ?*' he began. 'When? When did they leave here . . .?'

She shrugged, moving her hands. '*Soltanto cinque o sei minuti fa.*'

Five or six minutes. He had just missed them. His disappointment was like a weight upon him. He thanked her: '*Grazie, signora. Buona sera.*' Turning from her he moved to the cab, opened the door and got in. 'La Scala,' he instructed the driver.

Sitting back in the seat, he looked at his watch. Twenty minutes past eight. He felt suddenly very weary, added to which his head ached slightly, and his eyes itched. He needed to rest; he had barely slept the previous night at

353

the Bath hotel. He needed, too, a shower and a change of clothes. Also, he told himself, he could use a good meal; he had had very little breakfast and had merely eaten snacks at Heathrow and on the flight over. He lit a cigarette. Later there would be time to rest, time to eat.

Arriving at the piazza del' Scala, Guy paid off the cab driver and got out. The May evening was warm and pleasant, and the square was bustling with people. As he moved across it in the direction of the opera house his eyes darted from one to another in his search for Rossi, Mrs Bennett and John.

Reaching the opera house he looked for them in the booking office, then went back out onto the front steps and stood gazing out over the square.

The minutes passed, and there was no sign of them. If they were not there then he had no idea where else to look. If Rossi planned on taking Mrs Bennett and John to a hotel they could end up anywhere in the city.

As he stood looking out across the piazza he was struck again by the strangeness of Mrs Bennett's move in bringing John to Milan. It must have been an act born of pure panic. And, probably, considering that Rossi was familiar with the place, made at his suggestion.

But why should Rossi suggest such a dramatic solution to Mrs Bennett's dilemma? She might well not have been thinking rationally – she couldn't have been – but Rossi, uninvolved, ought, surely, to have been able to offer her some sound reasoning. Instead, he had brought her and John here to Italy.

As Guy pondered Rossi's own possible motives for the curious, and desperate, act he suddenly caught sight of them.

They were on the far side of the square, John walking between Rossi and Mrs Bennett.

Even as Guy ran down the steps he saw them disappear from sight around the corner of a tall building. He ran on, dodging the pedestrians and the traffic. Reaching the other side of the piazza he took the street the three had taken, and soon found himself in a busy, tall, glass-covered gallery with shops and restaurants on either side. Frantically scanning the faces of the evening sojourners, he continued on.

His feet carried him from the confines of the gallery out into another wide piazza, and he saw before him the high walls of the magnificent Duomo. The wide square was teeming with people. Eyes moving from one figure to another, he hurried forward.

In the middle of the piazza del Duomo he halted and stood breathless, looking about him. The three were nowhere in sight.

After a while, his breath recovered, he set off slowly across the piazza. Taking a narrow street leading from it he found himself at last on a wide avenue where the traffic roared by, and all around him on the pavement the evening crowds moved to and fro. Without hope he stood for some minutes looking up and down the street, then set off again. At the next junction he stopped once more. He was quite lost now. More importantly, though, he had lost *them*.

He was just wandering, walking in no particular direction, when he saw them again. He spotted Alberto Rossi first. At the far end of the street he saw the Italian standing bathed in the glow of a brightly-lit shop window; standing a little apart from the other people who moved about, almost as if he wanted to be seen. Guy knew that Mrs

Bennett and John could not be far away. He set off at a run, and almost in the same moment he saw Rossi turn and move out of sight.

At the end of a narrow street, Guy found himself in another piazza, smaller than the piazza del Duomo, but almost equally busy. In the middle of the square stood a fountain around which a crowd of young people stood and sat talking and laughing in the warm evening air. Beyond it the high walls of a church rose up. He moved towards the centre. He could see no sign of Rossi, Mrs Bennett and John, though he knew they could not be far away.

Reaching the church he climbed the steps and stood with his back to the large, ornately decorated door and looked out over the square. And then he saw them. They were standing near the brightly-lit entrance to a restaurant on the far side. In a rush he was down the steps and dashing across the square.

As he drew near the fountain he collided with a youth who had sprung up from his seat on the steps to move towards a couple of girls who stood some distance away. The youth reeled from the collision, then, recovering, swore at him and moved on. Guy caught his breath then set off again. Now, though, as he ran towards the restaurant, he saw that Mrs Bennett, Rossi and John were no longer in sight.

Reaching the restaurant he came to a stop and stood breathless, turning on the spot to look anxiously about him. A young cyclist came riding by, so close that Guy had to step back to avoid him.

And suddenly he felt a sharp, thudding blow strike him in the upper abdomen, on his right side, just below his ribcage. Almost in the same moment there came the crack of a gunshot.

Propelled by the impact of the bullet, he staggered back a step against a short, dark-suited man who had just emerged from the restaurant doorway behind him. The next second the man was clutching at him, powerful hands gripping his upper arms from behind. Knees weak, hardly able to stand, Guy was held fast in the man's grasp.

Desperately struggling to retain his balance and free himself, Guy turned his head and suddenly saw, far away, the figure of his son.

'*John!*'

He was there; he could see him.

'*John!*'

With a sob and a great heart-surge of strength Guy tore himself from the man's grasp and lunged to his left. In the same moment a second shot rang out. The dark-suited man fell, a woman screamed, and Guy staggered three paces away and collapsed on the stone.

The scene in the piazza was pandemonium. People ran in all directions, roughly pushing each other out of the way as they dashed for cover and safety. Others cowered on the ground, hands and arms over their heads for protection or wrapped around the prostrate bodies of loved ones. The air was filled with cries that swiftly died to fearful silence.

And then, quite swiftly, the realization dawned that the danger was over; the runners slowed and halted, those who had thrown themselves to the ground began warily, nervously, to rise to their feet. The voices of the people rose again, now in wonder and growing relief.

Those members of the crowd who were nearest the restaurant swiftly converged on the two men who lay close to its entrance.

Gathering about the dark-suited man they saw at once

357

that he was dead. The second bullet had blown away almost half his skull. From the cavity his brains oozed while his blood formed a widening pool on the stone beneath his shattered head.

A few yards from the dead man a tall, fair-haired man staggered to his feet, one hand clutching his abdomen where the bullet had struck. Lie still, the gathered people urged him. But he would not listen. 'My son,' he said, thrusting away their reaching hands. 'My son . . .' Seeing that he was determined, they, afraid, shrank back a little, letting him through.

'What's happening, Gramma?'

'Mm? What?' Turning, looking down at the boy, Mrs Bennett met his curious, anxious eyes as they gazed up into her face.

They stood side by side, hand in hand, on a street corner. The pandemonium caused by the shots had barely touched them. They had heard the shots coming from the square nearby and John had clutched at her, momentarily afraid, but she had calmed him; it was nothing, it was nothing. They had moved on, hurried away, away from the excitement and the panic. And now Alberto had gone. 'I don't know,' she said, shaking her head, answering the echo of John's question. She gazed about her, bewildered. Where had Alberto gone to?

Alberto's behaviour had grown increasingly puzzling over the past hour. They had come to the city centre supposedly to inquire after tickets for the opera, but they had not done so. Instead he had led them in a wandering tour from the piazza del' Scala through a series of other streets and squares. 'Where are we going?' she had asked him, but he had either not replied or had brushed her questions aside. All the time he had been constantly

358

consulting his watch. His behaviour had been inexplicable. She recalled how, on leaving the last square, he had come to a halt beside her, head up, mouth set, as if listening, waiting. And then there had come the sounds of the shots and he had given a slight nod, at the same time briefly closing his eyes – almost as if in acknowledgement of the sounds. Then he had gone, melting away into the crowd.

'Where's Mr Rossi?' John asked, his fingers pressing hers. 'Where did he go?'

She shook her head distractedly. 'I don't know, dear. But don't worry, he'll be back in a minute. We'll wait here for him.'

She continued to scan the street with anxious eyes.

Hearing the shots Rossi had at once made inquiries to discover the facts. That done he had headed straight for a public telephone. There were three of them in a row, all engaged with callers. He did not hesitate but went to the nearest one where a young woman was in animated conversation. Taking the receiver from her hand he replaced it and grasped her by the shoulders. 'Get out.' He was barely aware of her astonished protests as he turned her bodily around and thrust her aside.

'It's happened,' he said when Rawlinson came on the line. 'And we lost.'

Silence.

'Did you hear me?' he said.

'Yes, I heard you.' Rawlinson's voice sounded weary. 'Are you quite sure?'

'Quite sure. Belliros's brains are all over the pavement. It's finished.'

Another moment of silence. 'What went wrong? Didn't you get Holman there?'

'Oh, yes, I got him here all right, and in the right place at the right time. After that it was out of my hands.'

'So Belliros got both shots?'

'Just one. But it was the one that counted. Right at the very last moment Holman went his own way.'

Rawlinson sighed. 'Well, we tried, anyway. Trouble was, everything was constructed on Holman, and right from the start he was unpredictable.'

'Right,' Rossi agreed. 'Anyway – I'm leaving here now. There's nothing more to be done.'

He hung up, stepped away from the phone. Out on the main street he hailed a taxi to take him to the airport. He had already made the reservation for his return flight to London. As he climbed into the cab he thought fleetingly of the woman and the child who waited on the street corner near the piazza. They might, the thought briefly went through his mind, make their way back to the villa on the via Soperga. If so they would find the apartment empty, locked up. Too bad. He dismissed them from his mind; they had served their purpose and he was no longer concerned with them. He sighed, his lips compressed; he was already thinking of other things.

Guy came to a stop and stood gasping. He realized dully that people were looking at him; some were pointing. He heard a woman remark, in surprise and horror: '*Guardalo – sanguina!*' For a moment he did not connect her words with himself, but on looking down he saw that blood was saturating his shirt front and running down the front of his trousers. He put his right hand to the wound and felt the blood hot and wet against his palm. He moved on.

At a public telephone near the piazza Mary Hughes dialled Crane's number in London.

Paxton's murder had resulted in Hughes being sent to Milan in pursuit of Holman; her task: to prevent at all costs his interference with the Belliros assassination.

She had got there too late. The 17.50 British Airways flight she took should have brought her into Milan around 20.45 local time, but with a delay caused by a minor air traffic control problem it had been after nine o'clock when the plane touched down. A further delay on the road from the airport had finally succeeded in turning her whole fraught and desperate enterprise into a waste of time; the taxi that carried her to the piazza dei Fiori had deposited her there only seconds before the shots. Nevertheless her discovery as to what had happened was beyond all her hopes and expectations.

As soon as Crane came on the line she said:

'Belliros is dead.' She tried to keep her voice calm, but there was no hiding the elation in her tone.

There was a pause, then, 'Good,' he said. 'You did well.' His own voice was a model of control.

'I didn't do anything,' she said, 'I wasn't able to get here in time, but it happened anyway. I don't know *how* but it did. Holman was here, right on the spot, but it *still happened*. Belliros was still hit.'

'You're quite sure of it?' Crane said.

'Oh, yes. I even managed to get through the crowd and see his body.'

'Fine,' said Crane. 'Then it's all okay.'

She gave a little laugh, infected by his calm in the face of the great victory. 'Yes, it's all okay.'

'And Holman got off scot-free. Well, it remains to be seen whether that's a good thing or not.'

'I don't know about his getting off scot-free,' she said. 'I'm told that another man was also hit. Whether it was Holman, though, I don't know. And I don't know where

361

Holman is now.' A brief pause. 'I hope the poor guy is all right.'

A man was standing before Guy, putting a hand on his shoulder, speaking in a strange language. To Guy's ears, and through the mist of his pain, the words, unintelligible, seemed to come from a great distance. And then he realized they were Italian. Yes, of course, the man was speaking in Italian. But Guy couldn't understand what the words meant – though it was something about getting help, getting a doctor. Feebly he shook off the man's hand. 'No,' he protested, staggering slightly. 'I have to – have to find my son . . .' He turned, lurching away, his blood leaving a trail behind him.

'Why are we standing here, Gramma?' John said. His voice now was slightly plaintive.

Mrs Bennett fought the rising irritation at his repeated question, looked down at his anxious face for a moment and then crouched before him. They had not moved from the spot on the edge of the pavement. She put her hands on his shoulders. She didn't know what to say. It was clear now that Alberto was not coming back for them.

'We'll go to the house we went to before, with him,' she said. 'He'll be there, waiting for us.' But she knew somehow that he would not. For some reason that she could not guess at he had gone; he had left them.

'And what if he's not there?' John said.

' – Then we'll go on home. We'll catch a plane. We'll get our case from the left luggage and go on home.'

'Yes, let's go home, Gramma. I want to go home.'

Home. Yes, they would go home. She straightened, standing before the child, hands briefly clasped lightly around the back of his head, on his soft hair. She should

362

never have brought him away in the first place, she said to herself. But in her desperation she had allowed Alberto to persuade her, make her believe that it would work, that in doing so she could save everything and keep John for herself. She knew now that it was not true. Within her heart she had known it all along.

'Yes,' she said, releasing him and looking down into his face. 'We'll go home, just as soon as we can.'

There they were.

Guy had turned a corner and, staggering to a halt, saw them ahead of him. He could make out their silhouettes against the lighted front of a café.

'*John*,' he murmured.

The image of them came and went, fading, surging, like pictures seen through water. He spoke John's name again, louder now, calling through the evening, past the figures that gathered about him, moving closer, their faces curious, solicitous.

Again he called out:

'John . . . John . . .'

And realized that his voice was making hardly any sound.

He started towards them, but somehow his legs, his feet, refused to move. And as he gazed at them he saw the two figures, the woman and the boy, turn and begin to move away. *No, wait. Stop, please – wait* . . . There was a sudden coldness against his cheek, and he realized in some vague, dull acknowledgement that it was the cold of the stone pavement. He closed his eyes; it was good just to lie there for a moment, not to need strength, to rest for a while. *But John* . . . He started up in an effort to stand, then sank back once more.

'Rest . . . Please rest . . .'

363

A woman's voice. He opened his eyes and saw the face of a blonde woman bending to him.

'Lie still,' she gently urged. 'You must lie still.'

The soft words came to Guy through his pain. Words he understood. He felt his head gently lifted, softness there as a cushion of some kind was placed beneath his lowered cheek. 'We'll have a doctor here for you any minute.' The voice again, the woman's voice, speaking English with an American accent. Comfort like an old pair of shoes or a familiar bed. Then her voice in Italian, asking whether a doctor, an ambulance had been sent for. '*Questo uomo sta molto male.*' This man is very sick? Yes, that was it: This man is very sick. He? Was she talking about him? Sick? Very sick? Yes, he was bleeding. This man is dying, he thought. But how could that be? Then he realized – ah, yes, there had been a shot. He had been hit.

The voices in the crowd around him whispered on while the blonde woman leaned above him, sweetly murmuring. He said to her, opening his eyes, looking into her plump, over-made-up face:

'I'm looking for my son.' His voice was very faint.

'Your son?' She had laid her coat over him, was holding his hand beneath it.

'Yes.' The word barely audible. 'My son John. I have to find him.'

He tried to move but her soft voice urged him not to. 'Lie still, Guy,' she said gently. 'An ambulance will soon be here.'

Mary Hughes had been looking for him among the streets around the piazza, and by some miracle he had come staggering into her path.

Now, on seeing the site of his wound, she was pretty sure that he had been hit in the liver. She was sure also that the bullet must have exited from his back, for now that he was lying supine the blood was pouring from the exit wound, filling the cracks in the pavement and forming a pool. He had lost so much already. He was on the point of death.

He opened his dry lips to speak again but she could not catch his words. She put her ear close to his mouth. 'What did you say?'

When she had heard his murmured words she smiled into his half-closed eyes. 'How do I know your name? Oh, I know. I know.'

He smiled; then, 'Am I sick?' he said. She heard his words clearly this time.

'Yes,' she said. 'But you'll be well again soon.'

He smiled faintly at the lie, closing his eyes in relief. 'When I'm well – ' his voice fading again now, 'I'll find my son.'

'Yes, you'll find him. I'll help you find him.'

'My son is *alive*,' he said, with a surprising little touch of strength. 'He's alive.'

'Yes, he's alive. Of course he's alive.'

' – And Sylvie . . .' his breath was fading now, 'she loved me. I never knew. But all along she loved me.'

'Yes, she loved you. I know she loved you.'

'You – know?' The faint glimmer of a smile again. 'You know that too?'

'Oh, yes, I know.'

His grip was loosening on her fingers and she held on, willing him to stay, but knowing that he could not.

'The man said,' he muttered, eyelids fluttering, 'the young priest – he said that Sylvie and I shall – shall meet again.' He frowned. His eyes were wandering now, rolling in his head. 'Could – could it be . . .?'

'Oh, yes. Oh, yes! Of course it could happen. It *will*

happen. It *will*. You must never doubt it.' Tears were running down her cheeks.

' – In Paradise,' he said.

'Yes,' she said. 'Yes. And you must believe it. It's true.'

'Yes,' he said. And smiled his last smile, a smile of the purest joy. 'It's true,' he said. 'I know. I know.'